A Wanton Adventure

The Brazen Curators, Book 1

Ramona Elmes

ARE YOU SIGNED UP FOR DRAGONBLADE'S BLOG?

You'll get the latest news and information on exclusive giveaways, exclusive excerpts, coming releases, sales, free books, cover reveals and more.

Check out our complete list of authors, too!

No spam, no junk. That's a promise!

Sign Up Here

www.dragonbladepublishing.com

Dearest Reader;

Thank you for your support of a small press. At Dragonblade Publishing, we strive to bring you the highest quality Historical Romance from some of the best authors in the business. Without your support, there is no 'us', so we sincerely hope you adore these stories and find some new favorite authors along the way.

Happy Reading!

CEO, Dragonblade Publishing

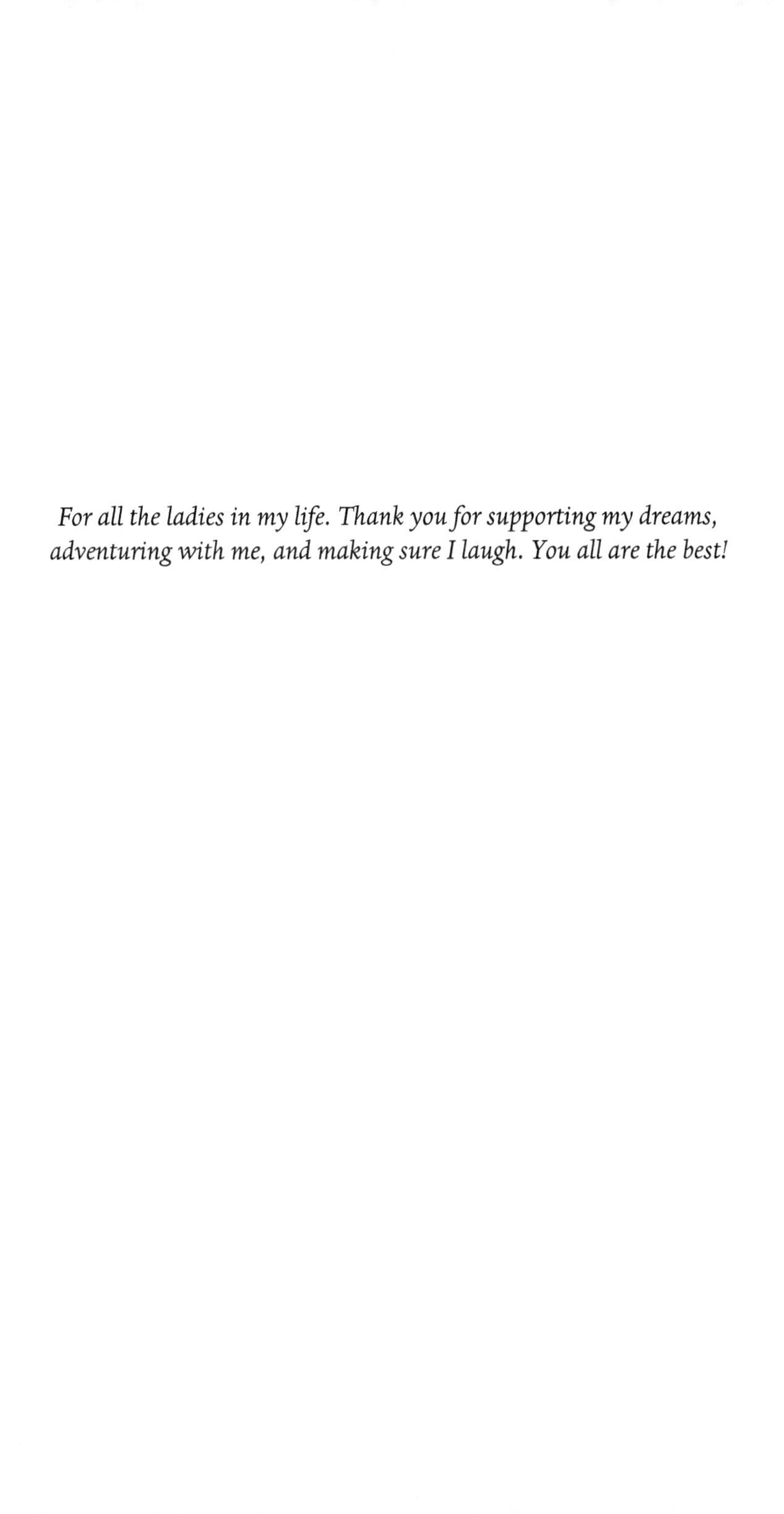

For all the ladies in my life. Thank you for supporting my dreams, adventuring with me, and making sure I laugh. You all are the best!

Prologue

London—1842

THE CARRIAGE RUMBLED away from the notorious gentlemen's club, the Den. Diana, the Marchioness of Hensley, couldn't believe she'd stepped into the place, but she had no other option. She needed to notify her brother-in-law that her sister was missing—no, not missing, but taken.

Diana wished Stuart was in London. Her husband had only departed a few days ago, but he was always much better in a crisis.

"Lady Hensley, Sam Kincaide will find your sister."

She glanced at Sebastian Devons, who sat across from her, startled to receive such reassuring words from the proprietor of the Den. He was a bit of a mystery in London—a rakish one. He couldn't be more than a few years older than she was, but he exuded confidence and worldliness that she suspected wasn't normal for someone in their mid-to-late twenties.

She forced a small smile onto her face. "Thank you. I know he will do everything in his power."

He nodded. "I'm confident she will be found."

While she appreciated his words, fear still clawed at her, but she forced herself to remain calm. The man was only trying to be kind. In truth, she was somewhat startled that Sebastian Devons had insisted on making sure she was escorted home safely. Diana hadn't expected that at all. Yet here they were, alone together in a carriage in the middle of the night.

Absurdly, she pondered if he often took ladies home at such a late hour. She suspected he did, but for other reasons. A blush tinged her cheeks, and she was grateful they only had the light from the full moon.

"It is very kind of you to offer the assistance of your investigators and guards to help my brother-in-law find my sister."

He nodded. "I will meet up with Kincaide after I see you home."

"My husband is out of town. If he were here, he would have gone to your club. I don't normally go to places such as your establishment."

Devons lifted a brow, and she added, "Not that there is anything wrong with your business."

A bark of laughter escaped him, and Diana felt her blush deepen. "I only meant to explain that my husband isn't here helping because he is traveling."

"I know your husband, Lady Hensley. He is a good man, and I have no doubt he would be assisting if he were here."

Diana smiled at his compliment of Hensley. "He didn't even want to go away. We have a son born only a few months ago, and I had to persuade him that his work still had to be done."

"I'm sure several lords and businessmen are grateful for your prodding. Hensley and I've only had a few conversations, but few could rival his mastery of the business world."

The emotions she was trying to control threatened to erupt within her. Right now, she wished she'd never encouraged Hensley to leave. Devons leaned forward and brushed away a tear from her cheek. She hadn't even realized she was crying.

"I promise you, Lady Hensley. Your sister will be found, and I will use everything in my power to assist Sam Kincaide."

She nodded, horrified to be such a mess in front of this man. "I'm sorry."

He shook his head. "Don't apologize. You've had a trying evening."

Diana took a deep breath. "Still, being this emotional isn't beneficial. Tell me something about yourself."

He wiggled his eyebrows boyishly. "You want me to tell you about my club?"

She laughed, grateful for the shift in the conversation. "Yes. Tell me, is it as notorious as all the ladies speculate?"

He smiled at her words and winked. "It is, but I like to explain it as a place where people can let all their inhibitions go and not worry about the judgment of others."

Diana smiled, amused at how he described his club. It wasn't how others gossiped about it. The carriage stopped, signaling they'd arrived at her townhouse. In truth, Sebastian Devons wasn't what she expected from all the chatter she'd heard about him.

He stepped out of the carriage and offered her his hand. Her fingers grasped his as she stepped down. She blushed, feeling unsure what to say to this man who had been so comforting. Devons smiled at her reassuringly. "Kincaide or I will send word once your sister is found. Do not fret. She will be home soon. I will leave a guard here just as a precaution."

Diana nodded and made her way to the door already being opened by a worried butler. Once she reached it, she turned back and saw Devons still standing outside the carriage, waiting until she was safely inside.

Their eyes met, and Diana suspected all that she'd heard of this man before tonight had been inaccurate. "Thank you for all your kindness, Mr. Devons."

He smiled at her. "Hopefully, this will all be over soon. Tell your husband he is welcome to visit the Den anytime. I will buy him a drink celebrating the arrival of your son."

"He would like that."

She walked into the townhouse and let the butler and housekeeper fret over her before she insisted on being left alone in the drawing room. Diana leaned her head back against the sofa and closed her eyes. She felt hopeful that Clara would be found and suspected it was because of Mr. Devons's reassurance.

The corners of her mouth curved up as she reflected on meeting London's most notorious club owner. He'd not been what she expected. She would be forever grateful to him for his kindness. She doubted they would ever speak again and would never confess this aloud, but she was glad to have met him, if only for a moment.

Chapter One

London—1850

DIANA, THE WIDOW of Lord Hensley and young mother of the future Duke of Huxton, smiled as she listened to Lady Prescott explain her plans for her next needlepoint creation. She smiled, but her mind wandered. It wasn't Lady Prescott's fault, or the topic for that matter. For years, she'd enjoyed discussions on needlepoint, but recently, such conversations left her restless. She was bored. The thought startled her. Diana had no reason to be bored. She was exactly where she should be, having tea with other ladies who were either married or widowed, their seasons long gone.

Yet at thirty-one, she had the alarming feeling she wasn't doing what she should be. The first few times she felt it, she assured herself it was only because of her grieving process. She'd lost her husband, Stuart, two years ago and even now still missed him fiercely. But deep down, she knew this was different. It was the blasted article. She didn't understand why it rankled her. It shouldn't.

"What do you think, Diana? Shall I do the landscape next or the dog portrait?" Lady Prescott said, snapping her out of her odd thoughts.

Diana smiled. "I think the landscape would be lovely and a wonderful gift."

Lady Prescott nodded. Diana wondered how old she was. She

couldn't be much older than herself. Diana's eyes roamed the room, taking in all the various factions of ladies congregating for tea at the Duchess of Peyton's home. Once mired in scandal, the duchess's events were now quite popular, and her invites highly sought-after. Diana was always invited as her sister married into the duchess's family years ago.

She continued to peruse the room, assessing the little groups that formed at these society gatherings. Standing in the middle of the enormous drawing room were the young ladies considered the smashing successes of the season. They would be married before the end of the year.

Her focus shifted to another group: the firmly on-the-shelf wallflowers who congregated at the tables closest to the room's walls. They sat with the ease of someone who accepted they wouldn't ever marry but understood they must attend the never-ending events of London society. Her gaze continued to the group that comprised the ladies who were neither smashing successes nor wallflowers. Diana, during her season, would have been considered one of them.

A sigh escaped her, and the ladies at her table glanced at her with concern.

"Is something amiss, Lady Hensley?" Lady St. James asked.

Diana flushed. "I'm fine. I'm feeling a little out of sorts. I think I will go for a walk around the room."

Diana stood, and Lady Prescott appeared ready to join her. "Please stay. I will return momentarily. I need a bit of move-ment."

Standing over her friends, some whom she cherished dearly, she could see a variety of lace caps pinned to their heads. The slips of fabric matched the ladies' dresses to perfection, just as hers did—the perfect accessory for a middle-aged married woman. A wave of restlessness shot through her, and she had the irrational thought that it was the dratted pieces of lace's fault. She turned and made her way not around the room but to the foyer. She needed a moment away from everything.

She did her best to walk gracefully, even though her mind screamed to run. Diana continued to survey the room as she walked, taking in her sister's group of friends. They were all married but somewhat different from Diana's circle. None of those ladies wore a cap or seemed as if their lives had passed them by. She frowned at her cruel thoughts. Life hadn't passed her friends by.

Diana tore her gaze away. The urge for silence and privacy intensified within her. A howl escaped the scandalous Lady Hawley while she spoke with friends. The woman's laugh was almost as notorious as her reputation. She didn't seem to mind that most of society found her unsuppressed chortling shocking. Or maybe she didn't care?

At events, Diana often spotted her laughing from the depths of her being. What must it be like to be so carefree, she wondered? Rumors of late suggested she was planning something over-the-top. Some said it was likely prompted by her fury at discovering that her estranged husband had taken one of her closest friends as his lover. Diana supposed eventually all would be revealed, but tonight the lady appeared completely unconcerned about society's opinions.

Lady Hawley's group consisted of married ladies who flouted convention. As Diana walked by, she spotted the much-talked-about woman, who smiled back. Diana's eyes widened. Not once could she remember a time that Lady Hawley had ever greeted her. The lady's smile dimmed at Diana's expression. Horrified that she may have unintentionally cut her, Diana smiled back, but Lady Hawley had already turned away.

It wasn't Diana's intent to ignore her. Regardless of one's reputation, she didn't believe in rudeness. She was just surprised the lady had said hello. In all the years they were both out in society, they'd never spoken to each other.

She continued to the door, finally arriving in the vast but quiet foyer. Sighing, she wandered before stopping at a massive gold mirror spanning most of the wall. She stared back at her reflection. Her eyes narrowed as she studied her perfectly acceptable features. She had a heart-shaped face framed by brown hair. Her eyes were probably her best physical trait. Her husband once said he had never seen a blue so lovely.

Yet as she gazed at herself, it wasn't her physical features she assessed. She pondered if the woman staring back at her was really who she wanted to be. It unnerved her that she was having such thoughts.

Her eyes moved to the lace cap on her head with small emerald bows. The dratted thing was both an annoyance she wanted to fling off and also something that gave her comfort. She pulled a piece of paper from the pocket of her skirts and unfolded it. Diana frowned at the caricature. It was a lady in a gown similar to her own with brown hair and a lace cap. She read the words under the picture.

The uneventful but much-needed steady ladies of London society

Sighing, she looked away from the annoying article, not needing to read anymore. Diana had studied it numerous times since it came out. It stated there was a group of ladies who were the backbone of London respectability. Without them, society was likely to fall into chaos and sin. No specific women had been pointed out. Instead, the writer provided a list of key traits that personified these types of ladies. All the qualities Diana embodied made a respectable marriage match: middle-aged, kind, elegant, morally strong, and content with their role.

She sighed. She was the epitome of a mature, uneventful, and proper lady. Yet an emotion stirred within her. One that challenged her to break free of the description that was very much her.

"Diana, are you all right?"

She spun on her heels to find her sister Clara in a lovely blue gown, minus the cap, frowning at her with concern. Her eyes flicked down to Diana's left hand, still clutching the article.

"Did someone say something hurtful to you?"

A laugh escaped Diana at the question, and her sister walked to her, more concerned.

"Diana."

Diana shook her head. "I'm sorry. No, it is nothing like that."

Not believing her, Clara said, "You must tell me what's wrong."

Diana handed her sister the article, and Clara read it. When she was done, she looked back up, still confused. "What does this have to do with you?"

Diana struck the same pose as the lady in the caricature, and a giggle erupted from Clara. She raised a brow, and her sister sobered.

"I'm this uneventful lady they are writing about."

Clara started to deny it, but Diana held her hand up. "Don't."

"There is nothing wrong with this type of lady," Clara offered.

Diana knew she was right. Yet for some reason, she had the urge to denounce this woman who embodied so much of who she was.

"It is quite insulting now that I think about it. Do you think this paragon explained in the paper can be broken down into these characteristics? I doubt it. I would say, 'Shame on this writer for portraying women as such simple creatures.'"

Diana smiled at Clara's attempt to write off the words that so strongly affected her. "Truth be told, I have always liked being this type of lady, but for some reason, lately, I feel adrift."

Clara's eyes widened at her revelation. Her sister took her hand. "You can be and do whatever you want, Diana. You are so young."

Diana snorted. "Not true."

"I mean it. There is a whole world to explore out there, but do it because you want to. Not because this article reduced your circle of friends to caricatures."

Diana squeezed her sister's hand.

"Are you missing Hensley?" Clara asked.

She always missed her husband. Even two years later, she wished he were by her side, but she couldn't shake the sense this was not because of his passing. This was something more, but she didn't know what.

"Of course, but this feels different."

Clara turned them so they looked in the mirror. "Diana, you can and should do whatever you like."

Diana smiled at her sister as their eyes met. "Thank you for your support."

Still, all she saw when she stared back at herself was the caricature of the uneventful lady. And, until now, she would have been fine with that lady. What changed?

⟫⟪

"DEVONS, OPEN THE door," his half-brother Malcolm, the Marquess of Derry, called from the hallway outside the apartment Sebastian Devons kept at their gentlemen's club, the Den.

Malcolm had a similar space but seldom spent time there now that he was a happily married man. Sebastian's brother knocked loudly, interrupting his thoughts.

A blonde naked minx groaned. "Tell him to go away."

Sebastian smacked her bottom. "Unfortunately, my sweet, I think I'm late for an appointment with him. We have business to discuss."

Abigail Spencer, a rising star of the London theater scene, rose from the bed and coyly asked, "Are you sure?"

The woman was a vixen and had been quite delightful over the past few hours. He leaned in and kissed her. She tried to pull him down, but another pounding on the door came again.

"Sebastian, we have a meeting."

He groaned. His brother used his first name. Malcolm never did that, which meant he wasn't going away. "My sweet, I do think you must go. I would suggest you dress before my brother sees you bare."

She sighed and jumped from the bed. "Brothers are no fun."

He chuckled as he headed to the door. Cracking it, he grinned at his impeccably attired brother, who glowered at him in return.

"We have much to discuss."

Sebastian rolled his eyes. "I'm busy."

Abigail giggled from within the room.

Malcolm's eyes flashed with annoyance. "Unbusy yourself."

"And to think you finding true love would make you less stuffy."

"Meet me in our office in ten minutes," Malcolm said before turning on his heels and stomping down the hallway.

After shaking his head at his brother's retreating form, Sebastian closed the door and turned to see Abigail, almost dressed in a lavender-colored frock that molded to her curves. The woman was a delight. She'd broken plenty of hearts since arriving in London. Sebastian wasn't one of them, but he appreciated the time they spent together, no matter how infrequent. He groaned and reached for her.

She giggled. "You have been summoned, Devons."

"Just one more kiss."

"Very well."

Thirty minutes later and twenty minutes late, Sebastian strolled into their office located on the second floor. Malcolm sat in a wingback chair reading one of the many London society papers.

"Anything good?"

Malcolm looked at him and frowned. "You look like hell."

Of course, he did, Sebastian thought. He'd been up most of the night entertaining Den guests and then decided to spend time with Abigail. He hoped he would be able to rest before Den patrons started arriving for the evening. He pulled his pocket watch out and flipped open the front case. It was two in the afternoon. If Malcolm left in the next hour, he could sleep for at least three to four hours.

"When was the last time you rested? Or did something besides Den business?" Malcolm asked.

Sebastian's fingers flicked the white dial forward and skimmed the text on the back case of the watch. *The measure of a man is defined by his actions.* Since receiving the pocket watch from his father at eighteen, he had a habit of opening the front and back cases and skimming the words within. He snapped the watch shut and dropped down into the other wingback chair. "Someone needs to keep our customers entertained."

"I'm here a couple nights a week and for any big events. You could do the same and focus on other efforts or initiatives you are interested in."

He looked at his brother skeptically. Their establishment was the most successful gentlemen's club in all of London. Most evenings, their venue was filled with the elite men of London, who placed bets, had drinks, and enjoyed their nightly entertainment. Sebastian couldn't remember the last slow night their club had.

Even if that ever occurred, the Who's Who of London paid astronomical amounts of money to utilize the decadent cottages scattered throughout the Den grounds for liaisons for which the club guaranteed absolute privacy. These little buildings were used and booked by both men and women.

Often, reservations for the year were arranged during one of the two scandalous balls the Den hosted in the fall and at the end of the season. Invites to the events were highly sought-after among the peerage and the wealthy. They promised a night of freedom for all attendees. Only three rules existed: no innocents, no violence, and no forcing anyone to do anything they didn't want to. They were currently planning the Ball of Misdeeds that would wrap up the season. Sebastian guessed at least half the cottages for the next few months would be booked by the end of the event.

Sebastian rolled his eyes at his brother's suggestion. "Malcolm, our success is because someone is always here."

"My point is it doesn't always have to be you," his brother countered.

"I'm not a lord like you and nor do I have a family. What does it matter if I spend my time here?"

His brother ran a hand through his brown hair. They were so physically different from one another. Malcolm had inherited their father's brown hair and fair skin, while Sebastian took after his mother, with black hair, dark-brown eyes, and olive skin. Yet their large builds and mannerisms would suggest a familial connection to any observer. "I worry about you. You work and play, never leaving the grounds of the Den. Lately, it has been more so than normal. You are burying yourself in this place to avoid what happened with Lady Wesley."

Sebastian scowled at his brother. He never wanted to speak of the lady again. She had been a liaison he thought was more until the lady picked a marquess to wed. He'd been about to propose to the widow when she'd shown up at the Den to wish him goodbye and to let him know that, perhaps after her first child, they could resume their affair.

When he mentioned proposing, she'd laughed and said she couldn't marry the by-blow of a lord. It was beneath her. He'd been a damn fool, thinking the dowager viscountess would wed him. Yet for a moment, he believed that they had something more. That she thought he was worthy of more.

He pulled his watch out again, flicking back and forth between the back case and the front case. Not really looking at the words but needing something to do. A sharp pain sliced across his chest, and he rose, moving to the table where brandy and glasses waited. He poured some into a glass. His brother made a disapproving sound, and Sebastian turned. "Don't judge me, brother."

Malcolm frowned at him with concern. "I don't. I worry about you. She—"

"I have no desire to talk about her," he said harshly.

Malcolm pressed his lips together and studied him silently.

Finally, he said, "Don't stay cooped up here. She isn't worthy of this punishment you are inflicting on yourself. Never leaving the Den, that is."

Annoyance flashed through Sebastian. "I do other things. You and I are involved in multiple ventures that have nothing to do with the Den."

"Yes, but if we are honest, your focus lately on anything but the Den, liaisons, and drinking has been minimal. You are drawing yourself into vice to forget her. Acknowledge the pain she caused you and move on."

Sebastian's lips twisted into a smirk. Lilah hurt him, and he'd been a fool to think her affection for him was more than an affair. It had been rash of him to assume she didn't care about status because she was a wealthy childless widow. He didn't want to think about any of that and pushed the thoughts away, focusing on his brother. Who the hell was Malcolm to judge? He was his partner in this very building of vice they were sitting in. "Are you judging our club now that you are married? Too much sin for your liking?"

Malcolm glared at him. "I care about the club. I built it with you from nothing and I'm honored to be part owner with you. All I'm saying is it would do you good to take a break from it. We could hire some gentleman in need of money or a merchant looking to chat with some lords to keep people entertained. It doesn't have to be you every night."

They recently had this discussion more than once. Sebastian couldn't fathom hiring men who likely had the world handed to them and wasted it to take his place.

As if reading his mind, his brother said, "They wouldn't replace you, but it would give you the ability to venture out. I can't remember the last time you stayed at your townhouse in Mayfair or left London?"

Sebastian rubbed the back of his neck, staying silent, not wanting to confirm his brother's points.

"Just think about it, is all I'm saying. There is more to life than ruling the Den all night, taking a companion home for a couple of hours, sleeping, and then starting all over again. You know that, Sebastian. Snap out of this wallowing or whatever it is."

Sebastian scowled at him. "I'm not wallowing."

His brother snorted. "Removing the topic of Lady Wesley, I would like to see you outside of this place more. Is that so much to ask?"

Sebastian sighed. "Understood. Let's move on. Hopefully, this isn't the only reason you came to see me today."

Malcolm shook his head. "I wanted to talk about the Ball of Misdeeds and who the final invitees are."

Rising, Sebastian moved to the large bookshelves that contained their business papers, books, and ledgers. He grabbed a book with the list of invitees and turned back.

Malcolm was still frowning at him. "You will think about what I said?"

Tired of his brother's concern, he nodded even though he wasn't going to do anything of the sort. "Of course."

Chapter Two

Diana sat up in her bed and frowned. A feminine laugh filtered through her bedroom window followed by a louder one. She pursed her lips wondering where it came from. She lay back down, telling herself it had nothing to do with her. It could only be coming from the townhouse behind hers.

Years ago, Sebastian Devons, owner of a scandalous club and half-brother to the Marquess of Derry, purchased it. At the time, all her neighbors had been up in arms about someone with his reputation buying a home in the heart of Mayfair, but eventually, they settled down. Her mind flashed to the one time she'd met him. Almost ten years had passed, but she still remembered and appreciated his kindness.

A loud splash and shrill laughter caused her to sit up again. She should go back to sleep but knew she wouldn't. She climbed out of bed and pulled her wrap on before quietly making her way downstairs and to the drawing room. Once in the room, she reached for the handle of the door, leading out to the terrace. She hesitated and frowned. Why was she going outside? It had nothing to do with her.

It was so late it was almost morning. Even the fire the servants kept going in the hearth had gone out. Ladies didn't wander around in the dark by themselves, she told herself. Yet she was tired of doing what ladies should. She twirled the brown braid hanging over her shoulder. She imagined her hair looked a mess. It always fell out while she slept. She was a restless sleeper. Stuart used to joke that she never woke up in the same spot she went to bed in.

She pulled the door open, and the sound of more feminine laughter and splashing drifted towards her. A deep, rich, masculine voice rang out, but she couldn't understand precisely what the man said. Pushing aside her practical thoughts, she walked down the terrace steps into the garden courtyard.

"Come, my lovelies. Out of the fountain," the man cajoled.

"You said you were not staying at the Ball of Misdeeds, so we thought we would bring the fun to you."

Diana glided past her own fountain in the middle of her garden to hear better. Thick vines covering the ornate fence between her townhouse and the one behind hers blocked any possibility of a view, but she was confident the man was Devons. His club's success had only grown, and they now hosted two scandalous annual balls. From gossip, she knew the Ball of Misdeeds was one of them.

A memory of him wiping her tears during their carriage ride years ago appeared in her mind. It had been a crazy night, but he'd been correct. Clara had been found the very next day, and the man who had taken her was paying for his dastardly deeds.

To some, Devons was considered nothing but a notorious rake, but Diana's encounter that evening proved otherwise. For a moment, she pondered what he must have thought of her that night. Grimacing, she doubted it was anything memorable for him. She was, after all, one of the uneventful ladies.

She silently chastised herself for such musings. At the time, Diana's heart wholly belonged to Stuart. She gulped, her stomach dropping as it always did when she thought of her husband in the past tense. It had been two years since his passing, and she still missed him. She pushed the thoughts away as she reached the wall. She leaned forward, listening.

"My lady, you of all people know a townhouse in the middle

of Mayfair may not be the place to cause a scene."

"Devons, you are becoming a bloody bore," a woman said, followed by a loud smack. Something hit the ground.

Diana's eyes widened. She knew that voice. She inched closer to the gate that separated her garden from Devons. The gate had never been used and was overgrown with vines, but she tried to peer through them, wanting to confirm who it was.

He sighed. Another woman sang, "Yay! You are joining us."

Diana heard a deep chuckle and then more splashing. She peered through the gate and gasped. Lady St. James and Lady Clarrow stood in the fountain, one only in her chemise and drawers and the other with her skirts lifted to her knees. The sound of more sloshing water drifted through the gate, and her eyes widened as she witnessed Devons, only in his shirt and trousers, wading through the fountain towards them.

The ladies screeched as he got closer and darted to the other side. Diana almost giggled at the sight they all made. She leaned towards the opening between their gardens, and her foot hit a vine, causing her to stumble. She fell against the gate and any confidence the vines would keep it closed disappeared quickly. The metal door swung open, ripping the vines.

Her knees smacked the ground as she fell forward. Heat spread across her body. She glanced up, still on all fours, and saw all three of the fountain frolickers staring at her in open-mouth shock. She jumped up, and no one said a single word. She should say something. Her eyes darted to Lady St. James, dressed only in her undergarments. The lady appeared slightly embarrassed but shrugged and waved at her.

Diana's eyes met Devons's. He broke contact and perused her from her messy hair, lingering on the tip of her brown braid falling over her chest, and then continuing down. She sucked in a breath. The movement seemed to startle him as he jerked his eyes back to her face. His gaze made her tingle, disconcerting her. She flushed, horrified that he may be able to somehow understand how he affected her. "I apologize, Mr. Devons—"

"Just Devons is fine," he said, his voice rich and growly.

The other lady in the fountain asked, "Would you like to join us?"

Diana stared open-mouthed at Lady Clarrow, flushing even more. "I…well…I."

"Leave her be," Devons said to the lady before turning his gaze back to Diana. "Why don't you return home, my lady? I'm sorry if we woke you."

She studied him. For some reason, her eyes wandered down his form. She took in his broad chest and flat stomach, which she suspected was not only flat but firm, and then her eyes started to move further down.

"Lady Hensley?" he said, startling her.

She glanced back at his face. He smirked at her, cocking an eyebrow wickedly in some sort of invitation. She could feel her face turning red again. "Yes, you are quite right. I apologize for intruding. I promise tonight's events will be forgotten by the morning."

Lady St. James appeared relieved, while Lady Clarrow and Devons seemed not the least bit bothered either way. She turned and heard Devons's footsteps following behind her. Diana spun back around to tell him it wasn't necessary that he escort her and accidentally smacked his chest with one of her hands. Flustered, she took a step back.

"I don't need you to walk me to my terrace doors," she insisted.

"Lady Hensley, I will see you to the door as I did once before."

Diana's eyes flew to his, startled, he remembered. Devons smiled, amused by her surprise. Unsure what to say or do, she simply nodded and crossed her garden. He followed at a more leisurely pace. As she reached the door, she turned back to observe him standing at the foot of the stairs, watching her. "Good night."

Devons nodded and spun on his heels, returning to his own

garden area. Diana entered the drawing room and shut the door, leaning against it. What a strange night. Her mouth tilted up in amusement. Lady St. James was certainly not an uneventful woman. Perhaps her sister was right. No one could be put into such simple categories. A chortle escaped her, as she really thought about the absurdity of the situation. Diana wondered how often Devons pulled ladies out of his fountain.

She studied herself in a mirror and squeaked. Her hair was everywhere, and her wrap was gapping in the front, revealing her nightgown. Diana should be horrified but she imagined Devons had seen plenty of nightgowns and tousled hair. Diana wondered what she must have looked like through Devons's eyes but eventually pushed the thought from her mind. Why was she thinking such a thing?

SEBASTIAN STOOD IN his second-floor study, watching Lady Hensley playing with her son in her garden. Before last night, it had been years since they'd spoken. When he'd read about her husband's passing, he'd been tempted to send her a missive or call on her to pay his condolences, but he'd worried about how that would look, not so much for him but for her. She was a highly respected lady, and he was the main provider of vice to London society.

The corners of his mouth twitched upward, reflecting on the previous evening. It had been shocking when she fell through the opening between their gardens. Her chestnut hair had wildly fallen out of a braid, and she'd been dressed only in a wrap and bed attire. She looked so drastically different from the woman he now observed.

Today, she appeared very much like any other proper lady, every hair in place and a little cap at the back of her head. He didn't understand why married women chose to wear lace caps.

Was it an unwritten rule that once they wed and reached a certain age, out came the pieces of fabric? He was being unduly harsh. Not all ladies wore them, but the ones the peerage deemed to be paragons of society certainly did. Those caps seemed to be used to signify their standing among the peerage, even if it was a farce. He smirked. Lady St. James often had one fashioned to her head, and she was no saint.

Sebastian frowned as he stared at the contraption on Lady Hensley's head. It was none of his business but, for some reason, he was fascinated with the two sides of her. The one from the previous night was so completely undone and the one today was extraordinarily proper. Which was she? Why did he care?

He should go back to the Den to review how the club fared now that the Ball of Misdeeds was over. Uncharacteristically of him, he'd departed the ball while the revelry was still going on. Sebastian didn't know why. Normally, he would entertain his guests until the last person left, usually when the sun came up. Yet as the night wore on, he'd wanted to be anywhere but there, and that is how he found himself at his townhouse.

Sebastian remembered when he bought the place. He'd done it to prove that he could afford anything the lords and ladies of London could. He smirked. Sebastian hadn't expected Lady Clarrow or Lady St. James to show up at his residence. Still, it was common knowledge he owned a townhouse in Mayfair. He imagined a staff member let it slip where he went.

He'd fished the ladies out of the fountain and sent them home, both disappointed not to be staying. He blamed his lack of interest on being interrupted by the widow he now watched. In all honesty, Sebastian wasn't sure if she was the cause. Even though he'd been charming to the ladies, he'd not been elated to see them. Lady Hensley grabbed her son who hid behind a bush. "I've got you!"

Her son laughed. He didn't appear much older than six or seven. "Now, your turn, Mother."

She smiled and shook her head. "I think I need a rest. Why

don't you play with your ball for a bit."

The boy shrugged and ran over to the ball, kicking it against the wall between their gardens. Sebastian studied her more. She looked so matronly this morning, with a muted brown day dress and her hair tied back severely at her nape. Was the woman trying to appear older?

Sebastian flipped his pocket watch open and closed, causing his man-of-affairs, Curtis, to sigh. He held back his laughter. The sound Sebastian's habit made drove him crazy. He walked to the door, and Curtis glanced up from his ledger. "Shall I follow you?"

He shook his head. "No, I will only be a moment."

Sebastian headed to his terrace doors and walked through his garden to the metal gate between their yards. Gone were most of the vines, and he could see the lady and her son quite clearly. He wanted to apologize and make sure she was fine. He pushed the gate open, and the boy grinned at him. "You're our neighbor."

Lady Hensley stood, shocked to see him. Sebastian smiled at her but turned back to the boy. "I am."

"What is your name?"

"It's Sebastian Devons."

"Hello, Sebastian. I'm Robert."

"Robert, you are to address him as Mr. Devons," Lady Hensley said firmly.

Sebastian glanced at her, once again startled at how different she seemed today. "Your mother is right, and I should address you as Lord Robert."

The boy scrunched up his nose but moved on to the next topic. "Do you want to play ball with me?"

"I'm sure Mr. Devons has more important things to do," Lady Hensley said before he could speak.

Sebastian winked at the boy. "I think I have some time to spare, but if it's fine with you, I would like to speak with your mother first."

Lord Robert's face lit up. Sebastian glanced at his mother, who appeared sad for a moment, but quickly replaced her expression with the unemotional, serene look that most ladies of the *ton* had mastered. The boy kicked his ball down a garden path as Sebastian made his way over to Lady Hensley. She flushed.

"My lady, I wish to apologize for last night."

She shook her head. "There is no need. I was somewhere I wasn't supposed to be."

"Why were you there?" he asked.

The flush deepened. She shrugged. "I'm not sure, but don't worry, it won't happen again."

His eyes roamed over her, and he had the insane thought to tell her she was welcome anytime. He was going mad. Lady Hensley was not his type. Moral paragons of London society did not appeal to him. He only had two aversions when it came to spending time with women. Overly proper was one of them.

The other was insincerity. He suspected the reason the situation with Lilah affected him so much was because he hadn't seen the fakeness in her until the end. He'd been charmed by her. He didn't mind a good time but appreciated frankness from his partners. She'd toyed with him.

Yet as he studied Lady Hensley, his body stirred. Annoyed at his reaction, he begrudgingly thought his brother may be right. He was partaking in too much vice and spending too much time at the Den. Lord Robert laughed, and she glanced his way. Sebastian caught sight of her lace cap. He frowned, irritated that she wore the thing.

"Why do you wear that piece of lace fabric in your hair?"

She gasped, startled. "That isn't your concern."

He rubbed the back of his neck, confused by his actions. "You have lovely hair. You shouldn't hide it."

Her flush that had never gone away was now the deep red shade of a strawberry. "You are mistaken."

"No, I have seen it twice now. Once at the Den and last night."

She glared at him, and his eyes flicked down upon her. She was a petite but curvy woman. He started to wonder about what was under her practical, muted dress when the realization of what he was doing hit him. Christ! She was not for him and, again, not his type. He pushed the strange thoughts from his mind. "Please disregard my remarks. I shouldn't have said that."

Lady Hensley nodded at him but still looked perturbed. "Thank you. Have a wonderful day, Mr. Devons."

He bowed and made his way to Lord Robert. He began to take his jacket off when Lady Hensley marched over to him. "Mr. Devons, what are you doing?"

"I promised Lord Robert we would play."

"That's unnecessary. I will play with him."

The boy stopped dribbling with his feet. "Please, Mummy. You aren't very good."

The lady glanced away, embarrassed, and Sebastian did his best not to laugh. He'd already offended her. She didn't want him there but acquiesced to her son's request. Lord Robert clapped as his mother went back to the table she was sitting at.

The young lord leaned in and said, "You can call me Robert."

He winked at him. "You can call me Sebastian."

Chapter Three

DIANA ROLLED HER eyes at her Aunt Winifred as they made their way through the exhibits.

"It's an innocent question. Why is it acceptable to look at all these naked statues, but women must have layers and layers of clothing? Goodness, it's so hot."

Diana slowed and glanced sideways at her aunt. "It isn't the same."

Her aunt snorted. "When I'm in the country, I often go without unnecessary undergarments."

A smile tugged at Diana's lips. "Well, thank you for wearing all the proper garments today."

"You are most welcome."

Diana shook her head and continued. She'd received a message from Lady Hawley that she had an exciting venture to discuss with Diana, but first, she wanted her to visit the London Society of Antiquaries grand hall, which housed hundreds of artifacts and antiquities. The lady had finished the missive, explaining she would be in touch soon. Diana would be lying if she said she wasn't intrigued. Still, most of the exhibits appeared dreadfully dull.

She leaned in to study a manuscript written in Latin. The volume was stunning, even without her understanding the words, but she suspected the value was derived from the text. She wished there was a translation.

"Of everything you could find fascinating, you're looking at an old piece of parchment," her aunt complained, disappointed.

"What should I be looking at?"

Aunt Winifred moved closer and said, "The naked statues, of course."

Diana flushed. Her aunt winked at her before her eyes darted behind her. "Or maybe that man. He's so wickedly handsome. And the stories they tell about him are delicious."

For some reason, Diana suspected her aunt was talking about Sebastian Devons. She turned and saw him standing by another exhibit, laughing with the Marquess of Derry, his half-brother. They were once considered something of a scandalous family. Their father had chosen to live openly with his mistress, Devons's mother, while the current marquess's mother lived abroad.

Studying them both, Diana didn't sense any animosity between the brothers. If she remembered correctly, Sebastian Devons was the oldest. He didn't seem bothered that his younger brother held the family title. She wondered what his life was like growing up. How did that shape the man rumored to be one of the biggest rakes in London?

She'd enjoyed watching him play ball with Robert yesterday. His enthusiasm to engage with her son had seemed so sincere. Her son had gone to bed delighted their neighbor was now their friend. Diana flushed, still perplexed by the man's comments over her hair. Still, she couldn't be too upset. She had spied on him.

Diana studied him. He was tall and much broader than most of the men in the room. Even without the height, he would have stood out with his square jaw and dark hair.

"You find him attractive, too," her aunt said before guffawing.

The sound caused both the marquess and Mr. Devons to turn their way. Her eyes met his. He nodded, and she smiled in return, before turning back to Aunt Winifred.

"You are causing a scene."

"I'm an old lady, and I'm allowed to."

Diana shook her head. "You are only fifty-two."

"One foot in the grave."

How was her aunt so different from her mother? They had the same parents. Diana didn't understand it and once asked Aunt Winifred that very question. She'd said Diana's mother was her parents' favorite. Aunt Winifred was mostly an afterthought to their mother and father, spending most of her childhood with distant relatives. Once she became an adult, she was married off. After her wedding, Aunt Winifred happily moved overseas with her husband and stayed there until he passed away two years ago.

Her aunt had reached out to her, Clara, and Henry upon her return to England last year. Initially, they'd all been suspicious of her, but she'd gradually won them all over. Now, Diana couldn't fathom her aunt not in her life.

"I think he is coming over here," her aunt whispered excitedly.

Diana spotted him making his way to them and turned, not wanting him to think she was watching him. Her eyes landed on a young woman furiously scribbling on a pad as she observed a Grecian statue. Opposed to the rest of the visitors, who seemed to be there to be seen and socialize, the woman was working. Diana wondered what she was doing.

"Lady Hensley, I didn't know you were a lover of history," Devons said, bowing before her.

Diana took a deep breath and turned. "The same could be said about you, Mr. Devons."

He grimaced. "Please, just Devons is fine."

She sighed, and he chuckled. It was a deep, rich, alluring sound. "I'm not a formal man."

She smiled. "Very well."

"Diana, you must introduce me to your friend," her aunt said, even though she knew very well who he was.

Diana stopped herself from rolling her eyes. "Devons, please meet my aunt, Lady Clark."

Devons bowed again. "It's nice to meet such a lovely lady."

Aunt Winifred tittered. "Oh, you are delightful."

He winked at her, and her aunt grinned as if she'd received a puppy. She fanned herself and turned to Diana. "I think I will get some punch. Would you like some?"

"I will go with you."

Aunt Winifred shook her head. "No. Stay and talk."

Her aunt smiled impishly at her and left. Diana frowned at her retreating figure. What was she up to?

"You didn't answer my question. What brings you here?" Devons asked with a smile.

"A friend recommended I attend."

He looked at her with a wicked grin. "A gentleman?"

She blushed, which he seemed to take as confirmation. She wasn't outraged by his improper question. She didn't know why because they barely knew each other, but a sense of familiarity and ease seemed to exist between them.

"He should have escorted you."

Not wanting him to get the wrong impression, she said, "A lady friend. I was hoping she would be here."

Just then, they were interrupted by Lady Wesley and Lady Mattle. "Lady Hensley, it's so lovely to see you."

Diana forced herself to smile even though she wasn't fond of Lady Wesley. The lady was beautiful, but she'd always struck Diana as intentionally mean. Devons stiffened next to her. Lady Wesley's eyes raked over him as if she knew him far better than she should. Diana flushed at the obscene perusal, preparing to leave.

Devons's bearing turned cold, and he appeared unaffected by her stare except for the tightening of his jaw. Something was amiss, but she didn't know what. The lady glanced between her and Devons, her smirk turning colder the longer she studied them. "I see Lady Hensley found you. I recommended she spend time with you."

His hard facade cracked for a moment, and he frowned at

Diana. She looked back at him, confused. What was Lady Wesley talking about?

"She asked me about you. I told her we were on a little break. That you were wonderful to have fun with but to make sure you understood your place."

Diana gasped. "Lady Wesley!"

She had no idea what the viper was up to. She'd never talked to her about Devons. In all honesty, she rarely spoke with the lady.

"Don't be shy, Diana," the lady said, winking at her as if they were friends.

Devons's eyes darted between the ladies, and he emanated with anger.

"Devons—"

"If you will excuse me," Devons said before Diana could deny the lady's words.

He walked away as if he had no worries, but Diana sensed it was a show. She wasn't sure what Lady Wesley was up to, but the woman had used her. Fury swelled in her. "How dare you! We are not friends, nor would I be friends with someone who treats others in such a way."

The lady's eyes raked over her. "Devons is mine."

Had the lady insinuated they were friends to Devons so he wouldn't speak to Diana? And what must he think of Lady Wesley that she was confident he would behave that way? A dark laugh escaped Diana, drawing stares their way. "I hope he has enough sense to choose better."

She spun on her heels and headed in the same direction as Devons. Diana needed to explain she was not friends with Lady Wesley, and they'd never discussed him. She flushed. He couldn't think she'd planned to proposition him. She was one of the uneventful ladies, the moral backbone of society. She quickly made her way down the hallway she saw him take. She didn't know what she would say to him but she—

Diana let out a gasp as strong arms from an alcove grabbed

her and pulled her against the wall. Her eyes widened in alarm as she stared up at Devons. He looked furious as his black eyes assessed her. She flushed.

"So, you were talking with Lady Wesley about me?"

Diana shook her head but froze as Devons leaned in and nuzzled her neck. Her stomach dipped. "Do you think of me when you're alone?"

She felt his lips graze her neck, and Diana trembled, causing him to chuckle darkly. "Is this what you want, my lady? A tryst in a darkened corner?"

He nipped at her ear, and she let out a moan, shocking herself. "Do you wish I would have taken you to bed that night all those years ago when I brought you home from the Den? Your husband wouldn't have ever known. What a charmed life that would have been. Married to a soon-to-be duke and taking the King of the Den as your lover."

Devons's last words chilled any desire racing through her body. She would have never betrayed Stuart. What was she doing? She was almost ready to submit to a man who thought she would betray the one person who had held her entire heart and still did. She pushed at his chest. "Release me."

He stepped back and smirked at her. Gone was the charming man she observed in the fountain or the man who spoke with her son. Now, he was replaced with a hardened person that she didn't like—no different from Lady Wesley herself.

"You're an arrogant ass!" she hissed.

His eyes widened at her use of profanity. She stared at him haughtily, not embarrassed. He leaned against the other wall, his eyes raking over her. "I can tell you desire me by how flushed your cheeks are and how you tremble when I lean into you."

"Unlike you, Mr. Devons, I require more than physical attraction to bed someone. I came here to apologize for what Lady Wesley said, but now I see that the two of you deserve each other. I suddenly don't feel the need to explain anything to you."

She pushed past him, hating him but also hating herself because as much as she wanted to deny it, her body had reacted to him.

SEBASTIAN STORMED INTO the Den. He climbed the stairs leading to the walkway overlooking the club's main hall two at a time. His eyes swept over the room. It was late afternoon, but some gentlemen were already starting to arrive, ready to play at the card tables. He hated that Lilah had gotten a rise out of him. To be honest, it wasn't she who affected him.

Lady Hensley had triggered his fury. Though he didn't know her well, not once had he assumed she was friends with Lilah or viewed people the same way his ex-lover did. He didn't care that she played the proper society lady. Plenty of women did. That was one of the primary reasons the Den's decadent balls required masks. What Sebastian couldn't tolerate were lords and ladies who believed they were better than others because of their untainted lineages. Beliefs held by Lilah and, from what he gleaned, Lady Hensley as well.

He shouldn't give a damn about what the mousy woman thought of him. Then why was he thinking of her? He knew why. He desired her. Sebastian scowled, denying it to himself. She wasn't his type. A flash of the lady in her wrap and her disheveled hair falling around her shoulders appeared in his mind. He pushed the thought away. It didn't matter. He had no plans to see her again.

Sebastian turned to one of the four doors along the walkway and made his way to his office. He threw himself into his chair and grabbed the stack of messages left for him. Most were requests asking for an extension on credit. Even Lord Wesley was on credit at the Den. Yet he had been good enough for Lilah. Her words from their last night together attempted to push to the front of his mind, but he wouldn't allow it. He had never felt bitter that he wasn't a lord and wouldn't now.

He stared at the familiar scrawl on one envelope and smirked. What did Addie want? There was gossip she was up to something. Sebastian still couldn't believe her husband had taken her best friend Eleanor as his lover. The *ton* was all agog over it. He had to admit it was rather shocking. He liked both Addie and her husband Lord Hawley. The man never struck him as someone who sought attention, so the fact he'd committed such a public transgression was rather appalling.

It shouldn't be such a scandal. They'd been separated for a decade, but Addie loved to thumb her nose at society. In return, they gleefully shared any disparaging gossip they could about her. He opened the envelope and pulled out her message.

Devons,

I have an exciting venture I must speak with you about. I promise you won't want to miss out. Please pay me a visit on Thursday afternoon to learn more. I can't wait to share with you the adventure that awaits you.

Lady Hawley.

Sebastian shook his head as his lips quirked up. He would call on her even if he wanted nothing to do with her venture. They were too good of friends for him not to. He leaned back in his chair as his mind went back to earlier events. Lilah had riled him up. It still embarrassed him that he'd been so wrong about her. Their time together had seemed as if nothing mattered but the two of them. Today, she'd been cruel, and he hadn't seen a glimpse of the adoring lady he remembered.

He'd also misjudged Lady Hensley. Sebastian was still surprised about the association between the two ladies. Before today, he would have guessed that Lady Hensley was more proper than anything. He smirked. She could still be judgmental even if she were the moral paragon of society. Still, no matter what she thought of Sebastian, the lady had wanted him. The sound of her moans, when his lips touched her skin earlier, flashed in his mind.

"I've been looking for you," Celeste Hathaway said from the doorway, startling him.

She was dressed in a rich red silk gown that accentuated every one of her curves and highlighted her rich blonde mane. He smiled at her wickedly. "Here I am."

The tempting woman rolled her eyes. "I'm not one of your ladies. I'm immune to your flirting."

And she was. They would be a perfect match. Both were children of lords, sired outside of marriage. However, Sebastian felt fortunate that he grew up with his father. The research Sebastian had done on Celeste indicated her own father played cards at the Den. Not once had Sebastian seen him ever acknowledge her. He mentioned it once, and she cut him off before he could finish asking his question.

She deserved better treatment. Sebastian should marry her and make her the wealthiest woman in all of London. "Why have we never gotten together?

Celeste pursed her red lips. "What is wrong with you? You are still not pouting about your lady who threw you over for the very lord who can't seem to stop gambling in your club. It's her mistake. You must know that."

He sighed. "I don't wish to talk about Lilah."

She made her way to the desk and sat on the edge across from him. "She is—"

"You have asked me not to bring up your personal life. I'm simply asking you to reciprocate."

A sigh escaped the lady. "Donahue said you wished to speak with me."

Donahue had to be the most organized and thorough butler in all of London. When Sebastian and the other owners acquired the Den property, he'd come with it. They'd offered to give him an exemplary reference if he didn't want to be part of a gentlemen's club, but he refused. The man was the most proper thing about the Den.

Celeste lifted a brow, waiting for him to speak. He smiled at her barely contained impatience. "I wanted to see if you wished to play host one night a week."

"I'm the host for the gaming tables."

"I mean for the entire Den."

She opened her mouth and then shut it, shocked. Finally, she said, "When I first started here, you said no man but you would fill that role."

Sebastian's eyes swept over her. Shocking him, she blushed. "You're no man."

Celeste smirked. "No, I'm not. Why now?"

"My brother seems to think I'm afraid to leave this property."

"You have been fairly predictable in your activities. Spending a great deal of time enjoying the vice we serve to others."

"I too am allowed to enjoy myself," he stated.

She snorted. "That you have."

He sighed. Malcolm had already lectured him. He wouldn't allow Celeste to do it as well. "You are not here to talk about my behavior. Do you have interest?"

She slid off the corner of his desk and studied him. "I will do it, but I demand a raise."

Good for her, he thought. "Of course. We will meet with all the owners to discuss the specifics."

She nodded and frowned. "You do know you were too good for her."

Was it that obvious the lady hurt him? Did everyone think he was moping around? He rolled his eyes. "Out."

She smirked and flounced out of the room.

Chapter Four

DIANA WALKED WITH Arthur, the Earl of Tremont, along a pathway in Hyde Park as Robert raced ahead chasing squirrels. His governess, Miss Melanie, the saint she was, kept up with him. She smiled as he looked over his shoulder at Miss Melanie, grinning mischievously.

"It's a beautiful day to take such a charming lady for a walk," Arthur said.

They had long ago agreed to do away with formality when it was just the two of them. He'd become a dear friend as she dealt with the impacts of losing Stuart. In truth, before her husband's passing, Diana doubted she'd spoken more than a few words to Arthur, but death, she supposed, brought people together.

He stopped suddenly. Diana followed suit. Robert and Miss Melanie darted off to explore a wooded area.

Turning back to Arthur, she asked, "Is everything all right?"

He nodded and motioned to a bench. "Would you please join me?"

Diana frowned, perplexed by his actions. What she enjoyed so much about Arthur was how at ease they were with one another. He seemed nervous, making her anxious. Still, she sat, and he joined her.

"Diana—"

"Mummy, look at this beetle," Robert said, now only a few

feet away from them.

She'd been studying Arthur so intently she didn't realize he'd come to see them. She smiled patiently, leaning forward to examine the insect in his hand. It was a tiny thing, but Robert grinned proudly.

"It's lovely."

"Yes, I agree," Arthur said impatiently. He waved Miss Melanie over. "Can you please take him to play? I need a moment of his mother's time."

Robert's excitement diminished. Miss Melanie ushered him away, and Diana turned back to Arthur with a frown. He held up his hands. "I'm sorry. I have been building up the courage to speak with you for weeks, or I wouldn't be so dismissive of the boy."

What was he going on about? She shook her head. "I don't understand."

He took a deep breath and pulled a folded piece of paper from his pocket. Horror filled her as he showed it to her. It was the caricature of the uneventful lady. What was he doing with it?

"Diana, I admire you for all your wonderful qualities. You are a virtuous lady. Recently, I came across this article, and it only increased my admiration for you because you personify every trait that keeps society together. I shall read it to you."

"No! Please don't," Diana interrupted him.

The harshness of her tone caused Arthur to jerk back. She could not sit here and listen to him recite the list she knew so well. A list that annoyed her. She took a deep breath and forced herself to smile. "I have seen the article."

A smile appeared on his face, pleased. "I imagine you have discerned the similarities."

She suppressed the urge to rail at him that she was so much more than those few qualities. Her sister was correct. No lady should be put in such simple boxes.

"Well, I'm glad we are in agreement."

They weren't, but Diana said nothing.

He continued. "These last few months have been nothing short of perfect. We have come to know each other so well. Reading the article heightened my awareness of all your exemplary traits."

Arthur was going to propose! Diana blinked rapidly at him, willing him not to. The man just described her as the very thing she disliked. He sat up straighter and took her hand. "I think a match between us would be most beneficial. Lady Hensley—"

"I'm not ready."

He went rigid, turning bright red. Diana gasped, horror filling her that she was so blunt. "It isn't that I don't want to ever marry again, but I need more time."

Arthur took a deep breath as if composing himself. He smiled tightly. "I didn't mean to rush you. Still, I would be honored if you would consider me when you are ready."

"Of course, I would," she said, doing her best to conceal how overwhelmed she felt.

"You are the epitome of what a lady should aspire to be. Perfect in bearing, grace, and above reproach."

Diana wanted to scream that she was more than those qualities. Still, she remained quiet. She'd been raised to be the ideal lady and had excelled in her role. Her eyes roamed over him. Was she being unreasonable? Arthur was perfectly suitable and even handsome. He was tall, slender, with brown hair. Why did she feel like something was missing? Perhaps because he was so different from Stuart in appearance and personality.

Stuart was a short, larger man who, in all honesty, had won her heart over time. Theirs had not been a love match at first, but his gentleness, kindness, and interest in her thoughts made her fall for him. Diana was doubtful she would ever feel such devotion again. Still, shouldn't she feel something for Arthur? At least desire? Perhaps she was incapable of feeling such passion for another.

Liar. Liar. An infuriating man and his words flashed in her mind. *Is this what you want, my lady? A tryst in a darkened corner.*

She flushed, horrified she had a respectable man on the verge of proposing, and her mind was fixated on a rogue who operated a scandalous club. What was she doing?

Arthur took her hand. "Just know when you are ready, I'm here."

"You have my word. You are the first person I would consider," Diana lied.

Later that evening, Diana sat in her drawing room, turning the message over in her hand. Yes, if she weren't intrigued before, which she was, Diana was now. The missive requested that Diana meet with Lady Hawley at Seely House in three days to learn about an exciting new venture. Seely House was in the northwest area of Mayfair near Diana's home. The peculiar part was the building had been empty for years.

She should send a response stating she couldn't attend. Diana should be content with her life and accept Arthur's proposal, but part of her vehemently refused the idea. She wanted to be more than the traits the awful article listed. Was it ludicrous that she hoped whatever Lady Hawley was proposing would help her prove she was more than the caricature?

She reached into her skirt pocket and pulled out her copy of the annoying article. She unfolded it and frowned at the caricature. Arthur suggested it was her to perfection, but she disagreed. Diana balled the paper up in her hand. No longer would she allow herself to be so easily defined. She tossed it into the fire. It was time to try new things, starting with exploring Lady Hawley's venture.

⟫⟪

"HAVE YOU LOST your mind, Addie?" Devons asked his dear friend as he sat in her drawing room.

The voluptuous beauty rolled her eyes. "I'm serious."

"What do you know about artifacts or ancient texts?"

She rose from her chair and grabbed the brandy decanter, pouring him more before she added some to her glass. "I know enough, and what I don't know, I plan to have the best minds in England help me."

He raised a skeptical brow at her as she sat back down. She ignored it and continued, "Did you know the Duchess of Lusby, prior to her wedding, spent four years working at ancient sites cataloging artifacts."

"She's been married for at least a decade," he reminded her.

"Or that Sarah Martin, the daughter of the President of the London Society of Antiquaries, applied five times to be admitted to her father's club and was turned down each time. Her father is the president!"

"It's a men's-only club. I have no problem with that. I, too, own a men's only establishment."

She frowned at him disapprovingly. "Yes, but you employ women and hold events that ladies can attend."

"If you are asking if I'm some type of secret advocate of women's rights, I will be quite frank, it isn't something I spend much time thinking about."

"You are more of a supporter than you realize. I wouldn't be meeting with you if I thought otherwise. I need your help and involvement."

His eyes narrowed. Addie was a shrewd lady, and Sebastian didn't doubt there was a reason she wanted his participation. "What part am I to play in this escapade?"

She took a sip of her drink. "You are right to suspect I have hidden motives."

Sebastian snorted. Addie always had an agenda. She appeared carefree to all of London, but he'd known her way too long to believe the facade she presented to society. He'd seen the scandal sheets. He knew she was hurting because of what happened between Eleanor and Lord Hawley.

"Pretty brazen of you to take on his club."

Sebastian thought she would feign ignorance. She twirled her brandy glass silently but finally looked up. "He took Eleanor away from me. My dearest friend."

He pressed his lips together, knowing he couldn't do anything to prevent his friend's pain. Still, this was a complex venture and would require a great deal of work. He needed to know more.

"What is my part?"

She took a deep breath. "My goal is to have the entire club managed by a board of women. The problem with such an initiative is anything we own is the property of our spouses or guardians. I want to make sure they do not have the ability to gain control over what we build. I need you to be the sole owner and then we will draft up a trust, giving overall management to the board."

He was shocked. Sebastian and Addie were close friends, but he didn't realize she trusted him that much. He was honored, to be honest. A frown marred his face. "Do you suspect your husband would take this venture from you?"

She smiled sadly, and Sebastian had the urge to pummel Lord Hawley. "I don't, but I also never believed he would involve himself with someone so close to me. It is merely a precaution to protect not only me but the other ladies as well. Would you like to know what you will gain from this?"

Sebastian nodded.

Addie continued, "Prior to investing or splitting profits among the group, we would be willing to give you forty percent of all revenue generated."

Addie really wanted this, Sebastian realized. She was being far too accommodating. He took a sip of a drink. "What will the payout be for the board members?"

"For two years, we will reinvest any revenue back into the club and then, following that, split any profits equally among the board."

Sebastian was silent. He pulled his watch out and read the text from his father before flipping the cases open and closed as he pondered Addie's words. Eventually, he said. "I will forgo any revenue for the first two years and take an equal share with the board."

Addie beamed. "And that is why you are the only man I would trust in this venture. You, Sebastian Devons, are a decent man. A true champion for women."

He ignored her statement, not wanting to argue with her, and asked, "What will the name of this club be?"

"The Historical Society for Female Curators."

"Do you have the capital to start this?"

Addie grinned. "Some, but I also have an idea. I need your help with that, too. It is the bigger request."

An hour later, Sebastian sat in his carriage, still incredulous Addie convinced him to agree to her outlandish scheme. He wasn't sure if it was because he had Malcolm's voice in his head saying he needed to do something besides spend all his time at the Den or he wanted to help his friend pull off the impossible.

Regardless, he was committed now. He would need to see if Celeste would play host more than the one night a week she'd agreed to. Though it made him nervous to be away from the Den for so long, Sebastian completely trusted that Malcolm, Miller, and Celeste would be fine for two months. Malcolm was right. He was stuck in a rut. He needed this venture even if he still thought it was crazy.

What did he have to lose? He couldn't think of anything. Sebastian would spend two months touring far-flung lands with his good friend and then watch a group of ladies shake society up a bit.

Chapter Five

DIANA MADE HER way up the front path of the Seely House, joining another woman who was knocking on the door, but no one answered. She knocked harder.

"Perhaps we should go in. I don't know if there is a staff accepting visitors," Diana suggested.

The young woman turned to her, startled to see someone else. She was the woman from the exhibit Diana had seen sketching a statue. She nodded and pushed the door open. As they entered, Diana glanced around the two-story foyer, which had a split staircase leading into separate mezzanines. A commotion from the one on the left caused Diana and the woman to turn. Lady Hawley grinned down at them, waving exuberantly.

"Hello. You both made it. I'm so pleased. I'm sorry no one opened the door for you. My butler, Harrison, was supposed to do that, but he was so appalled at the state of Seely House that he became distracted cleaning it up."

The butler, Diana assumed, threw the doors of a room open on the first floor, shaking his head in disgust. "My lady, perhaps we should have your guests join you at the Hawley Townhouse."

She let out a shriek that echoed through the empty, expansive room before grinning. "Nonsense, it adds to the fun."

The butler looked like he was about to roll his eyes, but after quickly glancing at Diana and the other woman, he thought better of it. "As you wish."

"Good day," a woman said from behind Diana.

They all turned. It was the Duchess of Lusby.

"Your Grace," Lady Hawley said, curtsying. Everyone else followed her lead.

The Duchess of Lusby nodded in acknowledgment. She was dressed in a gray-and-purple frock, a sign that she was nearing the end of mourning for her husband. The duchess was a bit of a mystery. She'd fled England and stayed gone for a few years, then returned to marry a duke twenty years her senior. The couple only hosted one ball a year in London and spent most of their time in the country.

The duchess shifted, uncomfortable with the staring. "Lady Hawley, your message said you had a venture."

Their hostess descended the stairs. "Yes, that is correct. Please join me in this room right over here."

They all followed her to the space the butler had just emerged from. To Diana's surprise, the room had furniture and didn't look nearly as worn as the foyer. Perhaps Harrison could work miracles.

As they sat, Lady Hawley said, "Let me do introductions while we wait for the last lady?"

She looked at the young woman that Diana had seen at the exhibit. "This is Sarah Martin. She is a lead scholar in Roman art history. She recently wrote a paper proving there were well-regarded and highly sought-after female painters in ancient times. She has studied with some of the greatest scholars in England. Did I forget anything, Miss Martin?"

The young woman's eyes widened, shocked. Lady Hawley grinned at her before turning her gaze to the Duchess of Lusby. "Her Grace, while currently not involved in antiquities, spent several years traveling to various historical sites to catalog artifacts. It is rumored that she can look at an object and tell you what time period and civilization it is from."

The duchess frowned at her, not impressed with her

knowledge. Before she could respond, their host turned to Diana. A wave of anxiousness filled her. She was unsure and nervous about what their host would say.

"Then there is the Marchioness of Hensley, a highly respectable society member."

Diana winced, flushing. There was that blasted description again. The duchess rolled her eyes. "Are you saying the rest of us are not?"

Lady Hawley let out another guffaw. "Of course not."

The butler appeared at the door, interrupting them. "My lady, Lady Esme."

Diana knew the last lady quite well. Both she and Lady Esme's siblings had married into the same family.

"Sorry, I'm late."

Their hostess rose to greet her. "You are here now. We are in the middle of introductions."

Lady Esme took the seat next to Diana, smiling, relieved she knew someone. "And lastly, this is Lady Esme, a historian. I believe your interests lie in the earliest civilizations on earth and the building of their societies."

She blushed. "Well, not a real historian, more so self-taught."

"Only because you are a woman," the Duchess of Lusby said.

Lady Esme turned to her, surprised that she knew who she was. The duchess didn't explain any further. Diana studied those around her. There couldn't be a more different group of women than those sitting in this room. What was Lady Hawley planning?

"Harrison, can you prepare the refreshments?" Lady Hawley asked.

"Yes, my lady," he said from the foyer.

She took a deep breath. "I have invited you all here to ask you to be on my board for a new venture. I plan to establish the Historical Society for Female Curators, which will be based out of this very building. It will not be an easy feat, but I think it will be a worthwhile endeavor."

Stunned silence met her statement. Diana, again, didn't understand why she was asked to attend. She knew nothing about antiquities.

Lady Hawley continued, "Imagine this building filled with artifacts, ancient texts, and exhibits that make London giddy with excitement. Have you ever been to the London Society of Antiquaries exhibit? It's dreadfully dull."

"The study of history isn't a game," Miss Martin said judgmentally.

Their hostess rolled her eyes. "I understand that, but presentation is so important. We could use all of our skills to make this venture wildly successful. The Duchess of Lusby, Lady Esme, and you will ensure we provide worthwhile antiquities, and I will draw in visitors."

She hadn't mentioned Diana. What did the lady want from her? Perhaps her being here had been a mistake. She felt her cheeks heat, but then Lady Hawley fixed her eyes on her. "And you, Lady Hensley, will give us the appearance of respectability that we need to survive any insinuations thrown our way."

Ahhh…she understood. She glanced around the room. The women present were either considered eccentric, scandalous, or both. She was here to provide an image of high moral standing. Why did Diana want her attendance to be for something different?

"Will we be stakeholders in this venture?" the duchess asked.

Miss Martin added, "Will it be an all-women's club? Would our families need to be supportive of the venture?"

Lady Hawley smiled. "All wonderful questions. While I imagine most guardians, fathers, and husbands would be supportive, the plan would be to do this on our own. We would have overall control."

Lady Esme wrinkled her nose in confusion. "How would that be possible without the ability to legally own the club?"

Their host nodded. "You make a valid point, but after speaking with my solicitor, I believe I have found a solution. We have an investor who has agreed to back us and sign off on a trust, giving us full control."

Diana and the other women stared at her in shock. Diana asked, "Why would they do that?"

"They will get a percentage of any profits, but they also believe in setting up this club as much as I do."

The duchess frowned at her. "How do we know this isn't a passing fancy for you?"

Her comment hinted at the situation involving Lady Hawley's husband, but their hostess stared back at her innocently. "My only motive is to make sure women also have a club that allows them to be involved in the antiquities field. If we happen to do better than other clubs, that will only be an added benefit."

A skeptical snort escaped the duchess. "Are you expecting us to invest our own money?"

Lady Hawley shook her head. "No. The investor has agreed to provide some upfront funds to set up our club's location, which will be right here."

Diana glanced around the massive run-down building. It needed a great deal of work. She suspected the other women were thinking the same thing. As if not wanting them to dwell too much on it, Lady Hawley clapped excitedly. "I have also established another avenue to generate income while we get started."

"How?" Miss Martin asked.

Lady Hawley grabbed a document from a satchel. With a flourish, she placed it on the table in the middle of all of them. They all leaned forward and read it.

First Cruise of Its Kind!

Join the crew of the SS Lark for a leisure cruise to new and exciting locations. Stops include Porto, Sardinia, and of course the best place for respite, Tuscany.

Don't miss out on your chance!

Diana looked up at her. "How does this generate income?"

Lady Hawley smiled. "For our club, our investor and I will travel on this cruise containing new destinations. I have convinced two newspapers to publish a column generated from updates we send back at each port. The club will receive royalties."

"That will be good for short-term income, but it will be at least a year, likely two, to get the club up and running," the duchess stated.

Diana suspected Lady Hawley didn't appreciate the duchess's practical points. Her smile was becoming more forced. "You are quite right, Your Grace, but I have also partnered with the ship owner to potentially build a tour for ladies."

The whole scheme seemed rather outlandish to Diana, and she sensed from looking around that the others thought so too. Yet she hesitated to say no.

"Who is the club investor?" Lady Esme asked, changing the subject.

They had discussed so many things, Diana had forgotten they didn't know who he was. Lady Hawley shifted uneasily in her chair. "Someone who has agreed to own the club but won't have any say in how it is managed. And, most importantly for the cruise, someone all the ladies would love to read about as he goes adventuring."

"We would all need to have a solicitor review the trust and know who this investor is before agreeing to anything," the duchess stated.

"Of course," Lady Hawley said.

A loud pounding at the front door halted any further conversation. Their hostess's eyes widened. They were silent as they tried to hear what Harrison was saying. It was a male voice. Lady Hawley muttered under her breath and jumped up. The door was thrust open, and Lord Hawley stood in the doorway, scowling.

Diana gaped at him. She'd never seen someone in polite society appear so unhinged. His eyes raked over the ladies until they landed on his wife.

"A word, Lady Hawley," he bit out.

"I don't have time right now."

His eyes narrowed. "I insist."

Lady Hawley sighed and followed her angry husband from the room.

"What do you think that's about?" Miss Martin questioned.

The duchess shrugged. Lady Esme asked, "Do you think what she is proposing is possible? Could we really start up our own club?"

"Remember, Lady Hawley has her own agenda for doing this, and it is related to the man she is speaking with," the duchess said.

"But it would be quite the achievement if we pulled it off," Miss Martin said, her eyes filled with excitement.

"It is a rather bold endeavor," Diana said.

Miss Martin nodded. "While completely outlandish, she has done a great deal of work already. I would love to one-up the London Society of Antiquaries."

"Your father's club," the duchess said.

Miss Martin blushed but didn't respond. The duchess turned her gaze to Diana. "What do you think, Lady Hensley?"

What did she think? She thought it was an awful idea but was surprisingly still interested. Still, her practical side told her it was too much.

"I mean it, Adelaide!" Lord Hawley roared from the foyer.

Everyone went quiet, and the faintest murmurs and gasps could be heard. Diana and the duchess rose simultaneously, both concerned. The front door slammed, and the door to the room they were sitting in opened. Lady Hawley entered, looking dazed.

"Is everything fine?" Lady Esme asked.

Lady Hawley smiled sadly, "Perhaps this wasn't meant to be. Lord Hawley said he would drastically limit my access to our money if I went on the leisure cruise or left England. The money from the newspaper royalties and grand tours for ladies is what I hoped would sustain the club for the next two years."

"There must be another option," the duchess said.

Everyone's eyes darted to her, shocked. Was the Duchess of Lusby agreeing to participate? She pursed her lips together. "I don't like highhandedness. If we can find a way to still do the cruise, I will join the effort."

"I could go," Miss Martin said.

Lady Hawley shook her head. "I appreciate that, but you are not well-known within the right circles. I don't mean that as an offense."

Miss Martin sighed. "You are right. Well, what can we do? We can't let your husband dictate what we are allowed to do. It won't do."

All the women nodded, even Diana. She felt inspired and excited. Shocking herself, she said, "What if I went?"

Everyone stared at her as if she'd suggested the craziest notion. Then Lady Hawley guffawed. Her notorious laugh that she was known for traveled through the room. Diana flushed, embarrassed.

Their host shook her head. "I'm not laughing at you. I think it is perfect. You are the complete opposite of our investor. Are you sure?"

Diana would have to see if her sister would care for Robert while she was gone for the two months, but perhaps this was her opportunity to do something different, something radical. She nodded.

"So, we are doing this?" Lady Esme asked, somewhat dazed.

The duchess nodded. "As long as there are no issues with the trust."

Diana, along with Miss Martin and Lady Esme nodded. They were going to do this.

"You never said who the investor was," Miss Martin mentioned.

At that exact moment, Harrison stepped into the entryway and announced, "My lady, Mr. Devons."

Lady Hawley beamed at them. "He just arrived."

Diana's stomach dropped. It couldn't be him.

SEBASTIAN LOOKED AT the ladies who sat in the room, gawking at him. It was evident that if a flying pig had flown into the area, they would have been less surprised. He glanced back at Addie, concerned. She grinned at him and motioned for him to sit. Sebastian took a seat in one of the empty wingback chairs.

He looked around more intently, and his gaze ground to a stop at one brown-haired lady with one of those silly caps. It was Lady Hensley. What was she doing here? He doubted she and Addie traveled in the same circles. Their eyes met. She stared at him in horror. He turned back to Addie. "What have I missed, Lady Hawley?"

Addie beamed at him. "We have a change in plans, but not to worry, nothing that will impact you drastically."

The way she said it made Sebastian suspect it would significantly affect him.

"Has something changed with the leisure cruise?"

Addie's eyes darted to Lady Hensley, and she fidgeted. His good friend was never nervous. She looked back at him and smiled the way she did when she tried to charm her next conquest. He frowned back at her. While he could never deny Addie was stunning, her coquettish games had long ceased to affect him. He raised a black brow in response.

"Lord Hawley stopped by," she said and then sighed. "He is threatening to limit my funds if I attempt to leave on the *SS Lark* or leave England."

Sebastian's eyes widened. Hawley had never struck him as a controlling type of husband. In all honesty, he'd never seen him show any emotion related to his wife's antics.

"Yes, I can see from your expression you find it rather surprising. I did as well," Addie said as Harrison walked in.

The butler carried a tray of champagne and commenced handing them out. Sebastian took one and nodded thank you to the man. Sebastian doubted Addie paid him enough to put up with her escapades.

"I believe it is in the best interest of your club that, at a minimum, one lady from the board participate in the leisure cruise. It won't do for your all-women's establishment to publish a column only from a man's perspective. As we both stated before, I'm merely there to add more excitement."

She smiled at him, and he sensed trouble was afoot. Addie leaned over and squeezed his hand in reassurance. All the other ladies' eyes widened at her familiarity. "And we do appreciate your willingness. You are a true supporter of our cause."

The woman in mourning, who Sebastian believed was the Duchess of Lusby, snorted. His eyes darted to her. Perhaps she would replace Addie. Sebastian imagined he could make that work. He was just adapting to the idea when Addie said, "Lady Hensley has agreed to go in my place."

Sebastian froze and did his best to keep his expression shuttered. Addie could have said anyone, and he would have been less surprised. He lifted the champagne to his lips and drank the bubbly liquid, not pulling the glass away until he finished it all. His eyes wandered over to Lady Hensley, who was looking down, drumming her fingers on her white-and-green-striped dress. The color was lovely on her, and if she didn't have the blasted cap on or her hair so severely tied back, she would look quite beautiful today.

"You are up for taking this adventure with me, Lady Hensley?" he asked, the words coming out more suggestively than he meant.

Her head jerked up. She pursed her lips. He lifted a challenging brow and saw a bit of fire flare in her eyes. He forced himself not to smirk.

He wasn't sure how Addie convinced this woman to go with him. Perhaps Lady Wesley had been telling the truth. This moral paragon was looking for fun. He didn't judge her for that or the stench of hypocrisy that came with it, but he hated that she likely thought she was better than him. Her eyes narrowed as if she sensed the direction his thoughts were going.

"I agreed before I knew who my travel companion was to be," she ground out.

He smirked again but remained silent, wanting to aggravate her. Tension wafted between the two of them. Addie frowned. "You already know each other?"

"Mr. Devons is my neighbor."

Harrison stopped before him to refill his glass, and this time, he took a smaller drink. "So now that you know it is me to serve as your travel companion, what will it be?"

He expected her to blush and make up an excuse not to go. She was a leader of London society, and he was a rake who ran a scandalous gentlemen's club. Though, times were changing. He often found himself, over the last few years, mingling more openly with his brother and other lords. But Sebastian suspected that had more to do with the character of those lords opposed to any real societal change.

Shockingly, she stared back at him as if he had thrown down a challenge, and she would be damned before she backed down. Who was this woman? The fact he didn't understand her fascinated and unsettled him.

"Who it is does not influence my decision at all. I imagine we will get along fine when needed."

Addie tilted her head, studying both, and frowned. "You will be expected to spend a great deal of time together."

"Are you trying to talk them out of it?" the young lady who hadn't spoken yet muttered.

Addie smiled at her. "Of course not, Miss Martin. Still, each adventure they have needs to be told from both of their perspectives for this to work. The masses will be delighted to read updates from the most proper lady in all of London and the King of the Den. Lady Hensley will be a wonderful contrast to Devons, and her pristine reputation will deter any salacious gossip."

The sound of the lady's gasp, as he kissed and nuzzled her neck at the exhibit, bounced around in his head. She pursed her lips at Addie's description, intriguing Sebastian more. He suspected she didn't like being held to such a high standard. His body reacted in a way that infuriated him.

What the hell was wrong with him? This woman was not his type at all. Addie interrupted his thoughts by clapping, capturing everyone's attention. "So, we are all in agreement?"

"What will we do while they are on their leisure cruise?"

"Take our next step, of course, which is to turn this dilapidated building into the grandest antiquities club in all of England." Her eyes darted to Lady Hensley. "This will work out perfectly. Almost like it's meant to be. I can be here to plan out the exhibits with the other board members. Thank you, Diana, for volunteering to go. Is it fine if I call you by your given name?"

His new travel companion smiled. "I think we are beyond formality."

All the ladies nodded. Sebastian smiled. "I couldn't agree more, Diana."

She stiffened, and he had to stop himself from laughing out loud. He suspected he wasn't included in her previous statement. Too damn bad. Sebastian enjoyed goading the lady. He would continue to use her given name.

Addie beamed and lifted her champagne. "To our venture?"

Sebastian studied the women as they each raised their glasses. How had Addie convinced these ladies to join? He wasn't sure, but they all appeared as determined as Addie to succeed.

Chapter Six

"What have I done? I can't leave England for two months," Diana stated as she paced back and forth in her sister's drawing room.

Clara laughed at her frantic statement and her husband shook his head, frowning at her. Diana knew there was a reason she liked her brother-in-law Sam Kincaide. She stopped her pacing and put her hands on her hips. "This isn't amusing. I have committed to something without any thought of the repercussions. I don't do things like this."

"You told me only last week you were tired of life as it was. This is your chance to try something different. You would have never agreed to this, no matter how much pressure you felt if you didn't want to go. It will be a grand adventure! Remember when we were girls and you used to sneak those books from Father's library about faraway lands?"

Diana had forgotten about that. A memory of her staring at maps and studying information about various civilizations flashed in her mind. Eventually, her father found out, and she'd been punished for her curiosity. Her parents held specific beliefs about what ladies and girls should focus their attention on and it wasn't learning about the world.

"Robert has already been through so much with losing Stuart."

Her sister shook her head. "Sam and I will take him to the country. The season is almost over. He'll fish, go riding, and run free."

"I would be happy to leave sooner if you like," Sam added with a wink.

Clara rolled her eyes at her husband. Sam, over the years, had come to like the whirlwind of London less and less.

"Not to mention, Henry will be home from school. Robert adores him and they will have a wonderful time together."

Their brother lived with Clara and Sam full-time when he wasn't away at school.

"He would love that," Diana begrudgingly admitted.

Years ago, Diana's parents departed England surrounded in scandal and heavily in debt. Both Diana and Clara's husbands had agreed to make their situation right and provide them with an allowance if they never returned. After they left, Sam worked painstakingly hard with Henry to make his dukedom solvent again. Her brother was very close to him.

A shiver coursed through her. They'd not been the type of parents one loved or adored. They'd used their children as if they were pawns to help improve their status, completely indifferent to the impact their selfish choices had on her or her siblings.

Their final last dastardly deed had seen Clara almost lose her life. They'd attempted to marry her off to a deranged lord. Sam had stepped in and wed her, infuriating her parents. They'd disowned Clara for marrying him, a commoner. Their father had passed away last year, but Diana hoped it still rankled her mother that a man who she thought was so below them was the one who saved the dukedom.

A frown flitted across Diana's face. Recently, she'd received multiple letters from their mother about returning to England. Last year's revolutions seemed to cover the continent, including where she lived. Only now were things quieting down. The letters of late had been different from her mother's usual condescending missives. Even with all they'd put her and her siblings through, Diana wondered if her mother was well after her father's passing. An absurd idea popped into her mind.

"I could visit Mother."

Clara stiffened at her words and Sam finished the remaining portion of his drink in one gulp. Diana immediately felt bad. Still, if she was going to be in Tuscany, shouldn't she see her? "I will never forgive her for what she did to us, but aren't you curious if she is well without Father?"

"We know she is fine. That is what we hire investigators for. She spends her days entertaining all the lords and ladies who pass through Tuscany instead of suffering the consequences of any of her actions," Clara bit out.

Diana sat down in the sitting area. "I didn't mean to bring up hurtful memories."

Sam squeezed his wife's hand and rose. "I will leave you to discuss this more. For what it is worth, Diana, I think you should go on this adventure. I think Stuart would have found it rather delightful. But you owe your mother nothing, and Stuart hated how she treated you as much as I detested her treatment of Clara."

She and Clara said nothing as he made his way from the drawing room. Clara took another sip of her drink. "Do you want to see her?"

It was a difficult question. While her father had used Clara and Diana to improve his position in society, it was their mother whom they feared the most in childhood. She had been their punisher, leaving lasting scars they both still carried on their backs from her fondness for doling out lashes.

"I wonder if she has changed. Perhaps Tuscany has softened her."

Clara snorted. Diana didn't blame her. Their parents had preferred Clara marry a lecher instead of Sam. In their mind, a monster with the right bloodline was better than a commoner.

"I want her to know we are happy."

Clara took a deep breath. "Of the two of us, you have always had the bigger heart and the most compassion. She will use that to persuade you to allow her to move back to England. Both Henry and I have no desire for her to be in our lives. Remember, nothing she does is for the benefit of anyone but herself."

"Would you support her returning?"

Clara sighed. "Since news of Father's passing, I have suspected this would be the eventuality. Sam and I will still provide her an allowance."

Diana said, "She has expressed interest in returning."

Her sister snorted. "She will blame all that happened on Father and try to reenter society. The woman, even though she is our mother, is treacherous. Don't forget that."

Diana reached over and squeezed her sister's hand. "She can't hurt us anymore, no matter where she resides."

Clara squeezed her hand back. The wounds of their childhood still lived in them both. They were silent for a moment, and then Clara clapped, making Diana jump. "Let's not dwell on Mother. Tuscany is only one part of your adventure. There are so many other grand things to imagine. I still can't believe Lady Hawley is standing up this rather unconventional club and that the board will be comprised of all women."

"Besides our investor."

Clara smiled. "Fascinating. Who is he?"

"It's Sebastian Devons."

Her sister's eyes widened in shock. "He is an exceptional businessman. The club will do well with his support."

Diana hadn't revealed the other shocking bit of news. She took a deep breath and said, "Lady Hawley believes a column about traveling on this new type of leisure cruise would be best from the perspective of a man and woman. Mr. Devons will also be joining me on my adventure. He will be the other writer."

A gasp escaped Clara. "Devons is going on the cruise!"

Diana rose again, pacing. "It's a bad idea, isn't it?"

Her sister shook her head. "No! Not at all. I just can't imagine Devons out of London, let alone the country."

Diana stopped her pacing. "What of his reputation?"

Clara smiled. "Sam was a partner for a brief time with Devons in his club. He is a close friend of his. He may be rumored to be scandalous, but rest assured he is nothing but honorable."

Diana blushed furiously. "Do you think it will be perceived as scandalous for me to take this cruise with him?"

"You will be on a ship with hundreds of other people. You aren't sharing a bed with him."

Heat coursed through Diana at Clara's words. Her sister continued, "Perhaps if it were Lady Hawley going or someone else, but your reputation is above reproach, and I imagine you will bring a companion with you. I'm assuming Aunt Winifred would be up for the trip. No one would consider you to do anything improper."

There it was again, that assumption that annoyed her lately. Her mind flitted back to her moment with Devons in the alcove. She'd not been proper then. She'd felt hungry and wanton. It vexed her that she would feel such things for a man she immensely disliked.

"Perhaps Sam will speak with him about your trip."

Diana frowned at her sister, hating the thought of Sam doing that. She didn't need anyone speaking for her when it came to him. The man already made his conclusions about her, no matter how wrong, and he could continue to think them. Not all ladies were like Lady Wesley, and it was wrong of him to think so. "Please don't. I'm not a child."

"He will make sure no one takes advantage of you."

"What if I want someone to take advantage of me? To have some type of interlude."

Clara stared at her in amazement. "Truly?"

"Well, if the right gentleman came along. I am a widow after all." Diana blushed and added, "Of course, not with Mr. Devons."

Clara giggled. "He wouldn't dare with you being Sam's sister-in-law."

The man didn't seem to care in the alcove at Seely House,

Diana thought. She remained silent, reminding herself it was a brief thing. She wouldn't dare do anything else with him either. Still, she wasn't lying to her sister. Perhaps she could discover who the improper Diana was on this cruise. "I'm not sure. Will see."

Her sister frowned, worried. "You and Stuart had such a loving relationship. I imagine that carried over to your private moments. An affair is not the same. There is less emotion involved."

Diana rolled her eyes. "I'm not some naive miss. I understand that. And what makes you think I want any emotion if I were to have a…well…ahh…affair."

"Because you can barely say the word."

Diana looked down, studying her hands, before revealing the truth to her sister. "What if I want to be someone different on this trip? Someone who isn't afraid to say anything or try anything."

Her sister studied her. "You are thinking of that article again."

"What if, for two months, I'm not the uneventful lady?"

Clara leaned forward and grabbed her hands. "I say it's your choice, but no matter what, you must understand that no woman is as one-dimensional as the writer made society ladies to be."

Diana squeezed her hands. "Thank you for being the best sister."

Clara grinned and hopped up. "Now we need something stronger to drink to celebrate this adventure you are going on."

As her sister poured their drinks, she shook her head. "I can't believe Devons is going on the same trip with you. I bet you will be fast friends."

"Yes, I'm sure," Diana said, not believing her own words.

SEBASTIAN TOOK A deep breath as he stood outside of the Seely House. He still couldn't believe he was going on a two-month leisure cruise with Lady Hensley. Even more shocking, she hadn't sent word that she was backing out. The woman irked him. He sighed and lifted his hand to knock, but before he could, it was thrown open. Addie's butler stared at him in surprise. "Sorry, Mr. Devons. I didn't realize you were waiting."

Sebastian smiled at the man. "I only just arrived. Why does Lady Hawley keep dragging you out here? I imagine you have other duties."

The man who normally didn't reveal any hint of emotion, smirked slightly. "You are quite correct, but the lady of the house is a most decent employer, so I will do as she asks."

Sebastian laughed and slapped him on the back. "You are a good man."

Addie stepped out of a room, frowning. "Are you complaining, Harrison?"

The man sighed. "Of course not, my lady. What would I have to complain about?"

She smiled, amused. Sebastian suspected that her butler was not at all afraid to be sarcastic with her. Addie turned to him, beaming. She looked lovely in a crimson gown that highlighted both her curves and black hair. "You are late, sir."

"You know I do have a business I must make plans for so I can participate in your mad scheme."

"Oh, admit it, you want to be part of my fun," she said, flouncing back into the room she came out of, knowing he would follow.

She continued to a table where glasses sat with brandy and poured them each a drink. She smiled at him. "Thank you again for still agreeing to go."

"You tricked me."

Addie handed him the drink and shook her head. "I planned to go. You should have seen my husband. I have never witnessed him in such a state."

Devons still couldn't believe he cared. They had been separated for years. Changing the subject, he winked at her. "We would have had fun on a trip together."

"Not as much as London would have speculated." Her eyes roamed over him, and she sighed. "A spark of something between us is missing, or we would have taken each other to bed long ago."

"I'm willing to try."

Laughter erupted from both of them. She reached over and squeezed his hand. "I mean it, thank you. No one else would have signed on for this.

Sebastian squeezed her hand back just as Harrison declared, "Lady Hensley."

They both turned and the lady was looking at them as if she had just caught them tupping. Her face was the shade of a strawberry. Addie walked towards her. "Diana, please come in. I'm thrilled that you and Devons are going on this adventure."

For a moment, Sebastian thought she might make up an excuse that she had to leave, but then she took a deep breath and smiled. "I'm excited."

"Would you like something to drink? Perhaps tea or Devons and I are having a brandy."

She bit her lip, and Sebastian's eyes jerked to her mouth. "I will have a brandy as well."

Addie's eyes widened. "That's the spirit! You and Devons sit. I will join you momentarily."

Sebastian motioned for her to lead the way and followed. The coloring of her dress today, unlike a few days ago, was atrocious. It was a mustard-yellow color that did not suit her at all. She wore another lace cap. This one was all white. The cut of the dress did complement her form, he realized, as his eyes dipped down to her waist, where her hips flared out. She turned to sit in one of the chairs, and he jerked his gaze away before taking a seat on the sofa across from her.

He watched her in silence. She drummed her fingers on her skirt. Sebastian sensed she was nervous and that he was the cause. A tension emanated between them. She turned her head, looking out the window and he studied her hair so tightly bound to her head. He clenched his hand, itching to unbind it. Unbind her hair, what was he thinking? She turned and raised a brow. Did she feel the tension too?

"How are you, Diana?" he asked.

She stiffened at the use of her given name, but Sebastian didn't care. They were participating in this crazy plan together. He wouldn't spend the next two months calling her Lady Hensley.

"Fine. Thank you," she responded primly.

Diana excelled at playing the proper lady. He wondered what she would be like alone. How quickly would her pristine bearing fade away? Sebastian hated that she was friends with Lilah and that they'd discussed him. He could admit to himself it was because he was attracted to her. He wanted to bed her but he wouldn't.

Sebastian wasn't interested in fucking any woman who considered him beneath them, no matter how casual the encounter was. Naively, he'd not seen that Lilah held that opinion until it was too late. He wouldn't make the same mistake again.

"I can tell already you will become great friends," Addie said, interrupting his thoughts as she joined him on the sofa.

Sebastian and Diana's eyes flew to each other, perhaps feeling the only kinship they ever would. All centered on the fact that Addie had somehow lost her mind.

"We have finalized the contracts with the *London Illustrated Chronicles* and the *British Tattler*. They believe your accounts of the trip will be wildly successful. They love how different the two of you are. To stay in good standing with the papers, you will both need to send updates back at every stop. It is imperative that you spend as much time together as possible. The papers are looking to see the same excursions and sights from two unique perspectives. Are there any issues I should be made aware of before moving forward with our plans?"

Sebastian remained silent, waiting for Diana to respond. If she was going to back out, now was the time. The lady's eyes darted over to him and lingered. She frowned as if trying to work something out in her head. Finally, she turned back to Addie. "No concerns but I do have a question. How will we get our updates back to you?"

"Captain Monroe of the *SS Lark* mentioned he could assist with this. It isn't uncommon for travelers or the crew to send letters at the ports."

Diana nodded. "I will also have my Aunt Winifred with me. She will be my companion on the trip.'

Addie grinned. "Lovely. It just highlights how wonderfully proper you are."

A grimace flashed across Diana's face. The lady did not like this title Addie kept bestowing on her, Sebastian realized. To needle her, he said, "Yes, Diana, you are the picture of propriety."

A pink hue touched Diana's cheeks. "I try my best."

"I can't wait to receive your first letters," Addie said, her voice filled with excitement.

"How will we know what we should write about or what we should go see?" Sebastian asked.

"I will need to rely on the two of you to identify that. The planned port stops for the *SS Lark* are brand new for the ship. They are trying them out to determine if they can create a new route for leisure cruises. I have possibly convinced Captain Monroe that lady leisure cruises are a missed market. Diana, you will need to find excursions that will keep ladies entertained."

"And the captain is supportive of these types of sailings?" Sebastian asked skeptically.

He didn't know Captain Monroe very well and had only spoken with him in passing, but the man didn't strike him as someone who spent a lot of time catering to ladies.

"Well, no, not quite, but he did say that we could try."

Sebastian rolled his eyes, but Addie ignored him. "Diana, I believe, is more than up for the job."

Diana appeared unsure, but then she glanced his way and

suspected he doubted her. It seemed to increase her determination. She tilted her chin up. "I will do my best not to fail the club."

Addie beamed. "The readers will adore learning about your adventures. Your perspectives will be drastically different."

Shocking Sebastian, Diana frowned. "Will they?"

He cocked a brow at her, incredulous. "Come, Diana. You don't have to be polite. We are not the same."

She tilted her head and studied him. "How?"

"I own a gentlemen's club, and I am a lord's bastard," he answered bluntly.

He'd intentionally been crude. If his father was alive, he would give him a sound thrashing for describing himself in such words. She flushed but glared at him. "My point is you are successful and own a home in Mayfair. We are not so different."

What game was this lady playing? Addie shook her head. "No fighting you two. And Sebastian, don't use such appalling language around us."

He hadn't meant to upset Addie. "I'm sorry."

"You should be. You are one of the few men I trust and care for. I won't have you speaking about yourself that way."

"You know I would do anything for you," he replied.

Sebastian glanced at Diana. She was nibbling on her bottom lip. He suspected she thought something was going on between him and Addie. He had the urge to deny it but stopped himself. It didn't matter what Diana thought.

Addie rose and made her way to the door. Diana's eyes went wide. "Where are you going?"

"I have another meeting. I thought I would leave you two to talk since you will be spending so much time together. One week until you sail," Addie said with a wink before she departed.

Sebastian turned back to Diana, who glared at him as if he were the devil incarnate. He leaned back and stretched out. Her eyes moved down him. Realizing what she was doing, Diana snapped her gaze back to his face. She frowned.

"Are you really going?" he asked.

She bristled and pursed her lips. "What makes you think I'm considering changing my mind?"

He shrugged one of his broad shoulders. "I'm not sure if you are. If I believed Lady Wesley's words, it would be the perfect situation for you to spend more time with me without having to worry about what others think."

A pink hue touched Diana's cheeks, and she sputtered, speechless. Finally, she bit out, "You are so full of yourself. Do you think I would leave my child simply for an opportunity in your bed? You must think you are something magnificent."

Sebastian stood and made his way to where she was sitting. She glared up at him. "Still, it is tempting, isn't it? There is a connection between us. A quick tumble would probably cure it. Do you like playing the part of the moral paragon? I can't figure it out. Every time someone brings it up, it seems to bother you. Do you wish you were more like Lilah? Are you hoping to take a secret lover who will never meet society's standards of what is acceptable? Is that your interest in me?"

Her eyes flashed with fury. "You are misinformed about my association with Lady Wesley and drastically incorrect about your appeal."

He barely registered the first part of her statement, more fixated on the last bit. Did she believe that he couldn't tell she desired him? Unable to stop himself, Sebastian leaned down and did something that shocked them both. He nuzzled her neck again, like he had in the alcove.

She smelled like fresh flowers. With his face pressed against her neck, he cupped the back of her head with one of his hands, itching to pull her hair free. He placed his lips along her jaw, kissing the curves of her face.

Diana huffed. "You do not affect me."

He chuckled darkly. "Are you sure?"

A breathy gasp escaped her as his mouth trailed down her neck. He ran his lips back up and then pulled away, so they were only inches apart. This lady wanted him. Common sense told him to release her. Still, the temptation to see how wicked Diana could be thrummed through him.

His grip on the back of her head tightened. Would one kiss matter? His cock urged him on, but his common sense gave him pause. And then the decision was out of his hands because Diana shocked him and pressed her mouth to his. The heat of her lips on his caused him to growl.

Yes, his body roared! Sebastian teased Diana's mouth open and demanded more. He dominated her with his tongue. Breathy moans escaped her. He pulled her up, pressing her flush along his body. She gasped as his hard cock ground against her.

Finally, his mind caught up, reminding him that this lady thought no different of him than Lilah. Still, her body very much wanted him. Unable to not point out the hypocrisy of her actions, he smirked. "We can be honest with each other, Diana. You are not the first lady of the *ton*, playing proper, to want a tryst with a lowly commoner. I'm happy to accommodate. Just admit it."

She jerked back, and her eyes narrowed.

He continued with his vicious words. "What a shame it must have been to be wedded to Hensley. Don't get me wrong I liked him, but he was an awkward gent, always focused on numbers and investments. Is that why you are looking for fun now?"

She slapped his cheek. "How dare you!"

Diana walked away from him. Ignoring the sting from the slap, he smirked, certain she was embarrassed that he called her out on her hypocrisy. Eventually, she turned back to him. He expected rage, but he was shocked to see tears streaming down her cheeks and her eyes filled with despair. He frowned, unsettled.

"You are a fool and a cruel one. Judge me all you want, but my husband was nothing short of wonderful."

She frantically wiped tears from her face with her hands, taking deep breaths. Her despair became mingled with anger. "I don't know why you are so awful to me, but I suspect it has something to do with Lady Wesley. Everything she said to you at the exhibit was a lie. I have never once spoken about you to her."

The lady stalked back towards him until they were inches apart and glared up at him. "And not once have I ever thought of you while my husband lived. How dare you insinuate I would want you when I had him. You've done it twice. Not everyone is so enamored with your attractiveness. Honestly, it's a waste that you are so handsome when who you are inside leaves a lot to be desired."

Guilt crept through him that he'd made a terrible mistake. He'd taken Lilah's insinuations as truth, never doubting them. Had he been wrong? "Diana—"

"No! I don't care what you have to say."

Sebastian flushed. She spun on her heels and marched right out the door. He cursed silently but before he knew it, she was back standing in the doorway. Her eyes emanated with fury. "And don't presume that I will not be on the *SS Lark*. It will take more than a kiss from you to scare me off from going on this trip for the club."

He said nothing until he was sure she was gone, and then yelled, "Fuck!"

What had Sebastian done? He'd behaved atrociously. He ran a hand over his face.

Chapter Seven

Diana laughed as her father-in-law, the Duke of Wescott, yelled, "Snapped."

Her son exclaimed. "You are cheating, Grandad!"

He tipped his head back and chuckled. For a moment, he reminded Diana of Stuart. A small bit of pain ricocheted through her heart, but she pushed it away, knowing her husband would hate her sadness.

"Mother?"

Her father-in-law added, "It's time to count your pairs."

She smiled at her son, amused by his excitement that he may win the card game. This was their third game, and Diana and Wescott had both won once. She counted her matches. "Five."

Robert jumped up and danced around the table in the drawing room. "I have eleven, and Grandad has ten. I win!"

Both she and Wescott laughed. Robert returned to the table and started to organize the cards. Wescott shook his head. "No more today. Your governess has prepared a lesson for you, and I promised I would walk in the gardens with your mother."

Robert jutted his chin out. "I want to go for a walk too."

Diana leaned over and ruffled his hair. "Another time. Miss Melanie has been waiting ever so patiently to give you your history lessons."

As if on cue, Miss Melanie appeared smiling. "Come, Lord

Robert. I have an exciting event to tell you about."

He looked at her skeptically. She said, "I promise."

Diana's son sighed but followed his governess out. Her father-in-law rose and offered Diana his arm. They were silent as they made their way to her gardens. She had sent word to Wescott a few days ago about her upcoming adventure. He'd responded that he was looking forward to speaking about it during his weekly visit.

"So, tell me about this trip and how it came to be. Does it relate to an announcement I read connecting your name with some society for female curators?"

Diana nodded. "Yes, I will be traveling as part of my duties associated with the Historical Society for Female Curators. I had hoped to tell you more about it first. I apologize you learned about it by way of the press."

He chuckled. "Diana, I would never insinuate you have to discuss your choices with me."

She blushed. "I know, but as Stuart's father, I don't want you to think I don't value your opinion."

They stopped, and both sat on one of the garden benches. He smiled. "I think my son would be delighted about you joining this club. It will be good for you. Now, tell me about this adventure. How does it line up with your club?"

"The club needs ways to generate income and interest, so Lady Hawley coordinated with two newspapers to publish accounts about the ports of a new leisure cruise. She secured passage for me and my Aunt Winifred as well as our investor. Our investor and I will write about our travels, and the papers will publish them."

"Fascinating, and who is the investor?"

Nerves fizzled in Diana's stomach. "Sebastian Devons."

His eyebrows shot up. "Who else is on the board?"

Diana listed off all the ladies, and his brows drew together in confusion. "Only one man?"

"The club will be managed by all women. Mr. Devons is to

be a nonvoting member. We have entered into a trust with him."

Her father-in-law wasn't a half-wit. A look of understanding crossed his face. "Lady Hawley is preventing any of the board members' families from taking control."

She nodded. Wescott frowned at her. "Do you think I would ever do something like that?"

Her eyes widened at the question. She shook her head. "Of course not. I believe it is more of a precaution. If it were my choice, I would happily have you join me."

A smile filled his face. "No. It's a smart move on Lady Hawley's part. She's a shrewd lady. I'm not sure I would have gleaned that from my few encounters with her."

Diana bristled, feeling protective of Addie. It shocked her. She didn't know her well, but she suspected many judged her wrongly. "I think she is a lady that is often underestimated."

The corners of his mouth tilted up. "Thank you for correcting my inaccurate assumptions."

They sat silently for a moment, and eventually, Wescott said, "I didn't know you were interested in antiquities."

She played with the folds of her skirts. "I'm not, but I feel like I need to do something…something different."

"My son would wholeheartedly encourage you if he were here."

She felt tears sting her eyes but admonished herself. Diana would not cry.

Sadness drifted across her father-in-law's face. "Sometimes, I think Stuart being sick for so long was both a curse and blessing. I hated watching him waste away, but it also gave him time to share his hopes for you and Robert with me."

Diana's eyes widened. "You and Stuart talked about that?"

"We did. And he always said the same thing. He wanted you to explore more of the world. I don't think he meant travel so much as finding your interests. He said your whole life, including him, had been chosen for you."

Tears stung her eyes again. "I have no regrets about any of

those decisions. I would choose Stuart again and again."

He squeezed her hand. "I know. I don't doubt your love. Nor did he, but at the end of his life, the one thing he was cross with me about was how your parents and I maneuvered you into marriage with him. Something to the effect that a beautiful lady like you would have never chosen a shy, round man like him on her own. He told me that my only role after he passed when it came to you, was to make sure you did as you liked and you were happy. I was not to tell you what was right or appropriate."

Diana smiled. She wasn't surprised. Stuart had thought differently than most lords and ladies. She'd grown up in a family that only cared about titles and appearances. He'd been the first person ever to tell her none of that mattered. He truly hadn't cared about status, which shocked her in the beginning.

She hated that, at the end of his life, he still worried about how their marriage came to be. Their union was full of deep love and passion.

"I loved him quite desperately."

"He knew you did," her father-in-law said as he stood and held his hand out. "Enough of that. My point was not to make us both sad but to tell you that I am here to trust and support your choices."

"Thank you."

"Where will my grandson be while you are on this grand adventure?" he asked as they walked back to the terrace doors.

"He will stay with my sister and her husband at their country estate."

"I hope they like Snap."

Diana laughed.

SEBASTIAN LAUGHED, AND his brother glowered at him. He shrugged. "She is right. Both you and Miller are only here one night a week. Don't pretend that isn't the case."

Sebastian, Malcolm, and their other Den partner Simon Miller were meeting with Celeste about the management of the club while he was gone. They'd offered to raise her salary by fifty percent, and she'd asked them to double it. Malcolm had dared to question her lofty sum.

"I don't care how much either of you spend at the Den, my lord. My point is I will be spending the majority of the time playing host for Devons, so I think it warrants what I'm asking for," Celeste explained.

"When did you start calling him 'my lord'?" Sebastian asked her.

She glared at him. "I'm trying to be respectful."

"We will give you your requested increase, Miss Hathaway," Sebastian teased her.

Malcolm glowered at him, and Miller laughed. "Your brother is going to give you a thrashing. Am I correct, Derry?"

"I'm trying to be a gentleman in front of Celeste."

She snorted. "No need."

Malcolm sighed and shook his head. "Sorry, Celeste, I don't mean to be an ass. You are right. You deserve your proposed sum."

Celeste beamed at him and stood. "I must prepare for the evening. Customers will be in soon."

They waited until she left, and Malcolm sighed. "Did we really double her salary?"

Sebastian smiled. "She is worth it."

"Agreed," Miller added.

Sebastian rose and grabbed the decanter of brandy from a table. He refilled all three of their glasses before sitting back down. Both Miller and Malcolm studied him, glancing at each other occasionally.

"What is it?" Sebastian asked.

Miller cleared his throat. "We wanted to speak with you about Lady Hensley. She is a proper, respectable lady. We want you to be delicate with how you treat her and behave in her presence."

Sebastian's brows drew together in confusion. "What are you insinuating?"

Malcolm took a large gulp of his brandy and placed his drink on the table beside him. "I'm going to say it bluntly. This trip you are taking is an opportunity to take a break from all the vice you have been overindulging in. Lady Hensley is not accustomed to being around such things."

Little did they know, he had already made her accustomed to his antics. He took a sip of his brandy. "Perhaps you have the wrong impression of her? Maybe she isn't as proper as you think."

Both Malcolm and Miller tilted their heads back and laughed. He didn't laugh because the same guilt that clawed at him since his last encounter with Diana came rushing back. He flipped open his pocket watch, reading the phrase from his father. It was the text he tried his best to live by, except he hadn't with her.

He'd been awful to her simply because he thought she was friends with Lilah and viewed him as his ex-lover did. Had he made some wrong assumptions? No matter what, his actions towards her were appalling. His remorse increased daily. Still, he grasped for some justification. "She can't be that proper, and I assume, as a leader of the *ton*, she thinks someone like me is beneath her. She will probably try to avoid me while we are on the trip."

Malcolm looked at him, confused, and he was horrified to realize he might be blushing. His brother lifted a brow in his direction. Sebastian took another drink of brandy.

"She is the lady all others try to emulate when it comes to properness and decorum. In regards to judging you, I've never known or heard of her behaving in such a fashion. You knew her husband, as did we. He didn't see commoners that way," Malcolm said.

"We aren't accusing you of attempting anything with her. She is not your type, and you are not hers," Miller clarified.

Annoyance flashed through Sebastian. He ignored it, not wanting to delve any further into the uncomfortable emotion.

"She is friends with Lilah."

"Where did you learn that?" Miller asked.

"I saw them together at an event put on by the London Society of Antiquaries."

Malcolm snorted. "I'm not friends with everyone I'm seen with."

The guilt in him intensified. Lilah had not once ever mentioned Diana to him before that day. She'd likely made those comments to cause trouble and annoy him. She'd been livid when he informed her he wouldn't be continuing an affair with her after she settled into her marriage.

"Have care with your actions around her is all we are saying. I will see you tomorrow at the farewell dinner Addie is hosting for both of you," Miller said.

Malcolm rose as well and watched Miller depart. He turned back to Sebastian and frowned. "Do not seduce her."

Sebastian scowled at him. "Why would you say that?"

"You made a face earlier."

"No. I didn't."

"I know you better than anyone."

Sebastian's ears went hot, but he would be damned if he told his brother anything. He would turn over a new leaf. He needed to, especially with Diana. He took another gulp of his drink. "I think you and Miller are right. I have already decided to take a break from all the amusements I've been enjoying, which is not as much as you think."

Malcolm snorted. "Perfect. Until tomorrow evening, then. I'm off to meet Sophia."

After his brother left, Sebastian stood and made his way to the balcony overlooking the great hall of the Den. Customers were starting to arrive. As he perused the crowd, his mind wandered to Diana. He'd acted like an ass and taken too many liberties with her because of Lilah's tricks. He owed her an apology. Sebastian would be on his best behavior for their trip.

Chapter Eight

DIANA GLANCED AROUND Addie's massive drawing room before her eyes landed on her travel companion. He laughed with her sister and Sam. She took a sip of her champagne as her gaze roamed over Devons. His broad frame overpowered the space he stood in. His dark hair curled at the base of his head, tempting someone to run their fingers through it. He ran his hand along his jaw, drawing her eyes there. He was scruffier than she remembered. It intensified the air of wickedness around him. She sighed. There was no denying the appeal he had.

"He looks like sin but the best kind," Aunt Winifred whispered next to her.

A rosy blush appeared on Diana's cheeks, horrified that her aunt suspected where her mind was. Could others also read her so well?

"I can't believe we are traveling with him for the next two months. I would have so much fun if I were twenty years younger."

"Aunt!"

She laughed. "Oh, an old lady can dream. You are still young, though."

Diana's redness deepened. "Mr. Devons and I would not suit."

Her aunt studied the man and then turned back to her. "Why

not?"

"Well, because he is him, and I am me."

Her aunt lifted a brow at her. "Yes, two attractive people. I will enjoy watching what happens between the two of you."

"What will you enjoy?" Arthur asked, appearing in front of them.

Aunt Winifred's smile dimmed a little. She disliked Arthur and loved to tell Diana he was boring. Diana, horrified she would say something about Devons, quickly said, "Arthur, would you escort me outside to get some fresh air?"

He beamed. "I was just about to suggest the same thing, my lady."

Diana placed her champagne glass on a table and smiled at her aunt. "We shall return shortly.

Her aunt winked at her, likely knowing why she was fleeing. Diana and Arthur walked to the terrace doors, and she instinctively glanced back to where Devons stood but only saw Sam and Clara.

They made their way down the steps into the garden, joining other lords and ladies. What Addie called a small dinner was attended by far more people than Diana expected. Interest in their club and leisure cruise was already evident.

"I can't believe I will not see you for two months," Arthur lamented.

"It will go by quickly."

He frowned. "And that you are traveling with Sebastian Devons."

She sighed. Of everyone who knew of her adventure, Arthur took her leaving the hardest and was horrified to discover that Devons would be joining her. He'd told her ladies like her did not partner with such men.

He'd then questioned the characters of those in the club, making a snide comment about Addie. Diana had admonished him. The discussion was the only time they'd come close to being cross with each other. He'd eventually apologized.

She'd not wanted to leave with him so upset, so she reassured him that she would have her aunt as a companion and that she and Devons would be two of hundreds of people on the ship.

"I have already explained that we will see each other in a limited capacity. There is nothing to be worried about."

He sighed. "Thank you for trying to put my mind at ease, and I'm sorry I brought it up again. It only worries me because of his reputation. The man owns a scandalous club, after all. With a potential union in our future, I want nothing to tarnish your character."

Diana ignored his comment about marriage, instead focusing on his attitude towards Devons. "The Den is very successful, and as our primary investor, there is much we can learn from him related to business processes."

He nodded reluctantly, and they continued to stroll along the candle-illuminated paved pathways of the gardens. They walked silently for a while, smiling and nodding at other guests they passed. Unexpectedly, Arthur pulled her down a more private pathway, and Diana looked at him startled.

"I wanted us to have a moment alone."

She smiled, and he brought her to a beautiful, large, open area bordered by hedges lit by the moon. She turned to him, unsure what he was about. He was acting very unlike himself.

"Diana, you look very lovely tonight."

She smiled, happy she wore one of her favorite blue ball gowns. Diana had also forgone her cap, deciding to take a break from wearing it until she returned from her trip. She was going on an adventure, after all. Her lady's maid Audrey had worked some magic, twisting her hair up in luxurious curls on the top of her head while the rest trailed down her back.

"Thank you, Arthur. Your words mean so much to me."

He leaned closer, and Diana realized he planned to kiss her. Another kiss flashed in her mind, but she pushed it away, telling herself this was the man she wanted to receive such a gesture from. He whispered, "I would like to take liberties with you. Is that all right?"

"Yes," she said.

He brushed his lips across hers. Diana kept her eyes shut, expecting more. He laughed, causing them to flutter open. The kiss was over.

Arthur beamed at her, "Thank you for allowing me to be so forward. I hope it was to your liking?"

She was shocked by the chasteness of the kiss. Diana had expected something different. She flushed, embarrassed at her own thoughts. She'd wanted more.

"My lady," he prodded.

Diana forced herself to smile. "It was lovely."

He tucked her hand back in the crook of his arm. "That will help tide us over until your return."

A red glow across the clearing caught her attention. Her eyes narrowed, and she studied it. The light flared brighter, revealing Devons, smoking a cigar and standing in one of the alcoves formed by some hedges. That man! Was he spying on her? Had he witnessed the kiss? She turned back to Arthur. "Will you escort me back?"

He smiled and led the way. As they headed back to the lit area of the garden, Diana pondered why Devons hadn't revealed himself. She blushed, knowing he'd been watching them. She was so focused on him she didn't realize they were on a pathway with other people until Arthur said, "Stay here. I will fetch us some champagne."

Diana nodded and wandered over to the fountain of the central garden. Her body tensed as someone came to stand next to her. She didn't have to look at him to know it was Devons. She pursed her lips. "So, you have taken to spying on me now?"

He said nothing at first. She turned to him and lifted her brow. His eyes roamed over her, lingering on her hair falling over her shoulders. Finally, he said, "I was there first. I didn't realize you and Lord Tremont would be sharing an intimate encounter."

Diana flushed. "You should have announced yourself."

"And interrupted your tender moment?"

"It truly was."

He clenched his jaw but remained silent.

"Arthur is the epitome of the type of gentleman I would like to spend my time with."

She was being harsh but for once in Diana's life, she didn't care. She was determined to show him she wanted nothing to do with him. That the kiss she received from Arthur was what she desired.

He turned to her then. Fire flashed in his eyes. "No man should need to ask if his kiss was to a lady's liking."

So, he had heard everything. She had the urge to rail and yell at this man. Fury welled in her. Their furious eyes met. And Diana knew they were both thinking about the same thing. Their moment together. His gaze flicked to her mouth. Heat shot through her body. No! She wouldn't be attracted to this man, she told herself. Her stare turned haughty. "If the man were a gentleman, he would ask."

Devons dared to smirk at her, and she wanted to kick him. His eyes slid down her body, pausing at her bosom as she took a deep breath. He leaned closer, and for a moment, pure desire throbbed between them. It was so strong that it left Diana speechless and demanded she remove the space between them. She felt her body sway towards him just as Devons stepped back, shaking his head as if to make all the emotions disappear.

"There you both are!" Addie said, walking down the central pathway of the gardens. "I would like to discuss a few things with you both before you depart. Come with me."

Diana should wait for Arthur's return, but she needed to be away from Devons. Not sparing her soon-to-be travel partner another glance, she began to follow behind Addie, but he reached out, stopping her. She looked at him, confused.

Appearing more contrite, Devons said, "I would like to have a private word with you."

Diana had spent too much time with this man already. Starting in two days, she would be with Devons on a ship for months. "We can talk on the *SS Lark*. We will have plenty of time."

He frowned, but she didn't give him time to respond. Instead, she spun around and hurried after Addie.

The next day, Sebastian stood in his study, nodding in response to Sam Kincaide's words but not really listening. Instead, he watched Diana walk around her garden with Lord Tremont or, as she explained to him, the epitome of her type of gentleman. Sebastian assumed the man was spending one last moment with her before she left on the leisure cruise.

He shouldn't be watching them, but he remained baffled by what drew Diana to the man. Tremont was one of the few gentlemen who didn't frequent any of the clubs of vice that were so popular with the peerage. Sebastian knew that because of his own connections among the owners of the various establishments. Yes, from a societal standpoint, Diana and Tremont suited perfectly.

Still, the man's kiss was the most awkward token of affection Sebastian had ever witnessed. He almost felt sorry for him. Diana should want more than a brief kiss. Last night, he'd desperately wanted to show her the right way to kiss a lady in a darkened garden.

He would not act on his desires. Sebastian made a promise to himself that he wouldn't be improper around her anymore, and he planned to stick to it. He still owed Diana an apology. Embarrassment coursed through him that he'd fallen for Lilah's false words.

Diana and Tremont passed the gate at the back of his garden, and he leaned forward, studying them. She stopped and tipped her head back, laughing. Her hair was styled without the atrocious cap she usually wore. He rubbed his jaw as he observed her, wondering what Tremont had said to make her laugh.

"Devons, are you listening?"

He turned back to where Sam Kincaide sat in a wingback chair drinking a brandy. The man looked at him, puzzled. Sebastian pulled himself away from the window and joined him in the sitting area.

"Sorry, I've been distracted lately."

"A woman?" Kincaide said with a wink.

"No," Sebastian lied.

Kincaide laughed and shrugged. "If you say so."

"I'm sure this isn't why you came to visit me."

Frowning, his guest shook his head and took another sip from his glass. Was something wrong with Diana?

"Is it Lady Hensley?"

"I wanted to ask if you would look out for my sister-in-law. My wife worries she may be naive about certain aspects of life."

Sebastian lifted a brow. "You want me to act as her chaperone?"

Kincaide laughed. "No. She is a grown woman and should do as she likes. My wife insisted I emphasize that point. Still, if anyone dangerous or unseemly attempts to engage her, we are requesting you assist her."

Devons was already protective of Diana but wouldn't share that with Kincaide. "Of course."

"I knew you would. Thank you. I have one more matter to discuss with you. My mother-in-law may accompany Diana on the return leg of your cruise. If she appears to be up to anything, please send us word."

Sebastian's eyes widened. Many years ago, the Duke and Duchess of Claremore fled England for the continent with scandal chasing their heels. Why would they return? They'd tried to marry Kincaide's wife off to a madman. The lunatic, at one point, kidnapped her. Sebastian and his brother helped the Kincaide family track them down.

As if sensing his confusion, Kincaide added, "My father-in-law has passed, and the duchess wishes to resettle in England. Diana has agreed to assist."

"That seems very forgiving of her," Sebastian stated.

"Diana is perhaps the kindest person I know, which is why I worry my mother-in-law is up to something."

"You have my word."

His guest smiled, relieved. He raised his drink to Devons. "Cheers to you and Diana's trip. There is already a good deal of excitement about this leisure cruise. I'm looking forward to hearing about your adventures in the papers."

Sebastian held his glass up before taking a large drink of his brandy. He embraced the burn as it went down his throat. The more he learned about Diana, the more he realized how inaccurate his perception of her was. He was a scoundrel. Twice, he had dragged the proper lady into wicked fun.

No more mishaps, he told himself. He would be a well-behaved man in her presence. He took another sip of his brandy, trying to ignore his disappointment. Sebastian pulled out his pocket watch and opened the front case. His eyes flicked to the words contained there.

To my son, Sebastian Devons. Know you are loved by me.

—your proud father, the Marquess of Derry.

He flipped to the back case where the text he tried to live by was engraved. He would do better.

"So, who will be playing host while you are away? I imagine Miller or Derry won't be keen to stay away from their wives that much."

Sebastian snapped the pocket watch closed. "Celeste, our host for the card tables, will step in. She is more than adequately skilled to take my place. Truthfully, I'm worried I will return and will discover I'm unneeded."

Kincaide smiled. "I like Celeste, but I'm surprised you select-ed a woman. You will have society talking."

"They talk about me anyways."

A chuckle escaped Kincaide. "True. Enjoy the cruise. I was surprised you agreed to such an endeavor."

Sebastian was still shocked that he himself was going. He would never admit it to his brother, but he was right. The mess with Lilah had made him angry, spilling over into everything he did. He always enjoyed drinking, playing host to the *ton*, and the occasional trysts, but since Lilah, it had been at an excess he knew was too much. Still, he wasn't about to reveal that to Kincaide. Instead, he said, "You know Addie. She can be damn convincing."

They both laughed.

Chapter Nine

The Atlantic Ocean—June 1850

DIANA SPLASHED WATER on her face. She planned to leave her cabin no matter what. The past two days, she hadn't felt well enough to venture out, but tonight, she was going to dinner. Her stomach didn't gurgle like before, and as Captain Monroe promised, she'd started to adapt to the swaying. The ship's rocking also wasn't nearly as much as yesterday or the day they left.

Looking in the mirror bolted above the desk, she sighed. Her hair hung over her shoulder in a plait. She smoothed her green skirts, which contained far more wrinkles than she liked, but it would have to do. Her maid Audrey still struggled with sea sickness. Earlier, she'd made her way to Diana's cabin to help her dress, but Diana sent her back to bed. The girl could barely stand and was so pale Diana swore she was gray.

She crossed her narrow room, knocking on the door that connected her to Aunt Winifred's cabin.

"Aunt, are you going to dinner?"

"No," her aunt said from the other side of the door. "My stomach still hasn't settled."

Diana grimaced and turned around, bumping into the little table anchored to a wall. She'd been quite surprised by the size of the cabin. Diana expected it to be small but not so narrow. Her saloon cabin contained one bed pushed against the wall, a tiny desk, and a wingback chair. There was little room for anything else. Shockingly, Captain Monroe said the cabins bordering the saloons were considered the most spacious. What did the other rooms look like?

She wondered if Sebastian Devons was out and about. Nervousness shot through her. Diana was not up for another sparring match with him. A large farewell party saw them off, so they hadn't exchanged more than a few pleasantries since Addie's dinner. Robert had been delighted to see him and ran right over to Devons, leaving Arthur peeved. She wished Arthur engaged better with Robert. His lack of a connection with her son held Diana back from considering a real proposal from him. *That and he makes you feel nothing*, her mind whispered. She sighed.

After the ship made its way to the open ocean, the captain insisted everyone rest in their cabins. She smirked, likely because he'd been aware they would all be sick. Diana was happy the ship wasn't rocking as much. She stepped out into the narrow hallway bordering the dining saloon.

While the ship was owned by another, the Kincaide family built the *SS Lark*, and it exuded the elegance they were known for. Even the carpet and wood trim were as refined as any found in the finest London townhouses. Only over the last decade had ship travel become focused on leisure cruises. The Kincaide vessels were a shining example of what was required to cater to wealthy cruisers.

As she made her way closer to the dining room, she found that a steward had opened the door for her. She stepped through, and another man greeted her with a bow. "Hello, Lady Hensley. I'm Mr. Carlson. I will be seeing your meals while you are aboard our grand vessel, the *SS Lark*. Tonight will be a more informal fare with no set time for dinner. Starting tomorrow evening, we will host dinner every night at eight o'clock"

She smiled in return. "I can't imagine anyone is ready for an extravagant meal."

"I promise, my lady, the sickness will pass."

Diana nodded. "I feel better already.

He beamed at her. "Wonderful."

She followed him, passing several long elegant tables until he stopped at one in the corner. She was startled to spot Devons sitting there. Their eyes met and he stood. The man, even after days at sea, looked far too virile. Her stomach fluttered.

"I'm glad you are well enough to venture out of your cabin."

She didn't respond at first but glanced around, wondering if she could feign sickness. As if sensing her thoughts, he said quietly, "Lady Hensley, please give me a moment of your time."

Her eyes flicked back to his face, and she sighed. "Very well."

Carlson asked Diana, "Would you care for a glass of red wine?"

Diana's eyes darted to Devons and saw he was already drinking a glass. Her brows drew together in confusion. "How long have you been here?"

He smiled wryly at her. "A bit. I hoped to speak with you tonight."

She studied him, puzzled, and then turned back to Carlson. "Yes, that would be wonderful."

"I shall return with your wine and the first course."

Their table descended into silence, and eventually, Diana asked, "You mentioned that you would like to discuss something with me?"

Devons nodded before rolling his massive shoulders. He appeared nervous. Finally, he said, "I owe you an apology. I made some assumptions based on our interactions with Lady Wesley. I have since learned they were grossly inaccurate."

Something about what he said annoyed her. What was he apologizing to her for? For kissing her? Or because he now decided she fell in the category of the morally upstanding ladies who would never dare to do anything improper? "What assumption was that? That I was lining you up to be my lover?"

His eyes widened at her blunt words. Carlson returned with wine and soup for each of them, stopping the conversation momentarily. Diana smiled at the steward, but when she turned back to Devons, she fixed him with a glare.

"Let's be honest, Devons. You thought I was like any other lady you spend time with. And now you have decided for some reason I can't be that type of woman, someone who does…well…"

"Wicked things," he added, watching her in fascination.

What was the point she was trying to make? She should be happy that Devons realized she was a respectable lady, but it grated her. He tilted his head, still studying her, and slowly said, "I'm apologizing for assuming you view commoners the same way Lady Wesley did."

"Oh."

He leaned forward, his face filling with contrition. "And that my words about your husband hurt you so deeply. My innuendos were abominable."

Diana took another sip and, perhaps because of the wine, confessed, "When my husband died, so many acquaintances acted as if I was lucky and could now find someone more physically to my liking. That is why your comments upset me so much. Stuart may not have been what was considered handsome to most, but, to me, there was no man more desirable than he."

"I think your husband was a lucky man."

Diana swallowed the lump forming in her throat. She would not cry in front of this man who recently had wreaked havoc on her emotions. "We were both lucky."

"I'm truly sorry. My actions were caused by my own bitter thoughts and my own hurt."

Devons had a broken heart, Diana realized. "Lady Wesley hurt you."

He smirked. "I wouldn't normally admit it, but yes, she did. I thought we would wed, and she corrected my assumption by marrying the Marquess of Wesley. While we had a grand time together, my background made me unacceptable as a husband."

She almost placed her hand on his but refrained from doing

so. Instead, she made a disgusted face. "That woman is a viper."

A chortle escaped Devons, and Diana smiled at him. "You must know this. You couldn't have really given your heart to such an awful lady. I refuse to believe you loved her."

He took another drink and grimaced. "Perhaps I didn't."

Diana knew he believed he did. His heartbreak was written all over his face. This man, the king of one of London's most scandalous clubs, had been laid low by love. Surprisingly, her heart ached for him.

"I'm only sharing this because I wanted to explain my behavior. I'm sorry for our previous interactions. I've been drowning my sorrows in vice, leading to poor choices. This includes making bad assumptions about proper widows that led me to believe they welcome my advances. Going forward, I promise to be the most behaved man on this ship. It is one of my goals for our trip."

Why did his words fill her with disappointment? Still, it was for the best. Even if she wanted a tryst, Sebastian Devons was not the man to do it with, especially with him carrying around a broken heart. She glanced at him as he drank his soup. His large arms strained against his jacket, and his thick black hair fell over his forehead. No, the man sitting across from her was not who Diana should have on the top of her imaginary list for liaisons. He seemed altogether too much.

She sighed. "What a mess we are. You are suffering a heartbreak, and I am trying to figure out how to be less me."

He frowned in confusion. "What does that mean?"

Carlson arrived at their table. "Lady Hensley and Mr. Devons, we have two more guests joining you. May I introduce Mr. Spoor and Mr. Haggerty?"

"Perhaps we can talk more after dinner," Devons whispered.

She smiled.

SEBASTIAN ENTERED THE main saloon and spied Diana sitting with her aunt and Mr. Spoor. Lady Clark must have ventured out after they left the dining saloon. Though their arrival at dinner interrupted his and Diana's discussion, Sebastian enjoyed speaking with Spoor and Haggerty. They were friends who decided to join the cruise because Haggerty was a historian, and many of the ports were places he wanted to visit.

Spoor didn't seem to have the same love of history. Currently, he appeared to be very fascinated by Diana's aunt. The corners of Sebastian's mouth tilted up as he watched Spoor stare at the older woman with unconcealed adoration. The woman didn't seem to notice, or perhaps she was being coy.

His gaze shifted to Diana, and he perused her. Earlier, when she had entered the dining saloon, his body had instantly responded to her. What was it about the woman that tempted him so much? Tonight, her hair fell over her shoulder, plaited, giving her a carefree appearance. The vision stirred something within him. He clenched his hands as he watched her. He had an urge to wrap that braid in his fist while he—

"She fared better than I thought she would. She was one of the first ladies out of her cabin," Captain Monroe said from behind him, watching Diana as well.

A flash of anger shot through him at the way Monroe studied her. "Do you need something?"

Monroe smirked at him. "I do. I must speak with you and the lady. We need to talk about the ports. Some of them we've never visited. Perhaps we should go ashore first and identify a few potential activities for Lady Hensley?"

A frown filled Sebastian's face, knowing the lady would likely disagree with the captain's advice. Sebastian wanted to speak with Diana alone tonight. Not for vice or the trip activities, but because he was curious and puzzled by her statement about being less her. "Let's meet tomorrow. We are just getting acclimated to the ship."

The man sighed. "Fine, but no later than that. Also, the

weather deck is open for those interested in enjoying some fresh air this evening. The ocean is calm right now."

Sebastian's eyes darted over to the captain, but Monroe was already strolling towards a group of men playing cards. He moved towards Diana and bowed to both her and her aunt once he reached them. "May I join you? Or convince you ladies to join me for a promenade on the weather deck. It's a calm night, and Captain Monroe gave the go-ahead if anyone would like to."

Diana's face lit up, but Lady Clark shook her head. "I barely made it out of my room. I don't think I am ready to walk along the deck."

Sadness flitted across Diana's face, and her aunt smiled. "Go without me."

Sebastian could tell by Diana's expression that she was torn between doing what she liked and what was proper. She bit her lip, and he sensed she would decline. Disappointment shot through him.

Her aunt waved her away. "Go. Ship travel is different from all the events in London. There isn't enough space, and there are too many people for such rigid rules. You will be fine. I'm sure Devons will see to that."

Sebastian nodded. "There are plenty of people about. I wouldn't lead you into trouble. Remember my promise from earlier."

Diana laughed. "Well, how can I say no now?"

"You can't," her aunt said.

She stood and took Sebastian's arm. Lady Clark winked at him as he escorted Diana away. He shook his head, wondering what was going on in the lady's mind. They took the steps leading to the deck, and as they stepped out, Diana gasped. She tilted her face up to the sky, taking in the millions of stars stretching across the blackness.

The delight on her face took his breath away. Her mouth curved upwards as she glanced around. Diana turned back to him. "Isn't it stunning? It's almost as if someone or something took a handful of diamonds and threw them up into the darkness."

He forced himself to look away from her euphoric face and stare up at the sky. Sebastian had to agree he'd never seen the stars so clearly. "You don't see this in London."

They were both silent as they stared out into the black void. The deck was empty and quiet besides the two of them and the few words they'd spoken. The waves lapped against the ship in a calming fashion. Shockingly, Sebastian felt at ease and content in a way he'd not expected. They were new feelings for him. His club and other businesses didn't allow him to slow down.

His new emotions disappeared as Diana walked to the railing and peered over. Overwhelming fear filled Sebastian, and he had the protective urge to yank her back to him. He'd never been on a ship in the middle of the ocean, and it made him damn uncomfortable to watch her lean over the side.

She looked back at him and smiled. "It's as if I'm staring into nothing. Come look."

He grimaced. "Why don't you come back here?"

Her lips turned up in a smirk. "Is the King of the Den afraid of the ocean?"

Sebastian stepped closer to her, even though, in truth, he was. Not for himself but for her. "Fear is a healthy emotion."

Diana laughed. He held his arm out to her. "Please join me."

She grinned at him. "As you wish."

As they moved to the center of the deck, the tension in Sebastian subsided. Diana beamed at him. "Shall we return to the saloon?"

He shook his head. "Before we do, I wanted to know what you meant about being less you. You mentioned that earlier."

She blushed, shaking her head. "It's nothing."

Now, he really was curious. "I told you about Lilah."

Diana rolled her eyes. "I didn't ask you to share with me."

He winked at her and smiled. "Yet I did."

She was silent but finally said, "A few weeks ago, one of the papers had a caricature of a lady who symbolized the moral compass of London society. Do you know who it looked like?"

Devons shook his head. Diana's eyes widened in disbelief. "Come now, you must know."

She believed it represented her, Sebastian realized. He said nothing, waiting for her to confirm his thoughts.

She pointed towards herself. "It's almost as if someone drew me, cap and all."

"I'm sure she was still beautiful."

Diana rolled her eyes. "It made me wonder, is that all I am? Just this perfectly behaved lady. Truth be told, that is who I have always been. That is even why Addie asked me to participate in her club. It wasn't because I had some useful skills like the duchess, Lady Esme, or Miss Martin."

"Is that why you agreed to do the cruise?"

She nudged him with her elbow. "It wasn't because I hoped to spend time with you."

He flushed. "I have apologized for that."

Diana laughed. "I know."

"Caricatures don't honestly represent anyone. I have known plenty of ladies who were the epitome of properness but lived much more, shall we say, colorful lives."

She sighed. "I'm sorry for sharing. I'm sure you would rather be hearing about anything else."

"Don't assume that," he said. "I confessed my plans for this trip. We are friends, correct?"

Diana's eyes widened at his words. But Sebastian did believe they were friends or would be by the end of their leisure cruise. They may have started their relationship on the wrong footing but no more.

Her face lit up. "Perhaps we could help each other."

He tilted his head and studied her. "How?"

"You can help me be less proper, and I can help you stay out of trouble."

There was nothing wrong with Diana. He didn't understand

what she wanted. "What are you hoping to accomplish?"

She removed her hand from his arm and paced back and forth. He waited for her to formulate her thoughts. Finally, she smiled at him softly. "I'm the mother of a future duke and a highly respectable lady. In truth, I enjoy those things for the most part, but I want a reprieve to allow myself the luxury of doing something that isn't what is expected of me."

"You need to give me more details. You will receive no judgment from me, Diana."

She was quiet for a moment and avoided making eye contact with him. Now, he was intrigued.

Sighing, Diana said, "Perhaps I am hoping for all the things you suspected. Not with you, of course. You need to mend your heart. But if I can feel something when you kiss me, maybe I can meet someone on this trip. A man I can have an interlude with."

Sebastian was shocked. Diana wanted a lover—not him, but someone she was hoping to find during their journey.

She added, "I will likely be courted when I return from this trip. I would never consider such improperness if I were betrothed or married. It wouldn't be fair to my suitor and eventual husband. Now is my only chance. Does that make me selfish?"

"Tremont is the suitor?"

Her gaze flew to his, and she blushed furiously but nodded. For some reason, he wanted to tell her marriage to the dull lord would bring her nothing but discontent, but he didn't. The lords and ladies of the *ton* often had loveless marriages. Still, the lady had known love with Hensley. Why was she settling? He reminded himself it wasn't his concern, and perhaps she did have strong feelings for Tremont. He scowled. She wouldn't be looking for a lover if that were the case.

Mistaking his unhappiness for judgment, she added, "Maybe not a lover but a kiss or a flirtation. But even if I don't find someone, over the next few months, I want to live as if society's thoughts on my actions do not matter. I want to allow myself to be more than the moral compass of London society."

She was a fool if she thought she was only perceived as that. Sebastian didn't see her as so simple. He moved to her and tilted her chin up, so he was staring into her eyes. "You are so much more."

A wave of desire drifted between them.

"How do you know that?" she asked softly.

Warnings fired in his mind that being this close to Diana was a bad idea. Hell, upon their return to London, it was almost certain she would enter into a betrothal with Tremont. While Sebastian was always up for a liaison, he suspected he wouldn't escape this without one of them or both getting hurt. He wouldn't endure that again. Not after the debacle with Lilah. He released her chin as he stepped back. Trying to lighten the mood, he said, "Because a lady who is the moral compass of society wouldn't spy on me in my gardens or join Addie in her crazy scheme."

A surprised giggle escaped her, and she grinned at him. "Guilty."

They were silent, both studying the night sky. Finally, Diana asked, "What do you say? Shall we help each other?"

Yes, the request. He'd somehow forgotten about it, or was he avoiding it? While he was taking this journey to be vice-free, Diana wanted his assistance to be a little improper but not with him. It was wise he wasn't part of her plans, but it still rankled him.

In truth, every part of Sebastian's being roared to tell her hell no because the thought of anyone even flirting with Diana made him see red. But he reminded himself they were just friends. He studied her face, so eager, and knew he would play this game with her, no matter where it led.

"I will help you, but I'm unsure how your assistance will benefit me. There are all of ten women on this ship. I don't think I will have much trouble avoiding liaisons."

"There are the ports. You could have a tryst at every stop.

I've heard the rumors about the King of the Den."

His face heated. "Most are likely not true."

Diana had the gall to look at him in disbelief. She shrugged. "Regardless, I will make sure you avoid any ladies hoping to catch your attention, and you can assist me in pursuing things that are…well…what is the word—"

"Wicked," he growled.

Her eyes jerked to his. She gulped. He waited for her to laugh and say she was only pretending or this was some sort of joke, but she whispered, "Yes, wicked."

Her uttering of the word made him want to show her how improper she could be. Damn it! Sebastian shouldn't be thinking such thoughts about her. They were only a few days into their journey. He reassured himself that he would get over this strange connection he felt for the lady.

"And I will make sure you are the opposite of wicked. Is there anything else you would like to abstain from? Drinking?" she added.

Hell no. He wouldn't get through this without a drink. He shook his head.

"Smoking?"

He shook his head again. "I think what we have agreed to so far is more than enough."

"Splendid. So, we are in agreement?"

Sebastian nodded, and she beamed back at him.

Chapter Ten

DIANA MADE HER way to one of the smaller saloons on the ship. The prior evening, Devons mentioned Captain Monroe wanted to meet with them. Since their departure, Diana had only spoken with the man a few times but was thrilled she was about to learn more about their port stops.

Entering the saloon, Diana realized she arrived first. She nodded to the staff who stood in the room, waiting to cater to her or any other passengers. One wall was covered in large mahogany bookshelves. She frowned and stepped closer, curious how the books were kept secure. She smiled. A brass rod at the bottom prevented them from flying out. Clever.

She made her way to a sitting area, and an attendant immediately appeared. "My lady, can I offer you some refreshments?"

"Tea would be wonderful, thank you."

As the man hurried off, Devons and Captain Monroe stepped through the door. The captain smacked Devons on the back, and his lips flattened into a straight line. Captain Monroe seemed oblivious to his annoyance. Her travel partner didn't appear to like him very much. As they reached her, they both bowed before sitting in two wingback chairs.

"Lady Hensley, I recently mentioned to Devons that I believe you have adapted to sea life better than any of the other women we have aboard."

Diana smiled. "There aren't too many of us."

"True. Only ten out of almost a hundred passengers. You are quite the adventuress. The type of woman a ship captain can't help but admire."

She blushed, and the man grinned at her cockily. The captain was attractive. Diana suspected he was a charmer in his free time.

"You wanted to talk about the ports, Monroe," Devons barked.

Diana's eyes darted to him. He leaned back in his chair with his legs out and arms folded across his chest, frowning at them. Well, he was in quite the mood this morning. The attendant returned with the tea and poured Diana a cup. Both men declined any.

"Lady Hensley, I was talking with Devons, and we believe for the first port you need to stay on the ship until we have identified activities of interest for you."

What? She would not sit on the ship while they went off exploring. Absolutely not. Her eyes darted to Devons, incredulous.

He held his hands up in denial. "I never agreed to that."

"Well, I assumed you would agree," Monroe muttered.

Diana pressed her lips together, considering what she should say to his suggestion. In any other situation in her life, she would have acquiesced, but not today. The Historical Society for Female Curators' board was relying on her. None of her associates would agree to Monroe's idea.

"I don't believe that is the right approach, Captain Monroe. Please keep in mind that, no matter what you discuss with Devons, I speak for the club. He doesn't. If we are to identify activities at these ports for leisure cruises for future ladies, I will need to be involved."

The captain shook his head and started to defend his points, but Diana interrupted him. "I must insist."

Monroe's eyes swung back to Devons, but he smirked. "She's the boss."

"Lady Hensley, the other women on the ship have agree—"

"No, I will go ashore when the men do. Not a moment later," she stated adamantly.

She glanced at Devons, and he nodded slightly, showing his support. Shifting the conversation, she asked, "When will we arrive at our first stop? I believe you previously mentioned it would be Le Conquet."

The captain frowned, displeased that she'd moved on from his suggestion. "Le Conquet is a very small village. There won't be much for you to see."

"You must have picked the port for some reason. What was it? Your ship is for leisure cruising. While your previous plans didn't include ladies, you must have a vision for this location," Diana said.

"You may as well explain your reasoning, as I don't think she will let it go until you do," Devons said, sounding amused.

Monroe sighed. "Le Conquet is called the *port du bout du mo.*"

"The port at the end of the world," Diana said, translating his words.

The corner of the captain's mouth tilted up. "You do impress me, Lady Hensley. Men are simple. I believe, regardless of how interesting the actual stop is, they will enjoy writing back to their friends and family that they visited the port at the end of the world."

Devons nodded, agreeing with Monroe's idea. "I agree that travelers, including women, will like your gimmick."

Diana smiled at him, appreciating his help. They still needed something else though. It wasn't enough. "But why is it called that?"

Monroe ran his fingers through his hair and sighed. "There is a peninsula right before the village that is the farthest-reaching piece of land for France. The location makes one feel as if they are standing at the edge of the world."

"I love it. Can we visit there?" Diana asked.

Monroe nodded. "It isn't too far from where we will dock. A

lighthouse was recently built in the area."

"I like it. Travelers will enjoy the trip since it's so close to the port. What about the actual village?" Devons said.

"The stone buildings of the area are also quite lovely."

Diana frowned. She needed an antiquities component. They were on the cruise for a historical society. "Are there any cultural or historical sites I can visit in the village?"

Monroe stared at her blankly. Diana suspected such topics weren't of personal interest to the captain. A chuckle escaped Devons. She and Monroe glanced at him. He smiled. "Perhaps, it is best to explore the village on our own to determine if there is anything of interest."

A scowl filled the captain's face. "We have never stopped at Le Conquet. You can't expect me to know everything."

Diana gave Devons a pointed stare before turning back to Monroe and beaming at him. She didn't want to upset him. "Of course not. I'm thrilled to find out more about Le Conquet and the surrounding area."

He smiled at her, and Devons rolled his eyes. She asked, "How long will we be at the port stop?"

"One day, and then the next day, we will anchor by a cove in the area for an afternoon."

That sounded delightful to Diana. "I'm very excited about our first two stops. After this discussion, I think we can all agree I don't have to wait on the ship. Do you concur?"

Monroe shook his head but admiration shined in his eyes. "As you wish, my lady. I need to check on some things. I will leave the two of you."

She had stood her ground. Diana felt proud of herself. She glanced at Devons, who sat quietly with his arms crossed. "What is wrong?"

He stayed quiet. She brought the tea to her lips as she waited for his response.

Finally, he asked, "Is Monroe a consideration?"

A gasp escaped her, and she coughed, trying not to choke on

her tea. "I beg your pardon."

"Monroe, could he be a consideration?"

"Hmmm…I'm not sure. Perhaps I should."

Devons frowned. "You will be on the ship with him for the next two months. I don't believe he is appropriate."

She looked at him, confused. "Should I not consider anyone on the ship?"

He opened his mouth to speak and closed it. She studied him. What was wrong with him today? Eventually, he said, "No, I'm not saying that, but you must work with Monroe and will likely continue to do so after this cruise. It may complicate your business relationship."

Diana hadn't thought of that. In truth, she hadn't considered the captain at all. She glanced at Devons with concern. He looked sullen.

"Did you sleep well?"

"I'm fine," he said sulkily.

SEBASTIAN ENTERED THE hayward saloon, where guests congregated for predinner drinks. He was resolved to be in a better mood and support Diana's endeavors. He'd promised her his assistance, and he planned to follow through, no matter how much it unsettled him. If she thought Monroe made an adequate choice for a flirtation, there was no reason he should stand in the way. He perused the room, searching for Diana, but only spotted Lady Clark speaking with Mr. Spoor. He ambled over to them and bowed. "Good evening, Lady Clark," he said before turning to Mr. Spoor. "Sir."

"Are you looking for my niece? She is off talking with Captain Monroe about our first stop."

He glanced around but didn't see them. Where were they? When he turned back to Lady Clark, her face contained an amused expression. He raised a brow. She took another sip of her champagne. "So, tell me, Devons, have you started to write your first missive to send back to England while we are in Le Conquet?"

"Not yet. Both Diana and I decided we would start sending them once we arrived at our second port."

Lady Clark nodded. "A sound decision. No one wants to hear about the first few days of travel."

"Letters to your family?" Mr. Spoor asked.

"Have you not heard? My niece's club, the Historical Society for Female Curators, partnered with Devons to provide the *London Illustrated Chronicles* and the *British Tattler* with a detailed account of our leisure cruise. They are calling it the next grand tour. They will present both a woman's and a man's perspectives. The money will go towards setting up their club's exhibits at Seely House in Mayfair."

"What a clever idea. Who came up with it?"

"Have you met Lady Hawley?"

"I'm acquainted with her husband, Lord Hawley. Isn't he a board member of the London Society of Antiquaries? Why would women want to stand up their own club?"

"Do you have a problem with that," Lady Clark said sharply. "Because I can't imagine anyone I consider a friend not supporting such an endeavor."

The man blanched and shook his head. "You misunderstand me. I'm curious why they didn't join the London Society of Antiquaries."

"That club is for men only," Sebastian explained, ignoring the part about Addie being hellbent on revenge because her husband took her best friend as his lover.

"Ah...there is my niece," Lady Clark said, glancing at the door.

Sebastian turned. Was the woman trying to bring him to his knees, he thought? He took a large gulp of his champagne, watching her. Tonight, she wore a blue dress that emphasized her curvy figure more than anything else he had ever seen her in. Her hair made a tempting sight, tied on top of her head in loops and curls, with a few escaping down her neck. She laughed and looked back at someone. Sebastian glowered. Monroe was the cause of her joy.

He took another sip. Diana glanced around the room, and their eyes met. She smiled softly at him. It did something to him. I mean, she bloody well did something to his favorite part of his body, it seemed all the time, but this was different. It was a dip in his stomach, perhaps a flutter. Damn it. He needed to bed someone and not Diana. But he couldn't. Why did he agree to their deal? He hated abstaining from anything. What was the fun in that?

Diana joined them, excited. "Captain Monroe provided some helpful news."

Sebastian was glad the man didn't follow her over. He annoyed him. If he was being honest with himself, his annoyance with Monroe was a new thing. The man often spent time at his club, and he didn't give him a second thought there. Sebastian simply didn't like the way he looked at Diana.

"What did he tell you?" Lady Clark asked.

"Mr. Haggerty is meeting with someone about very old manuscripts at a church in Le Conquet. The documents contain tales about various mythical creatures and are believed to have been written by local monks over two hundred years ago. I'm hoping we can convince him to allow us to join him during his visit to the church. What do you think, Devons?"

"That's a splendid idea," he said begrudgingly.

She nodded, her eyes alight with excitement. "What lady doesn't love a legend?"

He smiled. Clearly, Diana did.

"You will find Haggerty's historical studies very insightful. Those lackwits at the London Society of Antiquaries messed up when they hemmed and hawed about allowing him entry into their club. Now, he'd never join them," Spoor revealed.

Sebastian's eyes flew to Diana's, knowing that Spoor's revelation was something that she could use. She grinned back at him, equally excited.

Continuing, Spoor said to Diana, "Your aunt told me you and Devons are to write about our travels."

Diana beamed. "Yes. The proceeds will go to the Historical Society for Female Curators."

Spoor's gaze flicked to Devons. "And how did you become involved?"

Devons shrugged.

A frown filled Diana's face. "None of this would be possible without Devons. He's our silent partner in the club."

He knew what she was doing. Diana, like all properly gracious ladies, wanted to make sure he was acknowledged for his part, but he didn't need that. "Very silent partner."

"Very modern of you to be supportive of a women-only scholarly club," Spoor said to Devons.

He nodded. "I think it's a worthy cause."

An amused expression flitted across Diana's face. He lifted a brow at her.

Diana grinned at him. "Sebastian Devons, the champion of women."

If someone had asked him before Addie's crazy scheme if he held such beliefs, he would have laughed but now his thoughts had changed. Why should it be so far-fetched or shocking for women to have their own club? Mr. Carlson rang a bell to signal the start of dinner. He offered his arm to Diana, his friend, he reminded himself. "May I escort you?"

Chapter Eleven

Le Conquet—Late June 1850

EVERYONE ON THE weather deck applauded as the *SS Lark* docked at the Le Conquet port. Diana was excited to tour the village but also equally thrilled to visit the lighthouse. From the ship, the Port at the End of the World took Diana's breath away and she didn't want to miss a single thing. The jagged coastline was both stunning and treacherous. Captain Monroe stated at dinner the previous evening that the area was rampant with shipwrecks, explaining the need for the new lighthouse.

Diana's eyes wandered over the stone buildings of the village, hoping the history of the region was as fascinating as the scenery. Devons joined her. "Excited?"

She turned to him, beaming. "Of course."

His mouth tilted up, and his eyes roamed over her. "Excitement and travel suits you."

Heat rushed to Diana's cheeks.

"I'm not flirting with you. I'm simply making an observation," he added.

His compliment filled her with so much happiness that she had to remind herself he could be no more than a friend. She wanted a liaison but not one with someone nursing a broken heart. "You are too kind."

His smile turned into a smirk, and for a moment, Diana suspected his thoughts were not innocent. "Kind might not be the appropriate description."

"Devons," she scolded.

He sighed and changed the subject. "Where is your aunt? Is she unwell?"

Diana nodded to where Aunt Winifred, a recovered Audrey, and Mr. Spoor stood, watching sailors prepare the ship so they could all disembark.

"I wanted to say thank you for not siding with Captain Monroe. I need him to see me as capable of making itineraries for ladies interested in a leisure cruise."

"I know nothing about what interests a lady when it comes to travel," Devons said and then winked. "That isn't my expertise."

She blushed again and he chuckled. What was it about Sebastian Devons? Why was the man so handsome? No, that wasn't the right word. He was sinfully intoxicating. She turned redder. His eyes raked over her before looking away to stare at the port activity.

"You are a shameless flirt, Mr. Devons. How will I keep women away from you?"

"You have done an exceptional job so far," he said, turning back to face her.

She snorted. "There are ten women on the *Lark*, and one is my aunt and the other is my lady's maid. I don't think I have done anything at all."

"Are you suggesting, I'm going to step off this ship and women will flock to me? Am I that appealing?"

She let her eyes wander over him. Diana had no doubt that Devons knew he made a dashing figure in his tweed jacket and hat. A glint formed in his eyes and Diana realized he was enjoying her perusal. A warmth spread across her stomach and further down her body. No! She would not think about Devons in this way.

"I won't give your ego a boost by flattering you."

He leaned in a breath from her ear and murmured. "You already have."

Before she could say more, they were interrupted by the arrival of her aunt. "Mr. Haggerty is on the deck. Mr. Spoor has gone to fetch him for you."

Diana stepped away from Devons as if they had been doing something much more than talking. He smiled at her and the warmth flowing through her body intensified. She reassured herself it would pass.

Later in the day, after disembarking, Diana, Devons, her aunt, Mr. Spoor, and Audrey followed Mr. Haggerty as he was guided by a Monsieur Benard through the cobblestone streets to the one church in the village. The man had met them at the dock and said for a small fee, he would take them anywhere they like.

Diana ran her hand along a stone building as they walked. While the buildings weren't grand or opulent, they had been picturesque to see as they arrived in port. Diana spied the top of the church. She was delighted that Mr. Haggerty had invited them to join him. He'd been happy they were interested in the manuscripts.

She glanced back to see Devons in the back of their merry group of travelers, making sure no one was falling behind. Not only was he intoxicating but also considerate. The man was too much. He was made up of so many contradictions. Though, Diana supposed one could be roguish and decent. She smiled at the thought.

Monsieur Bernard halted, startling her. He spun around to face them. *"L'église."*

"What did he say?" Aunt Winifred said, sounding winded.

"The church," Sebastian drawled.

Diana's eyes darted to him, and he smirked. "You aren't the only one who knows French, my lady."

"It's called *Chapelle Dom Michel*," Mr. Haggerty said. "Please wait here while I talk with the priest. I want to make sure he is comfortable having so many visitors."

Aunt Winifred fanned herself. "I'm parched. Perhaps, I could convince you, Mr. Spoor, to accompany me to one of these *restaurateurs* instead of reviewing the manuscripts."

Mr. Spoor nodded. "I would be delighted, my lady."

As they started to walk off, her aunt turned back to Audrey. "Would you like to join us or sit in the hot drafty church?"

Devons chuckled. Audrey looked at Diana and she shooed her to Aunt Winifred. Diana's aunt had no interest in anything historical, but she didn't hold it against her. Diana wouldn't be on the trip without her. While, as a widow, she could travel alone, it was far more proper to do so with a companion.

As her aunt and the others disappeared, Mr. Haggerty and Monsieur Bernard walked out of the church. Their guide frowned, confused to see only Diana and Devons.

"They decided to visit one of the *restaurateurs* instead," Devons explained.

"Do they know which one is best?" Monsieur Bernard asked, clearly unhappy he wasn't consulted.

Diana and Devons glanced at each other and then back at him.

Pointing in the direction they left, Diana said, "I'm not sure but they went that way."

Monsieur Bernard nodded. "Do not worry. I will find them and help."

He wandered off, and Diana and Devons trailed Haggerty into the church. An older priest stood inside waiting for them. *"Bonjour."*

"This is Father Jean. He is one of the priests here fluent in English. He will be showing us the manuscripts today," Haggerty explained.

The man smiled before walking to a door at the end of the church. They followed him, passing into a smaller room. Laid out on tables were dozens of scrolls. They were beautiful, each decorated with vibrant colors and drawings. She moved closer to one, fascinated by the depiction of a very short mischievous man.

Father Jean joined her. "That is a *korrigan.*"

Devons and Haggerty moved next to her, and he continued

his explanation. *"Korrigans* are troublemakers. The writing explains one should hope to never encounter them. They cause all types of mischief."

Haggerty practically pushed Diana out of the way to stand in front of the manuscript. A flash of annoyance passed over Devons's face. Diana held back a laugh. Father Jean moved to another one. "And these are also at times called *korrigans* but mostly sirens. They are beautiful creatures that tempt men to their deaths."

Diana's eyes flicked over to Devons. He smiled. "I like this tale more."

Of course he did. She rolled her eyes. "You would."

Haggerty asked, "How old are these?"

Father Jean paused, thinking about his question. "Three hundred years."

"And you have them out in the open?" Haggerty said.

The priest shrugged. "Not all the time. I took them out for you to pick the ones you want to take back with you."

Diana's eyes swung to Haggerty. "You are bringing these back to England."

"Father Jean has agreed to loan them to me so I can better study the history of the region."

These manuscripts could be exhibited at the Seely House. Diana beamed at Haggerty. "Perhaps afterward, we could discuss an idea I have."

A few hours later, Diana took Devons's hand as she stepped out of the carriage. The ride to the lighthouse had been bumpy but short. Only Monsieur Bernard had joined them, the rest of their crew of travelers had decided to stay in the village enjoying the food and shopping.

Diana's eyes flitted around, taking in the rocky, rugged coastline, the stone fort, and the lighthouse jutting out at the farthest point of land. The area was both beautiful and terrifying. Perhaps it was the wind and overcast skies, but the setting reminded Diana of something one might read about in a Gothic novel.

"This might be my favorite part of our visit," Devons said as he took in the scenery.

"More so than learning about your sirens," she teased.

He grinned at her wickedly. "Maybe, I will see one. Monsieur Bernard is going to ask the guard at the fort if we can walk out to the lighthouse."

"Truly?"

Devons laughed. "You were so distracted by the sights I'm guessing you missed that. He also stated the lighthouse is yet to be open but will be by the end of the year. We will be some of the first people to stand at the edge of the world."

"I hope they let us out there."

An amused expression flickered across his face. Diana placed her hands on her hips. "What is so funny?"

He grinned. "I'm not sure I would have ever predicted how adventurous you are. It will be windy."

Diana's gaze flicked to the lighthouse jutting out of the coast-line. Perhaps, fear should be what she felt but instead, she was filled with excitement. She wanted to stand at the farthest point. Monsieur Bernard stepped out of the stone building, smiling and motioning them over. Both Diana and Devons joined him. Their guide clapped excitedly. "The guard said you may walk out to the lighthouse. You are lucky—if it were any windier, he wouldn't allow it. I will wait here. I don't like heights, and the wind will make me nervous."

Devons held his arm out to her. She laughed and took it. The wind battered them as they walked out to the lighthouse and Devons yelled, "Are you sure you don't want to turn back?"

"Are you scared?"

He grinned at her. "Not at all."

They continued, charging through the swirling air and across the bridge leading out to the lighthouse. They stopped along the wall of the stone building, facing the fort. Diana grabbed her hair. It had fallen out and now swirled around her shoulders. Instinctively she reached to find pins to fix it.

Devons stopped her. "Leave it. It will only fall out again once we go around to the other side."

They started to move to the side facing the ocean and the wind pounded against them, but Diana didn't care. The sight of the waves crashing against the rocks just below the lighthouse was exhilarating. A waist-high wall prevented them from tumbling onto the jagged rocks.

Devons, Diana was discovering, was a cautious man. He stood with his back flush to the lighthouse stone, motioning her to him. She laughed as her hair swirled around her. She threw her hands up and let the air batter them, as she stood looking at the ocean. Then she turned, wanting to feel the cool mist of the ocean on her back.

Her travel companion, the notorious King of the Den, continued to lean against the lighthouse wall with his arms folded. He was missing all the fun.

She held her hand out to him and hollered, "Join me!"

Devons was being too serious.

She pretended to fall, and he charged forward grabbing her hand. She laughed.

He yelled, "Minx!"

She didn't respond but held onto his hand and spun around. She forced their clasped fingers up in the air before throwing her other arm up, hoping Devons would do the same. He did. They stood like that at the farthest point on earth, letting nature batter them. Devons smiled at her, and she grinned back at him. Diana hadn't felt this alive in years.

THE FOLLOWING DAY, Sebastian smiled as he observed Diana in front of him on the rowboat. Her hat fell back, and she closed her eyes, tilting her face to the sky. He needed to stop studying her so much, even if he enjoyed it.

At the lighthouse, he'd been unable to look away. She'd teased him afterward about being scared, but the truth was he'd been transfixed by her and, for a moment, lost all awareness of anything but her delight in the wind and the crashing waves. They were friends. He could enjoy her happiness, he assured himself. This connection with Diana needn't become an infatuation or more.

He turned away and perused the scenery. The weather was perfect to spend the day in the cove Monroe ordered his men to anchor offshore from. The boat stopped and one of the sailors jumped out. The sailor turned to Diana and Lady Clark. "My ladies, I will carry you the rest of the way."

"How will we make it to shore?" Mr. Spoor asked, looking confused.

"One moment, sir. I will transport you as well," the sailor explained.

Sebastian snorted and started taking off his boots. He looked at the sailor. "Do you really want to carry me?"

The sailor shrugged but Sebastian wasn't doing it. He was a large man. He couldn't imagine how he would look being carried around by a boy half his size. He removed his jacket and rolled his pants up past his knees. Pulling his watch from a pocket, he turned to hand it to Diana who stared back at him wide-eyed. Her cheeks were flushed and a flicker of something thrummed between them.

Interrupting the moment, Lady Clark said, "Goodness, Devons. Quite the show."

He laughed, hoping to suppress whatever he'd just felt.

"Aunt!" Diana said.

Sebastian glanced at Diana. "It's fine. Will you hold this for me?"

She nodded and he passed his most prized possession to her. Their fingers brushed as he did so, and just like that the flicker of something came back. He hopped out of the boat as if running from it.

He grimaced. The water was higher than he guessed, and his pants were wet up to almost his thighs. Still, he would be damned before he would allow himself to be carried about. The sailor asked Diana to scoot closer to the edge of the rowboat.

"I will assist her," Sebastian said, wanting, he supposed, to torture himself more.

"Oh, no, you don't have to," Diana said, blushing.

He waded over to the side she was on and slid his arms under her legs. "Ready?"

"Yes, she is," her aunt said.

Diana frowned at Lady Clark before turning back to Devons. "Are you sure?"

"Wrap one of your arms around my neck," he said.

She leaned forward and did as he asked while her other hand held tightly to his watch. He should have left the damn thing on the ship but hadn't considered it. The gift from his father was always with him. He lifted Diana, pulling her towards him. Her body pushed up against his chest and stomach.

The woman in his arms felt like a perfection he didn't want or need. He could deny it or continue to insist his previous actions with Diana were caused by his attempts to mend his broken heart, but he knew what attraction was and his desire for the lady was real. The thought disconcerted him, and he clenched his jaw as he moved to the shore.

"Am I too heavy?" she asked before biting her lip.

He looked at her startled. "Of course not."

"You appear to be struggling."

He couldn't very well tell her he enjoyed her in his arms a little too much and was envisioning her legs wrapped around his body. His shaft came to life at the thought. As if she intentionally meant to torture him, though he knew she didn't, Diana wiggled up against him.

"I'm fine," he said through gritted teeth as they reached the shore.

They turned their heads at the same time and their lips were mere inches apart. A memory of their previous kiss flashed in his mind. He heard a hitch in her breath. He leaned forward but was brought back to the present when Lady Clark yelled, "I'm next Devons."

Diana blinked, startled. He laughed, releasing her so she stood on the beach. They glanced back to see Mr. Spoor being carried on the sailor's back. Laughter erupted from both of them.

He smiled wryly. "I'm a much bigger man than Mr. Spoor. Can you imagine that boy carrying me?"

She laughed more. "No."

Another sailor tried to assist Lady Clark, and she motioned to Devons. The sailor attempted again, and she batted at his hands, causing the young man to turn bright red.

"I have her," Sebastian said, wading back into the cold water. Assisting Lady Clark was what he needed right now. He needed space from Diana. He couldn't keep fantasizing about her legs wrapped around him.

Later in the day, Devons sat with Diana on a blanket, watching the men swim in the turquoise ocean. They swam in their pants and shirts, foregoing formality for a moment. He glanced at Diana who wistfully watched others splash in the ocean.

"Would you like to go in?"

Her eyes flicked down to her dress and she laughed. "I will sink to the bottom. The water is so beautiful. I have never seen a blue like this before. I may be a smidge envious that men can frolic in it."

He didn't know how he would do it but at some point, he would find somewhere for Diana to swim. She sighed and the yearning on her face disappeared. Sebastian, out of habit, snapped his pocket watch open and closed. Diana said, "Your watch is lovely."

He studied his timepiece with all of its ornate carvings, knowing none of that mattered to him. "It could be the ugliest of watches and it would still be special to me. My father gave it to me."

"Were you close?"

Sebastian raised a brow at her personal question. She smiled at him. "Are we not friends?"

Not many people asked him about his family. One didn't broach such topics when they were born out of wedlock and their father was a well-known marquess. Even more scandalous, Sebastian's father and his marchioness, Malcolm's mother, chose love over societal rules. The marquess moved Sebastian and his mother into his country estate with him and Malcolm, while his wife lived abroad with her companion.

"We were. I grew up at Derry Hall with my father, mother, and half-brother for most of my life. Well besides when we were away at school."

They were quiet for a moment, and he added, "The hall was like a sanctuary from the rest of society for my family. A place where my father openly loved my mother and where my brother and I were always treated as equals. It is still one of my favorite places to be."

He flipped open the watch and showed her the engraved words he'd done his best to remember every day of his life. *The measure of a man is defined by his actions.*

"Loving words for a man to tell his son. Your upbringing seems unique but wonderful."

Sebastian smirked. "That isn't to say there weren't dramatics and a price for living in scandal, but I'd like to believe my parents and Malcolm's mother, along with her companion, made the right choice. They chose love."

Diana smiled, amused. "You are such a romantic, Sebastian Devons."

He ran his fingers through his hair. "A practical romantic. I will only ever wed for love. I had a front-row seat of what can happen if you don't."

"You are lucky you are a man and can make that choice."

Sebastian studied her. "You could marry for love again. You loved your husband."

Sadness flickered across her face. "For ladies, especially the mother of a duke, marriage is more of a business arrangement."

She deserved to be loved again, deeply. Sebastian didn't say it, knowing that even though Diana was on this adventure she would go back to whom she had been before. They both would. Instead, he said, "I'm so sorry you lost him."

She glanced down, playing with sand as if thinking through her thoughts. Eventually, she looked at him. "Thank you. I'm happy I was able to experience love at least once, no matter how brief. We were lucky. I didn't choose him. My parents and his father made the match. His, because he was afraid Stuart would never marry as he was so quiet. Mine, because he would someday be a duke. Love grew for us."

"Sometimes that is the best way."

She flushed. "I had my own preconceived notions when I met him. He was not what I envisioned or whom I thought my parents would pick."

"What changed?" Sebastian asked, curious.

Diana pursed her lips and thought about it. "I had assumed he wouldn't want anything to do with me because of how transactional our betrothal was and that I was merely a means to carrying on his family's title. I was distant from him at first. But he shocked me. He insisted on speaking with me all the time. He wanted to understand my thoughts, my desires, and what would bring me joy. No one had ever asked me such questions. I had been raised to be whatever my husband dictated."

Sebastian discreetly reached over and squeezed her hand. She smiled and glanced at him with watery eyes. "We laughed a lot. We learned about passion together. Not only was I naive about such things but Stuart, until marriage, hadn't been terribly focused on it either."

She blushed a fierce red and added, "The books he brought home for us shocked me at first. My husband was a thorough man when it came to research. It was beautiful to explore and learn such things together."

"You make me wish my first experiences were more special."

She pulled her hand away and wiped her watery eyes. "I'm sorry. I can't believe I shared something so personal. Some days are harder than others."

"I apologize for bringing it up."

"It's fine. I have had plenty of time to grieve. He would be so upset with me for being so sad. When we knew the end was near, he made me promise I would be happy."

"I had heard he was sick for quite some time."

Diana nodded. "He kept passing out. The doctors determined he had a heart condition, and he wouldn't make it another year. He passed away six months later."

She wiped her eyes again. "Ugh…No more of this talk."

There was so much more he wanted to say, but Sebastian didn't. He stood and held out his hand. He didn't want her to end the day filled with such sadness. "You may be unable to swim in the ocean, but I think walking along the shore would be a wonderful reprieve."

Diana took a deep breath and allowed him to pull her up. Once she was standing, Sebastian tucked her hand in his arm.

Chapter Twelve

CAPTAIN MONROE ESCORTED Diana around the weather deck. She'd been surprised when an attendant knocked on her door to ask if she would entertain a walk with the captain.

"I feel I may have offended you by requesting you wait on the ship at our first stop. I want to apologize. It wasn't my intent to upset you. In truth, I want these types of leisure cruises to be successful. If you and Lady Hawley can help with that, I would be delighted."

Diana smiled, happy he was apologizing, but she was confused as to why it seemed so sudden. She supposed she should just be content that they were no longer debating the topic. "Thank you, Captain Monroe."

"Did you enjoy your time at the cove and Le Conquet?"

"I did, and I think travelers will love the area, especially the lighthouse."

"Good," he said.

They continued to walk, but Diana finally stopped. "What is it you really want, Captain Monroe?"

He rubbed the back of his neck and grinned. He was quite boyish, and Diana wondered if he was younger than her thirty-one years. Eventually, he said, "I was hoping you would accompany me to dinner in Porto?"

Her eyes widened. Was the captain flirting with her? She

smiled, flattered. But she hesitated. She wasn't sure why. "Perhaps you could take a group of us to dinner? I know others would love to join."

"Like Devons," he said with curiosity.

"Yes, he and I will be writing about all our stops, and it is beneficial if we go to the same places."

His eyes met hers. "Is that all it is?"

Was he asking if something existed between her and Devons? That wasn't any of his business, regardless of if there were or weren't. Diana frowned at him. "We are associates and friends."

He leaned in close to her. "Perhaps, then, you and I can share a glass of champagne one night."

The captain was flirting with her! She hadn't forgotten Devons's warning that a dalliance with Captain Monroe might cause complications for the club, but that wasn't what prevented her from agreeing. Something was missing. What was wrong with her? She wanted a flirtation, and here was a man interested in having one. Annoyed she felt like saying no, she instead said, "Let's make plans after we visit Porto."

He smiled, seemingly delighted with her suggestion. As they walked, he told her about Porto and what they could expect to see. Unfortunately, Diana was only partially focused on his descriptions as her mind kept going back to her discussion with Devons from earlier. She couldn't believe she revealed so much to him. He probably thought she was an emotional mess. Devons put her at ease in a way no one else could. Well, besides, Stuart. The thought disconcerted her. Well, not exactly like her husband. She and Devons were only friends, Diana reminded herself.

"Is everything fine?" Monroe asked her.

Diana blushed, realizing she had stopped with no explanation. "I'm sorry. Please continue."

She did her best to listen to Monroe but her mind flitted back to Devons. They'd agreed to be just friends, and Diana knew that was the best decision. He needed to focus on himself, and she wanted something brief. Still, they'd kissed. A kiss she hadn't forgotten about. Yet the thought of pursuing an interlude with Devons, she suspected, wouldn't be so simple. No, Diana didn't want or need anything that would prove to be complicated. She pushed away the absurd notion of having any type of liaison with Devons and did her best to engage with Monroe.

Later that evening, Diana sat at the desk in her room, trying to form her thoughts about what to share with all of London. This would be her first missive about their trip and the first one printed in the papers. She was nervous. She wanted it to be exciting, clever, and intriguing. Things Diana felt she was none of.

"Good evening," her aunt said, knocking on the door between them.

Diana rose and opened it for her. "I thought you were asleep, Aunt."

"I'm about to, but I wanted to say goodnight."

Diana smiled. "Thank you."

Her aunt studied her, and Diana shifted nervously under her intense gaze. "You have come into your own away from England."

"We haven't been gone that long."

"No, but I see it already. Travel suits you. And so does Devons," she said with a wink.

Diana's brows shot up at her statement. "I have no idea what you mean."

Her aunt smiled at her slyly. "I think the man holds a *tendre* for you."

A laugh escaped Diana. "That is ridiculous. He could have any woman he likes."

"Oh, calm down. I'm not saying he is in love or going to propose, but he desires you. You can see it when he watches you."

"He isn't interested in pursuing any type of relationship right now."

Her aunt tilted her head. "You two are becoming rather close.

What has he told you?"

Diana wouldn't reveal Devons's broken heart. That was his story to tell. She shrugged and said, "Nothing."

Aunt Winifred sighed. "Why must young people deny themselves what they really want?"

Diana flushed. "I'm denying myself nothing. I'm not interested in Devons."

One of her aunt's brows shot up in disbelief and Diana added, "I'm serious."

"Perhaps my ability to sense these things is slipping. Maybe I'm too distracted by Mr. Spoor."

It was Diana's turn to give her aunt a hard time. "You like him."

"I will allow him to entertain me while we are on our journey," her aunt said, causing Diana to giggle. "What are you working on?"

Diana sighed. "I'm trying to figure out what I want to share about Le Conquet for my first update on our trip."

"Well, you must tell them about Devons carrying us to the cove. That will make the ladies swoon."

Diana gave her aunt a pointed look. "I thought I would write about the *korrigans* and sirens in the manuscripts."

"Ugh…that is exceedingly dull," her aunt said.

Diana frowned at her. "The only reason I'm here is because I'm on the board of the Historical Society for Female Curators."

"That is true, but you are trying to gain the interest of ladies who don't normally care about a bunch of old artifacts. Who wouldn't love to hear about a scoundrel carrying some ladies? You are the most proper woman in all of London. No one will think it's anything more than that."

She winced at her aunt's accurate statement. "You make a valid point."

Her aunt made her way back to her room and winked before shutting the door. "Of course I do."

Diana smiled, took a moment, and then started to write.

Once done she looked down and read her words.

To the Ladies of London,

The SS Lark arrived in the fishing village of Le Conquet, a beautiful coastal setting comprised of small stone buildings. This area is known as the Port at the End of the World.

We were greeted by the friendliest individuals who helped us enjoy the most divine food. At our first stop, Chapelle Dom Michel, Father Jean shared with us manuscripts depicting tales about the mischievous korrigans and the tempting sirens of the region. The Historical Society for Female Curators may have more to share about them soon.

But my favorite part followed. Mr. Devons and I journeyed to the farthest point of land in France. A lighthouse stands there, and we stood at the very edge, allowing the winds to batter us. I won't tell you which of us was more nervous, Mr. Devons or me.

Our first official stop ended with a day of leisure in a cove with the most beautiful water I have ever seen. If you are wondering how my dear aunt and I made it to shore, Mr. Devons, our increasingly helpful travel partner, carried us. We are grateful he is on this trip with us.

Both Mr. Devons and I can't wait to share more of our adventures with all of you.

Lady Hensley

Perfect, Diana thought. She wondered what Devons would write about. They had agreed with Addie not to share their updates with each other. Addie suspected it would be more interesting and exciting that way. Diana sighed. Hopefully, this would entertain enough ladies to raise money for Seely House. A smile flitted across her face, feeling optimistic about this club in which she initially didn't think she had a place.

Sebastian stood leaning against the railing of the *SS Lark*, smoking a cigar. Even though it was a calm day at sea, he was the only one standing on this side of the ship besides a few sailors coming and going. He took a puff of his cigar before releasing the smoke. The door to the stairway leading to the saloon deck opened, and Diana stepped out, surprising him. Their eyes met, and she smiled at him.

His mouth lifted up at the corners, happy to see her. He waved her over. She smoothed her hands over the front of her beige-and-pink dress. It was lovely on her, made more so by all the color she'd gotten recently. He'd been tempted to tell her that he liked her freckles, but he suspected she wouldn't like that.

"Are you hiding from everyone? There are several games taking place in the saloons below."

"I decided to enjoy the sea air."

She peered over the railing and lifted a brow. "You are faring much better up here. I remember our first evening. You wouldn't even let me stand by the railing, and now you are leaning against it."

He tilted his head back and laughed before looking down at her. She looked out at the ocean. He nudged her with his arm and handed her his cigar. Her blue eyes widened. "I couldn't."

"Why is that?"

"Ladies don't smoke."

He snorted and took another puff. "Plenty of them do, including the proper ones."

She looked back at the cigar and then at him, biting her lip. He held it out to her, and unable to resist trying something new, she took it. His friend was becoming quite a risk-taker. Her fingers squeezed the cigar, and she asked, "What do I do now?"

"Bring it to your mouth and puff on it but don't suck in the air."

She did as he said, bringing it to her lips, forming an *O*. His eyes were transfixed by her mouth. He had to stop himself from groaning. She inhaled and immediately started coughing.

Sebastian leaned over and patted her on her back. Diana handed him back the cigar.

"That is awful."

He laughed. "It's an acquired taste."

She rolled her eyes. "If you say so."

"Would you like to go back down to the saloon? I will join you."

She nodded and he held his arm out to her.

"But before we go, I wanted to apologize for sharing so much with you yesterday."

Her face turned red, and Sebastian suspected she was embarrassed. He dropped his arm before tilting her chin up so their eyes met. "Diana, we are friends. You can tell me anything."

She clasped his hand and squeezed it. "Thank you."

A sailor shuffled by them, carrying ropes, and they sprung apart. Diana wiped her hands on her skirt and said, "Well, still, I appreciate you letting me go on and on. I certainly overshared."

He didn't want her to be embarrassed. "It sounds like you and your husband had a special marriage. Honestly, it made me rethink what my feelings were for Lilah. Perhaps you were right. Maybe what I thought was love was infatuation."

"I shouldn't have said that. Who am I to say if you loved someone or not?"

"I guess my point is if I were to ever fall in love, I would want something as special as you described."

Diana grabbed his hand and squeezed it. "You deserve that."

Their clasped hands set off a warning within him. He was in a treacherous area of feeling something he didn't want or wasn't ready for. This lady was not for him, and he wasn't for her. He suspected Diana felt something similar as she released his hand and stepped back. "Well, I'm happy we have that out of the way."

He nodded. Sebastian wanted her to understand she would always have a friend in him. "Agree, but I do mean it. You can tell me anything."

"Thank you."

He held his arm out to her again, and as they walked, Diana asked, "Have you written your update?"

"Not yet."

She frowned at him. "You must do it before we arrive in Porto."

He laughed. "I will. Come, let's go join the others."

As they made their way to the saloon deck, Sebastian's mind flitted back to Lilah. Had he loved her? He wasn't so sure.

Late that night, Sebastian Devons sat at the desk. Addie should like his first missive, he thought. He perused the letter again.

To the Ladies of London,

Lady Hensley is making sure we have the most entertaining adventure. Le Conquet was filled with the magic of the korrigans and sirens. After learning about them, we ate the finest food and were told even more stories about the sirens. These sirens are said to be able to tempt men to their deaths. I told Lady Hensley I wouldn't be tempted. She seemed doubtful. My ladies, can you believe she thought I couldn't resist these magical creatures? Why would she make such an assumption?

We traveled to what is considered the farthest point of land in France. Some call this area the Port at the End of the World because it feels like from the coastline, nothing else exists beyond the ocean. The day we visited, it was exceptionally windy. I was reluctant to venture too close to the water, but Lady Hensley assured me she would stop me from toppling into the ocean if we encountered a big gust of wind. The lady is very brave and quite the adventurer.

Hopefully, my travel companion also told you about the enchanting cove we spent time in. It was a spectacle to get us to shore, but we made it. I believe if all my other ventures fail, I can find employment carrying men and ladies about.

That is it for now. I bid you good day until my next letter.

Sebastian Devons.

Chapter Thirteen

Porto—Late June 1850

DIANA LOOKED AROUND her room at the hotel in Porto and sighed. While she had enjoyed their journey so far on the *SS Lark*, she was grateful for a night in a full-size room. Audrey was in the maid quarters one floor up, and her Aunt Winifred was located next door. Captain Monroe had planned a busy day of activities for all of them. Porto, he declared earlier, was one of the best cities on the continent.

Dazzling had been the word that came to mind as they arrived at the port. The rising sun had given the buildings a golden hue. Even Devons stated it was beautiful. The passengers, happy to spend a night on land, quickly disappeared into the city. Diana and Devons's group of travelers had been whisked away to a hotel that Captain Monroe coordinated for them. Diana smiled at the thought that, somehow, they'd formed a little group to spend time with during their journey.

Based on Monroe's actions, Diana suspected he believed Addie's idea of an all-ladies grand tour was a worthwhile venture. The captain also arranged to have an acquaintance show them around. She wasn't sure if his assistance was business-related or something else. Diana frowned, thinking about how complicated it may become if she had some type of liaison with him. Still, she was flattered by his notice.

It had been a long time since anyone expressed such interest in her. Diana looked in the mirror in the corner, acknowledging the changes she saw, staring back at her. She'd grown up with the strictest rules about appearance and often found herself trying to readjust something or fix something out of place.

Since leaving England, she'd let that go. Her hair, even when worked on by Audrey, had a wild look to it. Probably because the curls that seemed so manageable at home refused to do anything orderly. The sun had given her face color she normally avoided. Diana liked it.

A frown filled her face. She would meet with her mother next week, and she wouldn't like the changes. Why did it matter? Diana hadn't seen her in years. A nibble of hope bloomed in her that maybe she'd changed. Diana told herself not to get her hopes up. Kindness wasn't natural to her mother. A memory flashed in her mind of her telling Diana who she would wed.

"Diana, I will not explain our choice any further. Lord Hensley will be a duke soon enough. That is what is most important."

"Mother, he is everything you tell us not to be in appearance. He always appears rumpled. He is not what I envisioned."

Her mother's mouth twisted into a sneer. "Did you think you would get someone better? You?"

She flushed. "I thought—"

"At least Clara is beautiful. You are just plain, a plain proper lady."

Pain shot through Diana at her harsh words. Her mother glared. "Is there anything else?"

"No, Mother."

Shaking the memory away, Diana reminded herself that at least it had worked out because, in the end, Stuart had been everything she could ever want. Still, the words had been cruel. Cruelty had been constant from the woman who gave her life. She shook her head. Why was she thinking about all of this? She would not dwell on her visit with her mother and her potential return to England.

Diana made her way out of the room and down the stairs before entering the *Café Agueda* connected to where they were staying. The cafe was filled with both men and women from all social classes. Diana spied a woman sketching at a table and, at another, a group of men playing instruments. Monroe said Porto was a city for artists, and Diana could see why. She had the urge to sit in the cafe and observe but knew they had a full day of activities.

"What do you think?" Devons said, approaching her.

She swung around and grinned at him. "Is it wrong for me to love it here?"

A curl from her bun must have fallen free because he leaned forward and tucked it behind her ear. "I don't think so at all. Have you ever been to my club?"

"Just once."

"Ahh…I remember that night. The day you burst through my doors, ready to find your sister."

"You must have thought I had taken leave of my senses."

He shook his head. "That is not what I remember. I remember thinking, 'What a fierce woman.'"

She blushed at his compliment. At the time, Diana had been frantic with worry about Clara. She'd been willing to do whatever it took to get help, even entering Devons's notorious club, the Den. Getting to know him, she was now skeptical of its notoriety. He was a good man, even if he liked to pretend otherwise.

"Tell me about your establishment."

He lifted a black, silky brow. "Why?"

She shrugged. "I've only been there one time. I'm intrigued at how infamous of a place it could be after meeting you. I'm starting to doubt the rumors."

He smirked and leaned in. "Not all sin is evil. Vice can be enjoyed without it causing harm."

"Can it?" she murmured, her heart hammering. Why did his words cause her to tremble?

Just then, Aunt Winifred walked through the door. "Captain Monroe's friend is out here, ready to take us on a historical tour."

Devons stepped back and winked. "Another time I will tell you about my club."

"I would like that," Diana said, surprising them both.

And she would, Diana realized, but now was not the time. She and Devons followed her aunt out the door, where a dapper, short slender man stood. He beamed when he saw them. "Hello. My name is Senhor Martim Costa. Captain Monroe is a friend of mine and I told him I would show you some of the history of my wonderful city while he does whatever captains do."

"Lovely," Diana said.

"Where will we be going first?" Devons asked.

"A place that tells the most romantic story in all of Portugal," he said, holding a carriage door open.

Diana allowed him to assist her. She was then joined by Aunt Winifred, Mr. Spoor, Devons, and Costa himself. Once settled, he tapped on the carriage, and they lumbered down the street.

"Have you heard of Senhor Pedro?" Costa asked them all.

They all shook their heads, and he sighed, disappointed. "Of course not, but don't worry, I will tell you about him."

They all leaned in, excited. Diana glanced at Devons. Well, except for her travel companion, who sat with his ever-present half-amused expression. Diana wondered what it took for Devons to be enraptured or swept away by something.

"Senhor Pedro was the son of King John IV of Portugal, and even though he was married, he fell in love with another woman. Her name was Inés. He loved her desperately. Still, there wasn't much he could do as he was tied to another woman for life. That is until his wife passed."

"Did he marry her?" Aunt Winifred asked.

Costa shook his head. "His father was against them marrying and banished Inés from the court."

"Horrible parents," her aunt muttered, enthralled with the story.

Diana glanced at Devons. His half-amused expression was still there, but she noticed he, too, now followed the story closely.

Costa continued, "But Senhor Pedro's love was too strong, and he chose to live with Inés in sin."

"This is a rather salacious story," Mr. Spoor said.

Her aunt shushed him, causing Diana to laugh. Costa smiled and said, "All the best ones are."

The carriage came to a stop, and he jumped out. "Follow me to learn what happened to them."

They entered a beautiful building, and hanging on the back wall of the grand hall was a tapestry of someone's life. The lower part showed two large tombs within a monastery.

"So, they ended up together," Diana stated.

Costa smiled gleefully, and Diana suspected he had told this story more than once. Devons stepped up next to her and said, "I'm guessing they did not."

Diana frowned, disappointed.

"The king was so worried about his son's relationship with Inés that he had her murdered. Senhor Pedro was outraged, but he could do nothing about it, so he waited until his father's death."

"He must have been quite an angry man," Aunt Winifred remarked.

Costa nodded. "Once his father died and he became king, he had the assassins killed, some even saying he took part. Then he moved Inés's remains to the Alcobaça Monastery and made her the de facto queen even though she was dead. They are both buried there."

"He must have loved her deeply," her aunt exclaimed.

"He sounds unhinged to me," Mr. Spoor stated.

Aunt Winifred rolled her eyes. Diana glanced at Devons. "What do you think?"

Devons shrugged. "That it is a shame they couldn't marry. A lifetime of scandal is a heavy burden."

Diana knew he was talking from personal experience. He winked at her. "Though Mr. Spoor might be right. Senhor Pedro does seem unhinged."

She laughed, and everyone joined in. Costa smiled. "I hope you enjoyed my story."

"Is it true?" Diana asked.

He shrugged. "Perhaps."

Steps echoed off the stone flooring, and they all turned to see an elegant man entering the hall. He was tall like Devons but not quite as broad. He had a regal, handsome face with a head of black curls.

"May I introduce Count Lorenzo de Messina from Sardinia. He is accompanying the late King of Sardinia's sister while she handles the king's affairs."

The man's eyes moved around the room before landing on Diana. He briefly perused her, and a small smile formed on his face. He was certainly attractive. He bowed to all of them. "Good afternoon. I will be joining you for dinner and the theater tonight. Did you enjoy the tapestry? I find the story rather dark but also fascinating."

Diana nodded. He stepped closer to her, taking her hand and raising it to his mouth. "And you are?"

She blushed. "Lady Hensley."

"Are you here for the tapestry as well?" Devons asked in a growly voice.

Messina dropped Diana's hand and smirked at Devons. "This is where I'm staying while in Porto." And then added dramatically, "Dom Costa asked if he could bring you all here so he can tell his story of tortured love."

Everyone laughed but Devons. Diana, trying to ease the tension, said, "Mr. Devons and I are writing articles for two London newspapers about a potential new leisure cruise for ladies."

Messina's eyes flicked to Devons and back to her. "I understand why you are here but not Mr. Devons. He isn't a lady."

"No, but he is very well-liked by the ladies of London," her aunt piped up.

Diana gasped and frowned. Her aunt grinned and shrugged. "It's true."

Messina glanced around the room before landing back on

Diana. "Well, I look forward to our evening later. I have some dealings to handle. Goodbye until then."

"Goodbye," they all replied.

He glanced at Diana one last time, causing her to blush. Goodness, she hadn't expected them to meet someone new.

SEBASTIAN SAT AT one end of the table, watching both Monroe and Messina flirt outrageously with Diana. To say he was displeased was a gross understatement. He reminded himself this was what she wanted. It wasn't his place to interrupt. She seemed to favor the count more. Monroe looked as if he was on the verge of giving up.

In truth, Sebastian imagined Messina was the perfect person for her to have a brief flirtation with. The count leaned towards her and whispered in her ear, causing her to laugh louder. Aunt Winifred, who sat next to him, peered down the table. "He is certainly handsome."

He took a sip of his wine and grunted in response. She elbowed him. "Are you telling me that doesn't bother you?"

He flicked his dark-brown eyes in the direction of Diana's aunt. "Why would it?"

"Because you like her."

"We're friends."

She rolled his eyes. "You like her. Diana says you are not looking for a tryst. Why? You are one of the most notorious men in all of London."

He choked on his wine. Lady Clark patted him on the back and told the table, "He is fine. He took too big of a drink."

Everyone resumed their conversations. Lady Clark whispered, "Well, maybe not in so many words."

He looked at her skeptically, suspecting Diana hadn't shared any of their private conversations with her. "I'm taking a break from vice and interludes."

Disappointment flitted across the older woman's face. "What a waste. Why?"

Sebastian stopped himself from laughing. "I've had too much fun. A break is good for me."

Lady Clark snorted. "Or more like torture."

Sebastian couldn't let her make assumptions about Diana and him. "We are business associates and friends, that is all."

She sighed dramatically. "Well, at least there is Messina. He would be the second-best option and will be with us until we reach Malaga."

His brows drew together confused. "What do you mean?"

"Captain Monroe mentioned to me earlier today he would be joining us on the ship."

Sebastian didn't like that at all. He frowned at Messina and Diana at the end of the table. "I wasn't aware of that."

"Yes, it's a shame you are out of the game."

He glanced at her and saw a gleam of something in her eyes. Was she attempting to rile him up? He was tempted to ask her why. But he reminded himself that Diana and he had two different focuses. He was trying to be vice free while she was trying to live a little. Then why did he feel like he was the perfect person to show her all about vice, not Messina?

Later that evening, Sebastian sat next to Diana in a box at the *Teatro do Principe*, waiting for the opera about star-crossed lovers to begin. Messina insisted on sitting on the other side of her. He wanted to make sure Diana understood the scenes because they were in Portuguese. It was a damn opera. Most didn't need to be translated.

He'd only briefly spoken with Diana since leaving the hotel for dinner and the evening's entertainment. The count seemed to be happy to monopolize her time. Messina excused himself to fetch champagne. Diana turned to him. "I have so enjoyed Porto. Have you?"

"It appears you have enjoyed the count."

Her eyes widened at his words, but she didn't say anything. His tone had been unreasonably harsh. She didn't deserve that. He sighed. "I'm sorry that was very rude of me. I'm glad you are enjoying yourself."

"Even if Messina hadn't joined us, I would still think Porto was exquisite."

He forced himself to smile. "I apologize."

She nodded and was quiet for a moment but eventually said, "It's nice to have someone find me desirable after being alone."

Sebastian wanted her to have that. He couldn't comprehend how anyone wouldn't find her tempting. Hell, he'd found her desirable even with her damn cap. It wasn't her fault he was struggling with watching her flirt with the count. They'd decided they were friends and friends only. Sebastian should be happy as her friend she was getting her flirtation.

"I'm glad you are enjoying your time with him."

She studied him as if looking for something. He kept his face emotionless. He would never want Diana to think he was judging her. Hell, he had no room to judge her.

"Enjoy the evening, Diana," he said.

She nodded and turned back to the stage. Messina reappeared with their drinks as the opera started. Sebastian did his best to ignore him whispering in Diana's ear and her giggles. It had nothing to do with him, he told himself, glowering at the stage.

Chapter Fourteen

DIANA LAUGHED AS she sat on the blanket, enjoying the warm sun while listening to Costa's associate Dom Alido explain to them the history of the port. She touched her hand to her cheeks and realized she was hot but wasn't sure if it was from the sun or the port they consumed. She'd found Le Conquet fascinating, but Porto and the surrounding countryside had her heart. She wondered if she could bring Robert here someday.

Her mind flitted to Arthur. She hadn't thought much of him since leaving. His potential proposal still hung in the air. The man, on the surface, was her perfect match. She looked around and suspected he would find all of this not up to his standards. The thought unsettled her. Was her ideal partner someone who wouldn't enjoy this?

She glanced at Devons, so different from Arthur. He lounged on another blanket, sipping his port without a care in the world. She questioned if he were ever not comfortable. Even mending his broken heart, he seemed content. She wondered if what he said previously was true. Did he think his feelings for Lady Wesley were not as deep as he initially thought? Why did that stir something in her?

Diana's eyes flicked over him. She desired him. That was why. She could deny it, but no one intrigued her as much as he did. What was she thinking? He was the one man she shouldn't have a tryst with. He was her neighbor and friend and would be somewhat involved in the Historical Society for Female Curators.

One of the reasons she considered having a liaison on this journey was because she would never have to see the man again. It was simple. What she felt for Devons was already complicated. Not that it mattered. Whatever feelings or attraction she suspected Devons had for her seemingly diminished the longer they were on their trip.

"Now that I have taught you all about port, enjoy your remaining time here. If you walk past that tree line, you will find Roman ruins," Dom Alido said while pointing over Diana's shoulder.

Most of their group headed in the direction Dom Alido pointed. Diana frowned at Devons. He remained behind, lying on his blanket with his hat over his face. Was he sleeping? Diana rose and nudged his foot with hers. "Don't you think you should see the ruins?"

"No," he said in a muffled voice from underneath his hat.

"We won't write about the same things then."

He grunted and lifted the hat from his handsome face that right now Diana found rather annoying. "It will be fine."

She frowned at him until he sighed and sat up, readjusting his hat on his head. "Would you really like me to accompany you?"

"Of course."

He stood, grumbling about wanting to enjoy a sunny nap. He held out his arm. "As you wish."

Diana glared at him, tired of his moodiness. "Stay. I don't need you to join me. I suddenly find that my own company may be better."

She wouldn't cajole the man to spend time with her. She didn't need him, nor his disinterest. Ignoring his arm, she walked off, heading towards the ruins. She heard Devons utter a word unsuitable for any lady. Diana didn't stop, weaving her way through people. Once through the crowd, she paused to catch her breath.

A firm wall slammed into the back of her. Devons had been on her heels. He grabbed her waist to steady them both. She didn't turn around but bit out, "You can go back to your nap. I don't need your presence."

He released her and leaned against a stone wall. "Diana, I'm sorry. I'm a little weary of sightseeing today. I should have asked to return to the *SS Lark* early."

Diana didn't believe him. He'd been different since arriving in Porto, and she didn't understand why. She wondered if his mind was on the lady who hurt him. A pain pierced her heart.

"Are you thinking about Lady Wesley?"

His eyes flew to her face, and he laughed as if she said the most absurd thing. She flushed, embarrassed. Devons's laughter subsided, and his gaze turned intent. Finally, he said, "Are you enjoying yourself with the count?"

The question startled her. She shrugged. "He is charming."

His lips twisted into a smirk. "Perhaps a contender for an affair."

She felt herself go red again. Unhappy with his harshness and a tone she suspected conveyed judgment, Diana replied, "I don't know. Are you about to lecture me if I were?"

"That would be hypocritical of me. I just thought I would offer some advice."

Diana lifted a brow. "Continue."

Sebastian pushed himself away from the wall and leaned forward so his mouth was a breath away from her ear. "Remember that regardless of the partner, the dalliance you are seeking should be about your pleasure. Too often, lovers can be selfish. If you sense Messina may be that way, let him go. You want a man who wants to fulfill your desires. Don't waste your time on someone who doesn't do that. There are plenty of men who would be more than willing."

His words made Diana gasp. She stepped back, and they stared at one another. What was Devons up to? He disconcerted her, and Diana thought it was intentional for some reason. "I see no reason to suspect Messina would be selfish."

He pressed his mouth together, annoyed. Was the man jealous? He couldn't be. "Devons—"

"I think Messina is exactly who you are looking for. Then you can go back to London life with no one being the wiser. The proper marchioness with an impending courtship on the horizon," he said, interrupting her.

Her eyes flashed with anger. She was tired of his surliness. "Hopefully, once on the ship, you will return to your normal charming self. I'm not sure I like this moody Devons."

A smirk filled his handsome face, and Diana had the urge to snap at him but was prevented from doing so by the arrival of her aunt, Spoor, and Costa. Her aunt and Spoor continued on, not even acknowledging them. The two were whispering and giggling. Diana had seen Spoor in the area of their hotel rooms early this morning. He'd bashfully smiled and hurried away. It seemed her aunt had already accomplished what she was failing at.

"I hope you have enjoyed your visit, Lady Hensley and Mr. Devons," Costa said, interrupting her thoughts.

She forced a smile. "I have loved it."

Surly Devons grunted and Diana rolled her eyes, exasperated with the man.

Costa didn't seem to notice and continued, "I know I'm biased, as I was raised here, but I have traveled the world, and there is no place like Porto."

Diana nodded. "I couldn't agree with you more."

Devons gave his head a jerk, agreeing with them. Costa beamed, delighted they were enjoying themselves. "I heard Count Messina is traveling with you to Malaga."

"Yes. He mentioned he has business," Diana said.

Costa chuckled. "He has business everywhere. He deals in exports and imports of goods when he is not escorting the princess."

Diana's eyes widened, and her gaze swung to Devons before

turning back to Costa. "Really? What type of goods?"

"Antiquities."

"Of course," Devons muttered.

Her eyes flicked to him, and she frowned. The news had only made him surlier. Diana smiled at Costa. "Thank you so much for the information."

Costa nodded and held his arm out. "We should return. We will be leaving soon for your ship."

Diana looked behind her and saw Devons strolling along with them. She sighed and glanced away. She'd so enjoyed her time with him and hoped this grumpiness was momentary.

Sebastian made his way to the main saloon, where everyone was gathered for after-dinner games and drinks. In some ways, being on the *SS Lark* reminded him of the Den, except here, he didn't play the part of host, and shockingly, he didn't miss it. Perhaps because this wasn't his ship. He'd invested a monumental amount of time into making the Den a success because it was his.

He perused the room and found both Messina and Monroe keeping Diana company. Didn't at least Monroe have work to do? Sebastian gave Diana space, not wanting to interfere in her choices. In truth, he didn't like either one of them. He'd thought long and hard about his own feelings for Diana. Not feelings, he reminded himself, but attraction. He'd been tempted more than once to pursue her.

But a fling with Diana wouldn't end well. They had too many family members and friends between them. She was also his neighbor. And even more concerning to Sebastian, he could damage her reputation. Even though she hated it, she was highly respected within society, probably more than any other woman he associated with. This trip was a brief adventure into the risqué for her, unlike Sebastian, who operated in vice every day. If a hint that they were intimate got out, it would be scandalous.

Hell, when they'd departed on this ship, no one had suspected such a thing could happen because she was perceived as the epitome of properness. He would not be the cause of gossip about her. No, she didn't need that. Nor did the club that she and Addie were standing up for.

He glanced at her, reaffirming to himself that there would be no tryst or liaison between them. Messina or Monroe would be perfect. She could have a flirtation or something else and return to England with society being none the wiser. He simply had to move past his attraction to the lady. It was the only option.

He took a big gulp of his brandy, annoyed that he felt the desire to go to her. To sit with her. To talk with her. And that terrified him more than the lust coursing through him because it meant he liked her. Sebastian assured himself that it was only because they were stuck on this ship together that he had such thoughts.

She was the mother of a soon-to-be duke. Yes, she was a lady so far out of his league when it came to a real courtship that he couldn't allow himself to consider such an option. He'd been a witness to his own parents' scandalous life. He would never put himself in a similar situation.

As much as he admired her and truly considered her a friend, he needed, for now, to keep her at arm's length. Perhaps, he would find a woman to spend time with during their stay in Malaga that would cure him of his outrageous thoughts.

"You have been rather quiet tonight, Devons," Haggerty interrupted.

"Have I been?"

Haggerty chuckled. "I told Lady Hensley that her club can display two of the manuscripts."

"Well done, Haggerty."

"Do you think it odd that Lady Hensley was picked to be the face of this new club? I have seen her at other events, and I would have never guessed she had interest in such a lofty plan."

Devons suspected many people underestimated what Diana was capable of, including herself. But he also believed the Diana who left on the *SS Lark* wouldn't be the same one when she returned to London.

"I can't imagine anyone else fulfilling the role."

Haggerty looked at Diana and nodded. "Now that I have become acquainted with her, I think you are quite right."

Devons would keep her at arm's length, but he would support her and the club. He'd not only felt as if he was championing the club for Addie but now also for Diana.

A few hours later, Devons dropped his pen and stretched. He'd finished writing his next letter to the London newspapers about Porto. Of their two ports so far, Porto by far had been the best, but he wasn't sure if he felt that way because Diana had loved it so much. He'd been amused at her love of a city that in some ways seemed the exact opposite of her proper world in London.

Did she know that so much of what was found in Porto could be found in the city she lived in if one knew where to look? He smiled and looked down at his note.

To the Ladies of London,

What greeted us in Porto should be seen by all of you fine ladies. A romantic city with a hint of darkness. At this stop, we learned about a vengeful love-sick king who did everything to show his adoration for the woman he loved. Then of course, a visit to this lovelorn city is not complete without attending an opera at the Teatro do Principe. I fear Lady Hensley enjoyed that more than I.

We finished the visit with a trip to the countryside to learn about the process of making one of the finest drinks, port. Lady Hensley may be upset with me for revealing this, but I dare say even she enjoyed a sip.

Sebastian Devons.

Chapter Fifteen

L AUGHTER AND CHATTER echoed through the dining saloon as everyone ate the final course of dinner. Diana glanced down to the end of the table she was seated at. Devons was speaking with a man who accompanied them on the port-tasting excursion. Diana wondered what they were discussing. Devons smiled and smacked the man on the back. The man let out a bellowing laugh that was drowned out by all other noises in the room.

Frowning, she looked down at her plate. Devons hadn't spoken more than a greeting to her since Porto. Had she done something wrong? It irked her that she was so worried about the distance between them when he seemed content. Everyone started to stand. Messina, who was seated next to her, offered his arm. She smiled at the attractive count.

He escorted her to the main saloon. "I shall return after I visit the smoking saloon."

Diana nodded. "Thank you."

After he left, Diana walked back out the door of the saloon and made her way to the weather deck, seeking air. She stood at the railing, enjoying the wind on her face. A handful of other passengers wandered about, and she smiled at them but didn't engage them any further. It disconcerted her how much not speaking with Devons bothered her.

She frowned, knowing her feelings were foolish. The man

lived a vastly different life than she did. This infatuation she had with him was something he dealt with all the time from women in London. They'd agreed to a friendship and nothing more. Diana needed to be happy with that. Yet for some reason, she was skeptical that he didn't feel more. Their kiss continued to linger in her mind. A loud sigh escaped her. She was tired of thinking about Devons.

Diana needed to return to the saloon. Her aunt and Messina would be looking for her. As she turned, she spied a man smoking a cigar. Her eyes narrowed. It was Devons, standing at the railing. He'd said nothing, instead choosing to watch her contemplate life. Annoyed, she marched over to him and said, "Why aren't you talking to me?"

He brought the cigar to his lips and took another puff. "I have no idea what you mean, Diana."

Well, at least they hadn't resorted to being formal with each other. "You have barely spoken to me since Porto."

He sighed and ran a hand through his black hair. "What do you want me to say?"

"There is a distance between us, and I feel like you are intentionally creating it."

Tension swirled around them. He stamped out his cigar. "I apologize that I have no interest in watching Messina and Monroe flirt with you."

"Are you jealous?" she asked, the words escaping her before she had time to think if they were appropriate.

He frowned before stepping closer to her. "How could I not be?"

A mad thought sprung into her mind. She wanted to declare that she chose him for her flirtation. As if reading her thoughts, he said, "I want you, Diana, but I believe we both know any interlude between us would only lead to trouble."

She didn't understand him. He had dozens of liaisons, probably more. "Are you worried I will become too emotionally involved? That I'm not sophisticated enough to be one of your lovers."

He was silent for a minute and Diana stopped herself from demanding he say something. Eventually, he said, "I'm not the right man for you. Have your fling or flirtation with someone you never have to see again. Nothing on this trip is real. But when you return to London, you and I will have to see each other often because of the Historical Society for Female Curators. I don't want any awkwardness to exist between us."

Diana frowned at him. "So, you do think I'm not worldly enough for you."

Hurt and embarrassment welled in her, and not wanting Devons to see any of it, she spun on her heels, heading to the door leading to the saloon level. Diana heard Devons curse, and his footsteps followed her. Before she reached the steps, he stopped her with his hand. "Wait."

She took a deep breath and turned back to him, willing her humiliation away. "Yes."

He ran his fingers through his hair. "I'm making a mess of this. We are better off as friends. I value and respect you more than most individuals I know. I don't want to ruin that. But you deserve to live a little. You should have a flirtation with some-one."

"With Messina?"

He clenched his jaw and bit out, "With whomever you desire."

Was she being irrational? Maybe she was too naïve to have a tryst with Devons. She pulled away from him, but he stopped her. Her eyes flew to his face. He leaned in. "I want to be able to look across a ballroom or a business meeting and not see regret on your face. You are the mother of a soon-to-be duke. Right now, London seems so far away, but I promise it is there with all its judgment and damn rules. Even as a widow, it would do you no good to have speculation swirl around you that we are involved. I won't have that for you. I care for you too much to allow such gossip."

He was talking about society's judgment of him and how it

would impact her. Specifically, that ladies like her didn't dally with men like him. Men who were by-blows of lords. "You are a good man, Sebastian Devons."

Devons held up a hand as if to stop any further assurances. "I know I am. Yet I still would be unable to prevent the gossip that would happen if we were to become lovers and it was found out. You may be frustrated with your proper social standing now, but it is very much a part of who you are."

She wanted to tell him she couldn't care less, but Diana then thought of Robert. She wasn't sure and being on this ship had confused everything she believed. Perhaps Devons was right. An interlude between them was too much. He was the expert in vice, after all. Maybe in this area of their lives, they needed to keep their distance. "I understand your points. I think, maybe, we have started to overshare with each other. I think it is best when speaking we stay away from anything related to interludes or flirtations. You can do as you like, and I can do the same."

He frowned at her. "I'm only trying to do what I think is best for you."

She'd humiliated herself enough for one night. "I imagine the count is waiting for me."

His face became shuttered. "I imagine so."

Without another word, she made her way back to the saloon. An attendant reached out to open the door to the room for her, but Diana shook her head. "Please, just a moment."

Diana leaned against a wall, feeling foolish. She wouldn't think about her attraction to Devons anymore. He could do as he liked, as could she. Diana took a deep breath and nodded to the attendant. The man opened the door to the saloon. As she entered both Messina and Monroe turned and smiled at her. Yes, Diana didn't need Devons.

The next morning, she sat looking over her letter to the ladies of London. This was the priority. Raising money for the club. She and Devons could and would work together on that. Anything else she chose to do was only her business, not Devons's. She held up the paper and read it once more.

To the Ladies of London,

The city of Porto is a delight you can't miss. We were fortunate enough to learn about Senhor Pedro, the eventual King of Portugal, as well as see an enormous tapestry that told the story of his unrequited love for a woman he was banned from marrying. I hope if you join this leisure cruise, you will take the time to hear their tale.

Porto is a city like no other. Some call it the city of artists, and I can see why. We ended our time with a dramatic opera and a tasting of some of the finest ports. Not that I have very much experience, but Mr. Devons assured me it is the best. I imagine he is an expert on such things.

Next, we are off to Malaga.

Lady Hensley

Malaga—Early July 1850

THE WOMAN IN the red dress spun to the sound of the music while those around clapped and whistled. They were getting a presentation by Romas about a dance called the flamenco. Devons had to admit the dance was beautiful and sultry. The women twirled around as everyone cheered. Several of the passengers from the *SS Lark* watched the show hosted in the courtyard of an old stone building.

His eyes darted to Diana, who hadn't spoken to him more than a greeting since their talk on the weather deck. It pained him that the closeness they once shared was now missing, but it was needed. He'd already been hurt by Lilah, and Sebastian suspected if he became involved with Diana, it would be far worse.

What he hadn't told Diana was that he wasn't sure he could survive an interlude with her, and Sebastian refused to think they could have more than that. This trip deceptively made everything possible. Varying groups of people mingled that never would in England.

While Lilah had been a widow in London, she wasn't used as an example of the proper lady. Not like Diana, who was revered for her ladylike qualities. She existed in a tier of society that judged someone like him as unsuitable to be in their presence.

They were attracted to each other. Any denial from him at this point would be ridiculous. Still, she was untouchable, a temptation that would only bring him pain. And, more importantly to him, Sebastian was determined not to cause any gossip that would impact her or her family. Gossip always swirled around him, but he didn't want that for Diana.

He pulled out his pocket watch, flipping the front and back cases open and close while he frowned at Messina. The handsome Sardinian stood next to Diana, beaming at her. The man said he had business here, but he'd been by Diana's side since they'd arrived this morning. Sebastian clenched his jaw, wanting to join them. No, he wanted to push Messina out of the way but stopped himself. Diana could do as she pleased.

The woman finished her dance, and everyone applauded. Some of the Spaniards started to clap out a rhythm, and the woman in red pulled Diana and her aunt out into the middle of the courtyard, encouraging them to try the dance. Another dancer cajoled the remaining ladies out. Diana became flushed from the activity, and Sebastian couldn't stop the smile from spreading across his face. She lifted her hands, following the woman in red's movements with her hips and feet.

As her form spun and turned, Sebastian's body reacted to her. The woman in red gave a slight shimmy, and all the ladies did the same thing. But it was Diana he couldn't tear his eyes away from. He was so distracted that he didn't notice the woman wearing the bright-green dress in front of him until she pulled him into the middle. He glanced Diana's way, and Messina had joined her.

Sebastian tore his gaze away and looked at his dance partner.

She winked at him and nodded to Diana. *"Ella te gusta."*

He answered back in Spanish. "No, she is a friend."

The dancer smirked in disbelief. She moved him back and forth, teaching him the steps. Sebastian wasn't conceited, but he'd done fine with his dance lessons in his younger years. He caught on quickly to the movements she was showing him. The music started to play at a much quicker tempo.

The dancer motioned him to move quicker. Then she guided him to turn. He moved her around the dance area. He glanced at Diana and Messina, who were struggling to follow the steps. Sebastian was being an ass, but it pleased him that Messina wasn't doing so well. The dancer said, "You pay attention to me."

He turned back, focusing on her. She smiled. As the music increased in tempo, the dance became faster with them moving closer to each other. Those around them cheered and whistled. His dance partner laughed. Finally, the music stopped. She gave him a flirty wink and then glanced at Diana. She leaned into him and whispered in Spanish, "I think you are more than friends or should be."

Sebastian's eyes slid over to Diana. She frowned as her gaze flicked back and forth between him and the dancer. Finally, Diana forced herself to smile and said, "You did wonderfully."

Sebastian wanted to dance with her. He wished his body could rock against Diana's. He felt his member twitch at the thought. *Fuck!* He needed to stop focusing on her. Whatever these emotions and connections were, he needed to move past them. Still, it only confirmed that some distance between them was the best course of action. But not too much. Diana and Sebastian had spent so much time together at the beginning of the trip, he couldn't avoid her completely.

Within days of departing England, everyone on the ship had seemed to separate into little groups that did everything together. Sebastian didn't want to break that up. Even today, they'd traveled with the rest of their tribe, including her aunt, Mr. Spoor, and Mr. Haggerty. He glowered because Messina had joined them as well.

The dancer beamed at him. "You are a good dancer. I would ask you to accompany me to an event tonight, but I think you would decline."

Sebastian's eyes darted to Diana, who quickly glanced away. What was the blasted woman doing to him? He should have wanted to join the dancer, but he had no desire. The lovely woman's mouth stretched into an amused smirk. "Good day, sir."

Later that evening, Sebastian declined to go out to dinner with everyone. He wasn't avoiding Diana, but he was uninterested in watching Messina fawn over her. Agitation filled him that she hadn't returned to the hotel yet. He'd heard her aunt and Mr. Spoor in the hallway but not Diana.

Even though it wasn't any of his business, it worried Sebastian that she was alone with Messina. Diana and Sebastian's rooms were both located on the fourth floor of the hotel while Messina's was on the fifth. He would not interrupt her but would wait up until he was certain she made it to her room safely.

Sebastian poured himself a brandy, slowly drinking it. He tried to read a book but couldn't focus. Finally, a man's voice echoed down the hallway followed by a woman's. No, what he heard was Diana's voice. Sebastian stood closer to the door. Diana's laugh filtered into his room and then there was silence. Was Messina being inappropriate with her? Was he taking advantage of her? Unable to contain his concern, he yanked the door open, and Diana and Messina sprang apart.

She stared at him in shock. Messina scowled. Sebastian ignored him. "Are you fine, Lady Hensley?"

Diana's brows drew together in confusion. "Yes. I was bidding the count good night."

Sebastian became rooted to the floor. He folded his arms, leaning against the side of his room's doorway. Diana looked from him to Messina and back. He wouldn't leave until the count departed. He was being an ass and he knew it.

"Can you give us a moment?" Messina asked.

He shook his head, and the count sighed. He took Diana's

hand in his and said, "Good night, Lady Hensley."

She glanced at Sebastian before turning back and said, "Good night."

The count left and made his way down the hallway. When Sebastian turned back to Diana, she was glaring at him. "What are you doing out here?"

"Making sure you are unharmed."

"From Messina. He is a gentleman."

Sebastian snorted. Diana angrily pressed her lips together.

"I wanted to make sure he wasn't taking any liberties with you."

She sighed. "Maybe, I was hoping he would. Maybe, I have enjoyed being pursued by a man who is open with his feelings."

He scowled, knowing she was intentionally pointing out Messina's behavior. "Next time, I won't interrupt."

Diana pushed open her door. "Please don't. Good night, Devons."

Chapter Sixteen

DIANA TWIRLED AROUND, taking in the amphitheater. It was a stunning piece of history. The city of Malaga had taken great care in preserving the Roman ruins. The debris and layers of dirt had been removed to reveal what lay beneath. Messina told her the time-consuming task took scholars and antiquarians multiple years. She'd been surprised the project had been a collaboration between Spanish scholars and a group of English antiquarians involved in the transport and export business.

The world-renowned explorer Thomas Easton and his colleagues Benjamin and Rose Calvert were the English antiquarians who participated. Even Diana had heard of them. Thomas Easton was famous for having serials written about his expeditions and escapades, while the Calvert family was well-established in the antiquities community for translating ancient texts. They were a father and daughter duo.

Messina walked ahead of her.

Diana asked, "Have you ever met Mr. Easton or the Calverts?"

"I have. Easton is always traveling to some far-flung place. The Calverts travel but spend a few months of each year in Tuscany. If you are interested, I could try to set up an introduction while you are there. They would enjoy learning about your club."

"That would be wonderful."

Messina smiled and winked. "Anything for my favorite English lady. I wish I were traveling to Sardinia and Tuscany with you, but my businesses here in Malaga need me."

Behind them, Devons sighed. Diana frowned, wishing she could forget he was there, but no, he'd been a quiet, looming presence the entire time. Her aunt, Spoor, and Haggerty ventured off in their own direction, but Devons silently followed her and the count.

Turning to him, Diana asked, "Don't you think it would be beneficial for the club to meet with the Calverts?"

Devons was silent at first, as if he didn't want to give Messina any credit, but he finally said, "It would be quite a success if you were able to arrange some type of partnership."

"I agree," Diana said.

"I will have a courier send them a message about meeting with you."

"You are too kind," Diana said.

Devons sighed again. "I'm off to find your aunt."

Diana watched him stomp off. A bit of sadness washed through her. She missed laughing and talking with Devons. Hopefully, they could go back to that before the trip ended. For now, she would enjoy the amazing view. She slowly spun around one more time, studying the stone seating surrounding them. As she turned back, Messina held out his arm. "Walk with me. I want to show you one more area."

They left the amphitheater and wandered to a courtyard-like area. The natural growth in this area hadn't been removed, giving it an enchanted feel. Diana could still make out stone walls and pillars. It must have been a stunning structure at one point.

"It is an old bathhouse," Messina said.

Diana looked around again. "Yes, I can imagine that."

Messina stepped closer to her. "May I call you Diana?"

He gently grabbed her chin, and Diana knew he was going to kiss her. "Yes."

One of his hands slid over her hip, and he pulled her to him. Devons flashed in her mind, annoying her. Of late, the man had been nothing but boorish to her. She shouldn't be thinking about him. He'd told her she should pursue anyone other than him. Yes, this was the flirtation she wanted.

Messina's head dipped down, and he brushed his lips over hers before gently teasing her mouth open with his tongue. Diana kissed him back, wanting to be swept up in the moment and hoping to be overwhelmed by his kisses, but while nice, the connection she desired was lacking.

Messina pulled back and studied her. Could he sense something was missing? He stepped away and leaned against a pillar, still silent. Finally, he said, "Is it Devons that has you preoccupied?"

Diana shook her head. She didn't want anyone making such assumptions. "Of course not."

He smiled, amused. "I have been trying to figure out what is going on between the two of you."

"We are friends and business associates, that is all."

"I can tell when I kiss a woman, and her mind is elsewhere. It doesn't happen very often."

Diana lifted a brow at the conceited man. He flashed a grin. "I'm being honest."

"You are mistaken about Devons. My response has nothing to do with him," she said before adding, "I'm new to these types of flirtations."

He looked as if he was tempted to kiss her again. Diana wondered if he thought it would be different. Another kiss from Messina wouldn't change anything. Something was missing. She scrambled back a little. He didn't push her. "Let's join the others back in the amphitheater."

She nodded, relieved. They made their way through one of the tunnels that kicked them back into the theater. Sebastian stood in the center, talking with Haggerty. He turned to look at them. His eyes narrowed. Diana blushed. Her response annoyed her. She had nothing to be ashamed of. Devons was the King of the Den, after all! What could he really say?

Her blue eyes met his dark ones. He knew she'd just kissed Messina. She didn't know how, but the ever-present connection between them seemed to spark and sizzle angrily. He turned back to Haggerty, dismissing her and Messina. She glared at his back. A chuckle erupted from the handsome man next to her. She glanced at him. "It's hot, my lady, and it has nothing to do with the weather."

THAT EVENING, SEBASTIAN stomped into the gentlemen's club *La Casa del Lobo*. The place was recommended by Captain Monroe. He wanted to be away from the hotel, even if it was for a few hours. In truth, he needed to escape Diana. It had taken everything in him not to walk over and pummel Messina this afternoon. He'd kissed her. Sebastian had no doubts about that. He told himself it was none of his concern. They'd agreed to stay out of each other's business when it came to interludes and flirtations. Still, knowing the count had touched her enraged him in a way he was unwilling to analyze.

The club was the premier one in all of Malaga and Monroe had used his connection to gain admittance for Sebastian. He smirked. The captain seemed to know just about everyone. Monroe declined to join Sebastian, murmuring about meeting a woman. It appeared he'd had ended his pursuit of Diana.

Sebastian's eyes took in all the details of the club, comparing it to his establishment. A pang of homesickness washed over him. He hadn't felt it once since his departure until now. He missed his domain. The place he ruled. He studied the fine craftsmanship of the wood paneling, the opulent furniture, and the feel of the club. Sebastian smirked. Not quite as good as his own space but no place ever would be.

He weaved his way to a smaller card room and frowned. Standing by a faro table was Messina, laughing. For once, the count wasn't hovering around Diana. Messina gleefully cheered while a few men groaned. He spotted Devons and waved him over. "Join us."

Devons shook his head. "I think I will grab a drink."

The smirk on Messina's face grew larger. "That sounds like a brilliant plan. I shall accompany you."

That was the last thing Devons wanted to happen, but he didn't have a way to politely decline. And he didn't want to cause a scene. He suspected by the way Messina interacted with everyone that he was a frequent customer.

Sebastian shrugged as he found an empty sitting area. The chairs were covered in a deep-purple fabric. Situated in the middle of them was an elegant mahogany table with a crystal decanter and glasses. Messina plopped down in a chair across from him. "If you don't want brandy they have other options."

"This will be fine."

He poured himself and Messina a glass. They sat in silence until the count said, "You will be leaving for Sardinia tomorrow. Correct?"

Sebastian nodded.

Messina took a sip of his drink and tilted his head back against the chair, closing his eyes. "That is where I'm from. A lovely area but very rural."

"How did you end up in Porto?"

Messina's eyes flew open. He sat up and smiled bitingly. "The revolution."

The man had fought, Sebastian realized. He saw it in his eyes now. The look so many soldiers had after returning. All of England had watched as the rest of the world had one revolution after the other. Several areas, such as the Kingdoms of Sardinia, Sicily, and Tuscany, had fought to unify. But most of it had been suppressed.

"If it hadn't happened, I would have never left my family's

land. Maybe for a grand tour, but all that I desire is there."

"Yet here you are."

Messina laughed. "Here I am. My loyalty to the exiled King of Sardinia demanded it. I'm assisting in a few matters that need to be wrapped up. Once they are complete, I will return to Sardinia for good and marry."

"A nice Sardinian woman?"

Messina nodded. "Of noble blood."

Sebastian smirked, disgusted. The count was one of those men who valued bloodlines over everything else. He hadn't expected that from him. As if sensing Sebastian's thought, Messina shook his head. "I'm not a snob. I believe all men can better themselves, but I also follow tradition. In my family, men have always married noble women from my region. Not once in five hundred years has the tradition been broken."

"And Diana?"

Messina took another sip of his brandy. "A flirtation."

A surge of protectiveness filled Sebastian. Messina added, "I suspect what she is after as well. I doubt she is looking to marry a count from a land she's never been to."

Sebastian begrudgingly nodded. Messina winked at him. "But don't worry, friend. I have a feeling her desires remain firmly English."

"That isn't the relationship we have."

"Why not? Are you against such things?"

The corner of Devons's lips quirked up. "Not at all."

The count studied him. "Then it must be that there is too much at stake for you."

Sebastian shrugged. "We belong to very different social circles."

"You have already allowed yourself to care for her. Now, the heart wants what the heart wants."

A snort escaped Sebastian. "This coming from the man who will only marry a woman with the right lineage. Your advice is surprisingly romantic."

Messina laughed. "Unlike you, I would never be as foolish as you to allow myself to fall for someone unsuitable. Now you must pursue her."

Sebastian took a sip of his brandy "Our relationship is fine as is."

A smirk flitted across the count's face. "If you say so. She seemed distracted by you today. When I—"

Sebastian's face filled with fury and Messina didn't finish his comment. Instead, he chuckled into his glass. "You are a foolish man."

Chapter Seventeen

DIANA STROLLED INTO the main saloon, hoping to find a spot to read. The sun had only come up an hour prior, but she felt restless in her cabin. She entered the room and found Devons sitting in a wingback chair in the corner. He was reading a book and hadn't seen her yet. She quietly turned to leave.

"Lady Hensley," he said.

She closed her eyes, wishing she had been able to escape before he saw her. Diana took a deep breath and faced him. He was standing and, of course, made a dashing figure.

"Yes."

An amused smile flickered across his handsome face. "Join me."

"I would prefer to enjoy my morning. We've not been the best company for each other as of late."

His smile vanished. Diana turned to leave, but Sebastian turned to one of the attendants and asked, "Could you please bring Lady Hensley tea?"

The attendant nodded. Diana frowned at the man who'd spent the last few days being a surly beast. Her proper upbringing prevented her from leaving. She made her way to the sitting area Devons was at and plopped down in the chair, feeling grumpy.

He sat. "Why am I always apologizing to you?"

"Perhaps because you are the moodiest man I have ever met.

And men like to say women are irrational."

A rich throaty laugh erupted from him. She couldn't stop herself from smiling. She did love her friendship with Devons when they weren't fighting. He smiled. "I'm sorry we haven't spent as much time together the last few days."

She shrugged. "You said we needed distance, and we couldn't talk about certain things."

Devons leaned forward, staring at her intently. "I only said we should stay away from discussions of interludes and flirtations."

"Admit it, it is you who has been distant from me," Diana said, trying her best to keep her voice emotionless.

He nodded. "You are right. I'm not perfect. There is an attraction between us, and it wasn't easy for me to watch you with Messina. I don't like the pompous count. You deserve better even for the short time we are on this journey."

Diana wanted to annoy him and said, "I found him quite charming."

A grimace crossed Devons's face. "I'm sure you did."

They sat in silence, and Diana wondered what he was thinking. He sighed and opened and closed his pocket watch. Diana realized he did that when he was restless, upset, or nervous.

"Was there anything specific you hoped to speak with me about?" she asked.

He snapped the watch closed and put it back in his pocket. "I promise not to be so sour. Can we be friends again?"

Part of her angrily wanted to say no but she didn't. She adored her time with Devons and had missed it. "I never once considered us not friends. Though, you can be a surly beast."

He tilted his head back and laughed. She smirked at him. "I'm not jesting."

"I will be better. I was behaving unacceptably. You and I have decided anything more than friendship isn't a good idea. It isn't fair for me to be upset over your potential suitors. I want you to live a little. I apologize for acting as if that isn't the case. It's hypocritical of me to judge you."

Diana wanted to say she didn't remember ever agreeing to what Sebastian said, but she didn't. She didn't want to continue the fight. As much as she hated it, his previous points were valid. They would be working together when they returned to London. She didn't want any awkwardness between them after they returned home.

An attendant threw open the door and said, "Come quickly."

They looked at each other and rushed after him. They ran up the stairs to the weather deck and headed to the railing. What was going on? Once they made it to the railing, their eyes looked to where he was pointing. "Mermaids."

Diana gasped and grabbed Devons's arm. "Dolphins."

At least a dozen of them leaped out of the water next to the ship. Their gray skin reflected the sparkling ocean. It was a sight Diana wasn't sure she would ever witness again. She squeezed Devons's arm harder, and he clasped it with his other hand. She glanced at him, and he smiled in awe of the creatures.

"Those aren't mermaids, dolt," a sailor told the attendant.

"No, they are dolphins," Diana explained.

The sailor nodded. "They are good luck."

Diana and Devons continued to watch them until they disappeared. She glanced down and realized she was still holding on to him. She stepped back from him but grinned. "Did we really see that?"

He nodded, still amazed. Moments like this made her realize how much, during this trip, she had grown to adore being friends with Devons. She didn't want to lose that, especially for a tryst. Diana would follow Devons's lead and ignore their attraction. It would fade, and they would still have their friendship firmly intact. She nudged him. "I'm glad I got to see this with you."

"Me too."

He held his arm out. "Back to the saloon."

She took it. "I'll walk with you but leave you there. I want to write my next letter to the ladies of London with that fresh in my mind."

An hour later, Diana beamed as she looked down at her missive. She was starting to enjoy writing them. She shook her head still in disbelief at the sight she and Devons witnessed.

To the Ladies of London,

I have so much to tell you, but first, I need to share what I witnessed today.

Mermaids!

Well, dolphins, but that is what the ship attendant called them. They are considered lucky, a sailor told us. Both Mr. Devons and I were lucky enough to see them just after sunrise. Witnessing them frolicking in the water is perhaps the most beautiful sight I have ever witnessed.

Now, on to Malaga. This city is full of excitement. We learned several fast-paced dances. I must admit they would be considered quite scandalous in any London ballroom. Mr. Devons was far better on his feet than I. We finished our time in Malaga with a visit to a Roman amphitheater. I wasn't expecting to see such old ruins, but Malaga is indeed another perfect stop for those ladies hoping to do a similar leisure cruise.

During the trip, I've met many travelers that I think will become lifelong friends. I dare say that even Mr. Devons is becoming a dear friend to this proper lady. Ladies, he is a most decent and enjoyable travel companion.

Lady Hensley

"I still can't believe we haven't seen any since you saw them this morning," Diana's aunt said.

Diana laughed. They were seated in the dining saloon with their regular group of people. Devons smiled. "You have to wake before the afternoon to see them."

Lady Clark scowled at him. "I stood outside for almost an hour, hoping to spot dolphins. One of the sailors said they spotted one farther out. I think he was trying to make me feel better. Were they really that close to the ship?"

Sebastian's eyes met Diana's. They had been that close, and he was glad the two of them had witnessed the awe-inspiring creatures together. All day he'd been delighted that his and Diana's relationship appeared to be going back to normal. Well, what it was before the whole Messina debacle. His mood improvement likely helped the situation. It wasn't in Sebastian's nature to be so surly. Diana was only his friend. He shouldn't have behaved like such an ass.

"They were, Aunt," Diana said, laughter in her voice.

Monroe joined them. "You mostly see them at sunrise."

Lady Clark scrunched her nose up. "I can't rise that early."

"Why is that?" Diana asked Monroe.

Monroe smiled at her. "No one knows. The ocean is a mysterious place."

Sebastian rolled his eyes. Diana glanced at him and gave him a pointed stare. He grinned. Yes, their relationship was doing much better.

"Tomorrow, we arrive in Sardinia. The waters in the region are some of the most beautiful I have ever seen. I tried to convince Messina to travel with us, but he couldn't. Don't worry, his family will make sure we are taken care of. Also, Andria Porcu is from there. He can answer all your questions," Monroe said before nodding to one of the attendants removing plates from dinner.

"Perhaps, I will go swimming while visiting Sardinia. I have to try it somewhere," Spoor said.

Monroe nodded. "It is the perfect place for it."

Diana bit her lip, looking disappointed. Sebastian needed to figure out a way she could swim without worrying about her clothing. Maybe Monroe's attendant had a solution. Everyone rose to make their way to the other saloons. Sebastian hung back and made his way to where Porcu was removing plates.

"Good evening. May I have a word?"

The small man's eyes widened, alarmed. "Is something wrong?"

Sebastian smiled reassuringly. "No, not at all. I was wondering if you could help me with something in Sardinia. I need to find a secluded location by the water."

Porcu frowned as if he was up to something lecherous. For once, Devons wasn't. He wanted Diana to be able to swim. He decided to tell him the truth. "I need a place where Lady Hensley can enjoy the water, alone. She can't swim with the rest of the men."

Porcu nodded, understanding. "I will arrange it for you."

"You have a spot?"

The man beamed. "I know the perfect one."

Sebastian made his way to the main saloon, delighted with his plan. He spied Diana and their group in the far back corner. Diana was waving her hands frantically and everyone else was calling things out. He smirked, somewhat in disbelief he spent most of his nights on this trip playing innocent games like charades. Diana scowled and placed her hands on her hips, seemingly frustrated. He walked over.

Spoor yelled, "Tree."

"Yes!" Diana exclaimed.

Everyone cheered and Diana traded places with Spoor. Devons joined her on the sofa. She smiled at him before turning her attention back to the game. Devons studied her. Tonight, her hair was falling down her back in soft curls, and she wore the lightest-pink dress. His eyes wandered to her throat where a jewel hung off a piece of lace. She was bewitching.

"Devons, do you have a guess?" Spoor demanded.

He pulled his gaze away from Diana's neck. "Mermaid."

Spoor gasped. "Are you even listening?"

Laughter escaped Diana. Sebastian looked at her and she shrugged in return. Finally, Lady Clark declared Spoor was pretending to be a bear. Utter ridiculousness, he thought. But right now, he wouldn't want to be anywhere else, including the

Den. His eyes drifted back to Diana. He reassured himself he was happy to have her friendship, nothing more.

Later that night, Sebastian pulled the cravat from his neck. He smiled at his latest letter.

To the Ladies of London,

We witnessed magic early this morning. It's easy to understand how sailors throughout history have sworn they have seen mermaids. Elegant and mischievous dolphins are likely what they saw. These enchanting creatures rode by the ship for almost an hour jumping and flipping. I daresay both Lady Hensley and I were speechless.

Malaga was a wonderful stop for our trip. We learned the art of Spanish dancing, and I might be bragging, but I think I was rather decent. The city is filled with Roman ruins that both Lady Hensley and I enjoyed. For ladies traveling with husbands, there are plenty of clubs where a drink can be had or a game played.

While I have liked all of our ports, more and more, ocean travel has grown on me. I've made many friends on this adventure. Lady Hensley has taught this man that fun can be had anywhere.

Sebastian Devons

Chapter Eighteen

Sardinia—Early July 1850

DIANA AND DEVONS rode in the back of a wagon being driven
by ship attendant Porcu. She'd never ridden in a wagon
before and initially had been somewhat reluctant, but Devons
convinced her. The man had dangled a mysterious surprise in
front of her. They'd departed from Messina's estate in Sardinia,
where they were staying along with the rest of their group.

It was a stunning piece of property. The large stone manor
was situated on a cliff that overlooked crashing waves. Messina
had promised her she would be mesmerized, and he hadn't
disappointed. They turned down a steep road and Diana clutched
onto Devons's arm. He squeezed her hand reassuringly. Porcu
glanced back at them. "Trust me. It will be worth it."

"We will be fine," Devons said.

They reached the bottom, and the road spilled out into a cove
area. The water was crystal turquoise. Diana walked closer to
where the water rushed up the beach, considering taking her
shoes off to put her feet in. Porcu motioned for Devons to come
with him.

"I'll be right back," Devons said to her.

She wondered what he was up to. She tilted her head up to
the sky and closed her eyes, smiling. Her mother was going to be
horrified when Diana called on her in Tuscany. Diana's skin had
changed from a pale pink to a golden color with a smattering of

freckles. Her whole life, she'd been told to avoid the sun, and yet, after a couple of weeks of forgoing a hat, she never felt more lovely.

"Ready for the surprise?" Devons asked.

Diana opened her eyes, startled to find him standing next to her. "Of course. You are being so mysterious."

He winked at her. "I needed to make sure it was just right."

She glanced around and noticed that Porcu was climbing back into the wagon. Diana's eyes swung back to Sebastian.

"He will be back."

Laughing, she followed behind him. They moved down the beach and rounded some rocks. She gasped as they reached the other side. It was a pool of water that went all the way into a cave and in the center of the ceiling was a massive hole where sunlight beamed through.

"It's breathtaking," she murmured.

Sebastian walked to a basket and bag. "While I'm glad you find it beautiful, that isn't the primary reason I brought you here."

She frowned at him puzzled. He smiled. "I brought you here to swim."

Her eyes widened and she clapped, delighted, but then her common sense kicked in. "What if someone discovers me here?"

"This is on Porcu's family's land. He assures me, no one will see you."

"I have nothing to swim in."

Sebastian pulled a rolled-up dark men's shirt out from one of the bags. "You can wear this."

Diana took the shirt from him. A blush formed on her cheeks. The moment felt far more intimate than she suspected Devons was aware of. She was being naïve. Absurdly, she wondered how many women had worn one of Devons's shirts. *Stop*, she told herself. They were only friends. It didn't matter if all the ladies in London were familiar with his shirts. It was none of her business.

Devons started to walk back to the other side of the rocks. She frowned. "Where are you going?"

"I will wait beyond the rocks. When you are done swimming and dressed, I will join you for a luncheon."

She didn't want to swim alone. The shirt was long enough that it covered most of her intimate spots. Devon was a known rogue. It wasn't like he hadn't seen a woman's legs before. "You aren't going to join me."

"Diana, I don't think that is prop—"

"Devons, we are in the middle of nowhere. Who will know that you saw my legs? A man who has seen hundreds of legs."

He flashed her an annoyed look. "Not hundreds."

She didn't want to enjoy this moment alone. They were friends. They could swim together. No one would be the wiser.

"Please. You can stay in your pants."

He seemed hesitant but finally, he nodded. "I will give you some privacy to change. Do you need help untying anything before I leave?"

"Yes, please," she said and turned her back to him.

He released the ties of her dress and then huskily said, "Tell me when you are ready."

Diana shimmied out of her dress and the rest of her garments before pulling Devons's shirt over her head. She giggled at how massive his clothing was. She was a curvy woman, but Devons's shirt almost made her feel dainty.

Diana was behaving scandalously but she reassured herself that no one would know, and the female body was nothing Devons hadn't seen before.

"Ready!" she yelled.

He walked back around the rock, taking Diana's breath away. Nicely dressed, Sebastian Devons was a sight to see, but this bare-chested man left her weak in the knees. *Stop it*, she told herself. *Friends. Friends. Friends.* She chanted the word over and over in her head. Not trusting her eyes not to peek in places they shouldn't, she spun on her heels and ran to where the water met the rocks.

Sebastian followed her. "Do you know how to swim?"

She looked back and grinned. "I do. I didn't learn until Stuart and I were married though."

The water was much deeper than she expected. There was a natural step down that would put her hip level in the water and then it would likely be over her head. The crystal-clear liquid sparkled from the sunlight beaming down from the hole in the cave ceiling.

She stepped down and gasped. "It's cold."

"Too cold?" he asked with concern.

Diana shook her head. "No. It is perfection."

She lay back in the water and pushed herself off the step she was standing on, floating out to the middle. "Devons, you must come in."

"It looks wonderful," he said.

She glanced at his bare-chested form. How was he so broad and muscular? Her gaze flitted across his chest and down to his hard stomach. She had to stop. He needed to get in the water. She couldn't keep looking at him. She swam back to where he was. "Get in."

He stepped down onto the step and grimaced. "Very refreshing."

She splashed him with water, and he yelped, making her laugh. Sighing, he pushed off the step joining her. They floated on their backs in the middle of the water with the sunlight streaming over them. "This is one of the best surprises anyone has given me. Thank you."

He didn't open his eyes or stop floating but said, "You're welcome."

"What was it about Lady Wesley that made you care for her?" Diana asked, just as startled as Devons that she brought the lady up.

"She didn't seem to care what society thought, or at least I thought so at the time. She seemed to enjoy being with me. Even though she decided to marry Lord Wesley, when we were together, not once did she speak against my family or how my parents lived. I suppose I thought I found someone who understood me."

Diana stopped floating on her back and looked at Devons. "I'm sorry that she wasn't who you thought she was."

He shrugged. "I'm the bastard of a marquess and the owner of a gentlemen's club. It is no small thing to choose to marry me."

"It's not so difficult," she said, surprised by the conviction in her voice.

He started floating upright and smirked. "Now it's you who is being protective."

She blushed and swam to the step where they had entered the water. Finding a flat surface along the ledge, she sat, crossing her legs. Diana should have been horrified for Devons to see her in so little clothing but she wasn't. The man swam back and forth, and she watched as his muscles rippled with every stroke. Eventually, he made his way to where she was and hoisted himself out of the water, joining her.

"So, Messina kissed you."

Her gaze flew to his, startled. "I thought we decided to not discuss such things."

He shrugged. "Was it enough?"

A laugh escaped her. "What does enough even mean?"

He turned to her. Their legs bumped into each other. "You know what enough is."

Her heart pounded. She was confused about the direction this was all going. Was he talking about their kiss? She always assumed the wrong thing when it came to Devons. She wouldn't do that now. "The kiss was pleasing enough. Maybe, I should be happy with that."

He glanced away, staring out over the water. His jaw clenched. Eventually, he turned back. "You deserve more."

Diana's body started to hum. She was tempted to lean into him, to touch him, but didn't. "How should I want a kiss to be from a potential lover?"

He cupped her chin. "A kiss from a lover should make your

body come alive. Their lips should whisper unspoken promises of what is to come."

Devons's head dipped down further. A soft gasp escaped Diana's mouth. He continued, "It should make you squeeze your legs together in anticipation. You should want to press your form against his in frustration because no matter how close, it is never enough."

One of her hands moved to his chest. His lips grazed hers. She froze, shocked by his words and the overwhelming longing that throbbed through her body. He placed a kiss on the side of her mouth and then along her jaw. "But never should it be just pleasing."

Her breath hitched. "Devons—"

He didn't let her finish but claimed her mouth. Her need for him overwhelmed any rational thoughts she had. She shouldn't want this. It was too complicated but none of that stopped her from wrapping her arms around his neck.

He groaned and his hands threaded through her hair as he pulled her more flush to him. Devons's tongue plunged in and out of her mouth, desperately as if he could not get enough. Diana pressed herself against him, whimpering whenever his mouth left hers for even a moment. He fell back and she toppled on top of him.

Sebastian moved her legs, so she straddled him. Her most feminine spot throbbed as it pushed along the length of his hard shaft in perfect torment. Diana tore her mouth away from his, arching her head back as she rocked her body into him. He grabbed her hips as she rubbed against him. He was unyielding in his savage hold on her.

"Diana, kiss me," he bit out.

She whimpered before leaning back down to touch her lips against his. He pressed her firmly against him, so they were chest to chest while he sucked and tasted her mouth. His tongue tormented her with delicious swipes.

Devons flipped her onto her back, scooting her further up the smooth rock surface. He ground his cock, still contained in his pants, against her. The shirt she wore rose, leaving her bare from the waist down. Her quim rubbed against the fabric of his trousers, enjoying how hard he was for her. She whimpered for more. Diana thought she may die from the sensation of his desire for her.

He pulled back and Diana reached for the fold of his pants, but he stopped her with his hand. She moaned, needing him now. He rolled to his side while sliding his hand up one of her inner thighs. Her legs fell open wantonly. Her need for him banished any thoughts of modesty. Devons murmured, "So beautiful."

He fingered the nub of her feminine core, and she arched off the rock. His penetrative gaze stared at her intently. She was equally overwhelmed and excited by what she saw in his eyes. "I love watching you like this. Bare for me and so full of desire."

He slid a finger into her and then teasingly pulled it out.

"Do you want to fuck my fingers?"

"Please," she whimpered.

He leaned down and kissed Diana while taking turns between stroking and sliding his fingers into her quim. She bucked against his hand. He tore his mouth away to gaze at her. "That's right, my sweet."

He was destroying her. Her legs shook in anticipation. She was close. His fingers moved in and out of her. Her rocking became more frantic. A groan escaped Devons as if her pleasure enhanced his own. The ache within her found a precipice that took her breath away. And then it exploded, crashing through her body. She let out a strangled moan.

Devons slowly pulled his hand away from her form and her eyes flew to his face. It was filled with a hungry need that Diana wanted to sate. She wanted to be the person that drove him to completion. She reached for him but froze when she heard a commotion coming from the other side of the rocks.

"Mr. Devons," Porcu called.

Both their eyes widened in alarm. They scrambled to their

feet. Sebastian turned away from her, taking deep breaths. Finally, he said, "Yes?"

"Are you ready to leave?"

No! They needed to speak about what happened. Shocking her, he said, "Yes, please give us one moment."

He grabbed a bag and pulled a shirt from it, pulling it over his head. "Do you need help dressing?"

She shook her head. He whispered, "We will discuss this later."

Diana nodded. Confusion swirled within her.

"We'll leave when you are dressed."

She pushed her thoughts away as she watched Devons scramble over the rocks.

DEVONS STOOD ON the terrace, smoking a cigar outside the drawing room of Messina's manor house. Laughter and chatter echoed from within. A picture of Diana's face filled with ecstasy flashed in his mind. He would never forget the sight. The moment by the water crossed a line that he'd been trying his best to avoid. He was in danger of giving his heart to someone he could never have. She was a lady that was not obtainable for a man like him. She was practically betrothed to the lord who was always by her side in London.

But not yet, he thought. He closed his eyes. Now that he'd touched her, he wasn't sure he could resist her. Could he have a dalliance with Diana and keep it uncomplicated? No, he'd been a damn fool to plan the swimming adventure. The best option he had was to be distant. If he didn't, he risked giving his heart to someone he could never openly have. Never. He'd watch his mother live that type of life.

Earlier, on the ride back from the cove, he'd planned how he would apologize and explain why it should never happen again and why more space was the only choice for them. Unfortunately, once they returned, he'd been unable to because Lady Clark had been waiting on Diana. She wanted to show her ruins in the area. Diana had given him one last confused glance. He needed to speak with her.

He sensed her before she said anything and he closed his eyes, taking one more puff from his cigar.

"Devons."

He put it out, leaving it on a glass dish on the stone wall and turned towards her. She was breathtaking but he felt that way every time he saw her. Her dress was a pale, icy-blue mixture of silk and lace, and her brown hair swirled around her shoulders in large curls. Her sapphire eyes were filled with concern.

"Good evening," he said.

She stepped further out onto the terrace, and he turned back to look out at the greenery even though it was pitch black. She joined him. They were silent, studying the night. He shouldn't desire this woman. She was the mother of a soon-to-be duke. He needed to end this now.

"About this afternoon—"

He cut her off. "It can't happen again. It was a mistake."

"You have kissed me twice now."

He smirked. "I did more than kiss you this last time, love."

A flush ran over her, turning her lovely golden skin a strawberry shade. "Let me say this and then whatever happens, happens."

He tore his gaze away from the pitch black and turned to her. She shifted nervously under his stare. Sebastian lifted a brow, waiting for her to continue.

"You've mentioned anything between us would be far too complicated. I think you are wrong. We are compatible. Why should we not enjoy each other's company while on this trip?"

He didn't know what to say. Sebastian couldn't reveal to Diana that he already wanted her more than any other woman in his life. Crazily, even Lilah. For Diana, this would be a last hurrah before she joined her proper peers back in London society, but it terrified him that it may be more for him. The whole farce was fucking tragic. His mother fell in love with an unavailable lord and now he was in danger of doing the same thing with Diana.

He needed to end this now. "Diana, I'm not interested in anything with you. We do not suit."

Her eyes widened in shock. She looked away as if trying to take a moment to gain control of her emotions. Finally, she said, "I won't beg you for your companionship. Nor will I approach you about this again."

She took a step closer to him, and he sucked in a breath. "But you are lying to yourself that we don't suit. I wasn't the only one at the cove overwhelmed with desire."

"We are better off as friends," he insisted.

She made her way to the door but turned back. "I think you are a fool, Devons."

Without another word, Diana left him alone with his thoughts. What the fuck was he doing? He'd bedded countless ladies. Why was he complicating matters? Was he really denying himself the pleasure of being with her? Sebastian was terrified.

He took a deep breath and returned inside. He spotted Diana talking with her aunt and was tempted to go to her. As if sensing his presence, she rose and left the room.

Sebastian sighed and made his way over to Lady Clark who sat with Spoor and Haggerty. The men seemed to be heavily involved in a conversation on bird watching while Lady Clark appeared content to sip her champagne. He joined her, and the woman smirked at him. "What have you done to my niece?"

Sebastian looked around but no one was paying them any attention. "I don't know what you mean."

She shook her head. "I don't believe that."

He didn't say anything, but she leaned forward. "Can I ask you a question?"

A disgruntled sigh escaped him. She laughed. "You like her. It's evident. What is the harm in having this time to enjoy each other?"

"Your niece is a highly respected member of London society."

"So, who cares while we are away? So am I. Do you think I'm not enjoying myself?"

She studied him, making Sebastian squirm. "Ahh…you are afraid you will fall for her. That is a problem because she is expected to make an exceptional match upon her return."

He glared at her. She shrugged. "Diana's future is marriage to a distinguished lord. Proper matches have been ingrained in her since birth. Still, I find it foolish that you would deny yourself and her time together. Do you think it will prevent you from getting hurt? It won't. Trust me. Not only will you not have her, but you will be filled with regret for not enjoying the time you had."

He didn't say anything. It was as if Lady Clark was reading all his hidden concerns and doubts. He understood what she was saying. What was worse, never having this time with Diana or it being only temporary? He didn't know.

"My niece left early. She said she was feeling unwell."

Why did he feel like he was making a decision that would change his entire world? Yet he stood. "I think I will bid you goodnight."

Lady Clark smiled. "You do that."

Chapter Nineteen

WHAT HAD DIANA been thinking? She should have let it go. Clearly, Devons didn't want to talk about it. Goodness, what a fool she was. A soft knock startled her from her thoughts. She looked down. She was dressed in her wrap and nightgown. Sighing, she walked to the door and cracked it slightly. Her eyes widened. Devons stood there.

"Can you let me in, Diana? Before someone sees me."

Her eyes narrowed. As if reading her thoughts, Devons added, "Only for a moment, if that is what you want."

She opened the door and moved to the other side of the room, wrapping her arms around herself. "What do you want?"

"I want to apologize."

Her chin jutted out. "I don't need your words or your pity."

He sighed and took his jacket off.

She tilted her head. "What are you doing?"

"I haven't been honest with you," he said, loosening his cravat and tossing it on a dresser.

Diana gulped. "I mean it, Sebastian. I release you from any misguided obligation you have acquired for me during this trip."

He pulled his shirt free from his pants. "The thing is, I don't pity you. I've spent most of this trip avoiding this pull between us. Frankly, it hasn't done any good."

Her stomach dipped. "It hasn't?"

He sat on her bed. What was he doing? Her heart fluttered. He started to pull his boots off. "No. From the moment you fell into my garden, I have wanted you. I have tried to deny it to myself and to you. Hell, I even convinced myself, briefly, that I finally reached the tipping point of my life of vice because of the many things I desired to do to you."

"What type of things?"

He walked to her and grabbed one of her hands, kissing her fingers. "To touch you. To taste you. To be deep inside of you."

A warm sensation pulsated through her body until it pooled at her most feminine place. "Why have you been trying so hard to deny it?"

His hand clutched one of her hips and he pulled her to him. "Because the need I have to bury myself in you over and over again, terrifies me."

She didn't understand what he was saying. She held his face in her hands. "Why?"

"I don't want a liaison to ruin our relationship. We are neighbors, business partners, and, most important to me, friends. I don't want anything we do to change that."

Diana felt the corners of her mouth tug upwards. "Do you have these conversations with all your lovers?"

"No, but I haven't been this tormented by a woman in a long time."

Diana's body hummed, feeling empowered by his honesty. "You have done the same to me."

He ran his hand slowly up and down her waist and the curve of her hip. "I mean it, Diana. Someday, you will be married to another lord, and I will be back to running the Den. I don't want to see you at an event with hurt feelings or awkwardness."

Diana didn't want to think about marriage or where Sebastian would be. She didn't. "I vow that no matter what happens on this trip, we will end this adventure as friends. I want you to promise me that while away from London, we will embrace what this is and not focus on London or the future."

He stroked her cheek. A bit of sadness flickered across his face. She frowned. "Sebastian—"

"I promise," he interrupted her. Then he reached out and started unbraiding her hair. "I have hungered to see you with all of your hair down since that night in my garden."

She wanted to ask him what was wrong. He shook her lush curls free. "Damn it, Diana. You are a temptress."

Desire replaced concern. She ran her fingers down his chest and his stomach. He groaned. "We need to remove these clothes."

Sebastian untied her robe, and a blush bloomed on her cheeks as she shyly allowed him. Diana wasn't a young woman. She'd carried a child. She imagined all the ladies in Sebastian's life. As if reading her mind, he grabbed her chin and planted a kiss on her lips. "Don't do that. I need to see you. Seeing you in my wet shirt earlier, as it clung to your curves drove me mad. Don't deny me the opportunity to look at you."

He pushed the robe from her shoulders and ran kisses along her throat until his lips met hers. Sebastian teased her mouth open. Diana moaned as he leisurely explored her. His tongue sparred with hers, promising wicked intentions. She bent her body into his, feeling as if it wasn't enough. In truth, Diana was unsure if it ever would be.

She deepened the kiss. A laugh escaped him at her pushiness. Taking control, he grabbed her hips and ground Diana against his cock while owning and claiming her mouth with his tongue. Sebastian released her and she gasped. He stepped back, leaning on the dresser. He took his shaft out of his pants and stroked himself. "Take your gown off."

His eyes glowed with desire. Her eyes lingered on his member, and she licked her lips. What was it about Sebastian Devons that made her want to be wicked?

Diana grasped her nightgown and tugged it over her head. His gaze roamed over her body hungrily. "I knew you would be beautiful. How will I get enough of you?"

He finished removing his pants and pulled her to him, rubbing his shaft against her quim. "Can you feel how badly I want you? How hard this cock is for you? It's always like that."

The ache within her most feminine place bloomed. "There are so many things I want us to do, but first, I want to bury myself in you. I need to take you, to feel that you are all mine. Do you want that, love?"

She nodded and he walked them backward until the back of her legs contacted the edge of the bed. She fell back, looking up at him. "Open your legs and touch yourself for me, Diana."

Oh, she was a wanton woman because she didn't hesitate. Diana spread her legs and touched herself while he stood in front of her wide-legged, stroking himself. "Is this how you play with yourself at night in your cabin when you are imagining me with my face buried between your luscious thighs?"

She nodded. He chuckled darkly. "Having you stare up at me like this is exactly how I imagined you. What do you want from me?"

A blush formed on her cheeks. "You know."

He pumped his cock. "I'm not sure I do."

She threw him a frustrated glance and his mouth tilted up in a wicked smirk.

"Sebastian, I want you in me. Please."

He moved between her trembling legs and grasped her bottom, pulling her closer to the edge of the bed. The tip of his large cock touched her core, and she whimpered.

"I'm not going to go slow. I need your quim now."

She nodded, unable to speak. He was torturing her. And then she went breathless as he slammed into her. He groaned. "I have dreamed of us together, and it still couldn't prepare me for this ecstasy. Nor how perfect your body fits with mine."

He wasn't lying. The same emotions filled Diana. The feelings both exhilarated her and sent a wave of alarm through her body. She didn't want to think about what it meant. Diana wanted to be lost in the moment, the beautiful breathtaking experience.

He pulled her legs up around his waist and entered her over and over again. With each entry, her whimpers grew louder and more demanding, as did his. The ache that had been a slow bloom in her core now pounded towards release, demanding what it wanted. She followed Sebastian's angry pace, feeding off of it. Until she let out a strangled moan as her body exploded. Waves of pleasure ebbed through her.

Sebastian grabbed the back of her head, kissing her deeply. His own strokes became frantic as she ran her fingers up and down his back. Racing to his release, he plunged into her with one more long earth-shattering stroke before pulling out and spending. He fell back next to her with a guttural moan.

Her body still pulsated from her release. They both lay their breathing heavily. "Damn woman. You may destroy me by the end of this trip."

She laughed shyly at him. He stood and grabbed a cloth, cleaning her, then himself. The gesture was intimate. For a mad moment, Diana felt as if she was looking at who Sebastian would be as a husband. She inwardly winced. They'd promised each other they wouldn't fixate on the future beyond their trip. He pulled her up and slid the bedding down. "Come."

She smiled, feeling somewhat bashful again. "What are we doing?"

"Resting and then we are going to do that again."

Diana laughed and moved beneath the covers with him. "Do you always spend the night when you do something like this?"

He wrapped his arm around her, pulling Diana closer to him. She thought he wouldn't respond but Sebastian said, "I find myself doing all types of things with you that I never do with others. Swimming in coves, flamenco dancing, listening to counts drone on and on about their traditions."

She burst out laughing. He leaned down to kiss her back and froze. Then he pulled the covers down. Diana remembered her scars and turned so her back pressed against the bedding. She looked in his eyes and gone was the laughter, replaced by fury.

"Who did that to you?"

Diana didn't want to ruin the moment. "Sebastian, please forget about it."

"Who?"

She sighed. "It's from my mother. When I was a young girl, she liked to punish me and Clara with the rod."

Shock flickered across his face. "Those are not small scars, Diana."

"I know. I should have prepared you, so it wasn't so surprising, but I was caught up in the moment."

He stroked her cheek. "You're beautiful. I don't care about them but my heart aches at what you endured. I know you are considering helping your mother return to England, but you should leave her in Tuscany. It is too forgiving of you."

Her brows shot up. "How did you know that?"

He sighed. "Your brother-in-law came to visit me before we left."

Diana threw a hand over her eyes, horrified Sam did that. "Did he ask you to look out for me?"

Sebastian winked at her. "Certainly not like this."

"No matter how charming you are, it is still embarrassing."

He laid back down and pulled her to him, kissing the scars on her back. "Don't be upset. They were just worried about you."

"I know."

He kissed her back again and she stiffened. She didn't want Sebastian to pity her. She hated the thought. "Don't feel bad for me, Sebastian. I'm fine. You don't need to kiss them. I want you to desire me, not treat me as if I'm fragile."

Sebastian pressed his hard cock against her. "Does this feel like I want to treat you like you are fragile?"

He nipped at her shoulder. "I want to fuck you, and trust me, I have no plans to treat you like you are breakable. Understand?"

She pressed closer to him. "Yes."

DIANA NODDED WHILE Signor Mura explained the origins of the ancient Nora civilization. Her face became heated, and Sebastian suspected it was the way he was staring at her. She glanced at him pointedly a few times. He smirked at her as he leaned against a tree. His body should be bordering on exhaustion as Sebastian had been in Diana's room until the early hours of the morning.

He'd done it. Sebastian gave in to the unrelenting temptation and took Diana to bed. He didn't regret it. Hell, he wished he would have acted sooner. Still, he reminded himself this interlude would end when they returned to London. Out here, it didn't matter that Diana was a lady, and he was a rogue and the illegitimate child of a marquess. Even now, he wanted to hustle her back to bed. He wanted to hear her whimpers of bliss and her pleading for more.

His thoughts flashed to the scars on her back. They'd been vicious deep marks that had shocked Sebastian. He'd seen some things in his life, but he was horrified that a lady of the *ton* could inflict so much pain on her daughters. There'd been rumors when Diana's sister had married Sam Kincaide about the duke and duchess's cruelty, but Sebastian would have never guessed the extent of it.

He shook his head in disbelief that Diana was considering helping her mother resettle in England. After everything the woman had done, Diana was still willing to be the good daughter. Their eyes met again, and she frowned at him. He realized he was scowling because of his dark thoughts. He gave her a flirtatious smile and she rolled her eyes.

Signor Mura broke their stare by pointing something out to Diana. Her eyes widened in delight. His smirk turned less amorous as he studied her. She was the perfect lady to be on this trip. Sebastian was glad Addie had been unable to go. His good friend, he imagined, was happily using the profits of the Ladies of

London column to move things along for the Historical Society for Female Curators. Sebastian suspected the difference between him and Diana would drive people to read the column about their exploits.

"Tomorrow, we board the ship for Tuscany. We are almost halfway on our journey," Monroe said, joining him.

"How long will we be there?"

"A week or two. It will be good for most of the passengers. It is like a little London there. Plenty of lords and ladies from England visit the area, now that the fighting has started to die down."

Sebastian nodded. Only a year ago, such a trip would have been impossible. It was strange or maybe surreal how fast the world seemed to move on from devastating events like the revolutions that spread across the continent over the last few years. Men had fought for freedom and rights. All things he believed in. While most hadn't been successful, it had changed how society viewed and included the common man. Time would tell how much or if for the better.

"She has changed since we left London," Monroe said, nodding at Diana.

Sebastian glanced at the captain, scowling as he watched his gaze roam down her form. Monroe chuckled. "No need to incinerate me with your stare. I have given up my pursuit of her. It's clear I never stood a chance."

"I don't know what you mean."

The captain slapped him on the back. "The two of you are safe on the ship. We are like our own little community but tread softly in Tuscany. The place is too much like London. Gossip travels fast."

Their bubble of privacy would end when they arrived at the popular port. He wasn't looking forward to it. Diana would visit her mother, and she may potentially return with them. He feared that his time with Diana may be cut short. *Would any amount of time be enough?* he thought.

The thought disconcerted him. They'd promised each other they would enjoy the time they had and not worry about the future. Another peel of laughter erupted from Diana. Perhaps, Tuscany wouldn't be that bad. Sebastian nodded tightly, appreciating the subtle warning Monroe was giving. "Is it really that full of lords and ladies?"

"Yes, there is a direct route by land once on the continent and several ships travel much faster paths than mine," Monroe said.

Fuck. He hated that his time with Diana could possibly end so soon. Lady Clark had been right. He'd been a fool, resisting the attraction that swirled around them. Monroe stepped closer to the crowd and clapped to gain everyone's attention. "Count Messina asked his family to throw you all a ball tonight. We will be heading back a little earlier than expected. Make sure you receive plenty of rest. It will be a late night before our departure."

Sebastian frowned. That likely meant he couldn't see Diana alone this evening. Both being unwell once was a coincidence, two nights in a row would cause speculation. He glanced around. Well, in London, it would. He wasn't sure about here or this trip. All the norms of society didn't appear to apply. He couldn't let that mess with his head. None of this was real.

He joined Spoor and Haggerty in a carriage, wishing he were with Diana.

"I would have rather stayed and studied the ruins longer," Haggerty grumbled.

"We have been looking at old rocks for days. It will do us all some good to have a normal night of socializing," Spoor said.

Haggerty grunted but didn't say anything. Sebastian didn't disagree with the scholar, though, his reasons for avoiding the event were selfish. He wanted to spend the evening with Diana, alone. He'd never felt so physically connected to someone.

The carriage stopped and the door opened. Sebastian stepped out, looking at Messina's manor house. It was an opulent old building. He could understand why Messina loved the place so much. He suspected it was older than even the Derry estate he grew up on with Malcolm.

Diana was still outside, he hoped, waiting for him. Sebastian walked to her and held his arm out. "Would you like to go for a stroll before you rest for this evening?"

"I would love that, Mr. Devons."

They wandered down to the gardens that sat in the back corner of the estate behind the house, passing a row of hedges. Once the house windows were out of sight, Devons grabbed Diana and pulled her to him.

She looped her arms around his neck. He trailed his lips down her throat. Diana sighed. "Why must we go to this ball? Tell me we should pretend to be ill again?"

"We should," he said as they fell against a stonewall.

"But we can't. People might talk."

At this precise moment, Sebastian didn't care who talked. He continued his onslaught of kisses on her neck and across her heaving bosom. She grabbed his hand. "Stop. I can't concentrate."

He chuckled wickedly. "Good. Don't be sensible."

"Truly do you think no one will suspect?"

Sebastian sighed. "No. We both should attend the ball."

She appeared so sad that Sebastian chuckled again and took her in his arms. "But at least I can dance with you."

Her eyes widened. "What are you doing?"

He started to hum a song, pulling her close. "Showing you how I wish I could hold you in my arms when we are dancing later tonight."

Laughter echoed through the garden, and he continued to hum. They swayed moving around the open area. He looked down at her and knew he would always remember this moment. His common sense told him to release her. He pushed the thought from his mind. There was tomorrow to think about the consequences.

Chapter Twenty

DIANA WALKED WITH her aunt on the weather deck. She couldn't keep the smile off her face. While she wanted to spend more time with Sebastian alone, to her surprise she'd enjoyed the ball at the Messina's estate. She suspected Sebastian did as well. They'd managed to sneak in a few secret moments but all it did was torment them.

"That is a gigantic smile you are wearing," Aunt Winifred said.

Diana looked at her startled. Her aunt stopped and pointed at two chairs. They both made their way over and sat. Diana couldn't believe how lovely the weather was. On land, July felt scorching hot but the breeze from the ocean took away some of the heat.

"You and Devons have grown close."

"Yes, I consider Seb—Devons, I mean, a great friend," Diana said, flushing at her flub of using his given name.

"His feelings run deep for you," his aunt remarked.

Diana shook her head. It was the trip, the sun, everything. She knew that. "You are mistaken, Aunt."

"Do you want to know a secret?"

Her aunt's tone left little room to say no, so Diana nodded. She sighed. "When I was a very young girl, perhaps eighteen, I fell in love with a man far beneath my station. I loved him fiercely."

"Before you met your husband."

Her aunt nodded. "I loved Lord Clark, but not in the way I loved this man. His name was Roger, and he was a barrister from the village by the family estate. We spent a summer in the country together."

Diana squeezed her hand. Her aunt turned towards her with watery eyes. "It was the most passionate experience of my life. If I close my eyes, I can still remember his touch. That is how much he has been seared onto my heart."

"Did he propose?"

Her aunt laughed. "Goodness, no. My parents would have destroyed his life. All of your mother's meanness comes from our parents. She is an exact replica of them. And even if we had somehow figured out how to make it work, he died in some rebellion in Africa."

Her aunt never rambled, so Diana knew she was trying to make a point. "Why are you telling me this?"

Her aunt grabbed her hand, squeezing it tightly. "Because I want you to enjoy your time with Sebastian Devons, but I would suggest you keep your heart locked up. It's what I wished I had done. I regret professing those romantic words to Roger. Some people can never be together, and as much as I wish that weren't true, we both know that is how the world works."

She wanted to laugh and deny such emotions existed between her and Sebastian, but the words wouldn't come out. Still, she told herself that she and Sebastian were only lovers. It would end after the trip.

"Aunt, it is only because we are on this journey."

Her aunt smiled sadly. "And for Roger and me, it was only a summer until it wasn't. In the end, instead of saying goodbye, we professed our hearts to each other. We never should have. It complicated everything."

"Well, there have been no professions of love on either side."

Her aunt released her hand. "Good."

"Would it be so preposterous if a successful businessman married a dowager marchioness?" she asked.

The words were out of her mouth before she could think about it. Her aunt's eyes flew to hers. Diana turned crimson. "Not that he would ever ask me."

Aunt Winifred frowned. "It wouldn't be easy or scandal-free for the owner of a gentlemen's club and the mother of a soon-to-be duke to wed. They would have to love each other very much to endure such gossip."

Diana was silent. Why had she asked that? Sebastian's feelings for her were not that deep, and hers for him weren't either. Them dancing around Messina's garden flashed in her mind. The joy she felt. No. She wouldn't allow herself to wander down this path. They were involved because of this trip. If it never happened, they would still be practically strangers. Maybe.

Her aunt stood and held out her hand to assist Diana to her feet. As they walked, she murmured, "It takes bravery to have a love like that, and if you can't be courageous, don't give him false hope."

Diana nodded. Tears welled in her eyes. She wasn't sure why.

Later in the day, Diana sat at her desk writing her Ladies of London letter. Her aunt's words lingered with her. Courage is what her aunt said it took to embrace a love between a commoner and a lady. Was it that scandalous? Would Robert be impacted by a choice like that? She tossed her pen on the desk. It didn't matter. She wasn't lying when she told her aunt there had been no declarations of love. They'd admitted they had an incredibly strong attraction to each other but nothing more.

They were having a tryst. That was all. The blasted trip made everything seem like so much more. Just like her aunt mentioned about her summer away from society with her barrister. She needed to guard her heart as her aunt suggested. As for Sebastian's heart, she would never hurt him. She wasn't like Lady Wesley.

She sighed, tired of her melancholy thoughts. Right now, she wanted to enjoy the moments she had left with Sebastian. Happiness was all she wanted on this trip. She smiled, thinking about how wonderfully perfect Sardinia had been. She reread her Ladies of London letter, wanting to ensure it was perfect.

To the Ladies of London,

Sardinia's soaring cliffs and beautiful water are a sight to behold. If any lady has the opportunity to visit, they should. Perhaps even bolder, they should dip their bare feet in the ocean. The shores are covered with little coves and caves that make you think Sardinia is Poseidon's paradise.

Also, on this beautiful island, we were introduced to an ancient civilization with its own story worth learning about: the Noras. I do hope at some point to bring some of this civilization to London as part of the Historical Society for Female Curator's exhibits.

We ended this visit dancing the night away at a ball put on by one of the families that have been here for hundreds of years. I even persuaded Mr. Devons to join in on the festivities.

Lady Hensley

THE DOOR OPENED, and Sebastian slid in, pulling Diana towards him. She giggled as their lips connected, and they tumbled onto the tiny one-person bed.

"Shh…you must be quiet."

"This is me being quiet. I feel like a young schoolboy sneaking about."

She pulled away from him, sliding off his lap, and raised a brow. "I imagine you do plenty of sneaking about."

He started to say something but thought better of it. It had been many years since he had to pursue a woman. She looked at him. "What were you going to say?"

"Nothing."

She slapped him on his arm. "Tell me."

"I own a club that hosts two scandalous balls a year most use to find their next lover. I don't need to sneak about."

He was silent, wondering if she would judge him. He glanced at her, and she burst into laughter. "The conceit you have is shocking."

A wicked grin formed on his face. "Maybe."

Sebastian needed to touch her. He leaned in and kissed her. A dominant pressing of his lips to hers. Her lips parted, and he overwhelmed her, plundering her mouth with his tongue. Why did it feel this spectacular with Diana? He pulled away, needing air.

"Perhaps the conceit is reasonable," she said with a smirk.

He winked at her.

She asked, "What are your scandalous balls like?"

Surprise crossed his face.

She nudged him. "Tell me."

He ran his fingers through his hair but finally said, "They are more theater than anything. There are acrobats, singers, dancers, and all types of entertainment. The food is sumptuous. All the men and ladies who attend must wear masks in public places."

How much should he tell her? He continued, "The Den gardens are quite expansive. There are small cottages throughout them. Often, they are used for liaisons. Trysts can sometimes be in a public setting."

Diana gasped. "Have you ever done that?"

He shrugged. "Not at the Den. That isn't my fancy. Some people like to watch and be watched."

"Goodness," she said, standing and pressing her hand to her cheeks. Then she glanced at him. "What are your fancies?"

He tilted his head and studied her. She blushed. "Stuart and I had a very healthy relationship, but I imagine nothing like what you have done. I worry this may all seem plain."

He rose and went to her, annoyed she would think that. She backed up, bumping into the wall. Sebastian rested one arm above her head, looking down at her.

"Nothing about this is plain. And what you had with Stuart and what you have with me are two different things. It's okay to want or desire something with me you didn't have with him and vice versa."

She smiled, seemingly relieved at his words. "You must believe me to be so innocent."

He stroked her cheek. "No, I just know how much you loved your husband."

Why did he have the urge to comfort her? He told himself it was because he was a decent man. His heart was not available to Diana. It couldn't be.

"Sebastian."

"Yes, love."

"Kiss me, please."

There was nothing he wanted more. He leaned into her and gave her a slow, lingering kiss. He kissed her jaw as his hands slid behind her to remove the ties holding her dress. The garment fell to the floor, and he kicked it away with his boots. She pulled his shirt from his pants, pulling it over his head and then tossing it.

His eyes flicked down to her front. The peaks of her breasts were pebble hard underneath her chemise. With one hand, he untied her petticoats and kicked them away. He purred in approval. "Lady Hensley, no corset. You have become rather bohemian."

She winked at him, playing along. "Porto, or maybe it was Malaga that turned me."

Diana, in her chemise and drawers, was as intoxicating as a naked Diana. He kissed her again and pushed his hard cock against her stomach. This woman drove him mad. He pulled his shaft from his pants and, in one motion, wrapped her legs around him while parting the slit in her drawers, entering her. She gasped as he pressed her back against the wall. At first, he entered her in deep, slow long thrusts, savoring the sensation of her around his cock. She cried out, but he placed a finger on her lips. "Shh...you have to be very quiet if you want me to stay buried in you. Is that what you want?"

He rotated his hips, and she whimpered. He pumped into her quickly, and he whispered in her ear. "Do you think you can do that?"

She nodded, and he rotated his hips again before entering her over and over again. She clenched his shoulders and murmured, "Sebastian."

Her quim clenched around him, and he could tell she was so close to climaxing. He pounded into her deeply and paused, staying lodged in her. He ground against the nub of her most feminine spot until she let out a quiet, strangled sob, peaking and crashing all at once. She sighed as he felt her pulsate around him. He leaned his forehead against hers, breathing heavily.

His shaft, still buried in Diana, throbbed with the need for release. Sebastian began to move again. His thrusts became deeper and more savage. She clenched her legs around him, urging him on. He wanted to sear this woman with his desire for her. That is all he thought about as he pounded into her. Sebastian gasped, on the verge of spending. At the last moment, he withdrew, releasing his seed before collapsing against her. Their hearts pounded in sync.

He gently slid her to the floor before gathering a cloth by the basin and cleaning them both. Diana leaned against the wall of the cabin, taking deep breaths. Her chemise and drawers were still on, and her hair had fallen out in large curls around her face. She was a vision. A vision he would never be able to forget. He sat on the narrow bed, content to watch her for the moment.

They were both silent, but eventually, Diana asked, "Sebastian, will we still be friends when we return?"

His eyes flicked to her face. "Why would you question that?"

She seemed reluctant to share more. "Just promise me all this won't make us hate each other."

Alarm filled him. He could never hate Diana, and he wouldn't be able to endure her feeling such an emotion towards him. "Come here."

She walked to the bed, and he pulled her into his lap before placing a kiss on the top of Diana's head. "All will be fine."

But deep down, Sebastian felt deceptive about promising her something he couldn't truly control.

The next morning, Sebastian sat in the main saloon, waiting for the *SS Lark* to dock in Tuscany. He'd struggled with writing his most recent letter for the column. He'd feared he would share too much. He wanted to write about his time with Diana at the cove or dancing with her in Messina's garden, but he couldn't.

After he left her the night before, he'd spent a few hours pondering his feelings for her. Sebastian was falling for her. What a damn fool he was. He'd told her yesterday it would be fine, but he'd lied. He was losing his heart to a woman he could never have. It would be wise if he ended their liaison, but he was too obsessed with her.

Every day he could spend with Diana he would take and deal with his heart later. He would find a way to make sure this all didn't end in catastrophe. He wanted her to walk away from their time happy. Sebastian needed that for Diana. He smirked at his letter. It was rather short but maybe Sardinia was just for him and Diana.

To the Ladies of London,

The water and cliffs of this island are delightful. While I enjoyed all the places we have visited, this one is truly the best stop. The water and the history are both perfect for any ladies hoping to go on an adventure.

But by far my favorite part of the visit was the dancing.

Sebastian Devons

Chapter Twenty-One

Tuscany—Mid-July 1850

THEY ARRIVED AT the hotel in Livorno in the early afternoon. While most of their stops were small cities or towns, Livorno was a lively, large port city in Tuscany. The buildings were a mangle of ancient structures and new ones being built. Diana was excited to explore the area.

As they were settling in their rooms, Diana received a missive from Messina stating the Calverts weren't in Tuscany. She sighed. It would have been quite the coup to have been able to develop some type of partnership with them. Still, all in all, the trip had been only beneficial for the Historical Society for Female Curators. She refused to be disappointed.

A knock on the door distracted her thoughts. She opened it and an attendant bowed. "My lady, you have guests."

Diana frowned. Her mother was in Livorno. Was it her? Diana assumed she would call on her tomorrow. Nerves filled her that she would be seeing her sooner. She made her way to the top of the marble foyer stairs and looked down. Her eyes widened in shock. Her mother did wait below, but Arthur was also with her. What was he doing here? He glanced up and smiled. "Surprise, Lady Hensley."

Surprise was certainly the word for it. She didn't know what to make of his sudden appearance. It was so out of character for him. As far as she was aware, Arthur had never been outside of

England. Her eyes flicked to her mother. She looked so much like her sister Clara. The same blonde hair, slender figure, and pale-blue eyes. Diana's eyes were the only similar trait she had with either of them. Her mother's eyes raked over her as she pinched her lips together.

From that one movement, Diana suspected her mother found her appearance unsatisfactory. She descended the stairs. "Good day, Mother. Lord Tremont, I'm shocked you are in Livorno."

He beamed. "I hope that you are delighted as well. I took one of the faster vessels. I arrived a few days ago. Your mother has been a gracious guide."

She smiled, not wanting to be impolite. Diana supposed his arrival wasn't that outlandish. He was a man who wanted to court her. But every part of her wanted to yell, *no, not yet*. Diana wanted more time with Sebastian. Her eyes swiveled around the room, looking to see if Sebastian had encountered Arthur yet. Nerves filled her.

"You have spent too much time in the sun, Diana," her mother said.

Diana couldn't believe that, after years of not seeing her, that was all the woman who bore her had to say. She forced herself to smile. "That is true, Mother."

At that moment, Sebastian, Haggerty, and Spoor entered the hotel from a side door. Sebastian laughed at something Haggerty said but then his eyes landed on Arthur. The laughter vanished. Next, his eyes flicked to her mother and then her. It may have been only Diana's imagination, but it appeared as if the entire foyer had grown silent. Sebastian clenched his jaw.

Arthur, oblivious to any tension swirling in the area, walked over to him. "Good afternoon, Mr. Devons. You and Diana are becoming quite the sensation with your column in London."

"That was the point," Devons said flatly.

Diana, unsure what to do, fell back on all her etiquette training. "Mother, may I introduce a few of my travel companions, Mr. Devons, Mr. Haggerty, and Mr. Spoor?"

All three men bowed. She nodded in return, her gaze lingering on Sebastian. Her mother's eyes narrowed as she perused him in a most unacceptable fashion. Her mouth pinched with distaste before turning back to Diana. "I've come to collect you in person. I insist you stay with me."

Diana's eyes darted to Sebastian's. He stared back at her, and she sensed he was thinking the same thing. Reality was quickly being thrust back on them. Diana was not ready. She would not be forced into anything. She shook her head. "Aunt Winifred and I are settled at the hotel."

Her mother's eyes widened. "My sister is with you. I hadn't realized she returned to England. Her husband enjoys living abroad."

"Lord Clark passed away a couple of years ago and Aunt Winifred decided to return to London. Since her arrival, we have grown close. She has accompanied me on the trip."

Her mother frowned. Her aunt always said she and Diana's mother were like oil and water, but she didn't realize how deep their dislike for each other was.

"I hadn't planned to have a visitor beyond you."

"It wouldn't be appropriate to leave her at the hotel alone."

Her mother sighed. "As you wish."

It wasn't a lie, but Diana also didn't want to stay with her. Partly because of Sebastian but also because she and her mother were not on good terms. She was playing as if they were, but Diana suspected that was only because she hoped to return to England. She needed Diana's support for that.

"Your mother has wonderful news," Arthur said.

"Yes, I would like to host you and your fellow travelers for dinner at my home in three days. Everyone is welcome," she said, her eyes flicking over Devons and the other two men.

Perhaps her mother had changed. She couldn't think of a time growing up when her mother would have allowed commoners to dine with her. Diana, still stunned, took a deep breath. "That is kind of you. We would love that."

Her mother nodded. "I didn't realize Winifred was with you. If possible, I would prefer to visit with you today alone."

"Mother, I have plans with my travel companions."

Annoyance flashed in the woman's eyes. "Diana, I have planned a full day for you, Arthur, and me."

Why was Arthur going? Diana's gaze flew to Sebastian. His eyes were filled with fire.

"We can all go together," Diana stated.

Her mother pursed her lips. "You have been with your travel companions for weeks. You can spend time with your mother and a close family friend today. I must insist."

Diana's gaze darted back and forth between her mother and Arthur. When had Arthur become a close family friend? She gulped, unsure what to do. She wanted to stay here with Sebastian. All of her etiquette training stopped her from declining. She nodded. Sebastian's face became shuttered. "If you will excuse me."

Diana watched him stalk off. She wanted to run to him and tell him it was only a few hours but didn't. Why did it feel like London society and all its rigid rules were back in full force? Annoyance and frustration festered within her.

"Come along, Diana," her mother said.

"Aunt Winifred is napping. Let me wake her and tell her you are here. She may want—"

Her mother shook her head. "Not necessary. We can become reacquainted at dinner."

Diana was flabbergasted that her mother didn't want to see her own sister. Wanting to move things along as quickly as possible so she could return, Diana nodded. She turned to Spoor and Haggerty. "Will you inform my aunt I will be back before dinner?"

Spoor nodded. "Of course. Enjoy your day."

Diana wasn't sure that was possible but smiled in return.

A few hours later, Diana sat with her mother and Arthur drinking chocolate in a cafe. The hot drink was decadent. Never far from her mind, she wondered if Sebastian would like it. Arthur arrived in Livorno three days ago and had decided to call on her mother. They'd appeared to have become fast friends.

All afternoon her mother and Arthur had chatted nonstop, no matter where they were—at a museum, a historic sight, and now at the cafe. Diana stayed quiet, lost in her thoughts that had nothing to do with ruins or antiquities but the displeasure that her society-free adventure was coming to an end.

"I have been speaking with Lord Tremont about my predicament, and he agrees with me."

Diana glanced between the two of them. "Your predicament?"

She daintily took a sip of her tea. "Yes, I barely survived the activities that took place between the Austrians and the locals. I don't think I can live through another revolution. I must return to England. We could have a flare-up of violence anytime."

Diana looked around at the quaint street outside of the cafe. She had to admit, she wasn't sure how her mother had managed over the last few years. A sliver of guilt shot through her. She pushed it down. She would not feel bad for the woman who had treated both her and Clara horrendously their whole lives.

"Mother, I'm speculating that you would need to have your household packed up. Maybe this spring would be a perfect time to return."

"Nonsense," her mother said. "I have instructed my servants to be ready to leave when your ship departs."

No. No.

"Lady Hensley, I think your mother returning with us would be the best solution. She has seen horrific things. Now that your father is gone, she shouldn't be alone."

She took another sip of her chocolate, trying to conceal her shock that Arthur would return to England on the *SS Lark*. Diana didn't want that but had no valid reason to stop him.

"I only want to retire to our family country estate. Nothing more."

She studied her mother. The duchess was still the perfect lady, but she did seem frailer. Was this a ploy? Diana's eyes darted to Arthur, who appeared to be siding with her mother.

"You will be prepared to leave when the *SS Lark* does?"

Her mother nodded. Diana wished she could speak to Clara about this. The duchess rose, and her lips trembled. "You are unsure if you want to help me? Why don't I leave you here with Lord Tremont? He is also staying at your hotel. He can make sure you are escorted back safely."

She left in a blur of skirts. Diana wondered if this show was for Arthur or was her mother truly displaying genuine emotion. She watched her departure before turning back to Arthur. He frowned at her. "She is your mother, Diana."

Diana bristled at his disapproving tone. Arthur had no idea how dreadful her mother was. She'd used her children as pawns and taught etiquette lessons violently. Diana still had the scars on her back from her many lashes. Both she and Clara did. The only people who knew about them were Stuart, Sam, and Sebastian. Her eyes flashed with anger. "You don't know what she has done to me or my sister."

Arthur's mouth fell open in shock at her fury. He cleared his throat. "I'm sorry. I shouldn't involve myself in something that is not yet my affairs."

The word "yet" caused a flurry of panic within her. They were not close to being betrothed. She couldn't discuss this now with Arthur. "I know you are trying to be helpful, but my relationship with my mother is complicated. There are things you don't know."

Arthur, contrite, said, "I'm sorry, Diana. Truly, I am. She has just been so helpful while I've been here."

Of course, her mother was. Arthur was a lord. Diana didn't want to discuss the topic any longer. She forced herself to smile, nodding.

Arthur, relieved, said, "Now, tell me about your travels. You and Mr. Devons have become quite the rage."

SEBASTIAN TWIRLED HIS wine goblet as he studied Diana while she laughed with Tremont at the other end of the table. They were being hosted by the Count and Countess of Demazz. Diana, Tremont, and Lady Clark sat closest to their hosts as seating was dictated by who was titled and who was not. Being untitled, Devons, Monroe, Spoor and Haggerty were located at the far end of the table.

Tremont gazed at Diana proudly. Sebastian's hand tightened on the glass. He had the overwhelming urge to smash in the man's face. The jealousy in Sebastian was startling and not something he was accustomed to. Diana and the countess looked his way, both smiling. Tremont frowned. The lord didn't like him very much and that was fine because Sebastian wasn't interested in befriending him. The lady of the house rose. "I would like to toast Lady Hensley and Mr. Devons's successful column about their exciting adventure. A few copies of the newspapers carrying the Ladies of London column have even found their way to Livorno. Lady Hensley and Mr. Devons, you appear to be quite the dynamic duo. I imagine there will be several women hoping to take a similar journey next year. Cheers to both of you."

Everyone applauded them and took a sip of their drink. Lord Tremont placed his hand on Diana's, whispering to her. She flushed and her gaze darted to Sebastian. He raised a brow. The host announced dinner was over and directed all the guests to different areas where they could enjoy their after-dinner drinks.

Sebastian decided to forgo a cigar in hopes of speaking with Diana. He hadn't seen her since early this afternoon, standing in the foyer of the hotel. Seeing Diana's mother had sent a surge of anger through him. He hated that she'd grown up with such a cruel mother. A picture of the white marks across Diana's back flashed in his mind. Her mother was lucky her daughter was so kind to consider helping her move back to England.

He wandered down the hallway, through one of the drawing rooms, and finally outside into a courtyard. To all the guests, it likely seemed like a casual stroll, but Sebastian was seeking Diana out. He spotted her talking by a fountain with Lady Clark. He made his way to them. Thanking those who stopped him to talk about the column.

Diana nodded hello at him as he arrived. Lady Clark grinned at him. "You are quite popular, Devons."

He laughed. "Apparently, the column is doing well if talk about it has reached the lords and ladies in Tuscany."

"I wonder what Addie has been able to do with Seely House," Diana said.

He laughed. "Addie can be determined when she wants to, and she is about your club. I have no doubt we will return, and several plans will be in the works."

Silence fell between them, and Lady Clark smiled. "I think I will go find more refreshments."

"My lady, I can fetch it for you."

She shook her head at Sebastian. "No, stay here and enjoy the breeze with my niece. I imagine you haven't seen her since my sister and Lord Tremont's sudden appearance at the hotel."

"I'm sorry I didn't retrieve you from your room."

Lady Clark shook her head vehemently. "No need. If she returns to England with us, the voyage will be enough."

Sebastian almost burst out laughing at her horrified expression. Diana sighed. "Well remember we are to dine with her the day after tomorrow."

"I am contemplating feigning sickness."

"Aunt," Diana reprimanded her with a frown.

Lady Clark rolled her eyes at Diana. "I wish our trip would have missed Tuscany."

A laugh did escape Sebastian then. He'd grown to adore Lady Clark. She didn't mince words. She grinned back at him. "Excuse me."

Sebastian smiled, amused, as the older woman strode off,

probably to seek out Spoor. The poor man was besotted with her. He turned back to Diana, still grinning.

Diana shook her head. "It wouldn't hurt my aunt to at least be polite."

Anger flashed through Sebastian. "If your mother treated Lady Clark anywhere close to how she treated you, I would say your aunt owes her nothing."

"You are only saying that because you have seen me in a state that isn't acceptable in public."

He leaned closer to her. "I have and it enrages me that a mother could dole out that type of punishment to her child."

"It's over, Sebastian."

They were silent for a moment. Eventually, he said, "I would like to visit you tonight."

Her eyes flicked to his. They were filled with a hunger that matched Sebastian's own desires. "I would like that as well."

"I want to feel your legs wrapped around me as I take what I want. It has only been a day, and I already miss your moans and whimpers," he whispered in her ear so only she could hear him.

She gulped, and Sebastian had the desire to kiss her beautiful throat. To feel the vibrations of her moans of satisfaction against his lips as he kissed and sucked there. He stepped back, knowing if this went any further, they would cause a scene.

"You, sir, are a tormenter—" Diana started.

"Lady Hensley," Lord Tremont called from the other side of the courtyard, where he stood with the hosts.

"That fucking man," Sebastian muttered.

Diana gave him a small smile. "I will see you later tonight."

After she left, Sebastian watched her with Tremont. They had a camaraderie that was different from what he and Diana had. He would be lying if he said they weren't well-suited. The thought caused him to take a large gulp of his brandy. After one day, he had to admit, he wasn't enamored with Tuscany.

He grabbed another drink from an attendant walking by, replacing it with his old one. He felt out of place, and he hated it because never in London had he cared enough that it mattered. But, seeing Diana with Tremont, he felt the difference in their classes. He was the bastard of a marquess watching someone he desperately wanted from afar while she mingled with her equals. He needed to get out of here.

Chapter Twenty-Two

DIANA AND HER group, minus Sebastian, headed out the front door of the hotel towards carriages waiting for them. Monroe had arranged for all of them to go on a sightseeing tour of the city. Signor Gallo would be escorting them. She glanced around, frowning. Where was Sebastian?

She hadn't seen him last night either. A blush spread across her cheeks. She'd expected him to visit her, but after several hours had passed, she'd given in to sleep. Diana should have suspected something was amiss when Sebastian left the dinner without telling anyone. Confusion and sadness filled her.

Her gut clenched that perhaps he had moved on to other things. If that were the case, Diana would accept it. They'd both agreed this affair would end once they were in London. Still, they were not in London, even if Livorno felt like it. As Diana waited to be helped into the carriage, Sebastian walked out the front door with a beautiful woman and an older man. He spied her and their group and smiled. Maybe he'd simply been tired yesterday evening.

Diana smiled back. "I worried you wouldn't join us today."

He laughed. "No. I found a club last night and met these two travelers. I was checking with Signor Gallo to see if there was room in the carriages for them to accompany us."

Arthur, along with Signor Gallo, walked out the door. Their

guide said, "I found one more person. Everyone, in the carriages so we can start our day."

Her aunt looked around at Arthur, Sebastian, the new couple, and Diana, and said, "I will ride with Mr. Spoor and Mr. Haggerty."

Signor Gallo nodded. "I will ride with you as well."

Diana entered the carriage, followed by the young woman and then the men. Lord Tremont joined her on one side, and Sebastian and the couple sat across from them. The woman was pretty, breathtaking even. Annoyance unfurled in Diana's stomach.

"Devons, do you plan to introduce us?" Arthur said in a tone that suggested Sebastian was behaving like a heathen.

Diana was still startled that Sebastian had been at a club last night. Sebastian smiled at him, but it had an edge to it. "I was getting there, Lord Tremont."

"Mr. and Mrs. Swinson, please meet Lady Hensley and Lord Tremont. Lady Hensley is the woman I explained I was traveling with, and Lord Tremont is a good friend of hers."

Her eyes flew to his face at the phrasing and tone he used for a good friend. She frowned.

Mrs. Swinson giggled. "We met Mr. Devons at the *Casa del Pavone.*"

Arthur's brows drew together. "What type of establishment is that?"

The woman Diana was starting to dislike clapped. "It's a gaming hall, but they shockingly allow women there as well. Can you believe it?"

Diana tried to ignore the hurt growing in her that Sebastian had intentionally chosen not to visit her the previous evening. Arthur pursed his lips in disapproval. "I'm not sure we should discuss this."

Mrs. Swinson snorted. "No one is an innocent in this carriage, are they?"

Diana shook her head. The woman continued. "Mr. Devons

is an exceptional card player. He was something of a one-man show last night, playing games and charming all the ladies in attendance."

The hurt in Diana turned to anger. Sebastian was flirting with ladies last night. Her eyes flew to his face. Shockingly, he blushed. "No flirting."

Mrs. Swinson nudged him with her shoulder and batted her eyelashes. "Admit it. You are quite the charmer."

Her older husband tapped his wife on her leg. "Leave the man alone, Jaqueline. You are embarrassing him."

The blonde beauty pouted but bounced back. "We should all go this evening."

"No. I don't think it is an establishment Lady Hensley and I would be interested in visiting," Arthur said with disdain.

Devons smirked at him. "Do you speak for Lady Hensley now?"

Arthur sputtered, "No. Of course not."

Mrs. Swinson giggled. Her gaze flitted between Diana, Devons, and Arthur. "Fascinating."

Her husband sighed. Sebastian's dark, piercing eyes swung to Diana. "Well, Lady Hensley?"

Diana glanced at Arthur, who frowned at her. Part of her almost agreed with him, but she stopped herself. She would not change her actions on this trip because he was here. She wanted to go to a gaming establishment. This was probably her only opportunity. Unless Diana visited the Den someday. She wondered, now, that she and Sebastian were friends if that may happen. She pushed the thought away. She wouldn't focus on the future. "I think I would like to attend."

Arthur's frown deepened. "Diana."

She shook her head. "I'm going."

The sides of Sebastian's mouth turned up in a smirk. She suspected it was because he was happy Arthur was annoyed. Diana wasn't sure if she wanted to attend because of her desire to see such a club or because she wanted to see all these women

Sebastian had charmed.

"Then it is settled. This evening, we will all go," Mrs. Swinson said.

The carriage came to a stop, and Diana was unsure how this day would go. Not well if Mrs. Swinson spent all her time ignoring her husband and smiling adoringly at Sebastian. But Diana had no place to be upset. She and Sebastian had no commitments to one another. Her gaze swung to Arthur, confident that his appearance in Livorno was key to this sudden change in Sebastian. Still, she didn't ask him to come. What a mess life had become in the last few days. The door was thrown open, and Signor Gallo yelled from outside, "Come, everyone. We have a busy day."

LATE THAT NIGHT, Sebastian walked through *Casa de Pavone*. Unlike last night, he hadn't come alone. The moment Lady Clark found out they were going to a gaming establishment that allowed women, she declared she would be going as well. That meant, of course, Spoor joined them, and surprisingly, Haggerty did as well. The only person who begged off was Mr. Swinson, who said now that his wife had friends, he preferred to stay in and read.

Sebastian liked the club and had been shocked to see so many women. Mr. Swinson, during the prior evening, stated the club was considered somewhat of an oddity in the area—a popular one, Sebastian guessed, based on the crowd that was in attendance tonight. Mrs. Swinson grabbed his arm, and he resisted the urge to pull himself free. He glanced back and saw Tremont was escorting Diana. His eyes met hers, and she looked away.

"Devons! Are you here to win more money tonight? Join us," an English lady hollered over the chatter.

Sebastian flashed her a grin. "Not this evening."

Lady Clark dragged Spoor and Haggerty off to a card table, leaving Sebastian, Diana, Tremont, and Mrs. Swinson. A man grinned lecherously at Diana, and Tremont stepped between them. An irrational urge to be the one protecting Diana hung over Sebastian, but he resisted.

"Shall we play faro?" Mrs. Swinson asked him.

Sebastian turned to Tremont. "Do you play?"

He pursed his lips. "No. I don't engage in such activities."

Was Diana going to marry this man? Sebastian hated him, and he promised himself it went beyond the fact that this man would become more to Diana than he could ever hope to be. He was damn boring. Diana would go back to being the proper lady she hated so much. The one the papers wrote about. He hated that for her. She was so different from that caricature of a woman. His gaze flitted to her.

She laughed. "I don't play, but I would like to watch and learn."

"Perfect." Mrs. Swinson said.

Sebastian leaned into Diana. "You will enjoy it. I can teach you the game once we are back on the ship in case you ever want to play again."

Tremont snorted. "That is unlikely."

Diana frowned at him and turned back to Sebastian. "I would like that. Perhaps I will play at the Den at one of your events that allows women. Maybe one of your balls."

Sebastian smiled. There was nothing he would have liked more. Tremont scowled but remained silent. They made their way over to a faro table, and Sebastian and Mrs. Swinson took a seat. He took his time playing and won several hands. Mrs. Swinson lost a good deal but didn't seem to mind. Sometimes, she followed Sebastian's lead, copying his bet and flirting with him. He thought it was mostly to rile the crowd up.

From what he learned the previous evening, her husband was involved in some type of wine business, and they didn't appear to be hurting financially. While she was a huge flirt, Sebastian believed it was all show. Sebastian suspected Mrs. Swinson was fond of her husband no matter their age gap. He saw it in her small actions and how she cared for him when no one was looking.

Sebastian placed his bet on the ten of spades. Mrs. Swinson placed hers on the same card. She beamed at him. "You are awfully lucky tonight, Mr. Devons. I can't help but follow you."

The crowd chuckled. He smiled and shook his head. The dealer flipped the two cards. The first was a five of hearts, and the second was the ten of clubs. Mrs. Swinson screeched and grabbed his arm, excited. Everyone around them hooted and hollered. Devons smiled, but when he looked behind himself, Diana was gone. He frowned and stood. "Mrs. Swinson, perhaps I can escort you to Lady Clark and the rest of the group. I want to see where Lady Hensley and Lord Tremont went."

A knowing glint flashed in her eyes. "Of course."

As they walked through the room, Sebastian's gaze swung back and forth, looking for Diana. Where was she?

"I believe they were headed to the front door. Lady Hensley remarked to Lord Tremont that she was feeling unwell."

Mrs. Swinson's words filled him with concern. *Fuck.* The woman sighed. "I don't think she liked my flirting. It was only a bit of fun, but I think it upset her. I spotted Lady Clark and the rest of our group. Go. I will make my way to them."

Sebastian wanted to explain it wasn't what she thought, but when he started to speak, she burst out laughing. "Don't deny it. Mr. Swinson may appear quiet but can be quite ferocious when concerned about me. You have a similar look right now."

Chapter Twenty-Three

DIANA STOOD IN her hotel room, staring out a window. She shouldn't have left the club in a huff, but seeing Sebastian and Mrs. Swinson together unsettled her. Her emotions could be considered jealousy, but it was more than that. Watching them side-by-side made Diana realize how well-suited the woman and Sebastian were.

She sighed, hating how she felt and wishing they had never come to Livorno. She knew their interlude would end but assumed not until they reached London. Now, Arthur and possibly her mother may return to England on the *SS Lark*. Maybe Sebastian had already decided to move on.

A quiet knock pulled her away from her thoughts. She moved to the doorway, suspecting Arthur was checking on her. He'd been concerned about her on the carriage ride to the hotel. She opened the door. "Arthur—"

"Why would Tremont be coming to your door so late?" Sebastian said quietly. A tenseness flowed off him.

Her own annoyance flared. He'd spent tonight and last night flirting with ladies at a club. He had no right to be mad.

"Sebastian, I don't have time for you right now."

He walked in, disregarding her statement. The annoyance in her shot to fury. He paced back and forth before leaning against the foot of her bed. "So, you are waiting for Tremont?"

Diana scowled. "That isn't your concern."

Her body thrummed as Sebastian's eyes raked over her. She was still in her gown from the club. He softly said, "Not my concern?"

"I'm sure any of the ladies you flirted with last evening could easily replace me for a brief interlude in Tuscany."

A black brow on his face shot up. "Do you think it is that easy for me to trade you out?"

His blunt words flared her anger. She scowled at him. "Apparently so, as you seem more interested in finding a new flirtation."

Sebastian laughed darkly. "Excuse me if I didn't want to run to your bed after you spent all day with Tremont."

"I had no control of that. I had no idea he would be here."

He smirked and shook his head. "Well, here I am, Lady Hensley, to do your bidding. You didn't even have to fetch me. I'm unable to resist you."

She was so angry with him but the ache in the southern region of her body flared at his words. "You probably just haven't found a new lady. You, no doubt, will have your pick in Livorno."

Diana didn't know why they were being hurtful to each other, but neither could seem to stop. He strode to her, his furious footsteps echoing on the floorboards. One of his arms looped out and snaked around her waist. He grinned at her cockily. "I could have my pick."

A furious gasp escaped her. She pushed against his chest with one of her hands. "Leave, Sebastian."

His mouth dipped down to her ear. "But I only want you. I'm standing here wondering how long it will take me to get between those lovely thighs of yours. Wishing that instead of your sharp tongue, I can hear your whimpers."

"My tongue may have been much sweeter had I seen you last night."

She was not happy with him. He growled, and her quim clenched. Sebastian nuzzled her neck. "Do you want me to go?"

Common sense told her to say yes, but her traitorous mouth whispered, "No."

He palmed one of her breasts as his tongue plunged into her mouth. Diana moaned, bending her body closer to his. Sebastian attempted to pull her flush but was prevented from doing so by her gown and petticoats. With a growl, he spun her around and undid the buttons going down her back. Frustrated, he hastily tossed aside her dress and petticoats.

His hand slid down the front of her drawers, and a groan escaped him as his fingers dipped down into her feminine folds. Yes. This is what she needed. Her body rubbed against him, enraptured by the sweet torment. "Sebastian."

He quickly removed the rest of her clothes before discarding his own. They toppled into the bed with him spooning her. His cock pushed against her from behind. "Please," she whimpered.

"You are mine until we return to London," he said bitingly as his shaft slid into her quim.

She pushed against him, wanting him deeper. He pulled her closer. "Say it. You are mine until we return."

Diana suspected she may be his forever but would never utter the words aloud. Instead, she simply said, "I'm yours."

His grip on her hips tightened as Sebastian pumped into her. He kissed her neck as one of his hands slid back up to her breast, pinching and teasing her. Diana bucked herself against him. The ache in her core intensified. She rocked harder as his fingers moved down to the sensitive nub of her quim. A loud sob of pleasure escaped her.

"You must be quiet, love. It torments me to say that because I have fantasized about letting you be as loud as you like. To have you unencumbered by the thought of someone hearing you is almost bordering on an obsession for me."

Diana wanted that, too. He continued to stroke her, eliciting more whimpers and cries of pleasure. She was beyond caring who heard her. He chuckled. "I shouldn't tell you about my fantasies. It only makes your cries worse. Are you close?"

She nodded, and he continued to tease her nub as he slid in and out of her from behind. The ache bordered on a delirious precipice that she wanted to crash over. She needed her release. Her rocking became more frantic. He littered kisses along her elegant neck.

She was a wanton mess and didn't care. Diana rocked into him harder until a strangled gasp escaped her. Her climax shattered and throbbed through her in millions of pieces.

His full hard cock was still buried deep in her. She pushed against him, and he groaned. "This is all I could think about since arriving in Tuscany."

"Good," she said, still vexed about Sebastian's flirtations.

Sebastian started to pound into her, taking what he wanted. She met him stroke for stroke. "Remember then, you are mine too until we return to England."

A surprised chuckle escaped him, but she wasn't joking. For now, he was as much hers as she was his. "I mean it."

Her words seemed to increase his desire as his cock swelled even more within her. Sebastian shifted her, grabbing both her hips and pounding into her even harder than before. He let out a strangled groan and released her, pulling out and spending.

Diana heard him rise and could tell he was cleaning up. She had an absurd thought that she wanted him to finish in her, to feel the closeness such a release between two people brought. The thought disconcerted her. They were only having an interlude, she reminded herself.

After seeing to them both, Sebastian rejoined her, cradling Diana along his hard, firm body. "You have me until we reach the shores of England."

What if she wanted him longer? She didn't dare say the words. Afraid she would appear naïve to a man whose frequent liaisons were widely known. He kissed her neck. "I don't like that Tremont is here."

"I don't like that you spent last night flirting with ladies," she responded tartly.

"I was being friendly, not flirting. I think Mrs. Swinson was looking to cause trouble."

Diana pulled out of his arms and turned so they were facing each other. "That doesn't explain why you went there in the first place."

He sighed. "This trip is somewhat of a fantasy. Tremont being here brought me back to reality. I needed time to mull that over in my mind. He may be your husband someday."

She frowned at him. "I have promised him nothing."

He stroked her face. "A man doesn't journey across the continent if he doesn't at least hope for more. He would be a good match for you."

His words were like a stab to the heart. She reminded herself this thing with Sebastian was only temporary. She said, "I would like to spend as much time together as we can, while we are here."

"Me too," he agreed before turning her around and pulling her against him.

Sadness filled Diana that her closeness with Sebastian would be coming to an end soon, and she had the overwhelming feeling so much between them had been left unsaid.

SEBASTIAN SAT IN the carriage, annoyed. Tonight, Diana's mother was hosting a dinner, and Tremont had insisted he and Diana depart earlier for the event than everyone else. A possessiveness swirled within him about the precious time he had left with her. Time that was slowly being taken away by Tremont. He was fortunate that, somehow, he and Diana had spent the last few days with their normal group sightseeing. Tremont wasn't present. Sebastian suspected he was more interested in socializing with his peers than touring any of the ruins of Livorno and the adjoining cities and towns.

They'd also managed to spend every evening together. He felt lucky they were staying on the same floor at the hotel. Tremont was always hovering around Diana when she wasn't sightseeing or in her room, but Sebastian did his best to tolerate it. Still, tonight, it annoyed him that Tremont would be escorting her to the dinner. Sebastian had no claim on Diana, he reminded himself.

The carriage came to a halt, and the door opened to a beautiful house. They were not the only ones arriving. A crush of people made their way into the event. It appeared the dinner was to be a grand affair. He helped Lady Clark out of the carriage. She grumbled, "My sister has to have so much pomp."

He smiled but said nothing. He'd come to adore this feisty woman. His mother would like her. He made a mental note to introduce them someday. They, along with Spoor, Monroe, and Haggerty, finally made it into the house. His group went off to find refreshments, but Sebastian stayed in the same spot.

His gaze wandered around the room, hoping to find Diana. Eventually, their eyes met, and she beamed at him. His stomach dipped. This woman was making him feel things he suspected would end up hurting him in the long run. Yet he walked towards her, unable to resist. As he reached Diana, her mother intercepted. "Diana, come. You must meet Lord Beaumont."

Diana's gaze darted to him, and it soothed him that he saw the same frustration in her eyes that he felt. He sighed and wandered to a billiards room where most of the men congregated. Monroe conversed with Haggerty in one corner, but Sebastian didn't feel like joining them. He leaned against a wall, grabbing a glass of wine from an attendant. Then he pulled his pocket watch out and casually flipped it open and closed, lost in thought about Diana.

"Do you play?" a man asked.

Sebastian glanced to his side to see the man leisurely knocking balls across the billiards table. He shook his head. "I'm rot at it."

The man laughed and grabbed his drink, walking over. "Thomas Easton."

Sebastian shook his hand. Why did his name sound familiar?

He remembered. He was the man Messina mentioned in connection with the Calverts. A few days ago, Diana received word from the count that the Calverts weren't in Tuscany. She'd been disappointed. Perhaps this man could help Diana meet them.

"I have heard of you from Count de Messina. He was hoping to introduce an associate of mine to the Calverts?"

He nodded. "They decided to travel to Damascus because of a new historical find. I'm headed there soon."

"When you have a moment, I would like to introduce you to Lady Hensley. She is part of a club called the Historical Society for Female Curators. They are looking to put together some antiquities exhibits."

The man lifted a brow. "Is this associated with the London Society of Antiquaries?"

"No. They don't allow women."

Easton laughed. "Still? What a bunch of old, stodgy men. Rose Calvert tried to submit a proposal for a lecture there once, but they turned her down. Something about it not being fitting for a lady to do such work."

"I bet she was livid."

"Furious. Lady Hensley leads this club?"

"She is part of a board consisting of five women."

"Unfortunately, I will have to decline the introduction. I will not be attending the dinner. I stopped by to speak with someone quickly and snuck in here to grab a drink before departing, but if you send a letter to the Hotel de Trevian, I can carry it to the Calverts."

Sebastian was disappointed he wouldn't be able to introduce Diana but happy the club would still be able to make a connection with the Calverts. "Thank you."

"So, are you here to enjoy a respite in Livorno?" Easton

asked.

"As part of raising funds for the curator club, I agreed to join a leisure cruise to test out new ports. Both Lady Hensley and I are writing a column about it in two London newspapers."

The man grimaced. "You're a reporter then."

"Hell no, but I'm a partner in the curator club. In London, I own a gentlemen's club called the Den."

"You are Sebastian Devons!"

Sebastian nodded, realizing he had never provided his name. Easton laughed. "You won your club's property off, my friend, the Marquess of Merry."

It was a small world. Sebastian chuckled. "How is Merry? I used to receive letters from him, but not anymore."

"He's well. Doesn't go by his title anymore. We do business together often. He will be in Damascus with the Calverts."

Sebastian smiled. Merry traveling to Damascus seemed so far-fetched for the young man he met long ago. He'd seemed so green when they played that card game that allowed Sebastian to take ownership of his estate. The property now housed the Den.

Sebastian never told anyone, but he had offered the estate property back to Merry. The young lord had laughed and explained losing it was the best thing that had ever happened to him and then he'd disappeared from London. Oddly enough, Sebastian had received letters and various gifts from Merry as if thanking him for taking the estate off his hands. It had been many years since he received the last one.

"The owner of the Den here in Livorno," Easton said, amused.

"Please tell Merry I said hello and I wish him well."

"Any interest in going to Damascus?" Easton asked.

Sebastian's eyes widened. "Are you joking?"

He smiled and shrugged. "Merry talks fondly of you. I think he would find it entertaining."

Probably in any other situation, Sebastian would have said yes, but he wanted to spend more time with Diana. "I can't."

"If you change your mind, let me know."

Sebastian nodded as Tremont entered the room from the corner of his eye. He should go find Diana now that the man wasn't hovering around her. The pompous man and a gaggle of younger lords made their way over to the billiards table he and Easton stood by.

"Nothing is official yet, but I imagine before Christmas, we will be betrothed or wed," Tremont told the men.

He glanced away from the group, and his eyes met Sebastian's. He knew without a doubt Tremont suspected something was going on between him and Diana. Sebastian didn't give a damn. He raised his glass to the lord, mockingly, before taking a large sip. Tremont scowled and turned away. His heart thundered. Would he really lose Diana to this ass?

Easton chuckled quietly. "You don't like him."

"Long story," Sebastian said. "Are you sure you don't have time to meet Lady Hensley?"

Easton drained his brandy. "I wish I could but I'm leaving now. I've stayed too long already. Send your missive for the Calverts to my hotel. I depart for Damascus in two days if you change your mind."

Chapter Twenty-Four

THE NEXT AFTERNOON, Diana and her aunt joined her mother and her friends for tea. She was exhausted from her mother's dinner the previous evening. It had run late into the night. Once she made it to the hotel, Sebastian visited her, but their lovemaking had been quick. A tenseness had emanated between them.

Sebastian had been upset that Tremont and her mother had monopolized her time. She'd barely been able to speak with anyone, not just Sebastian. She'd wanted to talk about it, but he'd been unwilling to share his thoughts. The longer they stayed in Livorno, the more distant they seemed to become. Diana hated it.

A mad idea sprang up in her mind. Could she and Sebastian become more than an interlude? Would he ever want more with her? The idea was preposterous but how she wished it could be. The way he touched her, spoke to her, and cared for her made Diana want so much more.

"Diana?"

She flushed, horrified she had no clue what her mother's friends were discussing. She glanced at the three ladies she barely knew, then her mother, and lastly her Aunt Winifred. Her aunt said, "Lady Beaumont asked if you enjoyed writing for the papers."

Diana smiled at her aunt, grateful, before turning back to the other ladies. "I do. I'm not sure I have any interest after I return, but the success means the Historical Society for Female Curators will have the funding needed to grow."

Lady Beaumont wrinkled her nose. "I heard about the club and that Lady Hawley created it to spite her husband because of an affair. Not that she should care who he is involved with, as she's rather scandalous. She should be happy her husband is so private about his discretions. She is not."

Diana gasped at the woman's bluntness. Her mother and her friends tittered. Her aunt frowned in disapproval at the woman.

"I can assure you the club isn't a game to Lady Hawley."

The tone Diana used seemed to upset the women as they pinched their lips together. Her mother said, "Come now, you don't really expect us to take your club seriously. Lady Hawley hasn't behaved in an appropriate manner for at least a decade. Your main patron is the owner of a scandalous gentlemen's club with an unsavory heritage. I wouldn't be surprised if the two are involved in a more intimate fashion."

Her mother smirked as a scowl filled Diana's face. Diana had no doubt her remark was meant to wound her. Her mother was a master at squirreling out secrets. She likely suspected there was something between her and Sebastian. Diana ignored her last point and said, "I can assure you they are both very dedicated to seeing the Historical Society for Female Curators succeed."

Her mother's friend Lady Hartley said, "My husband said it was a bunch of ladies playing at being scholars. The club would be lucky if it lasted a year."

"I will bet you a hundred pounds the club will survive through next season," Aunt Winifred said to the woman.

Lady Hartley gasped. "I can't bet that much money."

Her aunt turned to her sister. "How about you, Lisette?"

Diana's mother's eyes flashed with anger and maybe resentment that her sister had so much money. "No, I have no interest in your bet. It's a waste of time."

Aunt Winifred smirked, but Diana's mother changed the

subject before the discussion could go any further. "Ladies, I think we need to end our visit. I have some matters to discuss with my daughter."

Her mother's friends rose. Lady Beaumont beamed at Diana's mother. "I hope to visit you in England soon, Your Grace."

Her mother smiled demurely. Once her friends were gone, she frowned and took a sip of tea. "Diana, you shouldn't be so supportive of that Devons man. Think of your future marriage and Robert."

"I have only good things to say about Mr. Devons."

Her mother studied her. Her lips twisted with distaste.

"Well, Lisette, it's apparent even in Tuscany, you are still a cold, gossipy lady."

"You shouldn't speak to me that way," her mother snipped.

Aunt Winifred lifted a brow. "Why, because you are a duchess?"

A scowl broke across her mother's face. Her aunt said, "Be careful, sister. You are still trying to convince your daughter to help you return to England. Politeness goes a long way. I can only imagine the trouble you are hoping to cause."

Her mother glared at her sister. "I would like to see my family, especially my son."

"Mother, Clara is the only one who will decide that," Diana interjected.

Her mother's eyes swung to her. "She can't keep my child from me."

But Clara could. She wanted their brother to have nothing to do with her. Her aunt snorted. "What will you do in England? Aren't your friends here?"

Her mother frowned. "Most of them left during all the fighting from the revolution."

"Why didn't you ask for help to leave then?" her aunt asked.

Her mother glared at her. "The duke was unwell."

"So, kind of you to stay by your husband's deathbed," her aunt said, for once sounding sincere.

Her mother had regarded Diana and Clara as the means to further connections and wealth, but Diana did believe she cared for her father. He may be the only person her mother had true feelings for.

"I'm sorry you dealt with that alone," Diana said.

She swallowed and took a deep breath. "Yes, it was difficult. Part of the reason I wish to return home is because everything here reminds me of him."

Compassion for her mother coursed through Diana. Losing her father couldn't have been easy for her. "If I agree, you promise not to meddle in my, Henry, or Clara's life. You will retire to the country."

Her mother nodded. "Of course."

Diana glanced at her aunt, who was looking at her sister skeptically. Still, no matter what her mother had done to her, Diana couldn't leave her in Livorno. "We can try it. I think it is best if you finish prepping and move next spring."

Her mother's eyebrows shot up in alarm. "I can't. I have already packed my things and agreed to sell my house."

"To whom?" Aunt Winifred asked.

"Lord Hartley."

It was done then. Her mother would most definitely return with her. Frustration filled her even though she'd always known deep down that her mother's return was inevitable.

Her aunt scowled. "You were certainly confident."

Her mother ignored her comment. Instead, she said to Diana, "Tell me about Lord Tremont."

Dread filled Diana. A flush appeared across her cheeks. "He is a friend."

"He seems to want more and has exceptional family connections. An earl is a perfect option for you."

Who Diana married or didn't wouldn't be navigated by her mother. She frowned. "I have not started considering marriage again."

"It will be good that Lord Tremont is traveling back with us on the ship. I have seen the way Devons looks at you."

Diana's eyes met her aunt's, but they both remained silent. Her mother continued, "I imagine the options for female companionship on the ship aren't plentiful. How many ladies did you say were on the leisure cruise?"

"Ten," Diana whispered.

"Yes, it's very good that Tremont will be with us. I would hate for you to be seduced by such a rogue so he can satisfy his needs. The man can have anyone as his paramour. I wouldn't want to see you hurt once he discards you back in London."

"Lisette!" her aunt snapped.

Her mother stared back at her, unperturbed. "Yes?"

Aunt Winifred said nothing, not wanting to reveal anything else. Diana said, "You know nothing of Sebastian Devons's character."

Her mother sighed. "True, but he is a known rogue. I would hate to see you fooled by someone like him because he is bored, and there are no other ladies around. You, Diana, are not built to hold a man like Devons's interest."

"How—"

"It's fine," Diana said, interrupting Aunt Winifred. "Fortunately for me, there is nothing improper going on between us."

"Of course not. I wouldn't expect anything different from a proper lady like you," her mother said.

Silence descended upon the room as they sipped their tea. Her mother's words were always cruel, but her comments about Sebastian stoked her own fears. She wouldn't dwell on it. It didn't matter. It was just a tryst. Then why did her heart ache so much?

She glanced at her aunt, whose fury was evident. Diana knew the carriage ride home would be filled with the many reasons she should leave her mother in Livorno. Diana couldn't. Her mother was here alone. Regardless of how ridiculous it seemed, she felt obligated to make sure her mother was taken care of. Maybe Clara had been right that she was too kindhearted.

Once in England, Diana hoped to see her mother infrequently. Her cruel streak had not gone away.

SEBASTIAN SILENTLY CREPT down the hallway to Diana's room. Earlier, she'd not been at dinner, sending word through Aunt Winifred to their group that she was feeling unwell. When he asked Lady Clark, she'd shaken her head and said she had a trying day with her mother.

Throughout the meal, he'd been unable to focus on anything but Diana. He hated that he couldn't go to her immediately and was now sneaking about. He imagined her distress in a dozen different ways. Each worse than the other.

Then he'd been angry with himself because his overwhelming need to be with her made Sebastian realize he'd done the one damn thing he shouldn't. He'd fallen in love with her. Sebastian had been a fool to think he'd ever given his heart to Lilah because what he felt for Diana was so much more. He knocked softly, and his stomach clenched as he heard Diana pad to the door. She cracked it and gave him a small smile before stepping aside to let him in.

He frowned. She appeared pale, and there were shadows under her eyes.

"What is wrong? I was worried when your aunt said you wouldn't join us for dinner."

She pulled her wrap tighter around her. "It was a long day with my mother."

Anger flared in Devons that the cold woman had driven her to feel so awful. "You should leave her here."

Diana sighed. "My aunt said the same, but I can't. She is all alone. I want nothing from her except to see her settled in the country in England."

"You owe her nothing."

Diana's eyes flashed. "I know that, but she is still my mother."

He pulled her into his arms, holding her tightly. "Don't be upset with me. I'm only angry because I care for you."

"You are a true friend."

He flinched at her words. He fucking didn't want to be her friend. Sebastian wanted so much more. He wanted to be the man that comforted her when she needed it. Unable to hold back, he tilted her chin up and studied her. "Let me court you."

Her eyes widened in shock, and she pulled away, stumbling out of his arms. The piercing in his heart almost drove him to his knees. They stared at each other silently. Fear, concern, and perhaps excitement flickered across her face. "Why now?"

"I know I'm not a lord, and I'm asking a great deal of you to even consider me."

"Don't," she said, holding up one of her hands.

He went silent. She wouldn't even consider him at all. He tried to control the anger coursing through him. Sebastian looked away. When he turned back, she was frowning at him apprehensively. "Wait until we return to London."

He took a deep breath, hoping he was misunderstanding her. "Why?"

She hugged herself and said, "I want you to think about it. This all may seem less wonderful when we return. We can talk about it on the ship."

A bitter laugh escaped him. "In between your time with Tremont."

She flinched. "I can't control that he is returning with us."

"We could tell him we are betrothed."

Her eyes watered. "Be honest, Sebastian. Do you really want to marry me?"

He didn't understand what she was saying or why she didn't understand what he wanted. Maybe she was trying to turn him down delicately. "I wouldn't have asked if I didn't want to. Am I not even worthy of a chance, Diana?"

"It isn't that. How dare you insinuate I would think that way?"

He paced back and forth before facing her again. "Then explain to me why we need to wait."

"Once in England, you may think differently. This trip has placed us in a situation where, of course, we would fall for each other. We are always together."

Sebastian was a bloody fool. He'd fallen in love with a lady he could never truly have. Just like his mother with his father. "I have to leave."

She grabbed his arm. "Sebastian, please, can we talk about this?"

"No."

Sebastian pulled her to him, needing to taste her lips one last time. The kiss was brief but would be seared to his memory forever. She frowned at him. "I'm asking you to pause this and reexplore it in London."

He couldn't and it pained him that she was so unsure about what they had. He released her and walked to the door. She pleaded, "Please stay. Don't leave like this."

Sebastian didn't stop or look back.

Chapter Twenty-Five

"H AVE YOU SEEN Devons?" Diana asked Haggerty as they stood in the foyer of the hotel.

The man glanced at her, surprised. "Didn't you hear?"

Her heart started to pound. She shook her head. "Hear what?"

"He left on another ship. It was so early that Monroe closed his bill for him."

Diana looked around, hoping to see the captain. Sebastian couldn't have departed without saying anything to her. She refused to believe it. Last night, Diana had bungled things. Of course, she wanted to be courted by Sebastian. Diana loved him, but before he arrived at her hotel room, she'd spent all day thinking about her mother's words. Insinuations that suggested, in London, she wouldn't have been enough for a man like Sebastian Devons.

Her insecurities had roared to life. She couldn't stop thinking about the caricature of the proper lady and all the hurtful words her mother spewed during her childhood about her appearance being acceptable, but not much more than that. Why did she let the woman upset her? Sebastian looked at Diana as if he couldn't breathe without touching her. She knew that.

"Is Captain Monroe still here?"

Haggerty shrugged and frowned at her. "Is something

wrong?"

"No, but I was hoping the captain would still be here."

Haggerty pointed to the front door. "He just left. You may catch him before he gets in a carriage."

She rushed outside, glancing around before spotting Monroe about to leave. "Captain Monroe!"

He turned startled. "Lady Hensley, you shocked me."

Diana took a deep breath. "Haggerty said Devons left."

Monroe nodded. "The ship he is on should almost be underway, but don't worry, he gave me two letters for you. He left with Thomas Easton and mentioned that he hoped to meet with his colleagues, the Calverts. Read his letters. He said all the information would be in there. I dropped them off at the front desk."

Tears stung her eyes. *Do not cry,* she told herself. She needed to fix this somehow. "Can you take me to the ship he will depart on?"

His eyes widened, and he stared at her as if she'd gone mad. "It is about to leave."

"Please. You don't understand, we argued last night."

"It can't be that serious," he said.

She almost confessed everything to him, which would have been scandalous, but she stopped herself. "If you can't take me, can you tell me where the ship is?"

Monroe studied her. His expression softened. "It must have been quite the fight."

She nodded. He sighed and then held his hand out. "In the carriage, you go. Maybe we can get there before they depart."

Diana smiled at him, grateful. Monroe instructed the driver to a pier and joined her inside. The carriage sped through the town, and the captain smiled. "I told him I would pay him extra if he rushed."

"Thank you."

"I was surprised that Devons decided to leave with Easton."

She remained silent, too upset to say anything. He'd left.

Diana couldn't believe it. They rounded a large warehouse, and Monroe let out a curse. Far off the pier was a ship. It was Sebastian's ship. She would not cry.

"I'm sorry."

She shook her head. "It's fine."

But it wasn't. She was torn between feeling as if she failed Sebastian somehow and being furious with him for leaving. Only a few hours ago, he wanted to court her. The carriage came to a halt, and Monroe ordered the driver to take them back to the hotel.

"Thank you."

"If it is any consolation, he appeared just as wrecked as you seem."

She smiled, doubting that was possible. If it were true, he wouldn't have left. "May I make one more request?"

He nodded. Then she continued, "Could you not mention this to anyone?"

"Lady Hensley, your secrets are yours. Think nothing of it."

"Thank you," she said.

Once they arrived back at the hotel, she went straight to the front desk. The manager stated that the letters had been taken up to her room. She rushed to her room and found the two missives on the floor as if someone had pushed them under the door. One envelope had her name on it and the other was his last Ladies of London missive. She opened the letter addressed to her and read the messy brief words.

Diana,

I lost my head last night. I'm headed out for another adventure. All the best in your future plans.

Sebastian Devons.

She frowned. Monroe said Devons stated that everything would be answered in his letters. It explained nothing. Perhaps he had come to his senses. Pain sliced through her, but she took a deep breath. She had wanted a liaison, a flirtation. She would not hate Sebastian for giving that to her.

She ripped open his Ladies of London letter breaking their rule to not read each other's missives until they returned home. Diana hoped it revealed more than his hastily written note to her. This letter was neatly written.

To the Ladies of London,

My time on this adventure has ended. I'm traveling to Damascus with the famous explorer Thomas Easton. Have no fear, Lady Hensley will continue to keep you updated on ports during her return. Tuscany is a lovely region that those suffering from homesickness will enjoy. You won't have to journey far to find another Londoner or a peer on a grand tour.

Now that I have reached the end of my portion of the trip, I must admit Sardinia will always be my favorite location. If I had to guess, I believe it is Lady Hensley's as well.

Thank you to the Historical Society for Female Curators for allowing me to go on this adventure with them. Any tours the club develops for ladies will be a grand adventure, possibly the trip of a lifetime.

All my best,
Sebastian Devons.

Diana took a deep breath, folded the paper, and placed it back in the envelope. The letters explained nothing. Sebastian's had been written as if he couldn't be bothered to explain himself and his Ladies of London letter didn't fill in much more for Diana. She wiped at a tear rolling down her cheek. Perhaps the lack of details spoke for itself. He'd come to his senses. They were over. The tears fell faster, and she gave up on wiping them away.

THE SHIP ROCKED back and forth, making Sebastian's stomach

turn. He'd spent the first two days in his cabin barely suppressing his need to wretch all over the place. The *SS Ernesto* was not the *SS Lark*. For one, he was sharing a cabin with Easton. It had been a long time since he shared such close quarters with anyone, even his own brother. He supposed he shouldn't complain. Easton had taken his nausea in stride, bringing him food and making sure a clean pail was always by his side.

Unlike the *SS Lark*, the *SS Ernesto* was not built and designed to cater to passengers but to move as fast as possible. The primary purpose being to deliver mail. Sebastian opened the door of their cabin and made his way to the saloon. He spied Easton sitting at a table alone, scribbling in a notebook. He made his way over to him. "May I join you?"

The massive redheaded man grinned at him. "You are feeling better."

Sebastian grimaced. "A little."

"Sit," he said, motioning to a man to bring him food.

"I'm not sure I'm ready for a meal yet."

Easton chuckled. "It won't be anything extravagant. You aren't on one of the vessels built by the Kincaides. Probably some bread and stew."

His stomach growled at the words. Perhaps he was hungrier than he thought. As they waited for the food, Easton asked, "So what made you change your mind?"

"I needed space."

"From a woman?"

Sebastian's eyes jerked to his and Easton smirked. "You look like a man whose heart has been smashed to pieces."

"More correctly, I needed to give a lady space to think about what she wanted," he said.

He'd left because Diana wanted them to wait, insinuating that maybe the trip was the cause of his feelings. Sebastian knew what he felt for Diana would be with him for the rest of his life. He loved her. It was that simple. He wished he would have said the words to her that last night.

Still, after he departed her room, he'd thought about what she said and wondered if she doubted her feelings, not his. Maybe it was she who had gotten caught up in the magic of the trip. He wanted Diana only if she loved him. Sebastian would wait but he couldn't travel back with Tremont. He would likely toss the man overboard. Easton's offer had seemed like the perfect solution.

The explorer chuckled, jerking him out of his thoughts. "That is very noble of you."

Sebastian sighed, also wondering if he was daft for making such a decision. The man smirked but changed the subject. "Hopefully, we can catch the Calverts and Merry in Latakia. Damascus is a couple days' ride from the port city."

Sebastian hoped so. He wasn't sure if he was willing to journey all the way to Damascus. While he wanted to give Diana space, he still missed her. He'd poured his heart out to her in his letter. He didn't want to leave Livorno without her knowing how much he loved her and hoped to be her husband.

The ship Easton was departing on left at a time that didn't allow him to see her again. Regret sat on his chest that he hadn't been able to visit her one more time and tell her that he'd wait. He hoped his written words were enough to convey that. If he stayed in Latakia for a few days, he would only be a few weeks behind Diana's return to London.

"I think the Historical Society for Female Curators would be interested in partnering with you as well."

"After learning who the board members are, it is best the Calverts handle any partnerships."

Sebastian frowned. "Is there someone on the board that you have an issue with?"

Easton took a sip of his drink. "The Duchess of Lusby and I are old acquaintances. We aren't on good terms. I can almost guarantee she wouldn't want my help, and I have no desire to assist her in anything."

Sebastian was startled by the edge in Easton's voice. He'd been nothing but agreeable since they'd met. Hell, he even gave up part of his cabin so Sebastian could travel with him. What type of quarrel would an explorer have with a duchess?

"Before you ask, we grew up together. I wish her no ill will but think we are better off not interacting."

A man brought Sebastian his bread and stew along with some wine. After he left, Sebastian said, "Understood."

Easton smiled. "You will love Latakia. It's a beautiful city."

Curious, Sebastian asked. "Do you ever miss London?"

He was quiet for a moment but finally said, "My mother sometimes. But I was the son of a house servant in London and likely would have never become more than that if I hadn't left."

Sebastian suspected if he returned now, Easton would be one of the richest men in the city. His exploits, true or not, were well-known. "You have serials written about you. You are very popular."

Easton smirked. "Good. Still, I have no desire to socialize with the peerage. I learned long ago they aren't for me."

There was a story there, Sebastian guessed, but he wouldn't press the man.

Chapter Twenty-Six

Early August—Gibraltar 1850

A s Diana walked to drop off her and Sebastian's last missives, she surveyed the streets. Gibraltar appeared to be a contradiction of many things, both civilized and uncivilized. She wrinkled her nose at her disparaging thoughts. Maybe civilized was the wrong word, perhaps bohemian and proper. She suspected no one here was one or the other but a bit of both.

It was probably the same everywhere. Men and women weren't so one-dimensional they could be described as rogues or the perfect examples of a moral compass. Her mind flitted back to the caricature and article she'd agonized over a few months ago. Clara had been right. Shame on the writer for casting proper women as such simple beings. Looking back, Diana felt embarrassed that the article upset her so much.

"This place is awful. We should return to the ship," her mother said snootily.

There had been an issue with the *SS Lark*, so Monroe had all hands focused on that. He'd asked if she was comfortable enough to deliver her and Sebastian's last letters to one of the offices that handled mail and the shipment of goods. She'd agreed, thinking nothing of leaving the ship. Diana smiled, amused at how more at ease she was now with being abroad. She was by no means a travel expert, but somewhere along the way, she'd acquired not only her sea legs but also her adventure legs.

Diana couldn't completely disagree with her mother. A city like Gibraltar would shock most ladies. It seemed everyone mingled here. It was obvious there was still a class system, but no one paid much attention to it.

"Really, Diana, Tremont can deliver your letters," her mother added.

Diana glanced at Arthur, who appeared more uncomfortable than the duchess. She forced herself not to laugh at the absurdity of the situation. Neither her mother nor Arthur would have done well at any of their other ports.

"Mother, you didn't have to come with us. I requested you didn't."

Her mother pursed her lips. "I couldn't stay on that ship any longer."

The quality of everything on the vessel had been unsatisfactory to her. Diana had no doubt Monroe and his crew couldn't wait for her departure. She'd apologized multiple times for her mother's behavior, but Monroe insisted she should not be the one apologizing. Aunt Winifred had grown tired of her complaining and would shut it down every time she started.

Laughter erupted from a man and woman in the street. Diana smiled, suddenly thinking Sebastian would enjoy the chaos of this city. Her smile faltered as the lingering sadness she felt since he left became more pronounced. She missed him. Every day, she tried to stop herself from feeling anything for him, but it was still there. Hopefully, once back in England, she would be able to come to terms with the fact it was just a tryst. A magical moment she should cherish but was permanently over.

She spotted the office they were looking for. "We made it."

"I'm not going in there," her mother stated.

Diana sighed. Aunt Winifred, Spoor, and Haggerty had all begged off from joining her on her adventure into the city, and Diana suspected it was because of her mother. They didn't spend nearly as much time together. She missed her little group that had splintered since Sebastian's departure.

Arthur turned to her, horrified. "I can't let Diana go in there alone."

"Well, you can't leave me out here. I'm a duchess."

Her eyes flicked down her mother, who was dressed in a far too elaborate outfit, at least for travel. Diana touched Arthur's arm. "Stay here with her. You will be able to watch me through the windows."

Arthur reluctantly nodded. She entered the small office and took a deep breath. Happy to be by herself, even for a moment. Her mother or Arthur always seemed to be with her. She pulled two envelopes from her hidden pocket in her skirt. She'd resealed Sebastian's letter, but hers was still open. This was the last missive she'd send for the column. She supposed she could write one for Gibraltar, but it didn't feel right without Sebastian here. Pulling the folded paper from the envelope, she read her words once more.

> *To the Ladies of London,*
>
> *Tuscany is the ideal place for any London lady to arrive after so many adventures. It is filled with so many places to visit but also feels like home. It is certainly not a place to be missed.*
>
> *Yet as I sit here, thinking about all the ports I have visited, my favorite is Sardinia. The water, the sand, and the dancing made me believe magic still exists in this world, and it is no illusion but real.*
>
> *Soon these exciting ports will be available to you. Please visit the Historical Society for Female Curators at Seely House to learn more. I will happily detail my adventures once I return.*
>
> *Lady Hensley*

She closed the envelope back up. Sardinia would always hold a special place in her heart. Pasting, a smile on her face she handed the man in the office the two letters.

Latakia

SEBASTIAN HAD NEVER been happier to be on land. Latakia was a port under the Turkish empire but governed by the Syrians. Easton would be in the city for the next few days. Sebastian had already made the decision not to travel on to Damascus. He was antsy to return to London and call on Diana.

But first, he would meet the Calverts and visit with his old friend Merry. In truth, while he was amused to see Merry again, his real goal was to set something up with the Calverts for the curator club. He hoped they'd be interested.

He followed Easton into a small building and spotted men, shockingly, smoking from a metal contraption. Easton grinned at him. "It is a shisha."

"What are they doing with it?"

"They are smoking."

Sebastian had never seen anything like it. They made their way to a back corner where a man sat smoking, and two others drank tea. The man smoking rose and guffawed. "What are you doing here?"

Sebastian studied him. It was Merry! He was transformed from the young man all those years ago whom he won the Den from in a game of cards. Now, he was almost the size of Devons, tan, scruffy, and with shoulder-length hair.

"Merry?"

The man grinned at him. "Des, Desmond, or Keaton. I don't use that name anymore."

He blinked at him in shock. He sat back down and indicated for Easton and Sebastian to sit. Sebastian's mouth curved into a smile. Maybe the first real one since he left Tuscany. "You are not the same man I knew all those years ago in London."

Keaton laughed. "No, I'm not."

The older man in the sitting area asked, "How do you know each other?"

Keaton leaned back in his chair. "Devons here won my family

estate from me in a game of cards."

The younger man—no, not a man, Sebastian realized, but a woman muttered, "You must not have cheated back then as you do now."

"No, he was rather rubbish whether he cheated or not," Sebastian stated with a grin.

Keaton shrugged. "I don't play much anymore. Only with you, Rose, when we are bored."

She snorted. Sebastian studied her. She was tall and slender with dozens of freckles. Her hair was braided down her back. She wore a hat, but the most shocking thing was, she had on trousers. She stuck her hand out. "I'm Rose."

Sebastian took her hand. "Sebastian Devons."

"And this man is her father, Benjamin Calvert," Easton added.

Sebastian shook his hand as well, but his eyes darted back to Rose. She made a face at him, and he said, "I'm sorry for staring."

She sighed but waved off his apology. "You English are all the same. Horrified to witness a woman in pants. I bet you've done and seen far more scandalous things than me wearing trousers."

A bark of laughter escaped him at her blunt response. "You are quite right."

"What are you doing here?" Keaton asked.

Sebastian ran his fingers through his hair, unsure how to tell the complicated tale. "I've partnered with a group of ladies who have set up a club for female historians, curators, and scholars. The club decided to raise money by having me and one of the board members, Lady Hensley, write about a leisure cruise for two newspapers back in London."

Keaton gaped at him. "You willingly signed up to do this?"

Rose frowned at him. "How did you end up here?"

Sebastian sighed. "I didn't want to do the return leg of the trip, and Easton mentioned his journey here. I had hoped to catch up with Merry and perhaps create some connections between all of you and the club."

Benjamin chuckled. "Well, you have found us."

"What is the name of this club?" Rose asked.

"The Historical Society for Female Curators."

She smirked. "I hope they are making the London Society of Antiquaries nervous."

Sebastian's mouth quirked up in a smile. "It just formed, so they are looking to partner with people like you."

"Try this," Easton said, handing him the mouthpiece of the shisha.

Sebastian took it as Keaton explained, "It's kind of like smoking a pipe but not."

Rose frowned at his description. "No, it isn't."

Her father glanced at her, and she shrugged. "Not that I would know."

Keaton and Easton laughed. Calvert lifted a skeptical brow at his daughter, and she rolled her eyes. The older man turned back to Sebastian. "How is England? The London season will be starting soon."

Rose rolled her eyes. "Father, I'm not going."

"I think your mother would be beside herself to see you in pants."

She sighed. Sebastian took a puff from the mouthpiece and coughed. Easton slapped him on the back. "Welcome to Latakia."

"The season is still as busy as ever. It seems to start a little earlier every year," Sebastian responded to Calvert.

"That is how I met your mother during her season," Calvert said dreamily.

His daughter beamed at him.

"I never plan to go back to London. Too many rules for me," Keaton said.

"Me too," Easton added.

Calvert snorted. "You aren't going back because of a woman. I have told you time and time again you can't run from your feelings. Whether she is here or on the other side of the world, you are going to feel what you are going to feel."

Easton smirked but there was a hardness to it. "I'm fine.

Calvert, let it go."

The older man's words hit Sebastian in his gut. Likely because they were true. He missed Diana so much.

"Devons has women problems," Easton said, seemingly trying to shut up Calvert about his own secrets.

Sebastian frowned at him, but he shrugged and grinned.

"You do?" Keaton asked him and chuckled. "You do appear to have the same pained expression Easton carries around."

Easton glared at him, but it only made Keaton smile more broadly. Wanting to change the subject, Sebastian turned his gaze to the Calverts and said, "I hoped you would be interested in starting a correspondence with the curator club's board members to provide them artifacts to display in their exhibits at Seely House."

Rose Calvert stared at him, intrigued. Her father asked, "Who are the ladies standing it up?"

"Lady Hawley, the Duchess of Lusby, Lady Hensley, Lady Esme Tennis, and a Miss Sara Martin."

"Lisbeth is one of them!"

Sebastian's head swiveled to Rose. She was studying Easton, concerned. Calvert nodded. "Good for her. I heard her husband passed away a while back."

Rose scowled. "We aren't going to help them."

Calvert frowned at his daughter. "You used to be friends with Lisbeth."

Rose snorted. "No, I was friends with Easton. She came along with him."

"Am I missing something?" Sebastian asked.

"No," Easton bit out and turned to the Calverts. "It sounds like a worthy cause. One, I think, Rose, you would support as every paper you have written on the translation of ancient text has been turned away by the Society of Antiquaries simply because you are a woman."

Calvert nodded. "I agree. Rose, you could go to London to learn more about the club."

"No," Rose said, glaring at her father.

Calvert frowned at his daughter before pulling out a notebook and scribbling in it. He tore the paper out. "Please have the board send any correspondence to this address. I think we can arrange something."

"I won't be going to London," Rose said, sulking.

"We'll see. I have an idea," Calvert stated. His daughter rolled her eyes and muttered about bloody seasons.

Sebastian did his best not to laugh. He was delighted there was interest from the Calverts, well at least from the father. Sebastian nodded. "Thank you."

"Will you be going to Damascus with us?" Keaton asked.

"No. I hope to leave for London sometime during the next week."

He wanted to get back to Diana. Whatever her decision was, he needed to know. Calvert winked. "Smart man, not trying to run from his feelings."

Easton scowled. "Enough, Benjamin."

The older man laughed. He was right, Sebastian thought. He wasn't running. He was prepared to know where he and Diana stood. If she decided it was only a tryst, he would do his best to move on. Fear uncoiled in his belly because he didn't know how anyone moved on from the person they loved.

Chapter Twenty-Seven

London—Mid August 1850

DIANA GLANCED AROUND the grand foyer of the Seely House in open-mouthed amazement. She hadn't expected the club to accomplish so much while she was gone, but to her surprise, the building appeared to be almost ready to start showing exhibits. Addie, along with the rest of the board members, leaned over the railing of the mezzanine landing, watching her.

"What do you think?" Addie asked.

She smiled. "I think it is remarkable what you have accomplished."

Addie left everyone upstairs and met her on the first floor. "It wouldn't have been possible without the income we generated from the columns."

"It made that much money?"

"A wild amount," Sarah Martin yelled from the second floor, grinning.

Addie tucked her arm in Diana's and escorted her up the stairs. "We have so much to show you, but first, we need to discuss the future of the club."

"Where are we going?"

Their fearless leader winked. "Our office."

A laugh escaped Diana at the absurdity of what Addie said. They had an office. Once on the mezzanine level, Addie moved to the right but didn't enter the door where the rest of the women were. Instead, she turned so they were looking over the ornate railing, surveying the first floor.

"But first, let's envision what the board is thinking so far. In the entrance area below, we will have some type of grand statue. There is also room to have a few small displays for visitors to view as they move farther into the building. The two rooms on the left and the right will house our most exciting exhibits."

This was really happening. They would be an actual club. During the entire time Diana was gone, she'd known what she was working towards, but to hear and see all of this was incredibly empowering. Addie pointed to rooms opposite to where they stood. "On the mezzanine level, there will be a room for women to do research. Sarah Martin will head that up."

Addie pulled Diana into the office. Located in the room were six ornate desks and a sitting area. Diana brought her to one in the center of the room.

"This is yours."

Diana ran her finger along it and smiled. Somewhat in disbelief, she was part of this. She looked up and saw all the other board members in the sitting area, waiting for her. She blushed, embarrassed to be caught being so excited about something as simple as a desk.

She made her way over to where they sat and took a seat in a wingback chair. Sarah beamed at her. "It's rather exciting, isn't it?"

Diana laughed. "Yes. I don't think I realized how much so until I saw my desk."

"We all felt the same way," Addie said.

"How was your trip?" Esme asked as she sat.

Diana didn't know where to start. Instead, she simply said, "It was amazing."

"Your letters were all the rage here. Now, every lady wants to go on a leisure cruise, which is what we all hoped for," Addie said, beaming.

"Most would like Sebastian Devons to be on their trip," Sarah

Martin said with a wink.

His name caused flutters in her stomach. She would have to get used to hearing it. He was part of their club, and she would be in his presence again. Diana would never say anything bad about him. He was a decent man. Leaving Tuscany because his feelings were much more superficial than hers didn't change that. A simple affair is what they agreed to.

"He was a true asset on the journey. We had a wonderful time and enjoyed all the ports."

"Why didn't he return with you?" Addie asked.

She did blush then and didn't doubt it was a deep red. Everyone stared at her waiting for her to respond. Finally, she said. "I think travel agrees with Devons. He was likely hungry for more adventure."

All the ladies nodded as if it made perfect sense. Thank goodness.

"I believe he went to Damascus," she added.

Esme gasped. "Truly?"

Diana smiled. "Yes."

The young woman looked positively jealous. She muttered something about him being lucky.

"I loved your stop in Le Conquet. I'm so excited we will get to display some of the medieval manuscripts from the region," Lisbeth said.

The duchess was a known collector of many types of historical artifacts. Diana was thrilled that she was as excited. "We owe Mr. Haggerty a great deal of gratitude for allowing us to display the works. It is through his partnership with the church in Le Conquet that they will be our first exhibit."

"He doesn't work with the London Society of Antiquaries?" Sarah asked.

Diana smirked. "I think he was happy we were not part of them."

They all laughed.

Addie said, "One point for the Historical Society for Female

Curators."

Laughter erupted again. Finally, when Addie stopped, she said, "While you were gone, we tried to plan out what roles we would all perform as board members."

Diana bit her lip, wondering what role she would fill. Was she to be their paragon of properness? Hadn't Addie reached out to her for just that reason? Still, she didn't need a desk for that. Diana nodded, hoping her role would be more.

Addie continued, "Sarah will lead up the research department. She will identify ladies who want to work with us on historical studies."

Diana smiled at Sarah. "That makes perfect sense to me."

"Lady Esme will be in charge of exhibit designs, and the duchess will manage the finances for the club."

Disappointment filled Diana. If she helped with anything, she thought it would be their finances. Diana was good with numbers.

Addie pointed to herself. "My role will be the president, and I will also drum up customers for our exhibits. You will be the vice president and will do outreach to those in the field, convincing them to allow us to display their artifacts and antiquities."

Vice president? Diana hadn't expected such a position. "Why would you pick *me*?"

"While away, you identified two potential options for exhibits. It suits you."

Did it? She almost denied it but stopped herself. She had done that. Addie frowned at her. "Of course, if you don't think you can fill the position, we can think of something else."

She shook her head. "No, it's perfect."

Addie beamed at her. "We all thought so, too."

Everyone nodded. Sarah added, "The duchess and I may also have a list of potential scholars and antiquarians to contact."

Diana was ecstatic about her role. Addie pulled out a notebook and placed it on the table in the middle of the sitting area. "A few more things before we wrap up for the day. Both newspapers would like you and Devons to host a talk on your trip. We will have to wait until he returns but I don't think that shall be a problem. We can have it in one of the large empty exhibit rooms downstairs."

"Of course," Diana said.

She ignored the twisting of her stomach. It did no good to dwell on how it may be when she and Sebastian were together again. Instead, she would focus on her new, exciting role. Yes, Sebastian was never far from her thoughts, but Diana needed to move on.

Latakia—End of August 1850

"YOU ARE SURE you don't want to continue on with us?" Rose asked.

Sebastian liked her. She would be an oddity in London, but in this city, where a mixture of old and new abounded, Rose fit in perfectly. "No. It is time to return home. I have a business to run that I have been away from for far too long."

"Clubs are needed here as well," Keaton said.

"But they aren't my club."

Keaton laughed. "You truly do miss London. I can't imagine ever returning."

"I'm with you, Keaton," Easton said and then added, when Calvert looked like he was about to say something, "And no, I'm not avoiding anyone."

Sebastian wondered if that were true. He'd enjoyed his time with Easton, but the man was a legend in London. Something had to keep him from visiting, and with his personality, Sebastian doubted it was his adoring admirers.

"Thank you for connecting us with the club and also delivering my letter to the duchess," Calvert said.

Rose glared at him. "What are you up to?"

Her father frowned at her. "You don't have to know every-thing I do."

Sebastian chuckled. "I'm glad you are interested in forming some type of partnership. I will make sure your letter is delivered to the duchess."

Sebastian suspected Rose would be furious when she figured out what her father was up to. It had to do with sending ancient tablets she was keen on translating to London. Her father was determined to get her a season.

Easton stood. "I'll walk you to the carriage."

Sebastian said a final goodbye and walked with him to the line of carriages. As they approached, he said, "Thank you for letting me join you."

Easton laughed. "You seemed insistent that you wanted to be on any ship but the one you were supposed to be on. Will you see her when you return?"

He could feign confusion, but Easton wasn't a fool. "It's up to her."

"If she doesn't reciprocate your affection, move on. There is plenty of enjoyment to be had without the tender emotion wreaking havoc on your life," Easton advised before smacking him on the back. "Good luck, Devons."

"Thank you," he said.

Sebastian climbed into the carriage and leaned his head against the back of the seat, closing his eyes, both terrified and anxious to know where he and Diana stood. He'd completely fallen for her but would not live a life in the shadows with her and continue their affair, especially if she were determined to marry a lord such as Tremont.

The carriage came to a halt, and he stepped out. The *SS Stanton* would be his ride home to England. At least for this trip, he wouldn't share a cabin with anyone. The ship captain said they should expect to be back in England within twelve days. He took a deep breath. No matter what waited for him, it was time to go home.

Chapter Twenty-Eight

London—September 1850

DIANA SAT WITH her father-in-law in the sitting area of her townhouse. They both smiled as Robert raced from the room in search of some havoc to create. She and her son were once again settled in London. Diana had expected tears of joy when she returned from her adventure, but he'd acted as if she'd just left. Diana supposed that was the best way. He did adore her tales of all the ports.

This was the first time she'd been able to meet Wescott since her return, as he'd been away at his country estate. He'd only arrived in London a few days ago. The actual season had not started yet, but society was slowly returning to the city. Balls were beginning, and the government work was in full swing. Diana had been overwhelmed with invites to various events since her return. Everyone wanted to hear about her and Sebastian's adventures.

For the most part, she didn't mind all the questions except for one. When would Sebastian Devons return? Addie asked almost every time she saw her. She couldn't explain they'd fought, and he'd left the next day, only providing an impersonal goodbye missive. Instead, she'd guessed and told all who asked that he would return sometime in the fall.

"You have been spending significant time with Tremont."

She had. Arthur had been considerate and always willing to

escort her anywhere she liked.

"He seems to have a great deal of respect for you," Westcott added.

Diana shook her distracting thoughts away and smiled. "He is kind."

"If I were into making wagers, I would bet at some point he will propose."

Westcott studied her intently. Diana wondered what he was looking for. She squirmed under his gaze. "He has hinted at the possibility."

"Will he make you happy?"

That was a good question, Diana thought. Sebastian flashed in her mind. He was always in her thoughts, both while she was awake and sleeping. The man had left and not sent a single missive since. He should not be the one she was thinking about, especially since Tremont was doing everything one expected when being courted.

"Perhaps," she said.

Her father-in-law frowned. "Don't feel forced into marrying him."

She shrugged. "He does not lack anything I should want."

"You don't laugh or smile much with him. While society may say you must marry, I can assure you do not have to."

She smiled at Westcott, grateful to have such a wonderful father-in-law. "Robert and I are so lucky to have you in our lives."

"I made a promise to my son to make sure you are happy. I will do everything in my power to see that you are."

Diana had been thinking about Stuart a great deal. She always missed him, but in some moments the feeling would hit her and take her breath away. That had been happening often lately. In some absurd way, losing Sebastian also amplified the loss of Stuart. She sighed and Wescott's brows drew together in concern.

"I'm happy," she insisted, realizing she was causing him wor-ry.

He seemed skeptical. "Only marry if you think it will bring

you great joy. A lifetime is a long time to be unhappy. The older I get, the more I realize being miserable is rot."

Diana giggled. When she first met Westcott, she'd been terrified of the man. Not only was he a duke, but his bearing was formidable and of someone who shouldn't be messed with. Now, they were sitting here talking about happiness.

He tilted his head and smiled. "Now you seem happy."

She grinned back. "I was just thinking I'm most grateful that loving Stuart brought such a great father figure into my life."

The normally unaffectionate duke leaned over and squeezed her hand. "I'm grateful as well."

SEBASTIAN LISTENED TO his brother's butler announce him to those in the breakfast room. He heard Sophia gasp. He smiled as he stepped into the room. Malcolm rose and wrapped him in a tight hug. He'd decided to come straight to his brother's townhouse from the ship, needing a familiar face.

Sebastian laughed. "Brother, be careful. People might start to think you have a heart under your stuffy exterior."

"He has the biggest heart hidden behind all his arrogance," his wife said impishly.

Malcolm glowered at her, and she giggled loudly. Sebastian kissed her cheek and looked around. "Where are Penelope and the twins?"

"They are with their governess, being horribly punished," his brother said ruthlessly.

Sebastian's brows shot up in disbelief. "Truly?"

Sophia rolled her eyes. "If exploring the gardens with a basket of treats is a horrible punishment. That was your brother's idea of making sure they were disciplined for putting a hole in the wall at the foot of the stairs."

Some things didn't change. "Do I want the details?"

"Penelope taught them how to slide down the stairs on a pillow," Sophia said, unperturbed.

Chuckles erupted from Sebastian. "Pen might be my favorite of your children."

Malcolm rolled his eyes. "Sit. Join us. You and Lady Hensley are the talk of the town. You are supposed to host a lecture upon your return for the Historical Society for Female Curators."

Sebastian took a seat across from Sophia. "Am I?"

His brother and sister-in-law laughed at his question. He needed to visit Seely House and speak with Addie and the other board members. Perhaps, he would do that tomorrow. After breakfast, he planned to head to his townhouse and bathe, then call on Diana. He didn't want to wait any longer to understand where they stood.

"Even the paper today is talking about you and Lady Hensley."

"What are they saying?" he asked, sure it was some ridiculous drivel.

"All the papers are suggesting the same thing: send a rogue and the most proper lady in all of London abroad, and they will create the best grand tour of the decade."

Sebastian smiled, surprised it wasn't more salacious. "For once, the gossip sheets don't have something shocking to say."

His sister-in-law frowned. "What would they say? Lady Hensley's proper reputation could never be tarnished. She is almost a symbol to London society regarding how a lady should act. Also, everyone is all a titter because Lord Tremont followed her there. They keep saying a betrothal is imminent. Was his arrival as romantic as speculated?"

Sebastian felt as if the air had been knocked out of him. That couldn't be. Had his letter to her meant nothing? The crushing weight on his heart nearly undid him. He forced himself to smile. "Is he courting her?"

"Yes, they have been inseparable at the few balls and events that have been hosted since her return."

Sebastian couldn't believe it. He'd lost her to a man she held no desire for. Diana chose Tremont because he was a lord. He rose, his chair loudly sliding across the floor.

"I need to go the Den."

"The club can wait," Malcolm said, looking at him with concern.

Sebastian shook his head. "I only planned on stopping by briefly."

Sophia frowned. "Is something wrong?"

He needed to calm down. He forced another smile, hoping to ease their worry. "I'm fine. Merely anxious to resume life as it was."

Sebastian stumbled out of his brother's home. He had his answer about Diana. He would not dwell on it, he told himself. She made her choice, and he would go back to his life. A life enjoyed immensely before his entanglement with the most proper lady in London. He scoffed. A lady who was so much more complicated than what people saw. He'd once loved that about her, but right now, he wished she was not nearly as interesting.

Later in the evening, Sebastian sat in his office at the Den, drunk. He flipped his pocket watch open and closed. He'd put on a good show at the club tonight, laughing, joking, and entertaining all the lords with his stories about his and Diana's adventures. Diana's reputation was so pristine that no one had considered anything occurred between them.

Tossing the watch on his desk, he grabbed his brandy and took a large drink, savoring how it burned going down his throat. They'd all laughed about Tremont, an unadventurous sort, venturing so far away to see the woman he wanted to marry. Sebastian grinned through it all and even joked about Tremont being out of place in Livorno. In truth, that wasn't the case. He fit in fine with the rest of the lords and ladies touring the area.

A knock on the door interrupted his brooding thoughts. His butler Donahue entered. "Mr. Devons, there is a lady here who wants to speak with you."

Sebastian slammed his drink on the table and staggered to his feet. Diana had heard he was here. She'd come. "Let her in."

Donahue stepped aside, and the joy immediately burst. Before him stood Lilah, dressed in a provocative red gown. She smiled at him, her plump lips colored a vivid red to match her attire. He thought he loved this woman once and he felt nothing now. She walked to him, her hips swaying provocatively. "I've missed you, Devons."

He plopped back down in his chair, taking another large gulp of the brandy. "Have you?"

She pouted, leaning over his desk, making sure he had a clear view of her ample assets. "Don't be cross with me. I had to marry Lord Wesley. You know it is only you who I enjoy spending time with."

Fuck. How had Sebastian moped over this woman for so long? Her coquettish ways now annoyed him, yet at least she was here. That is more than he could say for the actual woman tormenting his thoughts.

She moved around the desk, trying to nudge her way between his legs. He stopped her with his hand. "Not now."

Annoyance flashed in her eyes. "Do you want me to beg?"

He didn't care what she thought, so he said nothing. She ran a hand up his thigh. "Lord Wesley has gone abroad indefinitely. Perhaps if not tonight, I could join you for the opera and we could become reacquainted. It would be like old times."

He wanted to laugh out loud hysterically. Emptiness filled him at the thought of doing anything with this woman. He nodded. She placed a lingering kiss on his cheek and sashayed out of his office. Sebastian took another sip of his drink. Maybe nothing was acceptable. It was fucking better than the pain that wouldn't ease in his heart.

Chapter Twenty-Nine

DIANA THANKED LORD Belmont for the dance as he escorted her off the floor. Lord Halethorpe's ballroom was packed. Diana smiled and greeted several acquaintances as she made her way back to her aunt and Arthur. She was still adjusting to all the interest from the success of her and Sebastian's columns. The first couple of questions on Sebastian threw her, but with each one, the pain at hearing his name became less and less.

The trip generated more interest about the Historical Society for Female Curators, as Addie suspected it would. The plan was to have a small grand opening at Seely House when she and Sebastian did their talk. The Le Conquet manuscript exhibit would be revealed at that time. Diana had reached an agreement with Haggerty that they would display the manuscripts when he wasn't studying them. He'd been reluctant to keep them at Seely House, but Sarah and Lisbeth amazed him with their diligent care of artifacts.

The London Society of Antiquaries boldly approached Haggerty to display with them instead, and he told them he had no interest, delighting Addie. Diana was actively lining up additional displays. While the manuscripts were a great start, they needed one grand exhibit. None of them had determined what that would be yet. She reminded herself they had time. They were only having a small opening when Sebastian returned.

Earlier in the week, Diana and Addie had met with Monroe about announcing a leisure cruise for ladies. They'd finalized their partnership with the captain for the first cruise the following year. While Monroe may have been initially skeptical of Addie's idea, he was now all in. A smile formed on Diana's face at the thought of Monroe taking so many ladies on a cruise.

When she reached her Aunt Winifred and Arthur, Diana almost laughed out loud at the relief she saw on both their faces. Since the journey back to London, Arthur had started to suspect Aunt Winifred wasn't a fan of his and was doing everything in his power to convince her she should be. Diana more than once wanted to tell him not to try so hard but didn't want to offend him.

She smiled at them. Tonight, Diana felt optimistic, and for the first time since returning to London, the ache clinging to her wasn't as pronounced. Even if she wanted to make more of Sebastian's short note, his lack of any correspondence since then was sufficient evidence he'd simply been caught up in the moment in Livorno when he asked to court her. While she hated her mother's explanation, she'd been right. Diana hadn't held Sebastian's interest.

"Diana, I was telling your aunt that at some point we will have to figure out how to get your mother back out in society."

Her mother's return had stirred up gossip in London but there seemed to be no indications she would be welcomed back among the *ton*. While she didn't care about her mother's social status, she did worry about the effect all the gossip about her mother was having on Clara and Henry. Both her siblings were reluctant to be around her. Diana didn't blame them.

Her mother had been staying with her and wasn't the easiest person to deal with. She hoped her house would be ready soon, but Diana suspected she was intentionally dragging her feet. Clara was livid she was still at Diana's townhouse and worried their mother planned not to leave. Diana reassured her more than once that wouldn't happen. She still carried the scars on her back from her mother's discipline.

Her aunt snorted. "She is blacklisted. That won't change."

"A good amount of time has passed, and we can't blame her for what were ultimately your father's decisions."

"Why would you think that?" Diana asked.

Arthur frowned. "Because the man is the final decision maker in a marriage."

Diana's mouth dropped open. Arthur flushed. "Of course, it would be with a great deal of input from his wife."

Aunt Winifred sighed. "I think I will fetch some punch."

"I will retrieve it for you," Arthur volunteered.

Her aunt smiled sweetly, and he was off. She fanned herself. "How do you tolerate him?"

"We can't blame him for believing Mother needs another chance. He barely knows her."

Aunt Winifred gave her a pointed look, but before Diana could respond, Addie appeared in front of them. "You will never guess the news I have. Devons is back in London"

Shock pinged through Diana. How could one's stomach flutter and drop at the same time? Arthur returned, handing Aunt Winifred her punch.

"He has been back for two days, and that annoying man hasn't called on us at Seely House."

"He is probably resting from his return trip. I'm sure he will make an appearance when he's ready," Diana said, ignoring the pounding of her heart.

Addie beamed at him. "No, he—"

She was interrupted when the butler announced, "Mr. Sebastian Devons."

The room went quiet, and everyone turned to the entryway of the ballroom. He took her breath away. His dark-black hair and dark eyes perused the room, and she insanely wondered if he was looking for her. *Stop it,* she told herself. It had been nothing more than a tryst. Still, if it was something so blasé, they could be friends, couldn't they?

Arthur moved next to her, placing her hand on his arm. She saw Sebastian focus on something, and Diana looked to see what it was. Shock rippled through her as she realized it was Lady Wesley. A flirtatious smile flitted across his face as he approached her. Diana tore her gaze away before he reached the lady, not wanting to watch anymore. She was so angry. Angry, not because he was flirting, but because Lady Wesley didn't deserve any of his attention. Why would he go to her?

"Travel seems to agree with him. Should we go say hello?" Addie asked.

The thought horrified Diana. Arthur stepped in and unknowingly saved her. "Lady Hensley has promised me this waltz."

She smiled. Addie nodded. "He will probably be engaged with all his adoring admirers tonight anyway."

Diana forced herself to keep smiling and allowed Arthur to guide her onto the dance floor. She would not look back to where Sebastian was standing. The waltz began, and she kept her attention on Arthur and the dance. As they moved across the dance floor with the other dancers, she kept her expression blank, but her mind was rampant with thoughts of Sebastian.

He had his own life to live, and if that included Lady Wesley, it was none of her business. Still, annoyance sizzled in her that he would allow himself to be used by her. Arthur escorted Diana off the dance floor, her eyes met Sebastian's. She forced herself to smile. His eyes raked over her, and without a smile, he nodded at her before turning back to Lady Wesley. Yes, waiting to decide on a courtship had been the best choice.

SEBASTIAN WAITED IN the drawing room of Diana's townhouse while the butler went to determine if she was available. He'd regretted not speaking with her last night. She'd openly acknowledged him, and all he'd given her was a curt nod. He hadn't been prepared to see her with Tremont or how familiar the lord had become with her. Still, Sebastian's actions were rude.

"Sebastian!" Young Robert exclaimed before shutting the door, seemingly hiding from someone.

He suspected it was a nanny. "Good day, Robert."

"I heard your voice."

A smile formed on his face. "We have only met twice, and you remember me?"

"I like you," he said, beaming before peeking out the door.

"Are you not supposed to be in here?"

The young boy wrinkled his nose. "My grandmother and my governess are looking for me."

He still couldn't believe the duchess convinced Diana she needed to return to England. The woman was awful for what she had done to Diana and her sister. Heels clicked on the foyer floor, and Robert's eyes widened. Sebastian raised his fingers to his mouth, shushing him. "Hide behind the curtains."

Seconds later, the door was thrown open, and the Duchess of Claremore stood before him looking as elegant and perfect as ever. He bowed, and her eyes narrowed as she nodded back at him.

"Can I help you with something, Mr. Devons?"

"I was hoping to meet with your daughter."

The woman entered the room, looking around. He asked, "Is there something you are searching for?"

Her lips pressed together in annoyance before she said, "My grandson is not behaving. He is hiding. Did he enter this room?"

Sebastian shook his head, "Not since I have been here."

She walked around the room. Anger emanated from her. Why did she care so much about her grandson's behavior? She'd only just met him. Sebastian suspected she was a woman who liked to break spirits. He hoped she wasn't staying with Diana long.

Finally, she turned back to him. "She is likely with her betrothed."

The words shocked Sebastian. He blinked rapidly, digesting her statement. Slowly, he said, "Betrothed?"

She looked at him with disdain. "Yes, Lord Tremont. They are keeping it quiet for now."

Diana had made her choice. It wasn't gossip but fact. He knew he shouldn't be angry, but he was furious. He took a deep breath. "Can you please let Lady Hensley know I called on her?"

Her eyes raked over him, her mouth twisting in distaste. Sebastian stared back at her, unflinching. Finally, she looked away. "I will let her know."

Later in the evening, Sebastian sat in the main hall of the Den. He was drunk but happy. He didn't need anyone. Just this club. He'd killed himself making this the most prestigious gentlemen's club in all of London. Fuck love! He took another sip of his brandy when Celeste appeared before him.

"We have a meeting, Devons. Can you please follow me?"

He took another sip of his brandy. "I don't remember a meeting. Change it to tomorrow."

She fixed him with a glare. "Now, Devons."

"Oh…you have done it now," a lord said.

While he had been away Celeste had done well as the host of the Den. The men who frequented the establishment regarded her with a mixture of fear, awe, and adoration. Sebastian shouldn't be surprised by her success. She'd excelled at managing the tables. He didn't want anyone to think he didn't respect her or her position, so he followed her without another word, causing more laughter.

They made their way up the stairs to the office spaces, passing hers and entering his. He stepped in behind her, running his fingers through his hair. She pointed to his seat at his desk, motioning for him to sit.

Sighing, he plopped into his chair, suspecting he was going to get a lecture. She was quiet for a moment but eventually said, "You told me when I started here we were not to be drunk around the guests. Drinking was fine as long as we could do it without becoming slushy."

"Your point?"

"You're drunk."

She wasn't wrong. He'd been drunk since this afternoon. He could lie, but he didn't. "You are correct. I won't go back downstairs."

She nodded. "I think that would be best."

"You have done an excellent job here, Celeste. I'm proud of you."

Her cheeks turned a rosy color at the compliment. He chuckled. "Say thank you."

She sighed. "Thank you."

Celeste had done so well that Sebastian decided he wanted her to take on a permanent role as host. "I know you think I'm in my cups, but I would like to speak with you about making your role as host more permanent. Not every night but a few nights a week."

She stared at him in shock but then frowned, shaking her head. "We will talk tomorrow."

He laughed, knowing she wanted him to remember what he was talking about. "As long as you say yes, tomorrow is fine."

She smiled and walked to the door but turned back, frowning. "Are you all right?"

He sighed. "Of course."

She studied him. "I have never seen you get so drunk with our guests."

"It won't happen again."

"But—"

"Good night, Celeste."

She sighed. "Good night, Devons."

Chapter Thirty

DIANA MADE HER way up the stairs to her desk in the Seely House. She smiled, still amazed she was a board member of the Historical Society for Female Curators. Stuart would have been delighted that she was part of this effort. As she entered the office, she came to an abrupt stop. Sebastian sat with Addie and Lisbeth in the sitting area, looking at a letter.

The package in her hands fell to the ground, causing them to glance at her. Diana flushed. Sebastian picked the package up and handed it back to her. She studied his face. He smiled, but it was a smile one would use when acknowledging someone they barely knew. It gutted her. "Diana."

"Devons," she said.

"I'm glad you are here. We may have an opportunity to one-up the London Society of Antiquaries," Addie said.

Diana looked at Sebastian's impassively polite face one more time before taking a seat in the sitting area. She asked, "How?"

Addie and Sebastian grinned at each other. A flash of envy shot through Diana at how comfortable they were with each other. It didn't help that Addie looked stunning today. She was dressed in a turquoise gown that highlighted her black hair and vibrant blue eyes. Married and single men adored her. She glanced at Sebastian, wondering if he ever had a liaison with her. It was none of her business, Diana reminded herself.

She sighed, causing everyone to look in her direction. "I'm sorry it has been a long day."

"There is talk about you and Tremont's lovely waltz last night."

Diana's eyes darted to Sebastian and his impassively polite face hadn't changed. She had the desire to rile him up but wasn't sure she knew how. She turned back to Addie. "Tremont is an adept dancer."

Addie laughed and then refocused her attention on Devons. "This man has brought us the best news."

The longer Diana sat there with the two of them, the more annoyed she became. She arched a brow. "Really?"

"During my follow-on travels, I traveled with Thomas Easton, and he introduced me to the Calverts. I know you had hoped to meet them in Livorno about a potential partnership. I mentioned this to them. They are interested. They know the duchess—"

"Lisbeth, please."

"They know Lisbeth well. Benjamin Calvert has proposed an option for an exhibit."

Addie, unable to contain her excitement, clapped. "They offered to allow us to display ancient stone tablets that Benjamin Calvert suspects is a love story. Ladies will love it."

"What do they want in exchange? Can we afford it?" Diana asked.

Lisbeth smirked. "Benjamin would like me to host his daughter for the season."

Sebastian shook his head. "I met Rose. She has no interest in visiting London."

Diana forced herself not to frown at his familiarness with the woman.

Lisbeth smirked. "No, she would rather be anywhere else, I assume. The tablets have not been thoroughly studied or translated. Rose will want to be the one to do that. Benjamin will use them to entice her to London. She will be furious with her father."

Sebastian laughed. "That is sneaky of Calvert."

The duchess was quiet for a moment but finally said, "Benjamin's wife passed away before I met him, but he used to always say she held big plans for Rose when it came to the London season. I think he wants to make sure he fulfills her dream."

"When will she and the tablets arrive?"

Lisbeth studied the letter again. "I think the tablets should be here within the week, and I bet Rose is not far behind."

"Is Rose a family friend?"

Lisbeth's face became shuttered. "Something like that. Rose is twenty-eight. She will come because of the tablets and attend a few balls to appease her father, but I doubt she has any plans to marry. I do think we should invite her to be part of our club."

"Are you sure you don't mind hosting her?" Diana asked.

Lisbeth shrugged. "I adore Benjamin. He was like a father figure to me when I was younger. I would host her for a season even without the tablets."

Addie nodded excitedly. "These tablets may be perfect for the grand exhibit. The next topic we need to discuss is the talk we are hosting about the leisure cruise. Can we be prepared in a week?"

They all looked at Sebastian since he had only returned to London a few days ago. He shrugged nonchalantly. "That's fine. Whatever Diana believes is best works for me."

"We wrote the column as partners. I would like your thoughts too."

He smiled at her politely. "Within the week is fine."

That smile was starting to annoy Diana. Addie, oblivious, nodded. "Perfect. I think we will have each of you describe your favorite ports, and then we will open it up to the audience. The interest in the leisure cruise is at an all-time high. The first cruise dates should be announced towards the end of the season. The talk will only make ladies want to sign up more. Can we be ready by next Tuesday?"

"I think so," Diana said.

Sebastian nodded and stood. "Really, whatever you think,

Addie. Just send me a missive, and I will be there."

"Where are you going? You've only just arrived. I want to hear about Thomas Easton," Addie complained.

He held his hands up as if it was out of his control. "I'm late for another meeting."

Diana wanted to throw something at him. Where was the Sebastian Devons she spent two months with?

SEBASTIAN SAT IN his theater box as his brother glowered at him from his own box. He suspected Malcolm was unhappy with his choice of companion. It wasn't as if Lilah were the only one with him. There were others in his box, including Celeste. Still, he knew they were causing a scene because Lilah was practically in his lap.

She giggled and rubbed her breasts against his arm. He felt nothing for her. It was a void of emptiness. Crazily, he wanted to feel something, anything. It was as if Diana had somehow broken him. Lilah whispered in his ear that she couldn't wait for later tonight. Celeste, behind them, sighed dramatically as if trying to warn him how bad of a choice the lady was.

Apparently, while he was away, Lord Wesley had been caught with an innocent young lady in his bed. She hadn't even had her first season. To avoid the scandal, he'd fled to America. Since then, Lady Wesley had been openly enjoying a plethora of lovers. She ran her hand over the top of his thigh. He sipped his drink, not engaging but not stopping her either.

His gaze moved back to Malcolm and Sophia. His brother's expression was murderous. Sophia whispered in his ear frantically. Sebastian suspected she was telling him everyone was watching. Malcolm, the marquess, wouldn't give a damn. He had the title to do as he liked. A twinge of guilt ebbed through him that he was thinking such harsh thoughts about his brother.

Sebastian sighed and turned away from him, focusing on the empty stage. When the hell would the show start? Tonight's opera was a drama about a sordid love affair between a prince and a farmer's daughter. Sebastian wasn't sure what made it tawdry. He imagined it was the different classes. He smirked at the ridiculousness of it all and took another sip of his drink.

Increased chatter drew his eyes to a box where opera watchers were arriving. His eyes narrowed as he realized it was Diana and Tremont. His stomach clenched at the sight. Yesterday, it had taken everything in him to appear unbothered at seeing Diana. He needed to get past this. There had to be an end to the madness of his emotions for her.

Lilah ran her hand down his thigh again. Sebastian forced himself to focus on her. He grinned wickedly at her, and she fluttered her eyelashes back at him. It seemed impossible, but Lilah somehow managed to scoot even closer to him. The play started but didn't hold his interest. His eyes sought out Tremont's box. Even in the dimly lit theater, Sebastian could tell Diana was staring at him.

Lilah leaned over and, with her lips practically touching his ear, whispered, "I've missed you."

He reminded himself that Diana had made her choice. He was free to do as he liked. Sebastian looked at her again. She still watched him. Lilah continued to whisper in his ear, but he had no idea what she was saying. He was too distracted by Diana.

Suddenly, she was on her feet, followed by Tremont, but she shook her head insistently. Tremont sat back down, and then she was gone. Sebastian stood. "Excuse me."

He made his way to the hallway Diana entered. He caught a flash of a skirt entering a side room and briskly headed in the same direction. The room had no door. It was more of an alcove than anything, but it was private.

"Diana."

She turned and fury flashed in her eyes. "Why are you with her?"

He stepped back, shocked at her angry tone. She marched up to him. "Of all the people to bring back into your life, why her?"

Anger flared in him, and it had nothing to do with Lilah. "You are here with Tremont. What does it matter if I'm having a tryst? You are to be married. I don't think you can dictate to me who I take as a lover."

She shook her head. Sebastian wasn't sure in response to what. She turned away from him. Again, he questioned, "What does it matter, Diana? We have both moved on. Why do you care?"

Diana spun back around. "Because I care about you. That viper hurt you, and you choose her of all people to bring back into your life."

He said nothing, and she added angrily, "Whether she is a tryst or more, you deserve someone who respects you."

Her eyes started to water, and Sebastian stayed quiet. She took a deep breath and looked up at him. "I'm your friend. That is why it matters."

"My friend?" he said skeptically.

She marched up to him and poked him hard on the chest. "No matter how things ended, I will only and always want the best for you. That woman who hurt you so deeply is not it."

"She is not the only woman to hurt me."

His words hung between them. Confusion flashed across her face. "What are you insinuating?"

The sound of frantic footsteps coming closer caused Diana to step back as Tremont rounded the corner. His eyes bounced back and forth between Diana and Sebastian.

"Diana, is anything amiss?"

She studied Sebastian for a moment. "No. I ran into Mr. Devons. We were conversing about his return trip."

Tremont moved to her, offering her his arm. "How about we fetch you something to drink?"

Diana accepted, and a polite smile appeared on her face. "Good evening, Mr. Devons."

Later in the night, Sebastian sat at his desk at the Den, playing with his pocket watch and drinking brandy. Diana and Tremont kept appearing in his mind. They were perfectly suited for one another. The gossip sheets had it right. They would make a perfect peerage match.

His door bounced open, and Malcolm stomped in. His eyes flicked around as if he thought he would catch Lilah lurking about. Sebastian had dropped an unhappy Lilah off at her townhouse after the theater. She'd expected to return with him to the Den, but Sebastian didn't have it in him to entertain her.

He wanted something he could never have, and it tore him up. His brother slammed his hand down on his desk. "What the hell is wrong with you?"

Anger boiled in Sebastian at his brother's arrogant tone. "Don't start with me."

"I will tell you when you are fucking up. Get a hold of yourself, man. She is not worth another moment of misery."

"Do you think it is so easy to forget her?"

His brother glowered at him and marched to his side of the desk, grabbing his brandy and finishing it. Sebastian rose to retrieve more, and Malcolm stopped him.

"Remove your hands from my person," Sebastian growled.

"She is not worth it!"

Sebastian grabbed Malcolm by the front of his shirt and slammed him against the bookshelf. "She is all I can think of. Don't tell me what her worth is. You are a fucking lord. My entire life I have never envied your title or resented you. Not once did I care that I was the bastard, and you were the son born within wedlock."

Malcolm grabbed his shirt and spun them around, slamming Sebastian into the bookshelf. "Enough!"

He shook his head and hated himself because tears pricked his eyes. "Right now, at this moment, I would do anything to have your title. I want it so badly it is destroying me."

His brother leaned his forehead against his and whispered,

"Stop this. She isn't worth this madness."

They stood like that for a moment, brother and brother. Their angry embrace turned to comfort. Malcolm pulled Sebastian closer to him. Eventually, Malcolm stepped back, giving him space to move back to his chair.

"It isn't Lilah."

Malcolm's brows shot up. He took a seat across from Sebastian. "Start at the beginning."

Chapter Thirty-One

THE DOOR TO the drawing room opened and Diana tensed. Her mother entered the room in a swirl of light-blue silk and lace. Even with the streaks of gray in her hair, the duchess's looks could rival any of the most talked about ladies of the season. She had the same beautiful but untouchable ethereal appearance as Diana's sister. The *ton* had given Clara the name Ice Princess during her time on the marriage mart. She hated it and, in truth, didn't deserve it. Their mother, on the other hand, was never swayed by emotion.

Diana poured them both tea. She was nervous. Today, Clara would be visiting them. Henry still wanted nothing to do with their mother, but Clara had shocked Diana and requested to see her before she retired to her country estate.

"Is Henry joining us?"

Diana shook her head. "He couldn't get away from his studies."

The only sign her mother was displeased was the pursing of her lips. "I can't imagine why Clara would like to call on me."

Anger surged within Diana. Didn't she want to see her daughter? "She is your child."

Her mother took a dainty sip of her tea. "She shamed our family by marrying that man."

"He has been an amazing husband to your daughter. She

would likely not be here if she ended up with the man you did your best to sell her to."

Her mother scoffed. "How did I raise two daughters who are so dramatic?"

The duchess needed to go to the country. She couldn't stay here. Diana didn't want Robert around her.

"When will the country house be ready?"

Her mother shrugged. "I'm sure in a few weeks."

"I would like you gone within a week."

Fire did flash in her mother's eyes then. "You all judge me so harshly. I made you a wonderful match. Perhaps even a love match, and you didn't have to slum it like your sister."

Diana placed her teacup on the table in front of her. It rattled. "Do not take credit for anything that occurred between Stuart and me. You chose him because he would inherit a dukedom. We found love. It had nothing to do with you."

Any further discussion on the topic was halted when the door of the drawing room was opened by her butler. Clara entered the room and frowned. She likely sensed the tension emanating in the space. "Diana, is everything fine?"

She nodded and Clara walked to the sitting area. Her gaze darted back and forth between Diana and their mother. At that moment, Diana wished she hadn't allowed her mother to return to England with her. This woman who always caused pain would be just that for Clara. Her sister sat and poured herself a cup of tea. The room was deafeningly quiet.

Finally, Clara said, "Hello, Mother."

"Good afternoon, Clara," their mother said, disdain dripping from her words.

Diana wanted to take her sister from the room. Protect her from this woman who still very much thought Clara made a poor choice by choosing a decent man over a title.

"Do you not have anything to say?" Clara said, her voice trembling slightly.

Their mother took a sip of her tea. "How is Henry? When

may I see him?"

After all these years and the pain she'd caused Clara, that was her first question. It shouldn't have been a shock to Diana. Their brother was the duke. She probably hoped to somehow work her way into his good graces. Her mother didn't realize Henry wanted nothing to do with her. He respected Clara's husband too much to ever allow someone who hated commoners in his life.

More importantly, Sam and Clara had shown him love. Something none of the Duke and Duchess of Claremore's children had known from parental figures.

Clara didn't flinch, smiling broadly instead. "Henry is doing wonderfully. I can't speak for him. He is the only one who will decide when he wants to see you. He did receive your letters."

"Good. I hope to help guide him with the estate."

Diana and Clara both looked at each other in shock. Diana shook her head. "Clara's husband helps him."

"A commoner."

Clara's eyes sparked. "My husband is the one who helped make the dukedom healthy again."

Her mother glared at her. "It wasn't ever unhealthy."

"Mother, you tried to wed me to a monster because you and Father were in so much debt," Clara said quietly.

"Why must you bring up such things? He had a great family and would have never hurt you if you married."

Clara rose and smiled at Diana. "Thank you for arranging this. It was right for me to come."

Diana stood as well. "I'm sorry."

"No, I mean it. I needed this."

Her sister departed and Diana turned back to her mother. "Within a week, you need to depart for the country."

"You would banish me because I don't approve of your sis-ter's marriage to a commoner?"

"I'm not banishing you. I'm choosing not to have you in my life. You were a cruel mother, and I will not have my child around you. My son will grow up valuing people for more than their titles."

Her mother scoffed. "And what will you teach him? That it is acceptable to associate with people like Sebastian Devons? Did you read the paper this morning? Both your club and his association with it are being questioned."

Diana frowned. "What are you talking about?"

Her mother grabbed the paper next to her and dropped it on the table between them. Diana picked it up and read the title.

Is a Club Owned by a Rake where Ladies should Spend Their Time?

Diana continued to read and gasped. The paper insinuated the club was used by Sebastian for nefarious reasons. It also suggested not even Diana's title could save it and she risked ruin herself if she continued to be associated with the Historical Society for Female Curators. A caricature of a proper lady holding on to several other ladies who were being pulled off a cliff by a rakish devil finished the article.

"You didn't think you would succeed with such a silly, pointless club, did you?"

Fury flared in her. Diana was done with her mother. "By next Wednesday, you must be on your way."

The duchess didn't say another word and walked out. Diana stared down at the paper, concern filling her because she knew gossip had the ability to end the club before it launched.

⟫⟫⟩✕⟨⟪⟪

SEBASTIAN SAT IN the carriage with his brother who scowled at him. He sighed and leaned his head against the back of the seat. He'd told Malcolm the whole sordid tale about losing his heart to Diana. His brother had been outraged that the lady discarded him so quickly for Tremont.

After their talk, Malcolm insisted Sebastian stay at his townhouse. He'd woken up and joined his brother and his family to discover the article that put the Historical Society for Female Curators on the cusp of failure. The damning words suggested he was somehow using the club to lure ladies into scandalous activities and Diana was the only thing stopping him, but she eventually would be dragged into his nefarious deeds. It was all lies.

"You should let the bloody club implode," Malcolm bit out.

Sebastian opened his eyes and glanced at his brother. "Diana is not the only one that is part of the venture. Addie is our friend. We can't let her fail."

"I don't think you are asking me to do this for Addie."

Sebastian wasn't sure why he didn't want to witness the club go under. Yes, it was partially because of Diana, but his desire to see them succeed was bigger than that. He pulled out his pocket watch, flipping it open and closed, pondering why it bothered him so much that gossipers tried to destroy the Historical Society for Female Curators.

"They have worked hard to make their club successful. No one should take that from them because they are women. It reminds me of when we first started the Den and some of the lords tried to convince others not to frequent our establishment. They'd done it for the simple reason they found it unseemly for the by-blow and the heir of a marquess to partner with each other. In their eyes, I should have been cast out and never acknowledged."

Malcolms scowled. "Our father raised us to always support each other."

Sebastian read the words inside the back of the pocket watch. *The measure of a man is defined by his actions.* He snapped it shut and stuffed it in a pocket. "He did. No matter how unconvention-al our family was, we were lucky to be raised with so much support and encouragement. The Historical Society for Female Curators has only me and now you. These ladies are being challenged because they aren't the right sex. It's wrong."

An amused expression flitted across Malcolm's face. "My brother, the advocate for women."

Perhaps he was. He certainly didn't like that gossipers were trying to stop them before they even started. "Thank you for doing this, and thank you for last night. I'm sorry—"

"Don't. You will never owe me an apology. Those words are never needed. I love you, and I would hate it if you despised me because of the title."

Sebastian grimaced. "I don't. I was drunk."

"She is not better than you and she is not worthy of you if she chose a title over love."

Diana had never said those words, but Sebastian didn't want to talk about it. He didn't want Malcolm to be angry when they showed up at Seely House. "I'm going to rest my eyes for a moment."

Malcolm sighed.

A short time later, they followed Harrison up the steps to the office in Seely House. All the board members were already there. His eyes met Diana's and worry filled her face. He clenched his fists as the urge to comfort her overwhelmed him.

"I was wondering if you would appear. We may be done for," Addie said, sounding defeated.

She looked tired as she stood rubbing her eyes and leaning against a desk.

"We can get through this," Lisbeth said, choosing to be optimistic, shocking Sebastian.

Of all the ladies, she seemed the most pragmatic to him. He didn't expect that. Sebastian ran his fingers through his hair and sighed. "I think I have a solution."

Addie motioned everyone over to the sitting area. The five board members sat on the two sofas and Sebastian and Malcolm took the wingback chairs.

"I would like to introduce you all to my brother, the Marquess of Derry."

Addie looked at Malcolm and Sebastian. "How is Derry going

to help us?"

Sebastian continued. "While he is still part owner in my club, the Den, he is a peer and, as a partner, could provide the Historical Society for Female Curators a level of respectability I can't. I've convinced him to partner in the club and use the same agreement I signed to make sure the board remains in control."

Lisbeth frowned and glanced at Malcolm. "Why would you do that?"

Malcolm's eyes flitted to Diana and back to the duchess. He shrugged. "My brother says this club is a worthwhile endeavor."

Addie beamed at Sebastian. His eyes flitted back to Diana who was frowning at him intently.

"You will hand over ownership of the club to the Marquess of Derry?" Sarah asked.

Sebastian nodded, and the group fell quiet. Shockingly, Diana said, "No."

Everyone's eyes flew to her. She flushed but still shook her head. "Why should we bow to these bullies? There are very few men who would have supported our endeavor and done so much for us. We can't simply end our association with Devons because of some article. It would make us no better than them. We are better than that. This board may be comprised of all ladies, but Mr. Devons has been our partner and our champion. As the board of the Historical Society for Female Curators, we should not turn our backs on him."

Sebastian stared at her in shock, and he suspected the rest of the ladies felt the same way as no one said anything. Malcolm said, "I promise I will be as dedicated as my brother. I have given him my word."

"Thank you, Lord Derry, but my vote is no. We started this with Devons. Fail or succeed, we end it with him," Diana said.

An impressed smirk filled Addie's face. "You are right. I vote no, too."

Esme said. "I agree."

"Me as well."

Lisbeth sighed and nodded.

Diana turned back to him and Malcolm. "We do not accept your plan."

Malcolm guffawed and everyone's eyes jerked to him. He held his hand up apologetically as he tried to compose himself. "I'm sorry. This is not at all how I planned this going today."

Addie shook her head. "You aren't alone."

Diana's gaze swung back to Sebastian. "We still should do our talk tomorrow. If we don't, they will think we are worried about the article."

Sebastian was stunned by the board's willingness to risk everything by continuing to partner with him."

"Diana—"

"I refuse to be forced to do anything because of what is printed in the gossip sheets. We should not change our plans. Will you be ready for our talk tomorrow?"

Even though he was still nursing his wounded heart, he couldn't help but smile back at her, impressed. "I will be ready."

She nodded. "Good, then it is settled."

Chapter Thirty-Two

DIANA STOOD WITH Sebastian, listening from the second floor of Seely House, as visitors made their way into the largest exhibit room.

"Are you ready for this?" he asked.

She was. The blasted article infuriated her and made her more determined than ever to see this club succeed with their existing partner. It enraged her that Devons thought they would give him up. That she would. He mattered so much to her. It took everything in her to not let the words fly out of her mouth. She smiled back at him. "More than ready."

"You are becoming quite the rabble-rouser."

Laughter escaped Diana at the absurd statement. She did not incite or cause trouble. Proper ladies didn't do that. Sebastian smirked at her, amused. "You really don't see it, but I do. You are standing up for me and thumbing your nose at society."

"Hmm…perhaps I am. No one should tell the Historical Society for Female Curators who they can partner with."

Silence fell between them, but eventually Diana said, "I wanted to apologize for my harsh words at the theater."

He shook his head. "You were right. I'm not seeing Lilah. It was a bad choice. One of many I have been making of late."

Diana had the desire to ask more but was interrupted when Esme asked, "Do you think they are here for the talk or because of the awful article?"

Lisbeth joined them, rolling her eyes. "What do you think? The column was popular but not that popular. They are here to gossip."

Addie appeared. "Are we ready?"

Diana glanced at Sebastian. Her heart did somersaults. The man was still so handsome. Standing this close to him, she had the desire to touch him. He smiled at her. The connection that she'd been trying to convince herself only existed on the trip bounced back and forth between them. Did he not feel it?

Diana nodded, and Addie motioned for everyone to start moving down the stairs. As they entered the large exhibit room, the buzz of chattering stopped. Diana tilted her chin up. She wouldn't let society dictate what became of her, Sebastian, or the club. She glanced around and was shocked that there were as many men as ladies.

Her eyes narrowed on a few who were members of the London Society of Antiquaries. In a far back corner, she spotted Lord Hawley. She turned to tell Addie, but she was already standing at the front of the room. She seemed oblivious to her husband's presence.

Nerves filled Diana, but as she looked closer, she realized more than a third of the room contained people that Diana, Sebastian, or the club would call friends or family. Their last-minute request for support hadn't gone unanswered. As she and Sebastian reached the front of the room, her eyes landed on others whose faces revealed disdain and contempt. What was it about London society that seemed to make lords and ladies thrive off cruelty?

Addie smiled at the crowd. "Thank you all for coming. Today, we will be talking about a leisure cruise Lady Hensley and Mr. Devons took. The Historical Society for Female Curators is currently working with the passenger vessel company to design a grand tour for women."

"Do you think that is the best idea with the existing reputation of your club?" a man asked.

Addie smiled wider. "I don't know what you mean. Now—"

"Are you planning to pretend you haven't seen the article?" Lady Dessup snickered from her chair. The crowd laughed.

Diana tilted her chin up, unwilling to allow this. "We have reviewed the article and the highly inaccurate statements in it. The board of this club has worked hard over the last few months to get the Historical Society for Female Curators off the ground. Mr. Devons has been by our side the whole way. The writers and source of that article can write as much inflammatory drivel as they like, but I challenge anyone in this room to point to anything factual. Additionally, I would ask that you judge us on what we provide, not speculation."

"Then partner with less unseemly characters," a man taunted from the back of the room.

Sebastian appeared prepared to take over, but Diana stopped him with her hand. "I don't know what you mean, sir. I once read that the measure of a man is defined by his actions and based on that belief, I must say there is no finer of a man than Mr. Devons. He has been an ideal partner and treats our club and board members with a level of respect you are lacking."

The room exploded into laughter. Diana grinned and looked at Sebastian. Shock flickered across his face. Diana wondered if it was because she'd used the words from his pocket watch. Their eyes held each other's for a moment but then Sebastian replaced his shock with a smile. He looked out into the crowd. "It seems today Lady Hensley will be my champion."

More than half the room applauded. Sebastian continued. "I'm honored. I hold her in the highest regard. I would ask you to allow this club to get its bearings and then decide if it should exist or not. Do this not based on gossip but on the value and enjoyment of what they provide."

More applause echoed through the room. As the room became quiet, Addie asked, "If there aren't any other questions, we shall continue with our actual talk about Lady Hensley and Mr.

Devons's leisure cruise."

"I have one," a man said from the back of the room.

"That is the vice president of the London Society of Antiquaries," Sarah whispered to Diana. She would know as her father was the president.

Addie smiled at him. "Yes, what is it?"

"What is the purpose of this club? A club for antiquities already exists. Why do we need another one?"

Addie frowned at him. "Let's discuss the leisure cruise. Afterward, our first exhibit will be available."

"I agree with Harston. Why do women need an antiquities club when they can attend the exhibits put on by the London Society of Antiquaries?" another man yelled from the back.

"Not all women only want to attend exhibits. Some of us want to be hands-on in the study of history and artifacts," Sarah said.

The room grew silent. Harston added, "It isn't right, or the way things should be done."

Annoyance flashed across Addie's face. Before she could say anything, her husband, Lord Hawley, of all people, said, "Harston, one would think you are afraid of what their club might accomplish."

Addie's eyes widened. Harston sputtered. "Of course not. They would never be able to compare to the London Society of Antiquaries."

Diana couldn't believe Lord Hawley defended them, and from Addie's reaction, neither could she. Hawley shrugged. "Then I see no need for you to question why they are starting the club. There are enough antiquities in the world for both clubs to coexist. Am I wrong?"

Harston shook his head but looked angry that Hawley had taken away his thunder.

"Wonderful. Lady Hensley and Mr. Devons, I'm looking forward to your talk and the follow-on exhibit. May we continue?" Hawley asked.

Sebastian smiled at him, amused. Diana stared at him in amazement. This man, whom Diana had only met once and at the time he'd been furious about their club had shut down his colleague for them. Sebastian lifted a brow. "Shall you start, my lady?"

Diana nodded and smiled at the crowd. "We will begin with our first port, Le Conquet."

SEBASTIAN STOOD ON the second-floor walkway that overlooked the main hall of the Den, watching men mingle in the packed room. It was a busy night for the club. All the game tables were full and those not playing were milling about, engaged in lively conversations. Sebastian loved this club. When he stood up here and saw the scale of what he and Malcolm had accomplished, it took his breath away.

They'd first started a tavern catering to the elite crowd, but Sebastian had wanted something grander. He and Malcolm first envisioned the Den when they visited the location that would become their club. It had been a night of debauchery hosted by the previous, now deceased, Marquess of Merry and his son Desmond.

While others had fucked and drank their night away, Sebastian and Malcolm had wandered around the estate with grand ideas formulating in their mind. They'd left, unsure if their dream would be possible. But then the marquess keeled over, and at an almost frantic pace, Desmond gambled everything away, including the grounds and building that made up the Den. Sebastian had taken the win of the property as a sign that his club was meant to be. He was proud of all that he and Malcolm had accomplished since.

Sebastian hated that he'd been brought so low by his feelings for Diana. He loathed how he'd treated Malcolm and how much resentment he'd allowed to fester. Never again would he allow himself to be driven into such a state.

His mind drifted to his and Diana's talk the previous day at Seely House. Once they'd made it through the debacle of questions from condescending pompous asses, their talk about the leisure cruise had gone well.

Sebastian couldn't believe how Diana defended him. She'd used the quote from his pocket watch. He pulled the item from his pocket and flipped it open, reading the words he did his best to live by.

"It looks like we will have a good night," Malcolm said, joining him.

Sebastian closed up his watch and put it away. "Yes, it does."

They stood there silently surveying the crowd. Eventually, Sebastian sighed. "What is it?"

Malcolm frowned. "Are you sure Lady Hensley received your letter? Could it have been replaced or lost?"

What was his brother getting at? "I have no doubt she received it. She sent my Ladies of London letter to the papers. They were together."

"She seemed so protective of you today."

A smirk filled Sebastian's face. "Now you like her?"

"Of course not. She chose that idiot Tremont over you. I could never forgive her for that. Did you see he showed up late to Seely House? What the fuck does she see in him?"

Sebastian didn't know, and his thoughts weren't much different from Malcolm's. He had wanted to speak with her after their talk, but he had been unable to pull her aside because Tremont followed her around like a lost puppy.

"She used Father's words to defend you. Her words contained a level of sincerity I wasn't expecting."

A flurry of anger swelled in Sebastian's chest. "Yet she went to Tremont afterward."

Malcolm snorted. "I'm not sure he gave her much choice."

"It's over. I'm moving on," he said and turned to leave.

Malcolm grabbed his arm, stopping him. "I'm not telling you to declare your love for her, but ask if she received the missive. You will harbor deep regret if you discover she never saw it when it is too late. Make no mistake, Tremont is making moves to marry her as fast as possible."

Sebastian walked away, not responding. Tonight, he wanted to do something that brought him great joy, entertaining the customers of his club. He didn't want to think about Diana. It was foolish and torturous. Malcolm was trying to give him hope but Sebastian knew there was none.

As his foot hit the ground of the first floor, several lords hollered his name. He grinned. "What type of trouble are you lords wanting to get into?"

Chapter Thirty-Three

THE MUSIC REACHED a soaring crescendo causing Diana to wince. The Duchess of Peyton's ball was brimming with a crush of the Who's Who of London society. Diana shouldn't have attended. Socializing was the furthest thing from her mind. In truth, she wanted to be anywhere else.

Arthur was not with her tonight, but Aunt Winifred and Spoor were. Since returning from their trip, her aunt had only grown closer to him. Finally, Diana spotted her aunt. She crossed the room and joined her.

Aunt Winifred smiled. "Spoor has gone to fetch me some punch."

"You two have become quite close."

Her aunt blushed but nodded. "There is something I wanted to tell you, and I haven't been able to because you have been so busy with your club."

Diana lifted a brow, curious by her serious tone.

"I was wrong to tell you to keep your heart locked up concerning Devons."

Diana was shocked by her words. Aunt Winifred continued. "I don't regret telling Roger I loved him. I tried to convince myself for so long that I did, but what I regret is not running off with him. Even if we had only a few years, it would have been worth it."

Diana moved further along the wall of the ballroom, and her aunt followed. She frowned. "Why are you telling me this?"

Aunt Winifred reached over and squeezed her hand. "Because when I saw you and Devons give your talk at Seely House yesterday, it became apparent how much you belong together."

Diana shook her head. "You are wrong."

Her aunt smiled at her in disbelief. "I don't think so. Have you told him how you feel?"

"Of course not. He left us in Tuscany. It was evident he was moving on."

"Tell him tonight. You will regret it if you don't. He just arrived," Aunt Winifred said, nodding to the entryway.

Diana followed her gaze and spotted Sebastian. He laughed at something the Duke of Peyton said before smiling warmly at the duchess. Her heart pounded wildly. "I can't."

Her aunt sighed. "One part of my advice remains the same. You and Devons come from vastly different backgrounds. To have a love like that, you will have to fight for it and want it desperately. If you can't even tell him how you feel, maybe you don't care for him as much as I thought."

Diana, needing to confess her true feelings to someone, said, "What if he doesn't feel the same way?"

Her aunt snorted. "Impossible and if I'm wrong, you still have Tremont. Though, if I were you, I would choose to remain alone."

"Aunt—"

"I'm simply saying you don't have to choose anyone. Someone like Tremont is not an asset for you. You, my dear, are the prize. Don't let him make you think otherwise. You have nothing to gain from him, but he has everything to gain from you."

Diana smiled. "Thank you for the bit of wisdom."

Her aunt winked at her. "Devons is headed your way. Tell him how you feel. I'm off to hunt down Spoor. I do enjoy that man, but he moves slower than anyone I know."

Diana shook her head and turned to find Sebastian standing in front of her. She sucked in a breath at the attractive sight he made. Memories of them flashed in her mind. He bowed. "Lady Hensley, I was hoping you would allow me to escort you to the Duke of Peyton's gallery room. They have new artwork to view."

She smiled but was nervous. "Yes."

Sebastian held out his arm, and she took it. They strolled from the room, out into the foyer, and into the massive gallery. The Duke of Peyton was known for his love of art. He and the duchess often hosted artists at their townhouse. The room wasn't as busy as the ballroom, but people still mingled about. Sebastian stopped in front of a landscape painting. Both studied it. Diana smiled. "Did you bring me here to study the art?"

"Definitely not. This landscape is dreadful, but at least we have a measure of privacy because no one wants to look at it."

A giggle escaped her. His brow furrowed as he looked at the art, and Diana wondered what he was pondering.

"Perhaps, a peculiar question, but did you receive my missive before I left Livorno?"

She gulped, trying to push away the hurt she felt anytime she thought of his brief words. Her gaze turned back to the painting as well, not wanting him to see the pain he'd caused her. "I did receive your short letter."

He frowned. "Short?"

She turned towards him. "Yes, that you lost your head when you proposed a courtship between us."

He stepped closer. "What? My letter said nothing of the sort."

Diana glanced around. They were the only ones left in the gallery. "Sebastian, it's fine. You are allowed to change your mind."

He shook his head. His jaw tightened. Sebastian stared into her eyes intensely. "In my letter, I said I would love you for the rest of my life. That I had been a fool to think I could simply have a tryst with you. That I knew from the moment you fell into my garden that you belonged to me, and I belonged to you."

Diana stared back at him, confused. "I don't understand."

Sebastian reached forward and rubbed away a tear on Diana's cheek that she didn't even know had fallen. He continued, "I wrote that I knew my asking about a courtship was sudden, and it was wrong of me to demand an answer right away. But most importantly, I loved you enough to give you time. Time for you to decide if you could marry a man like me, raise your son with me, have more children with me, and wake up in my arms every morning."

She stepped away, overcome with emotion and unsure how she received such a drastically different letter. Frantically wiping at the tears, she said, "None of that was in the letter I was given."

They stood facing each other, still in front of the awful landscape. Diana wasn't sure what happened, but she believed him. She could see the sincerity on his face. Someone read and switched out the missive. It was the only logical answer. Diana wanted to be angry, but all she felt right now was happiness. She smiled. "You love me."

He stepped closer. "How could you ever think I don't? Put me out of my misery, love, and tell me how you feel."

"I love you too," she said.

A rightness flowed between them. He reached to pull her into his arms but stopped, remembering they weren't alone. Hunger and frustration flickered across his face. Diana was sure she wore the same expression. Sebastian leaned in. "Meet me by the gates that connect our gardens in an hour."

She nodded. "I need to tell Aunt Winifred I'm leaving early."

ONLY IN HIS shirt and trousers, Sebastian walked through the gate, separating his townhouse from Diana's. He smiled, remembering her falling into his garden. At that moment, even though he didn't know it, his life changed. He saw a flash of white. Then there she was, in her nightgown and a wrap, walking towards him. He would love this woman and only this woman for the rest of his life.

She stopped in front of him and grinned mischievously. "So, the King of the Den, the most notorious scoundrel in all of London, loves me?"

He swooped her up in his arms. "A question like that shouldn't escape your lips."

She tilted her head, laughing, looking up at him. "Why is that?"

"Because you should never doubt that I am completely besotted with you and devoted to you."

"Those are quite the romantic words from someone so wicked," she whispered.

He needed her now. He kissed her and practically ran, still carrying her, into his house and up the stairs to his bedroom. By the time he shut the door with his foot, she was laughing hysterically. He placed her on the ground, not releasing her.

"We probably woke your servants."

He kissed her neck. "They know I appreciate discretion."

"Hmmm...I bet."

He pulled back and looked at her intently. "You are the first woman to be in this room."

She rolled her eyes. "I remember you fishing Lady St. James and Lady Clarrow out of your fountain."

"And I sent them home. This has always been my space. No lovers have ever spent time here with me. I always knew the only woman I wanted here with me was my wife."

There was still much to talk about, but that would come later. Right now, he wanted to make love to this woman and claim her as his. A hungry possessiveness coursed through him. He helped her remove her robe and nightgown before discarding his clothes.

His eyes lingered on all his favorite parts of her. Her soft hips that he dreamed about every night. The curve of her breasts and the way they felt in his hands. The thatch of curls that hid the part of her that he wanted to drive himself into. Sebastian sighed. "I think I must be the luckiest man that has ever lived."

His hand slid down her waist and to the curve of her hip. She shivered, and he smiled wickedly at her. Sebastian dipped his head down and ran gentle kisses across her collarbone and shoulder. She gasped, and he leaned further down, kissing and teasing the tip of one of her breasts before kneeling. He could feel the desire emanating from her. His lips pressed a smattering of kisses on her stomach before he grabbed her thighs in his large hands. He pressed a kiss at her core, nudging her legs further apart with his head.

She grabbed onto one of the posts of the bed. He smiled before going back to what he was doing. He licked and tasted her while she moaned. "Sebastian, I don't think I can stay standing."

He didn't let up, applying pressure and licking her as her hips bucked. When he knew she was on the verge, he teased the nub of her quim, knowing it would send her over the edge. She grabbed his hair tightly, causing him to wince, but he'd gladly take any pain to make her feel this way. She let out a lusty gasp, and he felt her body shudder and come undone.

Sebastian stood back up and surveyed her sated state. He smirked, satisfied with what he saw, delighted that he would be the man to make her look so completely satisfied for the rest of her life. He pulled her onto the bed and underneath him. His cock was begging for her sweet wetness. He entered her in one deep thrust and paused, groaning at the exquisite pleasure coursing through his body. Diana ran her fingers along his back as she rocked into him.

He grinned, realizing his temptress wasn't quite as sated as he thought. Sebastian started moving slowly at first, wanting to enjoy the feel of her warmth against his cock. She arched into him with every plunge. Her little breathy whimpers grew into moans. She met him stroke for stroke. His thrust became deeper, harder, and faster. His eyes met hers. They were filled with the sweet torture of being so close to coming undone. He didn't stop but kept driving into her. "That's it, my sweet. Let me feel you shatter."

Diana let out a guttural whimper, and he grabbed her hips, grinding into her. A strangled sob left her, and he pumped into her faster. This was a perfection Sebastian never knew he could have. He was ravenous for it. He continued his frantic pace until he was on the verge. Sebastian wanted to bury himself deeply in her, but there would be time for that later. For now, he withdrew and spent. Breathing heavily, he placed his forehead on hers. She laughed. "You are going to make me insatiable."

He kissed her. "I hope so."

Sebastian moved to his side, pulling her against him, enjoying the feel of her body.

"I love you," he said.

"You are my heart," she said.

He kissed the back of her head. "I will do everything to make sure marrying me is something you will never regret."

She pulled his hand to her mouth, kissing his knuckles. "I could never regret us. All I care about is getting Robert used to the idea. That will take time, and as much as it pains me, I think it would be best if we had an engagement for at least six months."

"Six months!"

He felt her laugh, and Diana said, "Yes, six months. Robert adores you, and I want to keep it that way. I don't want to overwhelm him."

"For Robert, I'm willing to wait," he said, kissing her shoulder.

"We can still see each other."

He kissed her neck. "I hope by that you mean like this in my bed."

"Of course I do."

He faced her and placed a gentle kiss on her lips. "You are giving up a good deal to marry me."

She frowned at him. "Nonsense."

He claimed her mouth.

Chapter Thirty-Four

DIANA STUDIED HER furious mother as she stomped into the drawing room. She was angry because even though she had attempted to drag out her stay at Diana's, the day was finally here for her to move to her own house. Her mother glowered at her. "Your servant said you wanted to see me."

Instead of answering right away, Diana made her way to the sitting area and poured them each a cup of tea. "Please sit, Mother. We are waiting for one more person."

Her mother's face filled with confusion. "Who are we waiting for?"

The butler interrupted them by announcing Arthur's arrival. Diana smiled. "Here he is."

Arthur bowed and joined them in the sitting area. "Aren't I the luckiest man? I get to spend time with both of you."

Her mother smiled demurely at him. Diana said nothing, sipping her tea. Once settled, he said to Diana, "Your missive suggested you had a matter you wanted to discuss with me. I hope it isn't anything serious."

"I called you both here to announce that I have accepted a proposal. I'm to be married in six months."

Arthur stared at her in open-mouthed shock. Her mother's only response was to press her lips firmly together. Diana smiled. "I won't keep you in suspense. My husband-to-be is Sebastian

Devons."

Arthur stood, his eyes flashing. "That is unacceptable, Diana."

"Please call me Lady Hensley."

He looked as if she'd slapped him. Sadness filled her that this was how her relationship with Arthur would end. He'd been there for her during her mourning, and she would forever be grateful for that. Needing to know, she asked, "Who decided to switch the missive from Devons?"

They both stared at her silently. Her eyes flicked back and forth between them. She wanted it to be her mother. Please let it be her, she thought.

"I switched it," Arthur said.

The sadness she felt for the demise of her friendship with Arthur became mixed with anger. She'd almost married this man and he'd been deceiving her.

She stood. "How could you?"

He scowled at her. "In every one of the Ladies of London articles I read, I could sense there was a growing fondness between the two of you. I hoped it was my imagination, but the way you looked at each other in Livorno, there was no denying it. What I did was for your benefit. He is not good for you."

"Who are you to determine that?" Diana asked, then spun to her mother. "Did you know?"

She shrugged. "Perhaps."

Arthur scoffed. "She put the idea in my head and also the plan for the scandalous article about your little club."

Any sadness she held about the demise of their relationship completely disappeared. How had she not seen this side of Arthur? The anger in her surged. "You are the source of the gossip?"

Arthur realized she hadn't known. "It was more your mother than I."

Diana didn't understand why Arthur would stoop so low. "You would have married me knowing our union was only possible because of lies? Why?"

He let out a frustrated sigh. "Our marriage would have made us one of the most powerful couples in London."

The sadness crept back, not because of the loss of her friendship with Arthur, but because he'd not even taken such drastic measures for love. He'd done it for social status. "I think it is time for you to go."

"You don't have to marry him. Even if you have been intimate with him, I would still wed you as long as you aren't with child."

Diana stared back at him, appalled and grateful she'd never accepted his suit. "Leave, Lord Tremont. I love Sebastian Devons, and he loves me. I choose him not because of some power grab but because my heart wants him."

"Be practical."

"Please go," Diana said more firmly.

Arthur looked as if he wanted to say more, but he shook his head and stormed out.

"You fool," Diana's mother hissed.

Diana spun around. "Enough. Had I known you were scheming behind my back, I would never have felt sorry for you and agreed to let you come back to England with me."

"Sebastian Devons is beneath you."

Diana could stand here all day and argue with her but realized it was pointless. Nothing she said or did would change her mother or make her a better person. She stomped to the door and stopped, studying the woman who had birthed her. Diana suspected this may be the last time she saw her. She should have felt sad but felt nothing but relief. "I'm honored to be Sebastian Devons's wife. Goodbye, Mother."

SEBASTIAN SAT IN Malcolm's drawing room, smiling. His niece Penelope frowned at him and whispered loudly, "What is wrong with him?"

His brother's wife, Sophia, shushed her. Malcolm laughed and said, "Well, tell us."

"I have proposed to Lady Hensley, and she has accepted."

Sophia clapped excitedly, then sprang from her chair and placed a kiss on his cheek. "That is wonderful."

Malcolm rolled his eyes at his wife's antics. She returned to her seat, grinning like a madwoman. His sister-in-law was mad for a love story.

"So, did she receive your letter?" Malcolm asked.

He and Diana had discussed his missive before she left his townhouse. It was clear someone had tried to keep them apart. Sebastian suspected Tremont. Diana had made him promise not to confront the man. Diana wanted to speak with him and her mother. For now, Sebastian agreed to her request.

"Malcolm said you would never wed," Penelope said. Sometimes, she called his brother and Sophia their names and sometimes referred to them as Mother and Father. She wasn't born to them, but they loved her as if she was.

Sebastian smiled at his brother. "Well, he is wrong."

"That was before he left for his trip and fell in love with the most proper lady in all of London," Sophia said, sighing dreamily.

He and Malcolm rolled their eyes at her dramatics. She continued, "We must write to your mother. She will want to return to meet Lady Hensley as soon as possible."

Sebastian agreed and had no doubt his mother would adore Diana. She didn't come to London often because she spent most of her time traveling, and she hated the gossip her presence stirred up. Even after two decades, London still liked to talk about how his mother had lived in scandal with his father.

Sebastian couldn't control the talk about his mother or his unconventional upbringing but was already making plans to sever any other ties that could impact Diana or Robert's standing in society.

"I do have upsetting news," he said to Malcolm.

Everyone at the table stared at him curiously. Malcolm turned to Penelope. "Pen, leave us for a bit."

"I want to know the secret," the girl insisted.

"Penelope," Sophia said.

The girl slid her chair back dramatically. "I'm not allowed to hear anything."

She stomped off in a huff. Malcolm and Sophia sighed. Sebastian laughed. "It's about the Den. I want to sell my percentage of the business."

No one said a word, and Sebastian sensed he shocked them. Finally, Malcolm said, "Why?"

"She is the mother of a soon-to-be duke. The least I can do is try to be more respectable. I'm not sure the owner of a gentlemen's club will ever be that."

His brother frowned. "It's the most successful club in all of London. Has she asked you to do this? If she has—"

Sebastian held up a hand. "No. She would never. This is my choice. There are things I can't change about myself, and she will have to endure them, but I can step away from the club."

"Maybe you should ask her first," Sophia said.

"No. I want to do this for her. I don't want her to feel as if she forced me to make a decision."

Malcolm rose and poured himself a brandy. Sophia frowned at him. "Malcolm, it is early."

He plopped back down in his chair. "Sorry. My brother is talking about giving up his business that he built from nothing. That I built with him."

"I love her more than I care about our business. I don't want to argue about this. I want your help to find a new partner in the Den who can buy me out," Sebastian stated.

Malcolm took a large gulp of his brandy. "If that is what you want, after the Ball of Sin, I will put some feelers out."

Sebastian nodded. "Thank you. I think I will also ask Celeste to take over as host for the Ball of Sin this year."

His brother sulkily shook his head. "If that is what you wish."

Chapter Thirty-Five

"ARE YOU READY for this?" Sebastian asked.

They were standing outside of Seely House. Today, they would tell Addie and the rest of the board members they were engaged. Diana worried that after their talk and the scandalous article, they would be livid that she and Sebastian hadn't revealed their relationship sooner. Still, Diana wanted all of London to know that she loved this man. She put aside her nerves. "Yes."

They entered the building, and Diana led the way to the office. They had a meeting scheduled for today, so Diana was confident everyone would be there. As they walked through the doorway, Addie looked up from her desk. She smiled. "I didn't know you would be visiting, Devons."

"There is something Diana and I wanted to explain to you all," he said.

She frowned and her face filled with worry. "Is something amiss?"

Diana motioned the ladies to the sitting area. Addie and Sebastian joined her right away and were then followed by Lisbeth, Esme, and Sarah. Sebastian flashed her an encouraging smile. Esme frowned at both of them. "Has another article come out?"

Diana shook her head and took a deep breath. "Devons and I are betrothed."

No one said anything. All the ladies stared back and forth between Diana and Devons. Suddenly, Addie burst into the belly laughter she was known for. Sebastian frowned at her as Diana flushed from head to toe. Lisbeth glared at her. "Addie."

"I'm not laughing at the match, I promise. You are perfect for each other, but I can't believe I didn't catch on sooner."

Diana smiled at her, and Sebastian shook his head. The other ladies beamed at them.

"I know this may cause trouble for the club, so we wanted you all to know as soon as possible."

Sarah shook her head in response to Diana. "You put everyone in their place at our talk. You will be the envy of the *ton* because you captured the King of the Den's heart."

Addie's eyes darted to her. "Sarah, I didn't know you followed gossip."

The young woman rolled her eyes. "Just because I'm a scholar doesn't mean I don't enjoy the London scandal sheets."

Esme laughed. Addie sighed. "So, tell us how this happened."

Diana looked at Devons. His eyes lingered on her for a moment with such adoration Diana thought she would float away with joy. He turned back to the other ladies. "Diana is my end and my beginning. There is no one quite like her."

They all sighed, shocking Diana. None of these ladies were the least bit romantic, but with a few words, Sebastian made them so.

"So, you aren't mad?" Diana asked the board members.

Addie laughed. "It seems scandal will follow our club no matter what. We should embrace it. I learned a long time ago that words and gossip can only hurt you as much as you allow."

Lisbeth nodded. "I agree. The gossip is only going to continue whether it is Diana or one of us."

Sarah Martin frowned. "What else could they say about us?"

Lisbeth lifted a brow. "You and Esme are both considered bluestockings, I'm considered peculiar with a secretive past, Addie is considered a flamboyant walking scandal, and now Diana is about to marry one of the greatest rogues in London."

Her soon-to-be husband's mouth tilted up in a smirk. "Not one of the greatest."

Addie snorted. "You are and I love that you lost your heart to the most proper lady in all of London."

Esme and Sarah laughed. Lisbeth just shook her head. "Who knew you were such a romantic, Addie?"

She shrugged. "I can admire a love story, especially when it involves a besotted rogue."

Sebastian's eyes met Diana's. "Completely besotted."

Later that day, Diana paced back and forth in her drawing room. She was delighted at how well received the news of her and Sebastian's betrothal had gone with the ladies of the Historical Society for Female Curators. Currently, she was waiting on Wescott. Sebastian had requested to meet with him to ask his permission to marry Diana.

While she found it to be a touching sentiment, Diana wanted the news to come from her first. She needed to know his thoughts before Sebastian spoke with him. The door opened, and her butler announced, "The Duke of Wescott."

Diana rose and smiled as her father-in-law made his way to the sitting area. "I was delighted to receive a missive from you, and I must admit, intrigued."

She laughed as they both sat. "Thank you for coming. I have some news for you."

Her father-in-law smirked. "I suspected you might. Recently, I received a request for a meeting from Mr. Devons."

Diana blushed. Wescott chuckled. "Every week when I read the column about your leisure cruise, I suspected that man was wooing you. I suppose I can meet with him and find out if he is acceptable."

She stiffened, concerned. "Mr. Devons is a good man. He may not have a title but—"

Wescott waved his hand. "I don't care about any of that. As you get older, Diana, you begin to realize how ridiculous and cruel the world can be. You either join them or try to be better.

Stuart would want you with someone who was the latter. Is he that?"

"Yes, he is. Stuart wouldn't be upset by our match," Diana said but then frowned. "I want you to know I will always love your son."

Westcott reached over and squeezed her hand. "Of course, you will, but that doesn't mean you need to live the rest of your life mourning him. I have two more questions for you. Do you love this Mr. Devons? Are you happy?"

"I do, and I am."

Her father-in-law nodded. "Then, when I meet with Mr. Devons, he will be given my blessing because my duty to my son is to make sure you are happy."

Diana's eyes watered. "Thank you."

SEBASTIAN LAUGHED AT something Lord Shipley said, smacking him on the back. The Den was packed. He'd slowly started to step back from the club, but tonight, he was playing host. Celeste had the night off. He grinned at one of the patrons while he silently admitted to himself that he would miss this.

This business had been his everything. He'd poured all his blood and sweat into it, and deep down, he knew it would hurt him when he let it go. Still, he was determined to walk away because he wanted Diana more. She was proper and the mother of a duke. It would destroy him if she ever felt shame or resentment from something his actions caused.

He pushed the dark thoughts from his mind. Getting rid of the club was a good thing, he insisted to himself. Sebastian joined Malcolm, who stood leaning against a wall, drinking a brandy. "I thought the role of host was to engage."

His brother rolled his eyes. "I cater to these fools in my own way."

"By lording over them," he said dryly.

They both laughed. Loud, angry footsteps struck the ground, and Sebastian turned to see who was barreling down on them. An enraged Tremont stopped in front of him.

"You will turn her into a disgrace!"

Diana had shared with him that Tremont confessed to the letter. He'd been livid. She'd made him promise he wouldn't spend his time worrying about the man or seeking out revenge. With that in mind, Sebastian fixed him with a cool menacing stare. "Leave, Lord Tremont. You are lucky that is all I have to say to you."

"Your union will bring her and her son nothing but shame."

There was only so much a man could take. Sebastian grabbed him by the cravat and pulled him up, so they were face to face. "The only thing stopping me from destroying you, Tremont, is my promise to Diana. Her kind heart is what allows you to walk away from everything you have done without any form of punishment."

Tremont struggled to get out of his grasp as Sebastian held tight, wanting this man to know who had the power between the two of them. He leaned in so only the wiggling lord could hear him. "Had you succeeded with your trick, make no mistake, I would have made sure your union with her ended."

Sebastian's grab on his cravat tightened. His brother said, "Sebastian, you need to release him."

Tremont started to choke, and he still didn't let him go. He glared at him and whispered, "And it wouldn't have been by divorce or annulment."

Sebastian's hand finally released its hold, sending Tremont staggering backward and crashing into a table and chairs. They were on the side of the main hall so most had missed the commotion up until his fall. Now the room had grown deafeningly quiet. Malcolm grabbed the angry lord and pulled him up by his arms. "Enough brandy for you, Tremont. Our staff will escort you out."

Tremont yanked away from Malcolm while glaring at Sebastian. "Don't bother. I can see my way out."

Sebastian watched him stalk out of the hall and into the night. The room was still silent. He clapped. "A free round on us tonight, gentlemen."

Loud cheers erupted in the room and any scene was quickly forgotten. The dramatic showdown may be over, but Tremont's words lingered with him. He vowed that he would do everything in his power to protect Diana and Robert's social standing.

The next day, Sebastian waited in the Duke of Wescott's study. He paced back and forth. Sebastian reminded himself he didn't need his approval, but he still wanted it for Diana's sake. She had a great affection for the duke, and the man was Robert's grandfather.

The door opened, and the duke walked in. He was a formidable presence and looked nothing like his son. He nodded to Sebastian and indicated for him to sit in the chair across from his desk. Sebastian took a seat and studied the man whose son married Diana. There was a hardness to Wescott, making him wonder why Diana cared for him so much.

"How can I help you, Mr. Devons?" he asked.

Sebastian considered what his next words should be. He could tell Wescott he had enough money that Diana would never want for anything, or he could explain his yearly income. He sensed the duke would care about none of that. Instead, Sebastian spoke from his heart.

"I'm here to ask for your blessing to marry Lady Hensley. I love her."

Amusement twinkled in the duke's eyes, transforming his face. He leaned back in his chair. "Will you make her and Robert happy?"

This was the question that mattered to the duke the most, Sebastian realized. He nodded. "I will try every day to make sure she and Robert are happy. It will be my greatest honor and duty."

He smiled. "My son, when he was very sick, told me that was

all he wanted for Diana and Robert. If you can do that, you and I will get along well."

Relief coursed through him. "Thank you. I also plan to step away from some of my businesses that may not be acceptable for Lady Hensley's social standing."

The duke sighed. "I'm not worried about that. The world is changing, Devons. No matter how many of my titled friends dislike it, what was once unacceptable is becoming tolerable."

The words shocked Sebastian, but he did want the duke to understand that he took Diana's reputation seriously. "Still, I will do everything I can to make sure that Diana's social standing isn't impacted by our marriage."

"Do not fret, Mr. Devons. The *ton* adores a love match. How about a drink to celebrate?" he asked, as he pulled a cord, summoning a servant.

Chapter Thirty-Six

DIANA FROWNED AS she stepped out of the carriage. She'd always wanted to visit the Den but hadn't brought it up to Sebastian yet. They'd been preoccupied with their news. Yesterday, Wescott gave Sebastian his blessing, and this morning, Diana explained to Robert that he hoped to be a permanent part of their lives.

The joy that had crossed her son's face caused her great sadness and happiness. The sadness came from knowing Robert didn't really remember his father. Stuart had not been far from her mind lately. She missed him but knew he would be happy that Diana found love again with Sebastian.

A butler approached her and bowed. "Lady Hensley, Lord and Lady Derry are waiting inside."

She nodded and followed him in. As she stepped inside, the building had an opulent small foyer, leading to a massive grand hall. It was as if the foyer was made intentionally small to highlight the staggering size of the next room. The grand hall was empty except for the marquess and marchioness. The butler said, "Lord and Lady Derry, Lady Hensley has arrived."

Diana knew both as her sister was married to Lady Derry's brother, but they were no more than acquaintances. Lord Derry nodded to the butler. "Thank you, Donahue."

"I appreciate the invitation to tour the Den, Lord and Lady

Derry."

Lady Derry beamed at her. "Please, you must call me Sophia and my husband Malcolm. We are to be family."

Warmth coursed through Diana at her kind words. "Thank you."

Malcolm sighed and his wife frowned at him. Diana wasn't sure what to make of the two of them. "Is something amiss?"

"My husband would like to speak with you, but first, we want to show you this place."

Diana nodded. "Of course."

Malcolm looked around as if to see where to go first. "We shall start on the second floor that overlooks the grand hall."

Diana followed Malcolm and Sophia up a grand stairway, leading to a second-floor landing, running the length of the massive room. The view of the grand hall from the second floor was breathtaking. It was clear this was the spot where Sebastian and his brother watched over their business. It was a kingdom they'd created with great care.

"It's stunning," Diana said.

Malcolm nodded. "It is. While Sebastian and I created all of this together, it was his vision and determination that made it the best gentlemen's club in all of London."

Diana turned to him. "Why do you want me to know this?"

"First, let's finish the tour, and then I will explain."

Sophia squeezed her arm. "Let him show you."

Diana nodded.

A few hours later, she sat with Malcolm and Sophia in an expansive study. They'd walked through the entire building and the grounds that housed several decadent cottages used for liaisons by lords and ladies. Malcolm handed her and Sophia a glass of wine before taking a seat in a wingback chair while holding a brandy for himself.

"Thank you for letting me walk you through the club."

Diana frowned. "I only wish Sebastian would have joined us. Does he know we are here?"

Malcolm sighed. "No. I asked you here, specifically, without him. He is planning to sell his shares in the Den."

Diana gasped. "Why?"

"He fears this business may impact your reputation and social standing," Sophia explained.

"I would never ask him to do that," Diana said, upset that Sebastian would think he needed to give any of this up for her.

Malcolm took a sip of brandy. "My brother has always had the stigma of being born out of wedlock hanging over his head. Even though we grew up with much love, society still judged him because my father chose to openly embrace him and his mother. I think he is trying to make up for the fact he can't change that."

Diana took a large gulp of her wine. Anger emanated through her. Did Sebastian really think she would care? She loved him. Both Malcolm and Sophia studied her. She raised the glass to her lips again, attempting to control her emotions but they wouldn't calm. "That daft man."

Her hosts' eyes widened in shock, and they burst out laughing. Sophia smiled at her kindly. "You don't care if he keeps the club?"

"Of course not. I'm insulted that he would think I don't accept him wholly. I didn't choose Sebastian with demands he should change. It isn't that I don't care. I do care. I want him to keep this club."

Relief filled Malcolm's face, and Sophia gave him a knowing, triumphant grin. The marquess smirked. "My wife believed you would say something to that effect."

It almost made her burst into tears that Sebastian would give this up all for her, but it also made her sad that he thought he needed to. "When is he planning to do this?"

"After the Ball of Sin," Malcolm answered.

Diana shook her head. She would not let the man she loved so much think she had shame for any aspect of his life. "This will not do. When is the Ball of Sin?"

Sophia looked at her curiously. "In two days, but Sebastian

will not be attending."

"Can you get him there?" she asked Malcolm.

He nodded and asked, "What is your plan?"

CELESTE FINISHED EXPLAINING the entertainment for the Ball of Sin. It appeared everything was ready to go for the scandalous event taking place tomorrow evening. Sebastian had done his best to stay hands-off, knowing he would not be a partner in the club for much longer. The Ball of Sin started the season, and the Ball of Misdeeds ended it. If Sebastian had to pick one, the Ball of Sin was his favorite. "Great job, Celeste. This year's ball will be the most elaborate yet."

Malcolm nodded. Celeste smiled. "Thank you. I know you will not be in attendance, but can I have your reassurance that if something is amiss, we can have a staff member fetch you?"

He frowned at his brother. Their other partner, Miller, wasn't at the meeting. "You and Miller will be there, won't you?"

"Of course, but sometimes you are the one the staff needs."

Sebastian nodded, knowing that if they needed him, he would be there. "Send word to my townhouse and I will come straight away."

An attendant stuck his head in the door, motioning that he needed Celeste. She excused herself. Malcolm frowned at him. "Do you really want to give this up?"

"It doesn't matter. I want my soon-to-be wife to be happy. I want her to not lose her place in society because she is married to me."

"Times are changing, Sebastian."

He scowled. "Not fast enough."

The Duke of Wescott had implied the same thing. Yet the lords and ladies of the *ton* appeared to be moving at a much slower pace. Those untitled and who earned money were still viewed distastefully from the higher echelons of London society. His soon-to-be stepson would be one of those lords someday. People would always question why his mother married a bastard and the owner of a gentlemen's club. He couldn't fix one of those things, but he could change the other.

"Have you mentioned your plans to your betrothed?"

"Leave it alone," Sebastian bit out.

"I think the lady loves you enough that none of what you are worrying about will ever matter to her. You are not the first untitled person or bastard to marry someone who is considered above their station."

"I don't need the club. I have plenty of money and other investments to live without it."

Malcolm shook his head. "This business holds a piece of your heart and if your lady loves you, she will want you to not lose it."

Sebastian rose. "I don't have time for this today. I'm leaving."

Chapter Thirty-Seven

DIANA SAT IN the carriage with Addie, Lisbeth, and of all people, her Aunt Winifred. Diana had confided in her aunt what she was doing, and she'd insisted she attend.

"You are going to take his breath away," Addie said dreamily.

Lisbeth snorted. "I'm still amazed our club is filled with so many romantics."

Addie rolled her eyes at her. "I like love. Stop judging me."

A laugh escaped Diana. She felt free. She was going to tell Sebastian she loved him in front of all of London tonight. It was important to Diana that he understood she wanted him, as is. She ran her hands down the dark-blue ballgown that glittered with crystals. Clara had helped her find a modiste who could quickly provide her with a decadent gown for the Ball of Sin. She had been equally shocked and delighted that Diana was marrying Sebastian.

Diana patted at the lace cap, holding back a portion of the curls on her head. She'd decided to wear one tonight as a reminder that even with her little cap, she was so much more complex than the caricature that she'd once worried about. It was her way of privately thumbing her nose at society. Amused, she wondered if Sebastian had been right when he called her a rabble-rouser.

"You look stunning. Are you sure you want Devons? You

could have your pick of anyone at the ball," Addie said with a wink.

"This will be the talk of the season," Aunt Winifred added giddily.

It would be, and she wanted it that way. She'd apologized to the board members in advance for any problems it caused with their club, but none seemed to be worried. The board had decided the choices they made for the Historical Society for Female Curators wouldn't be dictated by gossip. The carriage came to a halt.

"Everyone put on your masks. It's part of the rules," Addie explained.

They donned their coverings, just as the carriage door opened. Diana stepped out, looking around at the crush of people entering the foyer. The butler, whom Diana had met on the previous visit, made his way to her and her group.

He bowed. "Come this way, my lady."

Instead of going through the front door, Donahue navigated them to a hidden entrance, leading to the study. Sophia and Malcolm greeted them as they entered. Sophia beamed at her. "Are you ready for this?"

Diana nodded. The marquess smiled. "He may be cross."

She tilted her chin up, determined. "I don't care. This idea that my love is conditional ends tonight. I love him and I want all of London to know."

Her aunt sighed happily, while Addie giggled, and Lisbeth rolled her eyes.

"Good." Derry turned to Donahue. "Tonight, we will announce Lady Hensley's arrival in the great hall."

The composed butler gasped. "My lord, there are no names at the Ball of Sin."

"Tonight, there is."

The butler looked at her and an impressed smile appeared on his face. "As you wish."

They followed the butler to the grand hall's entrance. Diana removed her mask and handed it to Aunt Winifred. Addie asked, "Are you ready?"

Diana beamed. "More than ready."

Donahue loudly announced, "The Marchioness of Hensley."

The room went deafeningly quiet.

SEBASTIAN'S HEART SLAMMED against his ribcage. What did Donahue say? Did he announce Diana in the middle of the Ball of Sin? The hall was completely silent, even the music stopped. Lords and ladies turned towards the entryway. No, it couldn't be Diana they were looking at. The crowd separated as he walked to the front.

Sebastian wasn't even supposed to be here tonight. Celeste had requested his presence at the last minute. The realization that Celeste, of all people, never needed his help washed over him. Something was happening he wasn't in the know of. What was going on?

Those around him whispered Diana's name. No one was ever announced during the Ball of Sin. Names were kept secret and masks were left on. Diana had revealed herself. As the last bit of the crush of people parted, he gasped. She took his breath away and it wasn't the delectable dark-blue dress she wore but the look of love she directed at him. Sebastian went to her. There was no other option but to do so. Now and forever.

The whispers grew louder. He bowed before her. "Lady Hensley."

Diana smirked at him. "Mr. Devons."

"You look lovely, but you've broken the main rule of the night. You should be wearing a mask."

"The King of the Den needs no mask so neither does the queen."

It was true. He wore no mask and never did. It was his ball

after all. His lips twitched at her confidence. He liked Diana like this. He arched a brow at her. Her tempting lips, painted red, smirked at him. "Am I not to be your queen?"

"You are the only woman who will ever be."

A lady somewhere sighed, and Sebastian knew this night would be talked about for years. The night the most proper lady in all of London chose the King of the Den. He reached for her, pulling her to him. He leaned close to her ear. "What are you doing?"

She whispered back. "Malcolm said you were going to give this up for me. I wanted you to know that I choose you. All of you. Don't sell this for me. Don't be someone else."

Sebastian's eyes flicked to his brother who smirked back at him and shrugged. He turned back to her. "I wanted to limit the gossip I brought upon you."

Diana shook her head. "Let them gossip."

He laughed and someone in the crowd hollered, "What are they talking about?"

"No one can hear."

Diana grinned up at him. "But if we are going to create a scandal, it should be a worthwhile one. Don't you agree?"

He smiled wickedly at her, eliciting more sighs from the crowd. "What do you have in mind, Lady Hensley?"

She winked at him. "Well, you must kiss me like a man madly in love."

Sebastian pulled her flush. "There is nothing I would like more."

Their lips smashed together. He cupped the back of her head, kissing her as if only her mouth could sate his desires. And it was the truth, she was the only woman for him. He and all he had was hers. Applause thundered around them. Malcolm whistled loudly and yelled, "Ladies and gentlemen, in celebration of the King and Queen of the Den's love, enjoy a free glass of champagne."

They pulled apart, looking at each other, laughing. Sebastian shook his head. "You are insane."

She frowned at him. "You are. How dare you think I would ever want you to change."

Sebastian was a fool. He saw that now. "I apologize."

Even though Sebastian had always taken the words in his pocket watch to heart, in this moment, he felt his father's sage wisdom deep within his soul. Bloodlines, titles, and how one acquired wealth didn't matter. What was important was how a man lived, how he loved, and how he treated others.

"I love you, Diana."

Epilogue

DIANA LOOKED UP as Addie tossed a paper on her desk at Seely House. Every London paper hinted that a great scandal occurred at the Ball of Sin, but none had shared what it was. Those who attended feared they would never be invited to one of the Den's notorious balls again. While many whispered something had happened, no one dared to say that Diana had arrived maskless and kissed Sebastian in full view of the entire crush of people.

Addie grinned. "The *ton* is dying to reveal what they know."

She laughed. Honestly, if one looked close enough they would also see that each paper contained a betrothal announcement for Diana and Sebastian. It wasn't a stretch to guess who the scandal was about.

Lisbeth entered the office. "It was all unneeded drama in my opinion."

Diana rolled her eyes. The duchess was always so pragmatic.

"Admit it. It was rather romantic," Addie insisted.

Lisbeth shrugged. "I suppose."

"I'm just glad we've not seen a huge impact on the Historical Society for Female Curators," Diana said. "I would hate that."

Even though Lisbeth found her declaration of love for Sebastian unnecessary, she still smiled at her reassuringly. "We will survive any scandals thrown our way. Now, let's move past the gossip of the day and talk about the tablets."

Addie rolled her eyes at the no-nonsense duchess. "Sarah has preserved them. There are three. In Mr. Calvert's letter that arrived with the artifacts, he suggested there may be one or two more. He also said to expect his daughter to be very displeased to be in London."

Lisbeth shook her head. "Benjamin must really want her to have a Season to go to such desperate measures."

"Are the two of you close?" Diana asked, intrigued about Lisbeth's connection to the Calverts.

Lisbeth snorted. "No. She doesn't like me."

There had been rumors years ago about Lisbeth before she married. No one knew the truth, but the speculation was she'd disappeared and traveled the world with the Calverts and Thomas Easton. Diana guessed some of that was true based on her expansive knowledge of artifacts.

"Do you know Thomas Easton as well?" Addie asked.

Lisbeth's eyes flicked to hers. She frowned. "Why does it matter?"

"Why are you being so evasive?"

The duchess fixed her with a haughty glare. "Do I ever ask about the true reason you started this club?"

Diana smirked. Lisbeth didn't hold back. All the board members had the same suspicion of why Addie started this club, but Diana suspected that somewhere along the way, this all became so much more than a silly game of revenge for their club president. Addie winked at Lisbeth. "Keep your secret, duchess."

She smirked at her. "I will."

"Do you think the tablets will be enough?" Diana asked.

A sigh escaped Lisbeth. "Based on how all of London has lost their minds over you and Devons's match, I would say yes. Ancient text that reveals a love story, I can't imagine it not being wildly successful. Our club can make it so."

Addie smiled at the duchess. "I agree. I do hope Rose Calvert doesn't give you too much trouble during the Season."

Lisbeth sighed. "We should be very excited that she is deciphering the tablets for our first large exhibit and grand opening. I doubt anyone else, but your husband would have the skill to do so. Still, she will be nothing but trouble."

"It sounds like she will fit in wonderfully," Diana mused.

They all laughed.

Thank You for Reading!

I hope you enjoyed Diana and Sebastian's story. These two opposites were so fun to write. I loved dreaming up all their interactions and where they traveled on their leisure cruise. A Wanton Adventure is the first book in the Brazen Curator series. I can't wait for you all to learn more about the rest of the ladies trying to one-up the men's-only London Society of Antiquaries. I love these women and their happily-ever-afters so much!

Always feel free to check out my website for new information on the Brazen Curator *series.*

ramonaelmes.com

ABOUT THE AUTHOR

Since stealing her first historical romance novel from her mother more than twenty years ago, Ramona Elmes has been all in on the genre. Her infatuation with the historical and steamy stirred her to write her own romances.

Ramona loves to write happily ever afters set in the Victorian era. She believes this period makes an exciting backdrop for fast-paced storylines, steamy moments, dramatic endings, and memorable characters.

When not creating ways to entice and torture her characters, she spends her days in Georgia coordinating her family's crazy life, refereeing pets, hiking, and reading on her front porch.

Reading is hands-down her favorite way to relax, and she is an avid reader of all romance subgenres. Give her a dramatic storyline, a grand declaration, and heart-filled steamy moments, and she is in.

To get updates on Ramona's books, follow her on Amazon, Facebook, Instagram, or her website.

Instagram: elmes_ramona
Facebook: RamonaElmes
Website: ramonaelmes.com
Amazon: amazon.com/stores/Ramona-
Elmes/author/B08TTX6TJP
Goodreads:
goodreads.com/author/show/21134562.Ramona_Elmes